"Cribb writes very well, with a style reminiscent of historical novelists of a bygone era."

~ Foreword Reviews

"Thanks for taking me on a wonderful adventure, introducing me to interesting characters, allowing me to visit Ryeport and Nextwest and the Guiding Light Church, and providing me a mystery that kept me intrigued."

~ Lauretta Kraus

"I am just amazed by your story-telling abilities, not to mention your knowledge of life in 18th century England as well as ship lore….and how about that voodoo stuff!"

~ Pat Woods

"I started your book and after the first two chapters, I was caught! I went back to the beginning so that I could memorize all the characters and meet them! It was almost personal I had to get into their lives. Wow! What a beginning."

~ Elise

"Cribb's characters are likeable, his dialogue convincing and his knowledge of English history and ships impressive, adding to the main story's realism."

~ Blueink Review

"Readers willing to undertake this daunting tome will be rewarded with an engaging adventurous tale."

~ Kirkus Reviews

EAGLES NEST
WOODS
RIVER
ERNIES COVE
CARTERS ROCK

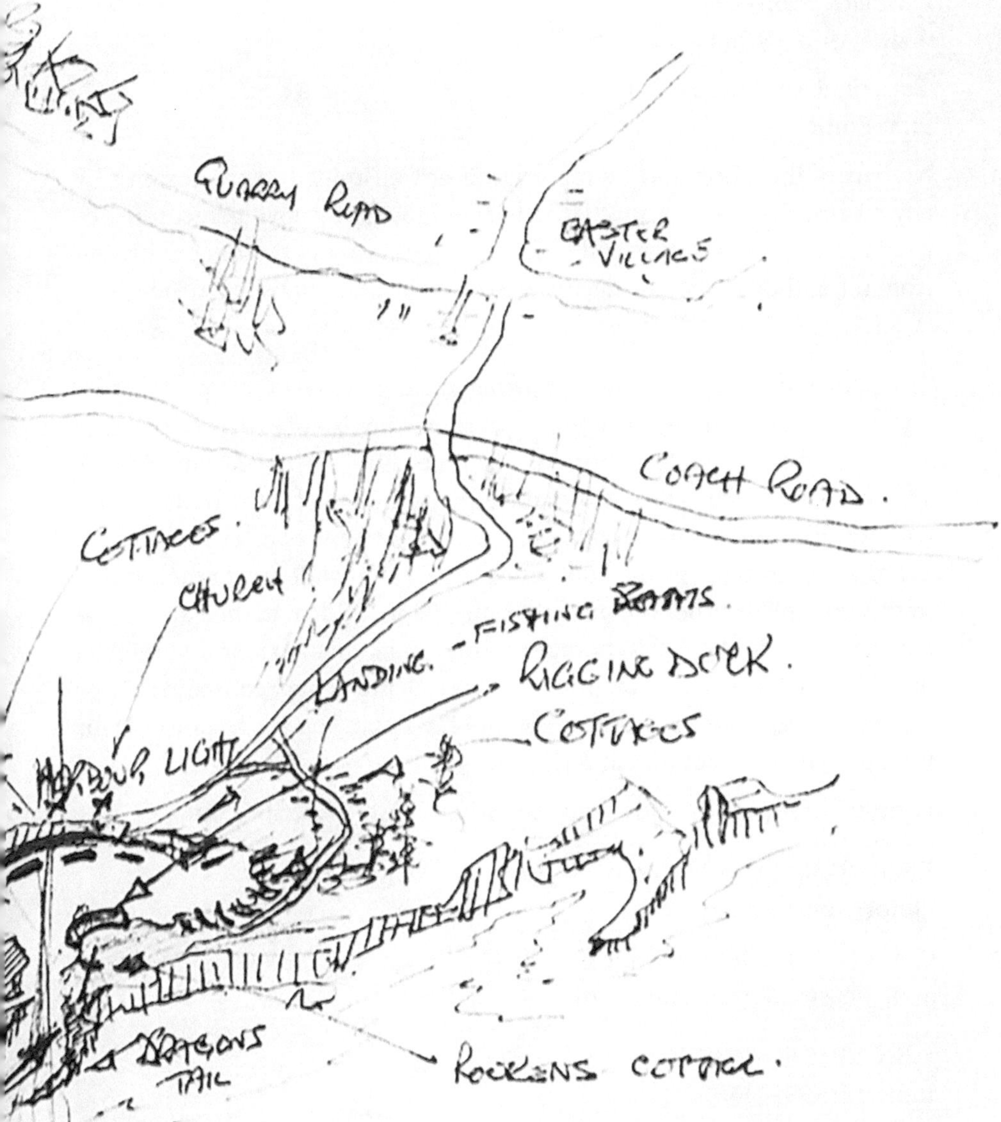

QUARRY ROAD

EASTER VILLAGE

COACH ROAD

COTTAGES

CHURCH

LANDING. — FISHING BOATS.

RIGGING DOCK.

COTTAGES

HARBOUR LIGHT

DRAGONS TAIL

ROCKENS COTTAGE.

RYEPORT

RYEPORT

*From the author's sketchbook*

Published by
Hasmark Publishing
www.hasmarkpublishing.com



Disclaimer



Editor: Janet-Lynn Morrison
jjlmorrison@gmail.com

Cover & Book Design: Anne Karklins
anne@hasmarkpublishing.com

ISBN 13: 978-1-989756-61-4
ISBN 10: 1989756611

THE RYEPORT REDEMPTION TRILOGY

BOOK 1

# THE VICAR'S JOURNAL

From the original novel
*The Fo'c'sle Door* by

## LES CRIBB

Hasmark
PUBLISHING
INTERNATIONAL

*With much love and grateful hearts we dedicate this book to our parents, Les and Joyce Cribb.*

*This tale sprang from our Dad's ever active imagination. We watched over many years as finally with retirement, he had the time to use his gifts as a storyteller to create this wonderful, captivating adventure.*

*We are very proud of his achievement and delighted to see it in print despite the many challenges that were thrown into his path. But the greatest gift he left us was a legacy of love and laughter. All of his funny stories, funny hats, funny songs and funny faces that he entertained us with brought so much laughter. His love for, and fierce dedication to his family and every one of his "Papa Hugs" will be with us always. Our beautiful Mum, was right there through every celebration and every crisis. With her gentleness, eternal patience and quiet strength she was always our port in the storm and a "guiding light" to us all. We were well loved.*

*It is our hope in finishing this part of Dad's journey for him that the reader will have a chance to experience how wonderful it is to get lost in a good book.*

Anne, Jackie, Lisa and David

# FOREWORD

In 1949, I first had the privilege of meeting Les Cribb during National Service with the Royal Navy on a training ship in Devonport, England. We were engaged on daily trips on a minelayer, laying cable and controlled mines for Harbour Defence. It was a very hard and dirty job, but as fit young lads of nineteen we now had to consider ourselves men. It was over a mug of hot tea on the mess deck of the training ship that I had my first conversation with Les.

We found that our hometowns in London were quite close to each other and we had a lot of similar interests. He was a very cheery chap and had a wry sense of humour, which always had me smiling. He was an able jazz guitarist and had been in a semi-professional dance band before being conscripted. The other members of the band were also engaged on National Service and planned to reform when they returned to civilian life.

In 1952, when we had all returned from the services, the band members began to rehearse. There was a pianist, tenor sax player, guitarist and drummer, but they realised that to have a credible group they required a bass player. By now, we were all good friends and although I was a very amateur dabbler in accordion, clarinet and guitar, I had no knowledge of double bass. I very rashly volunteered to purchase an instrument and take lessons. To their credit, no one raised an eyebrow at the ambitious suggestion. After taking lessons for a year, I was finally at a stage to join the band. We had a very successful five years together.

Les was a perfectionist, and whatever he embarked on it had to be right, otherwise it had to be redone. During his life, he acquired many skills, so it was no surprise to me that he had emerged as a skilled author. His diligence, historical research and knowledge of seafaring really pays off in this exciting and imaginative novel – to miss reading this book is to miss a journey of a lifetime, and I for one could not put it down. The first printing of this novel was published under the original title of 'The Fo'c'sle Door,' which to anyone with knowledge of ships is quite credible, but to land-lubbers it is not clear. Les' family are now relaunching the book under this new title and format.

Les passed away in 2016 and he is sadly missed. We and our wives were firm friends for over seventy years. A lasting memorial to a lovely man.

Goodbye, dear friend.

Harry W. Randall

# TABLE OF CONTENTS

R YEPORT  H ARBOUR

*From the author's sketchbook*

# CHAPTER 1

## *Two bizarre deaths*

Detective Inspector Pat Crowley was deep in thought when the ringing of his cell phone startled him back to the here and now. However, the phone was trapped by his seatbelt, so he had to pull his car onto the soft shoulder to retrieve it. "Crowley," he snapped irritably.

"Hawkins here, Sir," responded his station's desk sergeant. "Sorry to call you on your cell, but we've had a couple of strange deaths reported and I didn't want to put the information on the radio before you'd had a chance to check it out."

"Okay, Jack. What's up?"

"We have two dead men, Sir, on a construction site at the South West corner of the Fifth line and Ridge Road. This promises to be a weird case. One guy has apparently drowned – in an area where there is no water – and the other one died from a chest wound that looks as though it was inflicted by a long blade – possibly a sword. There's an exit wound in the guy's back. No sign of the weapon though. I don't remember there being any open water thereabouts; nothing deep enough to drown a man in anyway. The two deceased were part of a group eating lunch at the site but the rest of the group can't explain how these two ended up dead. The situation was reported by one of the group, an electrician that was working on the house. But he's not making any sense. He keeps babbling about an old sailing ship, fishing nets, and figureheads. I'm also concerned that he may have called a TV station before contacting us. That's why I avoided the radio. Too many people are listening in on scanners these days. I thought you'd want to check this out yourself, just in case any media show up. We are keeping the electrician at the station until he completes his statement."

"Okay, Jack, I'm on my way. Who do we have at the scene?"

"Saunders, Sir. He's a pretty cool guy as a rule, but seems a bit unnerved by this turnout and he's anxious for help. He said the man that drowned looks as if he's been dragged over gravel and the live people are all acting strange. One guy had his pants off and keeps doing squats and knee bends while another one is unresponsive to anybody and acts like he's swinging an imaginary axe at something. Saunders is having a job keeping them on site, Pat. I've sent two more cars, and requested a coroner and forensic team. We've also had a problem at the station. Sergeant Stanton collapsed a short time ago. He was out cold for a few seconds but seemed okay when he came to. I had Williams take him to the emergency room anyway; just to be safe. The doctors are keeping him for some tests."

"Good thinking, Jack. Keep me posted on that. Is there anything known about the deceased or anyone else at the building site?"

"Saunders believes the guy swinging the imaginary axe has a record, Sir. He remembers his face, but can't recall from where. We're checking that now. One of the names Saunders gave me was Earl Whitt, a real estate developer. This building lot is the site of Whitt's new house, which is almost complete. Pat, you will recall Toronto asking us to check on Whitt's wife about three months ago. Her lawyer had given them an address up here after her friends reported her missing. You had Stanton interview her, and he said she was recovering from a bad beating. He was so upset by the lady's injuries he wanted to go a few rounds with her husband himself. You spoke with Mrs. Whitt's lawyer after that, Richard Wellesley. Remember?"

"I remember. Is Whitt one of the dead?"

"Saunders didn't say, Sir. He had to leave the car and chase after someone trying to leave the scene. That was the last time I spoke with him."

"Okay, Jack. I'm on Ridge Road now. I'll get the rest from the guys on site. Keep me posted about Stanton."

"Aye, Sir."

Crowley well remembered how angry Stanton had been after meeting Mrs. Whitt. It was because of his anger that Crowley had made a point of visiting the lady's lawyer himself. Wellesley had told him: 'Mrs. Whitt left her husband after a bad beating. She also left a note on their fridge, stating that she would make no claims on him, provided he left her alone and didn't try to contact her. Whitt wanted the terms of her note converted into a binding legal agreement and asked a friend of mine, Bill Jones, to draw up a sort of retroactive, prenuptial agreement for her to sign, intending to deny his wife any access to his estate when they divorced. 'Jonesy' is a corporate lawyer, and didn't want the job. However, Whitt's partner, Chernak, who was already a client of Jones', persuaded him to look into the matter. Jones' enquiries led him to me and when he learned that Whitt was a wife beater, he wanted nothing more to do with him. However, his only contact with Whitt had been over the phone and so, as a courtesy to Chernak, he decided to give Whitt a chance to present his side of the story. I would have liked to have been a fly-on-the wall at the meeting.'

• • •

That meeting had actually taken place two months before the strange deaths on Ridge Road. Whitt, whilst pestering his partner, Chernak, to influence his lawyer to act on his behalf, had learned that Jones was a gourmet who delighted in new dining experiences. So, Whitt, who was a friend of the owners of an exclusive, gourmet restaurant 'The Victori-Anna', was determined to make a 'buddy' of Jones by treating him to a working supper there. The house had been converted into a restaurant of several intimate dining rooms where antique furniture, crackling fireplaces and lush area carpets, over polished wooden floors, gave the impression of an elegant private home, rather than a restaurant. Whitt was gratified by the lawyer's look of pleasant surprise when he greeted Jones there for their meeting.

Whitt waited for Jones to set his cutlery aside before asking: "So, how was your meal, Bill? It seemed to have your full attention, so I'm hoping it was as enjoyable as my own."

Jones' pleasant features lit up in a broad smile. He clasped both hands to his stomach before gathering up his wine glass, and relaxing in the comfortable, upholstered chair.

"Earl, that meal would have compensated for some of the worst days of my life. This has been a delight. Thank you for introducing me to this wonderful place. Converting elegant old houses into a restaurant of several intimate dining rooms is a well-established style, of course, but I've never been as impressed as I am by this one. I have a passion for good food." Whitt felt his muscles relax and tension slip from his body. This meeting was off to a good start. They both declined the tempting dessert cart, ordering liqueurs and coffee instead. Then Jones addressed the reason for their meeting outside of business hours.

"So Earl, I understand that you are leaving for England tomorrow, to be best man at Al Chernak's wedding. That promises to be an exciting affair. Al told me that the ceremony is to be in a unique church; in the West Country I believe."

"That's right! Al's fiancée comes from a fishing village called Ryeport, where an ancestor of hers designed the church and was later married there. That began a family tradition unbroken to this day, more than two hundred years later. I suggested that Al and Heather just live together. We all know how short-lived marriages have become these days. Heather, Al's fiancée, wouldn't hear of it. So, I suggested a quiet civil ceremony over here, with a more formal event in Ryeport later, when we weren't so busy. Apparently, her whole family ganged up against that idea. You'd think this marriage was the most important event of their lives. I could do without this fuss and interruption to my business schedule, especially now, in view of this problem with my wife."

Jones raised his eyebrows. "That sounds a bit 'Marley and Scrooge,' Earl. Surely, you must be flattered to be chosen as your partner's best man, especially for such a unique wedding. I understand Al stood up for you, when you were married. This offers you an opportunity to reciprocate."

"Al is a fool to get married. Especially since he's seen the problems I'm facing through legally tying myself to one woman, in such an outdated ritual."

Jones appeared at a loss for a response, and relieved to see the waitress arrive with the coffee and liqueurs. Their conversation paused until she left the room.

"Speaking of Millie," Jones said, "we really should get down to business. Earl, whilst researching the arrangement you requested, I uncovered some things I didn't expect. Just to ensure my facts are correct, I'd like to review my understanding of the situation and clarify a point or two. If any of my assumptions are wrong, I'd appreciate your corrections. Okay?" Whitt nodded his assent and Jones continued. "You have been married about two and a half years now, and your wife Millicent recently left you, without warning, and disappeared from sight. I have the copy of her note that you gave me, in which she stated that she would make no claims on you provided that you made no attempt to contact her. Okay so far?" Whitt nodded as he topped up their coffee. Jones continued. "Her friends were alarmed by her sudden, and unannounced, disappearance, and contacted the police. They suspected foul play." Jones paused, searching Whitt's face for a reaction. Finding none, he continued. "The police questioned all known associates, and her employer referred them to a lawyer: Richard Wellesley, who arranged for the police to meet Millie. Incidentally, her friends reported her missing before you did. Why was that?"

Whitt shrugged. "I thought she must be staying with friends. I had her note, remember?"

"Of course! The police met with your wife, confirmed that her seclusion was self-imposed, and that she intended to remain incommunicado at this time. They also stated that she was recovering from a severe beating." Jones fixed his eyes on Whitt again, obviously inviting a response but Whitt remained impassive, so again Jones continued. "Contrary to the terms of Millie's note, you tried to establish contact, but got no further than her lawyer whom, I must advise you, is a friend of mine. He told me that he reminded you of the terms of your wife's note and advised you to back off or risk a costly division of assets, and a possible suit for mental and physical abuse. However, you decided to engage a lawyer to convert the terms of Millie's note to a binding legal agreement. In fact, you wanted me to arrange a sort of retroactive, prenuptial agreement. Still on track?"

Whitt nodded. "Yes, I thought we had all this established."

"Mr. Whitt, you are going to have to level with me if we are to continue in this matter. Did you beat your wife?"

Whitt found the lawyer's eyes riveted on his face, as though daring him to lie. He was silent for a few seconds before raising the coffee carafe to Jones. The lawyer declined with a curt wave of his hand. "Whatever happened to Earl? Are we no longer on a first name basis?" Jones ignored the question so, with a wry smile, Whitt said: "We had a few quarrels. Contrary to first impressions, Millie is a hard woman to live with: very demanding, jealous and possessive."

"Did you beat your wife? Please answer the question." Jones' tone was insistent.

Whitt's athletic frame tensed as he leaned across the table to stare angrily into the lawyer's face. "Am I on trial here?"

"No, but you could well be and very soon, if I read Millie's lawyer correctly and he'll not be less direct." Jones appeared unmoved by Whitt's aggressive attitude, and his eyes didn't waver from their scrutiny of his companion's face.

Whitt shrugged and sank back in his chair. "I slapped her, a couple of times, nothing of any consequence. The woman was unbelievably irritating, always questioning my whereabouts. Certainly, there was no cause for her to leave. I gave her everything she wanted. I was even building a new house for her. What a bloody white elephant that will be! I even have to visit the site before I fly out tomorrow and I...."

Jones interrupted, "Nothing of any consequence, you say." He produced an envelope from an inside pocket, withdrew a photograph, and placed it in front of Whitt. "This photograph was taken in the Emergency Room of St. Mike's Hospital on the night that Millie left you. The picture is dated and signed by the attending doctor. Her doctor and the police don't consider Millie's injuries inconsequential. In fact one would have a job recognising her, because the severe bruising and swellings have so distorted her features."

"What does that have to do with me?" Whitt responded.

Jones spread more pictures in front of him. "The dates and doctor's comments indicate a progressive increase in the severity of the beatings over the past year. The doctor said she looked very frightened. On the face of things, if we were to believe these pictures and the statement of her friends and co-workers, one might conclude that you are a vicious, bullying, wife beater. But that couldn't possibly be true – or could it?" Jones gave a small, disparaging smile. Whitt raised his eyes from the pictures.

"I certainly didn't do that," he said. "She must have fallen down the stairs again. She was accident prone."

Now it was Jones' turn to lean across the table, as he stared into Whitt's angry face, as though trying to read his mind. "Wellesley has investigated this matter very thoroughly and, believe me, he deserves his excellent reputation. He has built a substantial file in preparation for this case and advised Millie to bring this matter to court. Initially she declined, but I believe it would be a difficult case for you to win if Millie decides to proceed." Jones appeared bored and that seemed to fuel Whitt's anger even more.

"You are supposed to be representing me! You act more like a damned prosecuting attorney, for God's sake. I hired you to secure a simple legal agreement. Millie had already proposed terms that were acceptable to me. All that was required of you was to draw a legal document in those same terms, and have her sign it. Stop treating me like a bloody criminal. I'm your client, the one who will be paying your exorbitant bill."

"Oh, Mr. Whitt, I wouldn't dream of presenting you with an exorbitant bill. After all, you are not yet a client. I only agreed to consider this matter as a favour to Al Chernak. I never accept a case before I check it out." Jones gathered up the photographs and returned them to his inside pocket. "Actually, this is not my area of expertise. I would never have considered the case at all, but for your partner's earnest request. Your wife's lawyer, on the other hand, is possibly the best in Canada in matters of physical and mental abuse. I have promised to return Millie's photographs to him." Jones rose from his seat. "Goodnight, Mr. Whitt. In my opinion, you would be wise to abide by the conditions of your wife's note and let the matter rest. Thank you for supper. In the circumstances, I shall consider that adequate compensation for time expended on your behalf. You will receive a letter from me declining to represent you in this matter. I shall, of course, hold my notes on file. Please apologise to Al for me. Tell him that I find your needs far exceed my expertise." He turned and left the room without looking back. There was no parting handshake.

Whitt stood, as though to follow him, but thinking better of it, angrily smashed his fist on the table instead, causing the coffee cups to rattle. He was having a hard time controlling his anger. "So much for the expertise of the great Bill Jones," he said. "Some bloody referral. Now I have to leave this matter up-in-the-air while I go to England for Al's stupid wedding." He looked out the window in time to see Jones enter his car. Light snow was falling, and the small flakes swirled and danced their way through the pools of light cast by the Victorian street lamps in the parking lot. "You double-dealing bastard," Whitt muttered, as he watched the car pull away, spinning snow from under its tires.

• • •

While Whitt and Jones had been enjoying the luxury of the 'Vic', the contractor responsible for completing Whitt's new house: Walter Wilton-Smythe – Smitty to his friends and creditors – was seating himself for his main meal of the day. However, the ambience of the Legion's beverage room paled by comparison to that of the 'Vic'. Smitty, chose a secluded corner, and placed his beer and paper plate on the arbourite-topped table. His meat pie was hot from the microwave, and his only side dish was a package of potato chips. He took a quick mouthful of beer before settling into his usual 'gun-fighter' seat; his back to the wall and facing the door. Carefully he placed his stiff left leg between the corner wall and the table so that no one could trip over it. That leg had been badly damaged in a motorcycle accident three years earlier and the knee was now inflexible, held together with screws and metal plates. Smitty tore the top off the bag of potato chips, and poured them onto the plate. The beverage room was quiet tonight, which suited the mood of this lean, six foot-two man perfectly. The last thing he wanted tonight was company. However, his solitude was short lived. He groaned and his shoulders slumped as he watched a familiar figure enter the room, buy a beer, and spotting him, cross to the table.

"Hi, Smitty!" Living high-on-the-hog tonight I see."

"Hi, Bert! I've got a lot on my mind tonight. I need some quiet time to resolve some private problems. I thought I'd find a quiet corner where I could focus on possible solutions, without interruptions."

Bert took the seat across the table – but not the hint – and studied Smitty thoughtfully. After a few seconds of reflection, he seemed to reach a decision. "Smitty, I've noticed a big change in you over the past few weeks. If you've got problems, I'd be pleased to help."

Smitty gave a shake of his head. "No, Bert! It's personal but thanks anyway."

"Come on, Smitty. We've been friends since grade school. You know I'm no gossip. Anything said here stays here. As I said, if I can help, I'll be pleased to. Trouble at work, is it?"

Smitty was silent for a few seconds, avoiding eye contact, before flipping his pie upside down and cutting into it with his plastic knife. Steam poured from the cut and the aroma of meat and gravy drifted across the table. Bert smiled. "Smells good, Smitty, but it won't be a patch on Amy's cooking. Why aren't you at home, where the food is better, and Amy can help you with your problems?"

"Sorry, but this is a private matter. I'm really not in the mood for questions tonight."

Smitty's surly manner left no illusions about his not wanting company, but

Bert refused to be put-off. "I bet it's got something to do with that bum of a helper you hired. Where is Robbie anyway?"

"Shopping!" Smitty ate a couple of potato chips. "I'll pick him up later. He'll call me here when he's ready."

Bert shook his head. "So, you are still acting as his private chauffeur. That guy is a real pain-in-the-ass. Everybody here knows that. They all wonder why you keep him on. Is he that good a worker?"

"No, Bert. Just between you and me, he's a liability. But he got us the job that we're working on and that's the crux of the matter! So, if anybody asks, you can tell them that I will make the hiring and firing decisions in my little firm."

Bert ignored the inference that he should mind his own business and leave. "That'll be the job in the valley – the job the black lawyer from England told Robbie about, when he accidentally bumped into him in the Orillia Legion." Bert gave a derisive, grunting, laugh. "Let's see if I've got this right? A lawyer from England just happens to be in the Orillia Legion, where he bumps into a stranger – an out of work ex-con, no less – and promptly offers him a fat contract. Not for him, but for you – another guy he's never met and who doesn't operate in the Orillia area." Bert raised his arms and his eyebrows in a gesture of total disbelief. "I wouldn't want that guy as my lawyer. I thought that profession was supposed to be more prudent than that."

"I don't know anything about the guy, Bert. I've never met him. Don't even know his name. Robbie couldn't remember it. Apparently, his firm handles all the legal affairs for Whitt's real estate company, including Whitt's new house. His original contractor quit when he was offered a fat bonus to work exclusively on another house that had a tight closing date. The bonus was to ensure there'd be no jumping from job to job. Whitt was mad as hell apparently, but had no written contract, so he needed a new contractor. When this lawyer – the black guy – 'bumped into' Robbie, he told him he needed a contractor in the Orangeville area to complete Whitt's house and asked Robbie if he knew me. I lost my previous helper, Andy, when he received an unexpected inheritance and the lawyer said he knew of me, because it was his firm that had helped Andy with his legal particulars. Anyway, Robbie piled on the bullshit, saying he knew all the contractors in the area, and got a phone number from the lawyer. Later, Robbie found me and told me the story. I called the law firm, Krueger and Johnson, and they sent me the specs for Whitt's house. So, I worked out a quote and called them back. Guess what? They didn't even want to hear my quote. Just asked if I would accept the balance of the work, for the balance of the originally contracted price. That balance was a lot higher than my quote, so it was a no-brainer. There was one condition; I had to employ Robbie for the duration of the contract. Obviously, I said yes. But if I'd known how much trouble Robbie was going to be, I would have turned it down. The fact remains though, that if Robbie hadn't brought me that lead, I might not be working now. But I often wish I hadn't taken the job. Whitt's a real bastard to work for and Robbie's shoddy work is causing lots of problems."

Bert was looking puzzled. "But why are you here now, Smitty? You and Amy make a great team. Since you met Amy, you shook off the 'macho-biker' mentality that cost you full use of your leg and became a responsible family man. And you got yourself a great, ready-made family to boot. Your friends were all happy to see you in such a good wholesome, relationship. Surely Amy could help you with whatever problems you've got?"

Smitty sighed and gave a shrug of resignation. Then he looked Bert in the eye and said: "Oh well, Bert I guess you'll hear about it soon anyway. Amy and me are splitting up."

"What?" Bert sat bolt upright, looking totally shocked.

Smitty looked glum as he continued. "Yeah, we had a bust-up over my getting home late the other night. The night you drove me home in fact. After work that night, I'd dropped Robbie off here and he insisted on buying me a beer for driving him around. We had a game of darts. One game became two, then three, and the beer kept coming. I played more games than I'd intended and got home too late to take the family to the show. I'd promised the kids that I'd take them and I let them down. Amy was annoyed. She said I was drunk, which I wasn't, and we ended up having a fight. I stormed out and had a few more beers. I thought I'd show her what drunk really looked like. That was the night you found me trying to get into my truck, took my keys away and drove me home, remember? Amy and me had another fight when I got home. She said she doesn't want her kids to hear us fighting, or see me drunk. 'My kids aren't used to that,' she said. 'And I don't intend they shall ever get used to it.'" Smitty waved his hand dismissively. "I can't blame her. She was absolutely right. The whole thing was my fault. Stupid really! I love Amy, and her kids. I'm really going to miss them. Anyway, Amy gave me an ultimatum. 'Get rid of Robbie, and quit the heavy drinking,' she said. 'All our troubles started when you hired him. Otherwise we'll have to separate.' So, I'm leaving! Tomorrow morning. It's her house after all! I am just the live-in boyfriend." Smitty picked at the pie with his plastic fork. "So now you know the whole story, Bert. But it's not for publication." He fixed eye contact, and pointed his fork at Bert – just to emphasise the point.

"Come now, Smitty. Surely, you're not going to throw away such a great relationship, over a few beers, and a louse like Robbie? For God's sake, dump Robbie, go on home and say you're sorry. Robbie's just using you! You need to get your priorities straight, my friend."

"Well, like I said, Bert, the contract guarantees his employment. If I fire him, I break the contract. I can't afford to do that. Every last penny I have, plus a massive loan, is tied up in Whitt's big house. Until it's finished, I don't get paid up, and I'm in debt up to my ears." Smitty's shoulders slumped, and he suddenly looked defeated. "I simply can't afford to break the contract," he mumbled. "I can't fire Robbie, and I'm also stuck with Whitt until the job is complete. The three of us might just as well be welded together until then." He looked tired and beaten but that only lasted a few seconds. Then he looked up, squared his shoulders and said: "So, if anyone asks, I'm still responsible for my little firm. I'll make the decisions – good or bad – not the guys at the Legion or my girlfriend. Sink or swim, it's up to me. Anyway, I need a helper. This gammy leg has robbed me of a lot of my independence."

Bert took a sip of beer before responding: "I'm sorry, Smitty; I'd help if I could. Can't you get your previous helper back?"

"No, Bert. I'd love to have Andy back, but I wouldn't even ask him. He had that inheritance, remember? Talk about coincidence! It was the same firm, Krueger and Johnson, that handled that too. Andy got a small farm willed to him. Well, to his dad actually but his dad died two years ago, so it passed to Andy. Right out-of-the-blue, that was. Just like winning a lottery with a found ticket. It seems an army buddy of Andy's dad passed away without leaving any relatives. Andy doesn't even remember his dad mentioning the guy. Anyway, we were working in Orangeville one day when this good-looking girl – Heather her name was – found us at the job site. She told Andy about the Will. Anyway, this girl, Heather, said that the farm would now pass to Andy. A conditional bequest I believe she called it.

It's outside Calgary somewhere! The farm I mean. Andy and me both stood there with our mouths hanging open, while she gave him the news. He had to go to Toronto the next day with proof of identity, and some army papers of his dad's. When he left here, he owned a farm. His first thought had been to sell it. But that wasn't allowed under the conditional part of the bequest. He had to live on the farm, and work it himself – no selling or renting the place. He's not allowed to change the farm to any business other than farming either. After three years, provided he shows a profit from the farm, the conditions will be lifted and he will become fully vested in the farm. He'll make it though. Andy is a hard worker – his girlfriend too. They make a great team. I'm happy to see good people get a break. But I was real sorry to lose Andy; he was a great tradesman and a good friend. And, to make matters worse, Robbie was his replacement. It seems that the big guy, upstairs," Smitty rolled his eyes towards the heavens, "must have decided I was having things too good since I found Amy and her kids, and decided to throw some crappy stuff my way, just to even things out. He overdid it though when he added Robbie to the mix. Andy learned, from this girl Heather, that this friend of his dad had always dreamed of owning a farm, and finally managed to buy this place just before he retired. Then the poor bastard got sick. He wanted someone else to fulfil his dream for him. So he willed the farm to his friend, but with those conditions attached. He didn't intend to give away a lifetime of savings and hard work to someone who would just cash-it-in."

Bert was looking glum. "Well, good luck to Andy for sure. But that still leaves you stuck with Robbie and you're still having to drive him all over the place. When is he getting his licence back?" Now it was Smitty's turn to look startled. "Get his licence back? I never knew he'd lost it! When was that?"

"Shortly after he got out of the 'nick,' Smitty. Drunk driving. And he was nailed for driving without a licence or insurance after that. Incidentally, he doesn't know that I know that. I had a friend of mine in the police check him out. His jail time was for grievous bodily harm, you know. He beat up an old variety store clerk for the cash in the till, and nearly killed the guy, all for about thirty bucks I believe. While Robbie was inside, his wife and kids took off. They disappeared down east somewhere. But I'd appreciate you keeping that information under-your-hat, Smitty. Robbie's got a reputation for back-alley methods of settling accounts."

Smitty was dumbstruck. "He never told me he lost his licence. He told me he couldn't find a reliable car that he could afford."

"Yeah, I know; that's why I checked him out. When my wife got promoted recently, a company car came with the new job. We had just had her own car completely overhauled, so I offered it to Robbie, at a really good price and I told him I'd take two hundred bucks a month. I thought that would help you out. That's some buddy you've got there, Smitty. With friends like him..." Bert spread his arms wide, "you don't need enemies. Watch your back."

Smitty ran his fingers through his hair, looking totally downcast. "Thanks for cheering me up, Bert. I feel much better now."

"You're welcome, mate! That's what friends are for! Seriously, though Smitty, if you can think of some way I can help, please let me know. I would hate to see you and Amy break up." Bert pushed back his chair, and picked up his empty glass. "Well, I'm off home, mate. Eat your pie – it's getting cold."

Smitty collected Robbie just before seven p.m. and dropped him off at his apartment. He declined the offered drink, saying he had to get home, but in fact, he had no intention of going home until Amy would be in bed and asleep. He wasn't sure how he would cope with this parting-of-the-ways, and certainly wasn't up to discussion with her tonight. He decided to waste some time in the Orangeville movie theatre until he felt sure Amy would be asleep. He bought some peanuts and settled in for the 7:30 pm performance.

• • •

As Smitty took his seat in the movie theatre, it was already 12:30 am, in Ryeport England, where Holly Maxwell, the new live-in barmaid at The Seahorse Inn, lay smiling in her bed. Holly was feeling safe and comfortable, for the first time in many years. She was relieved and grateful to have escaped from her previous job as a bartender at Freefrees, a sleazy nightclub at Plymouth. She had hated that place. Any conversation the regulars started with her usually included an offer to get laid, do drugs or go to a party, where you might be expected to rotate through all of the above. Had she not needed a job so desperately, she would have quit that place that very first night. But she had been single, living from paycheque to paycheque, while struggling to pay off the overloaded plastic her ex 'boyfriend' had left her, and she had to have a job, any job, to pay her bills.

On her last night at Freefrees, she had been trying, with such grace as she could muster, to escape the unwanted attentions of a 'macho-type' at the bar who was trying to sell her on the merits of spending the night with him, when the tall black man had entered the club. He had paused in the doorway for a quick survey of the room before making his way to the bar. The disdain on his face was hard to miss, especially as he paused to watch an effeminate, tubby man pinning zodiac buttons on various patrons. "Compatibility is so important, my dears," 'Zodiac-man' was saying, as he smiled his simpering smile. Holly had not been able to repress a smile herself, as she noted the newcomer's unmistakeable expression of disgust. The newcomer had appeared to be in his sixties; in good physical shape, well groomed, wearing an obviously expensive suit and looking too classy for that sleazy, 'meat-market' establishment. She recalled how out of place he'd looked as he seated himself at the bar and waited patiently for service.

But 'Macho-man' had her wrist in a firm grip, and seemed intent on holding her there until she gave him the answer he wanted. The black man waited patiently a while longer before interrupting. "Excuse me, Sir," he said, smiling at the man when he turned to face him. But he then addressed himself directly to her. "Could I have a Heineken please, Holly?" She jerked her wrist free, and rubbed it with her other hand. "Certainly, Sir," she said. "Coming right up."

'Macho' was not pleased and scowled as he faced the black man. "Why don't you bugger-off, spade," he'd said belligerently. "Don't you know better than to interrupt when a bloke's chatting-up a lady?"

The black man lowered his head momentarily. Then he stepped down from his stool and his expression was grim as he addressed him. "Obviously, you do not know of me," he said. His voice was quiet, but every word was slowly and clearly enunciated, as though to ensure no misunderstanding. "Permit me to introduce myself. Just to give you fair warning. I am known as 'The Sexton.'" He raised his eyebrows as he gave the familiar quote signal at the word Sexton. "In case you are unaware, a sexton is paid to put people in their graves. Sometimes, I work for free." He smiled a small but humourless smile, as he again raised his eyebrows. "Your bad manners could prove detrimental to your health. I would suggest, Sir, that you take your drink elsewhere. I'm sure that, if you have any friends or family, they would want that." 'Macho' hesitated, disturbed by the newcomer's confidence and unwavering eye contact. He noticed that the black guy had also returned one hand to his pocket. Could 'Sexton' be a street name for a 'hit-man'? This club was frequented by quite a few villains. The two men stared at each other for a few seconds before 'Macho' picked up his glass, and walked away. "She's not worth the bother," he mumbled.

"Thank you, kind Sir," she'd said, with a theatrically coy response, batted her eyelids and gave a small curtsey, holding the forefinger of her right hand under her chin. She had followed that with a quiet laugh. "Frankly," she'd said, "some of the people here are quite scary, especially when they hear the word no." She'd placed a napkin on the counter and poured the newcomer his Heineken. The black man had smiled as he said: "Holly, I have something here that I think might interest you." He unfolded his newspaper and drew her attention to an advertisement for a live-in barmaid at The Seahorse Inn in Ryeport. "Ryeport is a small fishing village west of here," he explained. "The village has an interesting history of smuggling and seafaring adventures. In a couple of months they will be exploiting that history by opening a vacation park; a modest sort of theme park for tourists." He'd smiled again. "No threat to Disney World, you understand but it should prove an interesting and lucrative enterprise. Anyway, the inn will need an experienced barmaid to cope with the tourist business. At the moment, their beverage trade is just draft beer and straight shots. Next weekend a few weeks ahead of the park opening, the inn will also host a wedding. A Canadian man will be marrying a local girl whose ancestor designed the local church. The church is unique and will also be a feature of the vacation park. The inn will be very busy Holly. I'm sure you'd like it much better than this place. The clientele will be more wholesome. By the way, my name is Sexton. Paul Sexton. And I am also 'The Sexton' of The Guiding Light Church, in Ryeport. So, I'm Sexton by both name and occupation." His smile had been warm and reassuring. He gave a small shrug. "I just steered your macho friend to a more sinister interpretation for my name."

She remembered smiling at his little subterfuge and watching his smile grow to a big grin, in response. "I wonder that I didn't see this advertisement myself," she'd said. "I've been looking for another job, ever since I took this one."

"It's a local paper." Sexton responded. "I don't imagine it's distributed here." She had re-read the ad. Compensation included room and board, plus a modest wage. The live-in aspect of the job would certainly be a relief. No more struggling for the rent at month's end or having to prepare her own lonely meals. And the biggest plus – she would be free of the inexhaustible supply of creeps at Freefrees. The pros easily outweighed the cons and she had applied for the job, in person, the very next day.

She recalled how she had checked herself out in the mirror before leaving her flat. "First impressions are important," she had told her reflection, as she dusted a piece of lint from her smart, dark green raincoat. However, she was disappointed in her first impression of the inn's owners, Sam and Sarah Bass. Sam was an overweight grungy looking individual, with a smile to match. It soon became obvious that he was not too bright either. Sam's wife Sarah, a short tubby woman, was pleasant enough, but when she learned that Holly was single, her questions focused more on her love life than her skills as a barmaid and that had given her the impression that Sarah might be concerned that an unattached barmaid might be tempting to Sam. Holly shuddered at the thought. However, she'd got the job. It transpired that Sexton had recommended her very highly and that his opinion carried a lot of weight in Ryeport. She had started the very next day, feeling strangely comfortable at the inn from the very outset. She was still smiling happily as her eyelids closed, and she drifted off to the land-of-nod.

• • •

At this time Smitty, who had spent the night on the couch, was sitting, alone, at the kitchen table in Amy's house in Bramalea, a mile or two east of Whitt's route. His right hand held a mug of cold black coffee. Two slices of burnt toast sat, untouched, on a plate he'd pushed away when the coffee had still looked appetising. Several partially smoked cigarettes lay crushed out in the ashtray. He had no appetite for anything. She had thrown down the gauntlet, by insisting he fire Robbie – without knowing, of course, that his contract with Whitt would have bankrupted him had he done so. Smitty's left hand was fidgeting restlessly with his hair – a sign that both Amy and Whitt had come to recognise as an unwitting signal that his confidence was low and that he would be indecisive and vulnerable.

Smitty was a ruggedly good-looking kind of guy – over six feet tall, with a rangy build and a thick mop of dark brown hair. But a few months after his motorcycle accident some stands of grey had crept into his hairline. Now there were two very distinct, almost white stripes, at his right temple. Amy said it looked distinguished but he thought it looked 'freaky' and that

Amy was just trying to make him feel better. That accident had robbed him of more than the mobility of his left leg. He had never been short of confidence before that.

The quiet creak of the bedroom door intruded on his thoughts and he raised his gaze to watch Amy enter the kitchen. She was wearing the rose-pink housecoat that he'd bought for her last birthday. Her arms were folded across her chest, head and shoulders bent forward, as though huddled against the cold. That self-hugging mannerism that made her look so vulnerable, together with her tousled reddish-brown hair and sleepy hazel eyes, would always be one of his strongest memories of her. As she entered the kitchen, her gaze rested briefly on two cardboard boxes that he'd left at the side door. The sight of them seemed to startle her, and she turned, as though to speak but paused, biting her lower lip, before saying: "I didn't hear you get up; I hope you weren't going to leave without saying good-bye." Her eyes took in the table scene and his obvious despondence and her voice cracked a little as she asked: "Any coffee left?"

"I was very late last night." Smitty responded. "I didn't want to wake you, so I slept on the couch. The coffee's cold. I'll brew some fresh, then I'll be on my way." He avoided her eyes and dumped the cold brew down the sink. "I'll make some fresh toast too. The coffee won't take long." Smitty thought of Bert's advice of last evening: 'You'd best get your priorities right.' Well, he knew they were right here but if he walked away from Whitt's house now, he'd be bankrupt, and have to find a new job. That certainly wouldn't help Amy and the kids. So, he had to hang tough for a while. He was desperately short of personal cash too. The material costs for Whitt's luxury house had all but drained his business, personal accounts and lines-of-credit. The payments that Whitt should have made at various stages of completion, should have kept him solidly in-the-black, but Robbie's shoddy work always gave Whitt the opportunity to withhold those stage payments, until that work was corrected. One such payment was due now. But Whitt would be in England for at least ten days, so Smitty would now have to pay Robbie's wages out of his own pocket. "Oh well, there's still Visa," he mumbled.

What did you say, Smitty?" Amy had detected his muttered undertones. "Nothing Amy, just thinking aloud." So, he poured the coffee. They left the toast to waste again and said their goodbyes; it was all very civilised. Amy shed a few tears as she gave him a quick hug. "Sorry, Smitty but I must consider the kids first. Take care of yourself. Please call me sometimes. Let me know how, and where you are, and how things are going. Please call. I didn't want us to split up."

"I'm sorry too Amy but I am running late and still have to pick Robbie up. We should be on the job by now. He gave her a last peck on the cheek. "Give the kids my love. Bye, Amy; thanks for everything." He turned, grabbed the boxes by the door and stepped out, into the minus twelve degree morning. Amy watched from the kitchen window as he threw his things into the back of the pickup. He was about to slam the tailgate when he paused. "Right now, this, plus my remaining equity in the trucks, and the used machines and tools at my shop, represents all my worldly wealth – maybe, twenty grand on the open market. What a loser!" He slammed the tailgate shut and hauled his stiff leg into the cab. "This has to change." He snarled, as he started the engine. He was all set to 'scream' the truck out of the driveway, when the frost covered windshield forced him to reconsider. His show of macho defiance would have to wait until he'd scraped the wind-shield clear and the pickup's heater was capable of keeping it that way. When he finally drove off, to collect Robbie, it also occurred to him that he had no idea where he would sleep tonight. He was desperately short of cash and there was little room left on the plastic. It was then that he realised that he'd been hoping that Amy would back down, and ask him to stay.

# CHAPTER 2

## *A case of déjà vu*

Holly Maxwell was an attractive woman and well used to compliments. However, vanity was not one of her failings, and she didn't take them seriously. From her own perspective though, she was too heavy. "I could do with losing at least a stone," she murmured, as she caught sight of her reflection in the bathroom mirror, then she added, with a wry smile: "Maybe a stone and a half. But, that's not so bad. I shouldn't expect to have a schoolgirl figure now that I'm forty-one. I'm just maturing, *like fine wine!*" She laughed: a bright and happy sound that was infectious in any company. Holly was looking forward to her new life in Ryeport, and knew that a little extra weight wouldn't spoil that. She dressed, brushed her shiny, auburn hair, added a light touch of makeup, and went downstairs to breakfast. Since Sarah Bass had made it clear that she would be doing all the cooking, that made the meal even more enjoyable.

The morning passed quickly, but she was pleased to see Sexton arrive for lunch. As she was clearing away his dishes, she said: "Thank you for showing me that ad, Sexton. This inn feels strangely warm and familiar to me – like an old friend. There's a comforting atmosphere about this place that I just can't explain. I really do feel at home here. I could hardly wait to start." She flashed a mischievous smile at him. "Do you think I'm a bad girl Sexton? I didn't give Freefrees any notice. I just phoned and told them I'd quit. They were mad at me, of course, and said I'd forfeit Monday's pay. But that's okay. I never want to see that place again. I left a letter for the landlord of my flat, giving him my furniture to compensate for the short notice. I only took my personal bits and pieces. I have no intention of going back there or leaving a forwarding address." Sexton smiled. "Tut-tut. Yes, you really are a bad girl Holly. But you've had a lot to put up with. Anyone who knows you would understand, and forgive, that little breach of proper behaviour." She laughed. "You must be my guardian angel Sexton. You appeared, out of nowhere, when I was so desperate for a better job. I'm so glad you found me." Sexton smiled as he responded. "My dear, I never lost you."

Holly was puzzled over those words, and wondered why she played them over, again and again, in her mind. '*My dear, I never lost you.*' Could that mean he'd been watching her? Following her maybe, or simply that he wasn't the one that had lost her...or what? The coincidence of this stranger turning up at Freefrees at such a low point in her life and providing an ideal solution to her problems seemed almost magical. She also recalled that Sexton had called her by name from the outset, treating her like an old friend – but she hadn't told him her name and that 'macho creep' at Freefrees hadn't used it. So, how had he known it? It was all rather strange – not scary strange – but puzzling nevertheless.

The lunch customers drifted away and Holly found herself with time on her hands. Sexton was now the only customer left in the bar and looked depressed, and rather tired. Holly took a bowl of peanuts to his table. "A penny for your thoughts, Sexton. You look quite fed up. How can I cheer you up?" Sexton returned her smile. "You already have Holly. Your happy personality brightens this gloomy room for all us patrons of the 'Harbour Light'."

"Well, thank you kind Sir," she replied, adding her trademark curtsy. "But I'm serious. You do look quite miserable."

"Oh, I've had a disappointment, Holly. A good friend of mine from Canada, had planned to vacation here in time for the wedding this weekend. But just this morning, he emailed me to let me know his vacation had been cancelled. Instead he has to substitute for another lecturer at a seminar in Boston, Massachusetts. He will be involved there for the whole week that the wedding guests will be here. Apparently the original speaker was badly injured, almost killed, in a freak accident." Holly looked concerned. "What a shame! But surely he'll be able to come over later, after the seminar perhaps?"

"Possibly, but this is very bad timing. I really needed him here for the wedding." She smiled. "He's not the groom is he?" Sexton laughed. "Not likely Holly. Father Charlesworth is a Catholic priest."

"Oh! So why is it so important that he be here for the wedding?" Sexton's face creased in a broad grin. "Boy, you are full of questions today, Miss." She coloured a little. "Sorry, Sexton. I didn't mean to be nosy."

"That's okay, Holly. It's just that I've been trying to get Father Charlesworth to Ryeport for more than twenty years now. We've been good friends for over thirty but we only see each other when he is over here on business, or when I go to Canada. And every time we try to arrange for him to visit here, something always crops up to spoil our plans. He's never made it yet." Holly repeated her earlier question. "Why is it so important that he comes to Ryeport?"

"Well Holly, Father Charlesworth is an expert on the paranormal. He's also well versed in reincarnation theories and related subjects and there are some intriguing stories about this old inn and 'The Seahorse', a ship that was wrecked here about two hundred years ago. Her salvaged timbers were used to build the extension to this inn you know. I'm sure my friend would be very interested in this place and I would love to hear his opinions on those stories and some of the artefacts salvaged from that old ship. Ryeport's history and the supernatural stories about this area, and this inn, are a hobby of mine."

"Ooh!" Holly shuddered. "I wouldn't want to get mixed up with any of that supernatural stuff. Too creepy! Excuse me Sexton. I've got a customer." Holly hurried to the bar, leaving Sexton gazing after her with an amused smile on his face.

• • •

Whitt's first-class flight to Heathrow was smooth and on time. Bearing in mind the limitations of an aircraft galley, the food had also been acceptable. That, plus generous complimentary beverages, were responsible for his relaxed mood. The tension that had plagued him since Jones' rejection had slipped away, and he had been dozing comfortably until wakened by the flight attendant's call: "Please fasten seat belts in preparation for landing." He even managed a smile for her when she handed him a note. "We have a message for you, Sir." Chernak had arranged for Whitt to be notified on the plane.

> *Earl: "Regret that I can't meet you as planned. Long story. Will explain later. I have arranged for a car and driver to take you to Ryeport. All is well. Some last-minute changes demanded our personal attention. See you tomorrow.*

*My apologies. Your driver, Dave Trelaw, will meet you when you clear
Customs. It's all arranged and paid for. Thanks for your understanding.
    Al."*

Whitt was met by a well-groomed, casually dressed young man, holding
a large card bearing his name. "Good afternoon Mr. Whitt. I hope you
had a pleasant flight. Mr. Chernak asked me to offer his apologies for the
inconvenience and change of plans. Totally unforeseen he said. My name is
Trelaw, Mr. Whitt...Dave Trelaw. If you wish we can leave directly, or I can
arrange a meal or refreshment first."

"Let's go Dave. I'm thoroughly sick of travelling and looking forward to
a big steak and a few drinks when we arrive. And they'll all be going on
Chernak's tab."

"Yes, Sir. Mr. Chernak did advise me of that." Whitt thought Trelaw's smile
was a little too 'knowing'. "Have you ever been to Canada Dave? Have we
met before? You seem familiar somehow." Trelaw shook his head. "No Sir.
But I do hope to go there someday. I love to travel."

· · ·

While Trelaw was loading Whitt's luggage into the boot of the rental car,
Al Chernak and his bride-to-be, Heather McDowd, were trying on shoes
and costumes in a London theatrical costumers. Heather caught her fiancé
checking his watch for the third time in half an hour. "In heaven's name Al,
quit worrying about Earl? He's a big boy and quite capable of looking after
himself. I'm sure he's landed safely and Dave Trelaw (poor soul) has met
him. They will soon be on their way to Ryeport. Then Sexton will look after
him, 'til we get back. He'll fill him in on the changes, and, undoubtedly,
look after his cranky needs and complaints." She gave a short laugh. "He
may even straighten out some of them by the time we get back. Let's hope
so. I think Earl will meet his match there. Anyway, this is our wedding. It's
supposed to be the most important event of our lives, not Earls. So, don't let
him spoil it!" Chernak managed a wry smile. "You know how he is Honey.
Not the sweetest guy in the world when things don't go his way."

"Who cares? I think he was a rotten choice for best man anyway. He doesn't
even believe in marriage. As poor Millie found out the hard way! Are your
shoes okay?" Al nodded. "Yep, they'll do."

"Fine, then please go into the next room and check that all the gear for the students is packed and ready. Use Sexton's checklist to make sure every-thing's correct."

"Yes Ma'am!" he said, and snapping to attention, executed a nifty 'Benny Hill' type salute. "On the double. Left-right, left-right." Heather didn't even look up.

• • •

Whitt heaved a sigh of relief as Trelaw turned off the motorway onto the secondary road to Ryeport. The long journey, plus the unexpected changes, had left him feeling very unsettled. Trelaw was a good driver and pleasant enough, but they had little in common and conversation had dried up many miles back. Whitt was looking forward to relaxing with a couple of stiff drinks and a good meal, followed by a good night's sleep. Last night certainly hadn't been restful. From Trelaw he learned that Chernak was expected back tomorrow afternoon. That meant he would be denied the satisfaction of complaining about the discomforts he'd endured on his friend's behalf for yet another day.

This new road was narrow and winding, with high hedgerows and no sidewalk or shoulders. There were some stretches where they drove under overhanging trees that made a patchy tunnel over the road. Some of the trees had obviously been pruned to provide clearance for taller vehicles. They crested a rise in the road, breaking out of the 'green tunnel'. A church steeple appeared on the left, then some irregular roof lines on the right. Only when Whitt felt his shoulders relax did he realise how tense the drive had made him. "We're almost there Sir."

Trelaw's smile looked a little artificial; riding with Whitt had not been a relaxing experience and his tension had been contagious.

"Boy! I could sure use a drink, Dave. Can I buy you one?"

"No thanks, Sir. I have to leave right away to pick up Heather McDowd's grandparents. They will be staying at Heather's parent's place, in Ryeport, for the wedding. They don't drive anymore. She is dying of cancer and only has about three weeks to live. When I return I'll leave this car at the inn for you. The keys will be at the bar." The high hedgerows gave way to more open countryside, providing a clear view of a long kidney-shaped harbour, ahead on their left. On the right, across from the wide harbour, stood an irregular assortment of buildings, some stone, and some beam and plaster buildings, with clay tiled roofs. Whitt noticed small clumps of moss growing on some tiles and stone walls they passed, as he sought his intended resting place, and that long awaited drink. "I expected that we would see the sea by now Dave."

"Oh, the harbour is actually enclosed by cliffs, Sir. There is a dogleg passage between the cliffs that leads out to the sea, at the far end of the harbour. Can you make it out yet? I always think of the harbour, and its' exit as resembling my old 'bullseye' putter. The shaft of the club being the seaward passage, and the head of the putter is the calm, protected, pool of water. The shaft of the putter has a bend in it though – just like my old putter." He grinned, "Just joking, Sir. Actually, it's my driver that I'm often tempted to wrap around a tree. At this end of the harbour – the toe of the putter – is a shelving sandy beach. The locals call that 'The Landing'. Farther along, a jetty divides deeper water from The Landing."

"So, you're a golfer Dave?"

"Just a weekend hacker, Sir. On a good day, I'll break a hundred. But golfing is a pleasant way to spend time in good company." He smiled: "I always do well at the nineteenth hole though."

At The Landing, a number of small boats were lying, tilted at various angles, just as they had been left by the receding tide. But Whitt was surprised to see a three-masted, square-rigged, tall ship tied up to the dockside wall, closer to the seaward exit. "That tall ship is a real 'blast from the past' Dave. Looks like the reproduction of The Bounty that I visited in Florida. Obviously, there's deeper water under the ship."

"Aye Mate," responded Trelaw, with a smile. "There might even be a press-gang waiting for us at the inn." Then Whitt spotted the inn. It was only a hundred yards ahead now and reminiscent of many calendar pictures of old country buildings. Whitewashed walls between black posts and beams, dominated its other features. The doors were short but wide, and the small windows were fitted with diamond shaped grids of glass and everything looked a little off-square or plumb. There was also a shortened bowsprit, protruding from the ceiling level of the second storey. Slung beneath the bowsprit, was a figurehead – a golden seahorse. Some of the rigging, including the martingale (dolphin-striker, he believed the Yanks called them) and chains were still in place. Certainly there was no mistaking the identity of the inn. "The inn looks to be below the sole of the putter and in line with the shaft Dave," said Whitt. "But you know, that figurehead seems strangely familiar. Maybe the inn has been used on calendar pictures."

Trelaw's expression was puzzled too. "Funny you should say that Sir, I also find that familiar." They turned into the small, gravelled, parking lot. A quick glance at Whitt's face told Trelaw that his passenger was not impressed. And with good reason; the whole village appeared bedraggled, and under repair. There was even some waste building material piled against the side of the inn. "If Chernak has booked me into some grungy dump, he'll get the rough edge of my tongue." Whitt muttered. "A favour is one thing but I'm not prepared to live in a fixer-upper while I'm doing it." Trelaw pretended he hadn't heard. "I'll get your bags, Sir, then I'll have to push off, or I'll be late for my next pickup."

"Okay Dave. Thanks for the ride." Whitt pulled out his wallet.

Trelaw raised a restraining hand. "Mr. Chernak has already taken care of everything, Sir. I'll see you at the wedding. I'm one of the attendants. I hope you enjoy your stay. I'll put your luggage inside the kitchen door; someone will take it to your room for you. You'll need to register at the main entrance. That's the large door, to the left of the small one." Trelaw opened the smaller door, put the bags inside and called out: "Sarah! Mr. Whitt's here. Luggage is at the side door." Whitt heard a muffled response. Then Trelaw gave him a quick smile and a wave. "I'll be away to pick up Heather's grandparents now Sir," he said as he reversed out of the parking lot and headed back towards 'the green tunnel'.

Whitt stood for a while, studying the harbour and the tall ship. "My God, I've been sent back in time. By at least a couple of centuries," he exclaimed. He hoped that the inn's, quaint, but uncomfortable looking exterior would not be representative of his lodgings. On the wall beside the door, was a weather-beaten sign displaying a flaming brazier, and the words: 'The Harbour Light'. It was obviously original and very old. The paint was chipped, and the colours faded, despite the protection of several coats of shellac. That too had crazed and yellowed with age. The sign struck a familiar chord in his memory. "Same name as the Salvation Army building, in Toronto," he thought. "That must be why it seems familiar. I wonder if the accommodation is the same too. My guess would be that the 'Sally-Anne's' is better." The doorknob turned easily under Whitt's hand but when he pushed the door, it jammed at the lintel. A second, harder push caused the bottom of the door to move in just a little, and vibrate noisily but it still stuck on the lintel.

"What's the matter out there? Didn't you 'ave yer 'Wheaties' this morning? Give the door a decent shove for Gawd's sake." The sarcastic voice from behind the door had a heavy and unfamiliar accent. "Obviously a local yokel," thought Whitt as, for his third try, he struck the top of the door with the heel of his left hand as he pushed with his right. This time, with a protesting squeal, the door scraped free of its frame. Whitt ducked under the lintel and stepped down onto a brick floor. The floor was a good six inches lower than the door's threshold – but he had known it would be so – and that realisation stopped him dead in his tracks, just as the sense of déjà vu struck. He had ducked under the lintel, and his step down had been fluid, almost practised. He recalled a warning: '*Watch your step. The floor is a goodly step down inside.*' Or did he imagine that? After looking into bright sunlight during the long ride from Heathrow airport, this room was extremely dark, and his eyes struggled to adapt. That near blindness must have heightened his other senses, because it was a confusing mixture of smells that struck him next. At first it was a damp, musty, mix of odours that seemed to come at him from all directions. But he soon managed to isolate and identify some of them. The strongest was a very distinctive, earthy smell, most likely from the brick floor, then the stale smell of spilt beer. Then, there was the smell of damp hessian, probably from the scraps of carpet now coming into focus in front of the bar. Sunlight had penetrated the small window on his left, and illuminated a truncated area of brick floor, filling that lighted patch with the elongated shadows of the diamond-shaped, leaded, windowpanes.

Whitt's eyes were adjusting now but the powerful sense of déjà vu was unnerving. The familiarity was so strong that it confused him. He knew there would be another patch of light on the floor to his right, behind the cluttered post that was doubling as a coat rack. Beyond that there would be a rough wooden table, and two benches. At the end of the room, there would be another plank door, similar to the one he'd just struggled with. His eyes had completely adjusted now, and he was able to pick out more detail in the gloomy room. Neglected brass horse ornaments and plates contributed their dull reflections in the shadows of the room. There were miscellaneous dishes on shelves and disused copper cooking pots hung on ceiling beams. "I don't recall those," he murmured.

A heavy Cornish accent intruded on his muddled thoughts. "Well don't stand there all day, man. Put the wood back in the 'ole. Or don't you 'ave enough strength left after fightin' so 'ard, to get it open?"

"The local yokel's giving me the gears," thought Whitt, struggling to comprehend the overwhelming flood of recognition that had struck him on stepping through the door. "I've never been here before," he muttered. "Never been in England before! How the hell can this seem so familiar?"

"Watcha say mate? Talkin' to yerself now are ye? Big boy like you should know better. You know what that's a sign of don't ye?" The sarcastic voice belonged to Sam Bass: owner of The Seahorse Inn. He was standing behind the cluttered bar, wearing a soiled white apron and a grungy smile.

Whitt's stomach was sour with the unpleasant sense of panic that had accompanied the onset of the déjà vu. For the first time in his life he felt disoriented, and scared. "This must be part of some forgotten dream," he mumbled. "But I remembered that unusually deep, step down, onto a brick floor and my entry through that awkward entrance seemed almost practised. He recalled another warning: from a different voice: '*Be careful! The floor inside, is about six inches lower than the doorstep. You have to step down, onto a hollow pounded into the brick floor by hundreds of left feet that have entered here for two hundred years*.' Still confused, Whitt turned and closed the door behind him. Then he peered around the 'coat rack' to see if his mental picture of the table and benches, patch of light, and the door at the end of the room, matched the facts. The patch of light was there right enough but no table or benches. Instead, an old ship's companion ladder occupied much of that space, obviously leading to the second floor. There was an arched opening in the wall where he expected to see the door and through the archway he could see stacked tables and chairs, and new carpet. He gave a sigh of relief. In a way he was disappointed that his precognition was uncorroborated, however, it was a relief to be wrong and the knot in his stomach unwound a little.

Now that the door was closed, and Sam's confrontational voice was silent, the locals lost interest in him and resumed their conversations, but even the buzz and pattern of their chatter seemed familiar. The strong smell of wood smoke was another memory. "Well, wood smoke smells the same wherever you are," he rationalised. "But this room was bad for that. The smoke stung my nose and eyes. Bad chimney I guess." He shuddered, shocked to find that he was accepting the déjà vu as a remembered experience. Two patrons, a short, tubby man and a taller, stiff looking fellow, sitting close by, looked familiar. "They must have been sitting there for centuries," he muttered. "Now why would I think that?"

"What'll it be then? If you've finished all your sniffin', an' mutterin', per'aps you could buy a drink." Bass had been watching Whitt, wearing an expression of pained disbelief all the time. "You should leave some of the atmosphere for others to sniff up ye know. Shouldn't hog it all for yourself. Maybe you could find the strength to hoist a pint?"

"Okay. Give me a beer," said Whitt.

"'alf, or a pint? Best bitter, or scrumpi?" queried Bass. His nose was twitching now. Testing the air to see if he could determine what it was that the newcomer had found so engrossing.

"Make it a pint of bitter," said Whitt.

Bass extended both hands towards Whitt; one held the glass jug of beer, handle towards him, the other, an open palm. "That'll be two quid if you please. Cash up front! No tellin' if ye'll 'ave the strength to pay for it after you've drunk it." Whitt had had enough. The panic in his stomach was a bad addition to his normal bad temper. He felt nervous, and threatened, and the adrenalin was pumping hard. This scruffy slob had got away with his smartass comments long enough. He grabbed the tankard with his left hand and a handful of Bass' shirt with the right, jerking him up against the bar so hard that one foot left the floor and struck a cupboard behind him with a crash. Everyone in the room turned around and the buzz of conversation abruptly ceased.

"Now look here you stupid, unwashed, son-of-a-bitch," said Whitt. "I use maggots like you for fish bait, and I never pay for something until I'm satisfied with it." He raised the jug, with the apparent intent of pouring it over Bass's head. But a firm grip restrained his arm just in time, effectively staying the anointing. Whitt scowled, and turned to face the owner of the hand.

"Come now, Mr. Whitt. There are less expensive ways to give poor old Sam a bath. Besides, your way would be a waste of good beer." The owner of the restraining hand was an older, black man. His relaxed features wore a slightly amused smile, but there was a definite sense of strength and purpose behind both his grip and the friendly expression.

"Do I know you?" Whitt was getting that uneasy feeling in his stomach again. Not the same sense of déjà vu this time, but there was a familiarity about this man, as if from a partially remembered dream. The black man smiled. "I really can't say, Sir. But if we have met, it would seem that, for you at least, it was not a memorable experience."

"Then how do you know my name?"

"Your friend, Al Chernak, asked me to look for you. He couldn't be here to meet you himself so he asked me to cover for him until he got back. His description of you was very accurate, right down to your short fuse. Why don't you put Sam down? After all, you don't know where he's been; he might be contagious. You could possibly catch something nasty. Please… bring your beer to my table to enjoy. Then I can bring you up to date on your friend's wedding plans."

Whitt gave Bass a final, belligerent, stare before releasing his hold. The innkeeper – relieved to feel both feet firmly back on the floor – avoided further eye contact with Whitt, straightened the front of his shirt and hurried to the other end of the bar as though to tend some forgotten, but urgent, chore. For the benefit of the locals, he did manage a wimpy smile, as he said: "Bloody Yanks; got no sense of 'umour."

The black man led Whitt to a table at the back of the room. With the confrontation over, the buzz of conversation resumed. "Bloody crazy Yanks." Whitt heard one man say. "Them bastards can't drink worth a shit. Just the same during the war! Two or three beers and they just go rangy." Whitt turned to locate the speaker, but the black man restrained him again. "Come, Mr. Whitt, you're too intelligent to be bothered by tavern banter. Just relax. Unwind after your long journey. By the way, you can call me Sexton. That's my job you know, my name too. I'm sexton of the church where Heather McDowd and your friend will be tying-the-knot on Saturday."

Once seated, Sexton inclined his head, querulously, and asked: "Mr. Whitt; you seemed confused, disoriented maybe, when you first came into the bar." He waggled his hand, palm down, indicating something unstable. "Are you feeling unwell? Or just tired perhaps, from the flight and the long drive? You would have been staring into the afternoon sun all through the drive from Heathrow. Perhaps it took a while for your eyes to adjust." Whitt took a long pull on his jug of beer. It had a much stronger flavour than he was used to and was quite warm. He gave it a disgusted look and put it back on the table. "I can see why he wanted me to pay in advance for this slop," he said. "No one in their right mind would pay for it after they tasted it."

"Oh, give it another try Sir. I'll admit it takes a little getting used to – especially after the sameness of the cold lagers of North America, but once you 'discover' the flavour, it'll be hard to put down I promise you." Sexton's manner was persuasive, and Whitt gave the brew another try – but only after peering into the glass jug, and examining the beer from every angle. "I guess if you are thirsty enough, even swamp water would be acceptable," he said. Sexton's answering smile was mechanical, and devoid of humour. He repeated his earlier question. "When you first entered the bar, Mr. Whitt, you seemed disoriented. Are you okay now?" Again, Whitt ignored the question. "Why isn't Chernak here? When will he arrive?"

"Oh, he had to go to London for a couple of days Mr. Whitt. He needed to get fitted with new clothes for the wedding, plus attend to some other chores that needed his attention. I will explain in more detail shortly. But first, please answer my question. I'm charged with your wellbeing, and therefore, rather concerned. When you first entered the bar you did seem unnaturally disoriented. Are you okay now? Are you feeling quite well?"

Whitt was tired of being forced to answer questions that he would rather ignore; first Jones, and now this black guy, Sexton. "Mainly the sudden darkness after driving so long into bright sunlight, I guess. That plus some travel fatigue. Strangely enough, I experienced a feeling of familiarity when I first came in here. Stupid really! This is the first time I've been in England. I have never been in here before, or there wouldn't have been a second time." He took a longer drink from his jug.

"Well, some say that déjà vu is a memory from a previous life Mr. Whitt. Perhaps you spent some time here in a previous incarnation. This inn would certainly cover a few lifespans – especially since they used to be so much shorter." Whitt, gave a short: "humpff", and gave Sexton a disdainful look. "You're not serious I hope. I wouldn't figure you for someone that would buy into that reincarnation crap. Especially, since you're associated with the church."

"Oh, but the church used to accept the reincarnation theory Mr. Whitt. Right up to the fifteenth century I believe. Then they blamed that theory for some loss of control over the worshippers. They found that too many people were 'slacking-off' in this life, believing they'd get a chance to make amends in the next. Today, we might consider that a credit card approach towards claiming a place in heaven. Play now, pay later! To combat that attitude, the Church started preaching hellfire and damnation. More potent, it produced better results, and gave them stronger control over the ignorant masses." Sexton raised his hand, and Bass quickly arrived with two fresh beers. Whitt was getting used to the brew and grudgingly conceded – but only to himself – that the flavour was 'moreish', once you got used to it. But it was still too warm. He gazed at Sexton over the rim of the mug. "Dead, is dead, my friend. You go around once. There ain't no heaven, and there ain't no hell. Look out for yourself first, last and always. The devil takes the hindmost."

"Oh, he'll do that for sure; actually, the foremost too, more often than not. But where did you get the devil from, in an existence that has no heaven and no hell."

"Just an expression! Heaven and Hell belong in the same bag as witches, Frankenstein, the living dead, voodoo etcetera – just different branches of the same gobble-de-gook."

"Really! So, you are familiar with all of this gobble-de-gook? Voodoo for instance?"

"Well, not familiar. I wouldn't waste my time on that stuff. Voodoo only works if the victim convinces himself that it does. Its power comes from the victim's fear, instigated by suggestion and theatrical mumbo-jumbo. It's that fear that produces the response the victim dreads. It's ridiculous to imagine that you could hurt your enemy by making a clay doll of him, and then by sticking pins in the doll, make the enemy feel the pain – that's naive. And how the hell would your friendly demon know who the doll is meant to represent anyway. You couldn't claim many instances of a good likeness. And that still ignores the fact that pain can't be transmitted through space."

Sexton leaned towards his companion a little. "Did you know Mr. Whitt that the black magic witch doctor – he's called Bokor by the way – includes in the doll, a piece of the person it's meant to represent – an identity tag of sorts. Some hair, or a piece of fingernail, maybe even a few drops of blood. Today we rely on such items for DNA evidence. It's positive identification! Sometimes even a scrap of clothing will do. The DNA can be picked up from perspiration, as I'm sure you know."

Whitt laughed, quietly. "You sound as though you believe in this garbage. What the hell is Mr. Demon supposed to do if he can't match the broken fingernail? Does he take it home to his hi-tech lab for identification? You've been watching too many late-night movies my friend, and what about the witch-doctor's dance?" He laughed again. "He shakes a rattle, sprinkles a little chicken blood and graveyard dust over someone, and that person becomes one of the living dead. A zombie! It's amazing how much acting talent you can buy for a bottle of cheap booze. Do me a favour Sexton. We do live in a more enlightened age you know. At least, outside of Ryeport we do. If there was anything to all that garbage, it would be taught in U.S. colleges by now. Just imagine, you might even graduate as a doctor of voodoo. Doctor Sexton V.D." He smirked, beginning to recover his usual self-assured manner. "There is no proven evidence to support the stories or claims of so-called witch-doctors."

"Surely Mr. Whitt, you can't believe that we know all there is to know about Heaven and Hell, whatever roles you may think those places play in the overall scheme of things. Let me play 'devil's advocate' for a while – just for the fun of it. As you know, very few ancient civilisations were able to record detailed instructions of their 'magical' practices. Knowledge was passed on verbally, often without explanation. That meant details were sometimes forgotten, or misinterpreted, and consequently, the 'spell' failed to work. Remember too, the witch doctor wouldn't need to know why his 'spell' worked. All he needed to do was remember the 'recipe', and where to use it. Hopefully, he would pass on that knowledge before he died. And remember, some 'dusts' are quite powerful. If you mix charcoal and salt-petre, with sulphur – only dusts, after all – you make gunpowder and we still use that today, even in our enlightened world, where atomic weapons have far surpassed gunpowder for destructive force. Perhaps, even chicken blood might contain useful chemicals which, when mixed with the right kind of 'graveyard dust', and combined by shaking in a rattle, might produce some sought-after effect, not necessarily a bang. For example: You might not be able to explain the explosion caused by gunpowder, but you could learn the 'recipe', and, to the unsophisticated, the explosion you create would seem magical."

"If I remember correctly, the chemicals that combine to form a human body are worth less than a dollar. But when mixed in correct proportions and with the wondrous addition of a divine catalytic spark they become living, growing, beings that are largely self-healing, can reason, and invent wondrous things; even vehicles that enable them to visit the moon. Pretty powerful results for a dollars worth of chemicals or graveyard dust. And those chemicals that combine to make human beings would have to be present in graveyards, wouldn't they? Surely their owners didn't take them with them when they died. Or did they? If so where did they go, heaven perhaps – or hell? A few decades ago, visiting the moon was deemed impossible." Sexton smiled. "One well-respected scholar said: 'It will never be done. We could never build a ladder long enough.'"

He tapped Whitt's digital watch. "You can alter the numbers on your watch, by pressing buttons. You make it happen, but I'd bet you couldn't explain how that works, either. Perhaps Voodoo is just like that, another technique we're not yet privy to."

Was it the warm beer or merely fatigue? Whitt was no longer interested in arguing with Sexton. He wanted his bed, but first he wanted to eat. "I want a steak!" he said, determined to end the conversation. "Then I'm for bed. I take it that this place does have a bed for me? Where the hell is Chernak? That S.O.B. was supposed to meet me here. It's dark outside. When is he coming? Or do you think some little witch-doctor has turned him into a doorknob? Come to think of it, he's been described that way on occasion." He laughed, and stood up. "I'm going to get my bag."

"Sit down Mr. Whitt. Sam's son has taken your luggage to your room. It's all arranged." Whitt wondered why the hell he complied so meekly. Sexton raised his hand to catch Bass' attention, and the bartender brought his stained smile, an oil lamp, and a large jug of beer to their table. Whitt addressed himself to Bass. "Where's Chernak? And, where's my steak? I want an aged, inch thick, medium rare sirloin, or a T-bone, a baked potato, with butter – not sour cream – vegetables, and garlic bread. I'm famished." Bass looked at Sexton, as though inviting him to respond. Whitt turned to the black man with a scowl on his face. "What now?" Sexton nodded to Bass, who took that as his cue to leave.

"Mr. Whitt. The reason Al and Heather are not here to meet you is that they are in London, arranging eighteenth-century costumes for their wedding." That remark got Whitt's full attention. "Eighteenth century? What the hell for? Chernak told me to pack my tux."

"Well this all came about rather suddenly. We thought that a costumed wedding, because of its obvious glamour, would help promote our village's entry into the tourist business. I believe you already know that your friend's bride to be, Heather McDowd, is a descendant of the vicar that founded our church. That was over two hundred years ago. Ever since then all their family members have been married here. It's a time honoured, and jealously guarded, tradition. Now that Church is to be the cornerstone of our new tourist attractions. We are hoping that our modest tourist park will replace fishing as the main source of income for the village. The attractions will be staffed by villagers in period costume. We even have a square-rigged tall ship – a three master – tied up at the harbour wall. I'm sure you saw it as you drove in. It's a replica of course – leased from a film company. Saturday's wedding date is only weeks before the official opening of the theme park. The wedding should be very colourful and your friend's name will become part of the history of the village, just as Heather's ancestors are.

By the way, Sarah, the landlord's wife, has prepared two guest rooms upstairs for yourself and Al Chernak. She's all aglow. It isn't often she gets to play host to visitors from overseas. I'm sure that you will reward her unsophisticated attentions with charm and courtesy. She is not like her husband. You won't need to grab her shirt although I suspect that Sarah might not complain."

Whitt's jaw clenched tight. He felt he was being manipulated again and the sense of panic was back, twisting his guts as before. His discomfort must have been obvious, but Sexton ignored it. Whitt sensed his companion was getting ready for another lengthy monologue, and fumbled for an excuse to leave. "I have to unpack. Excuse me," he said as he stood up. Just the act of standing restored some confidence. However, Sexton just smiled and waved him back to his seat. "I have taken the liberty of ordering supper for you Mr. Whitt. You can eat whilst I talk." It was obvious that Sexton expected compliance, and he got it. Whitt sat down. "Despite what you may think about this inn Mr. Whitt, Sarah is a good cook, albeit of plain fare, and you will enjoy the meal."

Whitt was now being told what food to enjoy, but he had lost all confidence in asserting any will of his own. As though on cue, a short plump lady emerged from the door behind the bar. She was carrying a steaming plate heaped with steak and kidney pie, mashed potatoes, cabbage and other vegetables. She looked flushed and nervous, and, as she set the plate before Whitt, she half curtsied. "I 'ope ye'll enjoy your supper, Sir," she stammered. "We don't often get the likes of you visiting our little inn. Oh! I'll get you a knife and fork." She turned and almost ran to the kitchen for the cutlery.

"What the hell is this?" fumed Whitt. "I ordered steak, not some house special. She can take this back."

"Mr. Whitt, no one here can afford steak. So the house doesn't buy it. If you want steak you will have to drive to Nextwest for it. That's about twenty miles away. I'm sure that's not an attractive prospect after the travelling you've already done today. Chernak said you were a good sport. Please, be gracious, and try Sarah's steak and kidney pie. You will enjoy it; I promise you." Sarah reappeared, with cutlery and some condiments. She trimmed the oil lamp and its light supplemented the recently lit, but rather dim, electric lanterns on the bar walls. This afforded Whitt the opportunity to get a clearer look at his companion's face. Sexton's features were quite young but his face was hard to put an age to, partly because of the generous amount of grey hair over his ears, and his eyes were strangely compelling. Whitt felt arrested by them. He had the disturbing feeling that those eyes were doorways to a different world. It took several seconds of concentrated mental effort for him to break eye contact, but in those brief moments, he was sure he'd felt the heaving motion of a ship's deck, smelled the sea, and heard the groans and creaking of an old tall ship. Whitt's sense of panic only subsided when Sexton closed his eyes. However, he suddenly appeared very tired as he lowered his head, and rested his forearms on the table, as if recovering from a strenuous physical effort.

Whitt's insides had again been twisted into that unpleasant sense of dread. This time it was so bad that it was affecting his breathing. His emotions were in turmoil and he wanted to leave this place. He had never experienced such a sense of panic before. He forced himself to a standing position, intending to leave. His back was to the rest of the patrons and the buzz of conversations continued unabated. Only Sexton could see his obvious distress, but he seemed unconcerned as he again fixed eye contact with him. "Please, Mr. Whitt, sit down and enjoy your meal. 'You-be-safe-from-the-storm-tonight', as we still say in these parts. You will enjoy the wedding and, despite your misgivings, find pleasure in your visit." Sexton's voice sounded, metered and, instructional and Whitt felt his pulse return to normal and his fears melt away. He felt fine. Just fine! But Sexton's speech pattern though had sounded robotic, almost like a recorded programming. "Someone should tell him about that," Whitt thought.

The smell of the food was inviting overriding his concerns of being manipulated. He dismissed all of his unpleasant sensations as fatigue. "Nothing to worry about, a good night's sleep will work wonders," he thought. Whitt forgot his discomforts and began to enjoy the appetising meal. True, it was unpretentious, but very flavourful. Sexton was right. Sarah was indeed a good cook and he certainly wasn't disappointed by not having steak. Nor did the drone of Sexton's voice interfere with his enjoyment of the food, or the constantly replenished jug of beer. "It's strange," he thought, "but the warm beer compliments the meal. Somehow it seems – just right." He tried to ignore Sextons voice. Once he'd finished his supper though, he grew anxious to leave again. Sexton looked at him and gave a quiet laugh. "No, you can't leave yet, Sir. I have been charged with the responsibility of entertaining you until your friend returns. And it's a duty I take very seriously."

"Why the hell didn't Chernak call me? I have things to do in Toronto that are a damned sight more important than swilling beer in a rundown English pub with some stranger."

"I've already explained that, Sir. It was a last-minute decision. And there is a letter of explanation, from your friend, on your bed, which I am sure, will confirm what I've told you." Sexton continued without further pause, ignoring his blustering companion. "And how sure are you, that we are strangers? If you search your memory – very deeply – you might discover me to be a long-forgotten acquaintance. Not such a stranger as you suppose. I believe your ancestors were from England, were they not?" His eyes searched Whitt's as if expecting some sign of recognition. However, he found none, so, giving a quiet sigh of disappointment, he continued. "Seriously, Mr. Whitt, how do you really feel about reincarnation?" Sexton's searching eyes made contact again and Whitt felt some of his new found confidence ebb away. He responded a little shakily, feeling as though he was living in a bad dream, wondering if this sensation was due to the unfamiliar brew. "Dead is dead," he said. "There ain't no heaven and there ain't no hell. No souls and no second trips around!" He hoped his adamant response would end the conversation. But Sexton didn't oblige. "Well! You are, of course, entitled to your opinion, Sir. I'm sure you are familiar with the word 'karma' Mr. Whitt? It's very prominent in some eastern religions. Some believe that your behaviour in this life will determine your quality of life in the next incarnation. They believe – and this is a liberal translation – that if you observe the doctrine, 'love-thy-neighbour', in its purest sense, then your karma will be good, and each successive life will be more rewarding until, eventually, your soul will attain Nirvana. Be villainous however and your karma will be bad, and it may take several painfully corrective lifetimes to prepare you for everlasting peace."

Whitt's eyelids were closing. The long journey, plus the beer and the heavy meal, had taken their toll. His chin sagged onto his chest and his breathing fell to a slower, deeper rhythm. He was asleep. Sexton's shoulders slumped as he realised that his companion's attention was now lost to him. "There was a time when I would have gained some satisfaction from your upcoming misfortune," he murmured. "But no longer. In fact, I shall have to share it with you. Never mind, 'Might as well be hung for a sheep as a lamb', was a favourite saying of yours, if I recall. In fact, you actually were, once."

Whitt was beginning to stir. No longer thirsty, he wanted away from the seemingly endless prattle of this old man. Sexton obliged. "Ah, you have come back to us Mr. Whitt. I think you could use a good night's sleep. Why don't you 'turn-in'? When you awake tomorrow, you will attribute much of today's confusion to unfamiliar brew. However, you will remember the "underlying sense of our conversation." Through the fog of his returning consciousness, Whitt construed Sexton's remarks as instructions rather than conversation. "Tomorrow I shall show you the interesting features of this village," continued Sexton. "Why don't you get to bed now? The room is not as luxurious as you are used to, but you will sleep well. Tomorrow, the Vicar will explain your duties as best man. I will meet you after breakfast, and take you to the church. I promise that you will find tomorrow interesting."

"More instructions," thought Whitt. Sexton raised his hand and, once he had Bass' attention, pointed to the ceiling. Bass called through the kitchen door and Sarah soon brought her flushed cheeks and shy smile to their table. "I will show you to your room, Sir." She led him back towards the door that had given him so much trouble earlier, but she turned left, away from that door, to climb the companion ladder that occupied the space where Whitt had expected to see the table and benches. He paused at the foot of the stairway, and pointed to the archway. "Didn't there used to be a door there?"

"Oh bless you, Sir; that was 'undreds of years ago. 'owever did you know about that? In the ol' days, there was a door there that used to lead outside, to the men's conveniences Sir. Or rather, to the convenient outside, if you get my meaning. There wasn't much in the way of sanitary convenience in those days, Sir. The original owner had the door taken out, after some spooky trouble they say. Over two 'undred years ago that was. I don't remember it of course." Sarah giggled. "Just a li'l joke, Sir," and she turned, to precede Whitt up the companionway, to the second floor.

"Just a little joke Sir," mimicked Whitt quietly, as with mincing little steps and an imitation of what Sarah had imagined to be a sophisticated smile, he followed her. But, as he grasped the rope handrail and his feet hit the treads, he thought: "They've changed the rope. This used to be a cotton rope." That unpleasant knot was back in his stomach again and it persisted until he was off the stairway.

Sarah was stammering her explanation of the facilities. "The bathroom is just two doors down the passage, Sir. It has a shower and everything. Just like mine and Sam's. Personally I prefer to lie in the bath Sir, rather than shower." Then she blushed at the thought that he might have a mental image of her in the bath. Her mind would have been full of images of this athletic looking guest had their situations been reversed. Sam had never been an attractive or imaginative lover and her mind did, sometimes 'wander'. She fell silent for a while, as she dealt with the images her mind had conjured up. Then, hurriedly, with her cheeks a few shades redder, and in a more officious tone: "There are extra blankets in the wardrobe drawer and extra towels on the washstand, Sir. Most guests don't use the washstand but they do like having antiques in their room."

Whitt's attention focused on the envelope lying on the bed. He recognised Al Chernak's familiar hand and thought that, thanks to Sexton, he could likely recite the message without opening the envelope. After announcing that breakfast would be at eight o'clock in The Seahorse lounge, Sarah bade him good night. Whitt looked around the primitive looking room and shook his beer befuddled head. One small dormer window poked through the sloping ceiling, overlooking the old, clay tiled roof. The bare floorboards were so worn that the knots in the wood stood proud of any softer, wider grain. The walls were of uneven whitewashed plaster between black posts. Limp, printed cotton curtains hung on an expanded curtain wire at the window. There was no socket for his electric razor, but the room did have a cheaply shaded electric light and for extra convenience, a cord dangled over the bed, to control the light. Whitt tossed his suitcase onto the bed and started to unpack. As he stepped close to the bed his foot struck something underneath. On lifting the overlay he discovered a chamber pot. He smiled as he remembered his grandmother referring to it as a g'zunder. 'Because it 'goes under' the bed dear,' she'd explained. "More antiques," he muttered. Sexton had said he would sleep soundly, and he did.

# CHAPTER 3

## *Coffee à la Sexton*

Whitt awoke to the cries of seagulls and the unfamiliar smell of the sea. The open window had kept his room refreshingly cool. He had no trace of a hangover from his warm beer episode of the night before and, despite the fact that The Harbour Light was no 'five-star hotel', he'd spent a comfortable night. Breakfast was also enjoyable, perhaps because of Sexton's absence. Fried bread with his eggs and bacon was a new experience for him, but he'd enjoyed it. Sarah had done an excellent job with the food but, of course, had failed to lay the table beforehand and had to 'bob-off' to get a knife and fork. There were no napkins either, but, when Whitt asked for one, she blushingly supplied a paper towel. She was refilling his coffee cup when Sexton arrived. The coffee left a lot to be desired, but that was the only low point in his morning – until Sexton's arrival that is.

Whitt felt unaccountably intimidated by this man, despite the fact that, as Sexton's 'programming' voice had instructed, most of the experiences that had unnerved him the previous evening he now attributed to the unfamiliar brew and fatigue. However, the memory of yesterday's déjà vu sensations, combined with the hammering his ego had taken over the last few days, had left him nervous. So, the unlikely pair sat drinking coffee at a window table in the newly carpeted 'Seahorse Lounge'. Whitt appreciated the difference in the atmosphere of this refurbished section of the establishment. The whole area was fresher, brighter, and more comfortably furnished than The Harbour Light lounge. It was no luxury hotel but he felt much more at ease here, and said so.

Sexton smiled. "Well this is a 'new' extension to the original inn, Mr. Whitt. This section was added in 1793 and, as you're aware, they've just refurbished it. All there was to the original inn was the building where you spent last night: The Harbour Light Inn. Then, in 1792, a ship named The Seahorse was wrecked in the blind bay just west of our harbour. Most of the salvaged timbers of that vessel were used to build this extension. In fact, when it was finished, the villagers said it was more Seahorse than Harbour Light, and so the inn was renamed. The bowsprit and figurehead still decorate part of the second storey. 'Waste not, want not', was almost a religious discipline in those tough times, and an ornament as grand as the figurehead, was too valuable a decoration to discard. The bar room of the old Harbour Light Inn became The Harbour Light Lounge. The original sign was taken from the post in the forecourt, and fastened by the door. It's still there today, thanks to several layers of shellac. That part of the inn would be more than two hundred years older than this extension. Not ancient by the standards of buildings in this country, but old enough to have an interesting history. Interesting, that is, if you like tales of adventurous sea voyages and smugglers and some of our villagers were no strangers to 'the Trade' – as smuggling was commonly known hereabouts. We even have some salvaged furnishings from the old ship."

Sexton rose from the window seat. "Come, I'd like you to see this old sea chest. It belonged to the captain." Whitt felt his stomach twist into that same miserable knot that had so unnerved him last night, as the image of an old sea chest formed in his mind. He was afraid that that image might match the antique that Sexton wanted him to see. Hesitantly, he walked to the end of the bar, where Sexton now stood, pointing into a dark corner behind the bar. The skin on Whitt's arms began to 'crawl' and he grew icy cold as he drew closer to Sexton. "Later," he gasped, "I have to go to the washroom. Too much coffee," and with a titanic effort, he managed to break eye contact with Sexton and head for the washroom, far too scared to face a possible déjà vu experience. Sexton appeared disappointed, but did manage a resigned smile. Whitt took his time in the washroom, splashing his face with cold water and holding a wet paper towel to the unaccountably stiff muscles on the back of his neck. Once he felt better, he left the building by the side door and walked around to the main entrance. Intent on avoiding another opportunity to view that old sea chest, he called from there for Sexton to join him outside. With a wry smile on his lips, Sexton met him in the forecourt.

A drizzling rain had begun to fall and Whitt commented: "Ah, the notorious English drizzle. Weather like this could really do a number on the wedding. Why don't we take the car? It makes no sense to get wet. It might be raining even heavier when we leave the church." Sexton nodded. "Okay, but I had anticipated you taking longer over breakfast. The vicar will not be expecting us for almost an hour. That will give me the opportunity to give you a quick overview of the village. The orientation centre for our 'park' tour is set in the village's original church. We have high hopes for the success of our tourist park: 'Ryeport Harbour'. Hopefully, it will become the mainstay of our village's economy."

Whitt was nervous of Sexton's motives, but, unable to think of a face-saving excuse, he nodded acceptance. They climbed into the car and proceeded a short distance east, along the broad harbour front, passing workmen working on a row of old cottages. "Most of these cottages are being converted into souvenir shops and cafés," said Sexton. "They are almost finished now. These original homes were small and very primitive.

"This was Ryeport's first church," explained Sexton, as they stopped in front of the largest of the local buildings. He unlocked the old oak door as he said: "Once the new church was built, this building became a community centre. Over the past two hundred years, it has served the village in various capacities. On a couple of occasions it became a morgue for victims of shipwrecks. The dead from the wrecked Seahorse were brought here, for instance." Whitt stepped into the hall, but had only gone a few paces when he was struck by an inexplicable chill. He froze, and shuddered violently.

Sexton paused in his explanations. "Are you okay?" he queried. "That was quite a shudder."

"Yeah. I just felt a sudden chill. Worst I've ever known."

"Really." Sexton sounded genuinely concerned. "It is a local superstition that only happens when someone walks over your grave." Then he smiled, and immediately resumed his explanations. "Anyway, this hall was more commonly used for Saturday night dances, bingo, and wedding receptions, etcetera. Now it will be a museum, detailing Ryeport's history.

"Now, here is what I really wanted to show you." They were looking down at a table mounted model of the harbour, as if they were viewing it from seaward. Sexton explained: "Ryeport is the only natural harbour for miles along this stretch of coast. It has the added advantage of being close to what was once a rich fishing ground. It's downside has always been that you can't see the harbour itself from seaward, because the only entrance is through an overlapping gap in the cliff formations. Think of the cliffs on either side of the entrance as gateposts to the harbour. Unfortunately, those 'gateposts' are deceptively similar to the cliff formation next door and they mark the entrance to the harbour's dangerous 'blind-bay' neighbour, 'Sorry Cove'. That similar appearance has been responsible for the loss of several lives, usually during a storm.

He pointed to the model of a square-rigged ship at the edge of the model. "Imagine that you were on this ship, and approaching the harbour." He pressed a button on a control panel, and the ship was illuminated. "As you can see there are three almost identical cliff formations ahead of you. The centre formation and the one on the right, are the 'gatepost' to the safe harbour. If, in limited visibility, you chose the left cliff and the centre one as your gateposts, you would be headed for disaster in the blind bay next door. In a storm the fishing boats might not realise their error until it was too late to make a course correction. I'm speaking of the days of sail of course. Powered vessels and radar have greatly improved the lot of today's fishermen.

So, pick the correct entrance and you would find calm water and a safe harbour. Choose the wrong one and your 'reward' would be almost certain destruction on the rocks of that blind bay called Sorry Cove. That similarity between the two entrances has proven disastrous in the past. Approaching this coast in poor visibility, made it almost impossible to distinguish between the two entrances early enough to correct an errant course. Sexton pressed a button marked HARBOUR on the control panel. A series of small white lights rippled outward from the model ship, through a gap in the cliffs, and then moved through a left-handed dogleg, into the safety of the harbour.

He pointed to the model again. "The entrance to Sorry Cove – that disastrous blind bay to the west – is almost identical. He pressed the button marked: SORRY COVE. This time a series of red lights flashed sequentially into the gap to the left of the true harbour entrance, culminating in a pulsating red glow that illuminated the skeletal wreckage of a ship in the rock-strewn bay. "This is where The Seahorse came to grief," explained Sexton, as he studied Whitt's face. "That bay was christened 'Sorry Cove' because you'd be sorry if you entered it. I'm sure you can appreciate how difficult it would be for a sailing vessel, during a flood tide, or strong following wind, to change course from close in. No space to manoeuvre. There was one, almost impossible, way to avoid being smashed and pounded on the rocks and that was to squeeze through this narrow gap in the cliff that divides the two entrances. Just here." Another button, THE CHUTE, illuminated a narrow gap in the centre cliff that connected Sorry Cove to the safe passage. Whitt noticed a rope suspension bridge over that gap; obviously it was intended to provide access to a small building with a huge chimney, on the island cliff-top.

"That gap is known locally as 'The Chute," said Sexton. "Shallow draft boats can navigate that quite safely at high tide. But it's rarely used. Sorry Cove is like the large open end of a funnel, and The Chute is that funnel's narrow outlet. The force of water through The Chute during a storm is tremendous. Given a calm sea and high tide, the depth of water in The Chute will safely accommodate a small fishing boat. But finding that opening in the cliff, in poor visibility would be like threading a needle blindfolded – mostly luck. And then, turning your boat into that narrow opening – almost at a right angle – and at precisely the right moment would be something of a miracle. However, one man has managed it – only one – in all the history of the harbour. That man was Tim Ozmund.

To overcome the problem of finding the entrance in poor visibility, the villagers used to light beacons – large wood filled braziers – on top of each of the two cliff-top 'gateposts'. Steering a centre course between them would keep you in the safe channel. Obviously, the fishermen would prefer to be safe in harbour before dark, but that could be costly if they found fish late in the day and then had to run for home with a small catch. Their greatest danger of course, was during storms because of the reduced manoeuvring options. But those storms would sometimes douse the fires. It was a miserable job to maintain the beacons, and generally left to volunteers. Then the fisherman named Archer, came up with the idea of building stone huts to protect the braziers and their minders from the weather. The seaward wall of the hut would be open, rather like a large fireplace, facing out to sea. This protection made the beacons more reliable by eliminating the risk of doused fires and wet wood." Another button illuminated braziers on the appropriate cliff tops. "The Western Beacon was a problem, because it needed to be on that cliff that formed the western gatepost and that piece of cliff had been made into a tall island by The Chute. So they built a sturdy bridge over The Chute to provide access. Maintaining those beacons would be a full-time job. Sufficient dry firewood would have to be cut in a local forest and stored at the beacon huts. It would require two men, full time, plus a horse and cart. The village never had enough money to pay for such a service. Then the innkeeper suggested that Archer – whose arthritis was making him stiffer by the year – and his tubby buddy, Jamie Rooken, should do the job on a full-time basis. Their income would be a small piece of the catch from each boat. It would be a village project to build the huts, and buy a horse and cart.

Those two old boys made quite a job of being 'Beacon Masters', as Archer dubbed them, and they certainly made the fisherman's lives a lot safer.

But finding the harbour entrance was not the end of the problem. The deep part of the channel into the harbour, was relatively narrow, and many a boat has come to grief on submerged rocks just when they thought she was safe. Finding that deep channel in the 'putter's shaft' was the problem. To prompt the boats to turn left at the correct point, and keep them in the deeper channel, the original innkeeper positioned another brazier in front of his inn, on the harbour wall. That's how the inn got its name of course: 'The Harbour Light.' As soon as this light became visible, it was safe for the helmsman to turn left and steer towards the brazier. The water in that channel, and the harbour, was deep enough for even tall ships. It worked very well for about three years, but then, one of the beacon lights failed. It was disastrous and it was that failure that motivated the vicar to design our unique new church. It made navigating the entrance, much safer and proved to be a turning point for the village.

Those were tough times in which to make a living from the sea, but the new church solved two major problems for the village. Today, we are again at a stage where this village is in crisis. And again, it's the village economy that's the problem. Fortunately, The Guiding Light Church has come to our aid once again. But you will learn more about that when you see the Church, and take a trip around the harbour. Come, we have time for a brief tour of the village, and then we should be off to the Church. The vicar will be ready for us by the time we get there."

Ryeport's community centre – the original church – was in the heart of the village. By contrast, The Guiding Light Church was perched way out on a cliff-top, at the most easterly point of the harbour entrance. It was little more than a quarter-mile walk from the inn, but that route involved climbing 'Jamie Rooken's steps.' If climbing ten feet of steep, irregular, steps cut into the side of the cliff was unattractive, there was a less arduous route. The long church driveway opened onto the road connecting the village to the main highway: the Coach Road. This almost doubled the distance, but was less strenuous. Whitt and Sexton took the car. That eliminated both the effort and risk.

From a distance, the church appeared to be an unremarkable, basically rectangular building, with an oversized belfry and spire at the seaward end. Whitt parked the car and they walked through a gate in the stone wall surrounding the small church yard. "Where's the unique design that the founding vicar got so much praise for?" Whitt commented. "It's a basic box with a belfry and spire."

"Have patience Sir. There is more to this place than first meets the eye," responded his guide. Closer inspection revealed fine craftsmanship in a building built of rough-cut local stone, but with the corners, doors and windows framed with carved ashlar. The glass in the windows was set in diamond patterned leaded frames, within rectangular, coloured, glass borders. The oversized belfry topped the roof at the seaward end of the building and a generous porch welcomed all-comers from the landward side. However, from Whitt's perspective, the church was basic and unremarkable.

The porch entrance was fitted with a large oak door hung on ornate black iron hinges. Whitt was impressed by the quality of the stonework and the doors. "The craftsmanship seems to be of a quality more befitting a cathedral than a small village church," he remarked. "Very perceptive Sir," said Sexton.

There were two matching doors, one either side of the altar, beyond the choir stalls. The door on the right opened as they approached, and a pleasant-faced young man emerged, greeting them with a smile and extended hand.

"You must be Mr. Whitt," said the vicar. "Welcome to our little village and, more particularly, our church. Sexton told me you would be here this morning. I trust you had a good flight and a pleasant trip down from London. It's not often that we have visitors from overseas. You and your friend have caused some pleasant excitement." Whitt responded with the usual pleasantries and asked the vicar's name. "I'm sorry," he replied. "How rude of me; I'm Reverend James Eggleton. Please, call me Jim. I'm happier without formalities when the occasion allows. Tell me, Mr. Whitt. Have you ever been 'best man' before?"

"No Jim, this is a first time for me," admitted Whitt. "But if we are to be on a first name basis, please call me Earl. But I should confess that I am not

particularly religious." At this point Sexton excused himself and, with a wave, disappeared through the door to the left of the altar. "Well Earl," said the vicar, "we are on fairly level ground. This will be my first time officiating at a marriage ceremony. On the other hand, as you might expect, I am particularly religious. I have practised the ceremony of course, and assisted at many marriages, so I am confident that I will tie the knot securely for your friends. If that knot is to remain secure and the union flourish, as I hope it will, it will require the constant TLC of the married couple. Guarantees on that score, I'm sorry to say, are beyond my capabilities." Then, suddenly, he appeared embarrassed. "Sorry Earl, I don't mean to sound negative, but I am very disturbed by the poor survival rate of modern marriages.

If I may change the subject Earl, I am very interested to learn how you took the news that this wedding will now be conducted in costume? The wedding party and many of the guests will be dressed appropriately for the period in which our little church was built, 1793. Personally, I find it quite exciting. That decision was made only a few days ago, so I understand that your friend had not time to advise you. I imagine you were excited when Sexton told you of the change?" Whitt had forgotten Sexton's references to costume changes last evening, but now that remark fully impacted on him. "Pardon me – costumes? I brought my tux, as Chernak requested. I hope I'll not be required to dress up. I assumed Sexton's passing remarks about costume changes referred to the bride's dress. I'm certainly not aware of any changes required for my clothing."

"Really? I thought that Sexton intended to brief you on that. Well, it should all be great fun. Your friend, Mr. Chernak, telephoned your tailor in Toronto and got your measurements faxed directly to the costume house where he and his fiancée are being fitted for the wedding. So you can be assured that your costume will be elegant and flattering. You are to be dressed as a ship's captain I understand. Very glamorous, 'Hornblower' style – apparently very dashing. Sword, too I imagine."

Whitt's flushed face and tight-lipped expression left Eggleton in no doubt that 'fun' would not be his terminology of choice. "Sexton was supposed to clue me in on all this, you say? Well he didn't. Not that I'm really surprised by that. What does surprise me is that the church would employ someone like him in the first place. All last evening, when he was supposed to be briefing me, he was bending my unwilling ear with tales of reincarnation and voodoo. Quizzing me to see if I knew how my digital watch worked and all sorts of irrelevant garbage. I couldn't get away from him. Did your people check him out before you hired him?" I can't believe he's religious! In fact, I wouldn't be surprised to see "voodoo priest' listed in his resume or find that his education was gathered from comic books, or TV's 'Twilight Zone' possibly during his commitment to the local funny farm."

Eggleton had taken a half step back at the start of Whitt's unexpected outburst, and still looked shaken as Whitt paused for breath. "Actually Earl, I was never involved with Sexton's hiring, although, I must admit that initially, I too considered him an unlikely candidate. I also wanted to see his resume." Whitt interrupted. "Aha! So you agree. The man is weird."

"He's different, maybe, but not weird. Not in a bad sense anyway. He was very well known to the church long before he applied for the sexton's position. Personally, I considered him over-qualified."

Whitt was looking very grim and intense. "And?"

Eggleton began to relax a little, as though realising he was comfortable with his ability to cope with his angry companion. "Sexton, until his retirement, was sole owner of a very successful law firm that specialised in real estate and investment counselling. In fact, his firm manages the resources of this church's 'Guiding Light' account and is responsible for the very fortunate financial position that we find ourselves in today. It is because of his firm's expertise we are able to finance the reorganisation of this village from a struggling fishing economy to a resort attraction. Not a cheap conversion I might add."

Whitt wasn't prepared to give up his attack. "Well I bet that he's been lining his pockets at your expense somewhere along the line. No one gives up a position as a successful investment counsellor to become a sexton of a church in a small fishing village."

"Not true, I can assure you, Earl. Independent auditors, employed by the diocese, verify the accounts annually. And they've always commended his firm for their expertise and ethics."

"Then explain to me why this man would want to become a sexton?"

"Oh! Mr. Whitt!" The vicar's shoulders suddenly slumped, displaying his impatience. "I feel that these questions are beyond the bounds of our relationship at this point. I shouldn't be discussing Sexton's business with you, especially without his knowledge and consent."

"Oh! Suddenly I'm Mr. Whitt. What happened to Earl? Did I touch a nerve?....Reverend Eggleton!"

Eggleton shrugged. "I find your attitude unjustifiably aggressive Mr. Whitt, but I will pass on to you what is a matter of public record concerning Sexton. Sexton – which also happens to be his legal name by the way – is a well-respected lawyer and financial adviser. Aside from his law degree, he also holds degrees in business administration and history. He is also a descendant of the sexton who was incumbent here in 1793, almost from the first day of this church, and is also a foremost authority on the history of this village in particular, and much of the West Coast. It has been his main interest and hobby since learning of his ancestor. I can assure you that his education certainly did not come from comic books or late-night TV and he is a very wealthy man in his own right. When our previous sexton retired a few years ago, Sexton handed the reins of his company to a very accomplished relative, who has worked with him for several years, stating that he wanted to experience the life of a sexton here and devote himself to the betterment of this village. He considered that ambition a form of self actualisation. Incidentally, his 'sexton's' income – at his request – is the same as that of his ancestor of two hundred years ago. As in that case, lodging is provided in an apartment right here in the church as part of his compensation. That much, as I say, is a matter of public record. He does take some time off on occasion to look after some private interests overseas. Apart from that, his time is generously spent on the needs of the village. I should also advise you that he has become a good friend and mentor to me. Now, Mr. Whitt, perhaps it would be more appropriate for me to brief you on the changes concerning the wedding rather than discuss Sexton's private life." Whitt looked angry but appeared at a loss to find a suitable rebuttal to the vicar's rebuke.

Eggleton took the opportunity to change the subject. "I'm really looking forward to the wedding. It will also be good publicity for our new tourism plan and the village will benefit tremendously from that. This happy and colourful event will provide an opportunity to publicise the refurbishing of this church, and the old beacons that guided our boats into the harbour, etcetera. All in preparation for the opening of our holiday theme park. The news media are very excited about the project." On this note, the two men retired to the vicar's office for a half hour chat. Whitt declined the proffered cup of tea. Once the briefing was finished, Whitt asked: "Since this is to be a costumed affair, surely there will be a dress rehearsal?"

"Of course, Earl. Sorry, I keep forgetting that you have not been privy to all the planning. We will have to wait for the bride and groom to set the time for that though. Depends on outside factors I'm told. I'm sure that Mr. Chernak will bring you up to date on everything later today though. Okay?" Whitt's expression was grim, but he nodded agreement.

As the two men were talking, Sexton was sitting alone in his apartment, mumbling to himself, and looking very troubled. Then suddenly, his expression brightened. "Perhaps he will reveal himself if I immerse him in the old village? I could try that…but not here. Not on consecrated ground," and he slumped into his fireside chair, looking very despondent again. "The vicar's cottage," he exclaimed suddenly. "That is outside the consecrated area. I could take the journal and my coffee there. I'm sure the vicar wouldn't mind." His expression brightened, and he left his apartment and knocked on the vicar's door. "Come in," called the vicar, and Sexton walked in, smiling apologetically, as he said: "Please excuse the interruption gentlemen. Father, as you know, I had intended to make Mr. Whitt some of my special coffee, but my percolator has chosen this very day to quit on me. I wondered Father, if – because of that – we might retire to your cottage instead so I could use your percolator. I also wanted to show Mr. Whitt the founder's journal, but I could bring that with me, as well as the makings for the coffee."

"Certainly, Sexton. But I thought you wanted to show Mr. Whitt your 'digs', and the special features of this church."

"That was my intention Father but then it occurred to me that Mr. Chernak hasn't had the tour either. I thought it would make more sense to show both gents around at the same time. By the way Father, I wondered if I should ask Sarah to serve us lunch at your place. I'm sure she will be happy to oblige. Provided you gentlemen agree, of course, I thought some of her homemade soup and a ploughman's lunch might be acceptable."

"That sounds like a good arrangement Sexton. Provided Mr. Whitt is agreeable?" Whitt nodded. "Then let's retire to the vicarage," said the smiling vicar. "The tour can wait 'til Mr. Chernak can join us." Turning to Whitt, he said: "I found Sexton's tour most interesting Earl. He is a walking history book when it comes to this village, and a fantastic storyteller. He has the ability to bring a story to life somehow and often entertains the villagers at the inn, with tales of smugglers, and seaborne adventures. I find myself so immersed in his storytelling that I feel I actually experienced it, rather than merely heard the story." He smiled, an enthusiastic, boyish, smile. "I just love listening to his tales, and Sexton will answer any questions in a most convincing manner. You would almost swear that you were hearing the story from someone who actually participated in the events." The vicar's expression changed for a while, and it appeared to Whitt that he was struggling to refocus a dim memory. Then, with a slight shake of his head, he returned to the conversation. "But I find all aspects of this village, and its history, interesting. Possibly, because I'm a direct descendant of the founder of this church and also distantly related to the bride to be. Actually, there are a number of coincidences surrounding this wedding that are almost... uncanny. If you had a suspicious frame of mind, you might suspect that some unseen hand was craftily choreographing a whole series of events just to help solve the present plight of our village." His expression grew thoughtful again. "Particularly in view of the financial help that was discovered so unexpectedly, that will now fund the building of our tourist park." He smiled again, rather sheepishly this time. "But there goes my imagination again. Sexton says I have an overactive imagination. He manages to find logical explanations for all of my puzzles and concerns. You know Earl, I feel as though we are all pieces of some large, jigsaw puzzle, and someone is trying to set the last completing pieces. Of course I would have to be one of the straight bits." He laughed, seeming a little embarrassed at his feeble joke.

•  •  •

While the vicar and Whitt were talking, the soon to be Mr. and Mrs. Chernak were finishing a late breakfast in the London Hotel. Despite the fact that they'd had almost ten hours sleep they were exhausted. A week of rushing between Ryeport, and London, plus all the aggravations and long hours spent acting as their own couriers, had taken its toll. They checked out of the hotel and drove their estate van back to the costumers to pick up the last of the altered outfits – an elegant captain's uniform, loaded with gold braid and complete with a sword. This was for their best man: Earl Whitt. "Are you sure? No...are you absolutely positive, that this uniform will now be a good fit for Mr. Whitt, the man whose measurements were faxed to you from Toronto?" Al Chernak asked the tailor. "Yes!" was the confidant response. Chernak looked hesitant. "Well, would you please be good enough to check it one more time for me before we pack it? Have you got the fax?"

"Mr. Chernak," responded the irritated tailor. "I'm absolutely certain that the clothes are correctly sized, just as yours were."

"Sorry, "he said, "but spending five minutes now could save days of grief later." Half an hour later they were loading the car, including the carefully packed, correctly sized, captain's uniform, leaving behind them a very annoyed tailor, muttering under his breath.

"Boy! This event is really cutting close to the finish line." Al said to Heather, as they squeezed the last few items into the car. "Now we face the long drive back to Ryeport. I'm not looking forward to that. Boy if this all comes together as planned, we deserve a medal," he said. "Wouldn't it be something if we go through all this, only to break up after a couple of months?" Heather hit him with her purse.

* * *

Sexton re-entered the vicar's office carrying an insulated carryall. "Gentlemen: I have all the fixing's for my coffee right here – also some excellent cheese and crackers. Shall we adjourn to the vicarage?" Whitt could hardly remember when he last made a decision for himself, but nodded agreement and the three men walked to the vicarage. They were soon relaxing in the comfort of the vicar's cosy kitchen. "The coffee smells great," said Whitt, as Sexton poured. "Oh, I do indeed, make a fine cup of coffee," responded Sexton with a smile and rubbing his hands together. Then, with a nod and a wink to Whitt, he said: "But I regret that there is no cream or sugar, James." Eggleton smiled. "That's no problem, I have cream and sugar."

"No. I mean no cream or sugar is ALLOWED in my coffee Father! Now don't look so downcast," he chided. "Allow me to show you how to really enjoy coffee. If it's not to your liking … Well… we'll review that matter after you've tried it. Remember, the old saying? Don't knock it 'til you've tried it?" He pulled an engraved silver flask from his inside pocket and poured a generous shot of dark brown liquor into each mug. "Pusser's rum," he said, with a chuckle. "It's the genuine stuff. 'Pusser' is just the Navy's corruption of the word purser. The purser was responsible for the ship's supplies you see, including the rum. This stuff is well matured. You would never believe how well matured – in the cask, of course. I still have enough of this good stuff left to last me out."

The vicar was looking most uncomfortable. "Come now Father," chided Sexton, frowning at the vicar as though he was spoiling the party. "There's nothing wrong with a cup of good cheer now and then. Your ancestor certainly subscribed to that point of view, as you well know from his journal. Do you really believe that I would lead you astray? Besides, it's ninety percent coffee. All I did was add a touch of Caribbean sunshine." Whitt, and the vicar, each took tentative sips as Sexton raised his mug to the unlikely pair and gave the toast: "Drive the drizzle from our bones," he said, savouring a more confident measure of the seductive brew.

"Well gentlemen, would you not agree that my special coffee drives the drizzle from your bones and warms the cockles of your heart?" He raised his mug and his eyebrows, to Whitt and Eggleton in turn, inviting comment. His companions were quick to agree. Their first tentative sips had validated the promise of the coffee's aroma, so they too raised their mugs to each other and repeated Sexton's toast: "Drive the drizzle from our bones." Without a doubt, it was the best coffee Whitt had ever tasted and he said so. He even asked Sexton for the recipe. "Surely it isn't just coffee and rum. I've had many variations of that before.

"I'm sure, but not this coffee and certainly not this rum. I have a friend in the city who imports coffee. This is his personal blend and the rum is very old. You wouldn't believe how old, but it's so smooth. My supply is almost exhausted, but, as I said before, it should last me out." Sexton smiled as he refilled the mugs. He then added a leather wing chair to complete a group of three seats around the table. "Come Mr. Whitt, you are our guest. Please, take the wing chair. The vicar and I will take the others and tell you something of the history of our church and the village. We even have the first vicar's journals here for reference." He patted two leather-bound volumes that he'd just removed from oilskin wrappings and placed them in front of Eggleton.

"Tomorrow, the weather will be more pleasant, and we shall take you out to sea so that you can experience the harbour the way the fishermen did, so many years ago." Whitt settled into the wing chair, as the vicar and Sexton took their places facing him across the table. Sexton placed the coffee pot between them. "Just a moment," he said, and left his seat to retrieve a small earthenware jug from his carryall, which he placed beside the coffee pot. "Now we are all set. The story of our church really begins with its first vicar, because it was he who conceived the idea of a church with a 'guiding light' and arranged for its construction, long before any lighthouse was ever built along this stretch of coast. That vicar's name was Rodney McDowd. Roddy, as he preferred to be called, was by nature, a waster and a womaniser. His journals here confess that." Sexton patted the leather bound, musty smelling journals affectionately. "You see these journals of his were entombed with him. His wife had them wrapped in this same oilskin, sealed in a brass box and placed alongside his coffin, in a special crypt in the lower part of this church – the lamp house – which they had arranged to share with their friend Gerry Mason; the man who built the church. The chamber is quite small, about eight feet square and seven feet high. Entry is by a short door, about five feet six tall and three feet wide and made of solid oak, of course. Roddy`s friend, the mason, who built the church was already entombed there when Roddy died. He had fitted the door with large strap hinges, and secured it with a heavy lock. The vault was not to be opened after Roddy and his wife were entombed there. Well, the sea air took care of that. It rusted the pins in the hinges and the lock mechanism, effectively sealing the crypt shut.

Then, quite recently – shortly after Father Eggleton joined us in fact – the strap hinge at the top of the door rusted right through. One morning I noticed the door leaning outward, away from the top hinge and when I pushed it back into place, the bottom strap broke too. The door fell and the locking bolt slipped from the mortise that was holding it. The tomb was open for the first time in nearly two hundred years. When I reported this to Father Eggleton he asked me to refit the door. But I was so intrigued I couldn't resist a look inside. When I saw the box beside the vicar's coffin, it occurred to me that he might have left it as a sort of time capsule. So I took a look. In a sense, that's just what these journals are – time capsules. His sexton left one too, in an identical brass box and that was sealed in the same way. But that ancestor of mine had decided to become a lawyer and resigned his position as Ryeport's sexton when he joined the law firm of Blackstock and Associates. That was the same firm that looked after our church's legal matters. Eventually my ancestor earned his lawyer's credentials and he bought out Blackstock when he retired. Successive generations of my family have inherited that firm until finally, it passed down to me. My ancestor's journal had been locked away in the firm's vault all those years. I was intrigued when I discovered my ancestor's mysterious box. I opened it and read the journal. That's how I became so involved in the history of this place."

The vicar interrupted at this point: "It's so strange that those hinges chose this particular time to finally rust through. If it had been arranged by some supernatural force it could have hardly been better timed." The volume and excitement in his voice faded as he became aware of Sexton's fixed stare.

"What the vicar is referring to Mr. Whitt is that right now, Ryeport is enduring a hard time financially. Fishing alone can no longer support our village. Our small boats can't compete with the factory ships that operate today, and to make matters worse, fish stock are dwindling as a consequence of overfishing. But discovering the journal has provided a solution.

Back in the 1790's, fishing was still a reasonable, though dangerous living. Roddy McDowd saved Ryeport back then by providing safer access to the harbour. Now we have Roddy's descendant here," he indicated Eggleton, "to lead us through this new crisis, but in a totally different direction.

Once reliable electricity became available, the authorities installed high powered electric channel markers to guide vessels into our harbour. Then army engineers blasted away any dangerous, submerged rock, as a training exercise and the village didn't need The Guiding Light anymore. Consequently, it fell into disuse. That Trust Fund – created to provide lamp oil and maintenance, in perpetuity – had grown exponentially. Initially the amount of money was quite small. But the Trust's real estate holdings made it very rich.

There was also a clause in the trust agreement that allowed encroachment on the capital, 'to beneficially maintain the community of The Guiding Light Church'. Those last words were our saving grace. '*To beneficially maintain the community*'. Use of the money needn't be restricted to lamp oil and maintenance.

The beneficial executor of that trust is currently, me." Sexton was enjoying himself telling his story, and the vicar was becoming more and more relaxed with every sip of 'coffee'. In fact, Whitt thought, Eggleton's eyelids were looking quite heavy.

Sexton was droning on. "So you see, when we say that you have arrived at a very historical time we were not blowing smoke. For the 'good and wellbeing of the community' we have restored The Guiding Light, and arranged for the harbour and the village to be turned into a small theme park: 'Ryeport Harbour'. The beacon huts that were used before the church was built are already restored. The mirrors and oil lamps of The Guiding Light have all been refurbished. Everything is now as functional as it used to be back in the seventeen nineties."

Whitt was starting to doze off when he noticed that Sexton was giving him a prolonged stare. He nervously shook his head and apologised. "Sorry, Sexton; the warmth, and the coffee are getting to me. I'll sit up, and try to master the jet lag." Sexton, acknowledged with a curt nod, and continued: "In good weather we will be able to take tourists out to sea, feed and entertain them. We'll bring them back in after dark, using The Guiding Light as a closing highlight of the day.

The costumed wedding of your friend – to a descendant of the founding vicar – with the ceremony performed by another descendant – was a marketing opportunity that will get us off to a great start with free advertising. Media people from all over the country are anxious to cover the event.

Let me top up your coffee gentlemen, and then I think the best way for us to tell the story of our village, and The Guiding Light, is for our vicar to read directly from Roddy McDowd's journal. Only by understanding that man can you really appreciate this church and the spirit of this village. If it were a movie I doubt it could be more entertaining." Taking this as his cue, Jim Eggleton stretched, rubbed his weary eyelids, and prepared to read from the journal that Sexton had placed before him.

# CHAPTER 4

## *A musty old journal*

Jim Eggleton cleared his throat and began to read: "I, Rodney Jacob McDowd, begin this, my journal on this 25th of May in the year of our Lord 1791, having assumed my duties here as the vicar of Ryeport, in the County of Cornwall, on the 9th of May 1791. Only two weeks have passed since that beginning – although it feels more like two years – my life here continues to be uncomfortable and boring in the extreme. Most of the villagers treat me more like a social outcast than a valued member of the community and ignore me whenever possible. I am left with the feeling that I have been condemned and relegated to this remote and God-forsaken place, so that my very existence can be denied. There are no pleasures for me here, no social contact and nothing to look forward to in my present existence. How I hunger for even the smallest distraction to help break the monotony of my dreary routine."

Sexton interrupted, smiling, as he waved his hand in Eggleton's direction. "Our new vicar is a true descendant of the man that wrote this very journal and roughly the same age too. In fact, it would be easy to accept him as that same eighteenth-century vicar, as he speaks those written words. But that coincidence helps breathe life into the tale. Wouldn't you agree?" Sexton was staring intently into Whitt's heavily lidded eyes as he continued in a quiet, but insistent, tone: "The very essence of those earlier days is with us here today, because of this book. It leaves one with the impression that it is possible to step back into that distant past, and experience the life and times of those early villagers. Touch this journal, and you touch history itself. You can actually experience the years in this book, if you simply relax and allow it. And I don't mean just the musty odour of this old book either. That is simply an invitation. Those times will actually come to life if you open your mind and allow it. Relax Mr. Whitt; allow the story to transport you. Relax, close your eyes, and touch the journal; allow the story to envelop you. Go ahead man – touch it!" Sexton's manner was quietly intense, almost demanding, as he continued: "You will inhale the ambience of those times with every breath you take. Relax, and touch the journal. You will experience the past as though you actually lived in those times."

Whitt struggled to resist what he considered another of Sexton's 'programming' directives. How he resented his easy compliance as his eyes closed and he reached out and touched the cover of the old journal. His fingers seeming unnaturally sensitive to the leather, experienced a tingling sensation, more like a mild electric shock. He quickly jerked his hand away, but, feeling rather sheepish, he hastily resumed contact. It was bizarre, but touching the book did seem to stimulate his senses. At first it was just the damp, musty odour of the pages that seemed to grow stronger, but gradually a blend of other smells began to envelop him. First the smell of the sea, unfamiliar until this visit, grew more intense, then a background of other odours, fish and wood smoke mainly, but much stronger than in the village presently. The cries of the seagulls too, were louder and more profuse. Startled by the intensity of the experience, he shot a quick glance at Eggleton hoping for the reassurance of a shared experience, but instead, he was alarmed to see the vicar's image become vague and hazy. His next look at Eggleton did nothing to reassure him because, although the vicar's image was firming up, he was now wearing apparel appropriate for an eighteenth-century vicar and mouthing the words his quill pen was scratching into the journal: "My days here are miserable, and lonely in the extreme and it is largely from a need to occupy my time that I set pen to paper this day. However, I am also resolved to examine these records periodically, to measure both my improving morals and the benefits that I shall bring to this congregation. For, without those improvements, I shall never impress my father well enough to earn my reinstatement in his will."

The vicar still appeared to be Eggleton, despite his figure remaining 'vaporous', but there was something very different about this man. Was he really the same man that had joined him in sampling Sexton's coffee? This man's face, though very similar in features, was less boyish, and his manner more assertive. There was also a fine white scar running from just under his right eye, almost to the corner of his mouth. Whitt waited for the image to solidify, but it didn't. The vicar continued muttering as he wrote, pausing only to dip his pen into an ink pot. However, this voice lacked the soft 'Cornish' accent of Eggleton. His voice had the harder, more 'clipped', tones of a Londoner.

"For my periodic self-examinations to be effective and fruitful, I must be painfully self-critical, completing these records with all the fidelity I can muster. Therefore, I shall begin frankly with the admission that I am, at heart, a waster and philanderer; a spoiled and wanton 'child' of twenty-four years, given to self-indulgence and the pursuit of love, or rather, love-making. I confess that my intense pursuit of such pleasures made me inconsiderate, and unconcerned for the needs of others. Obviously that must change – *or, at least, appear to change* – if I am ever to gain restoration to my father's will. I do recognise however, that my largest problem will lie in the fact that I dearly enjoy that lifestyle, and am most reluctant to give it up."

Whitt's mouth was agape, as he looked around him, hoping for some clue that would save his sense of reason. Sexton was standing behind and slightly left of the vicar but he had now been joined by a shorter, shadowy figure and they were both staring at him. Sexton turned to his new companion and said, in a hushed voice, "My first thought was to do this in my 'digs', but I'd overlooked the fact that that was on consecrated ground, so I had to bring Whitt here. But we now have less than two hours." The shadowy figure gave a nod of understanding, and then spread his arms wide, as if indicating the whole area of the kitchen, then swiftly raising his hands above his head he snapped his fingers and disappeared. Whitt couldn't be sure if he had actually seen, or merely imagined the man and began to wonder if Sexton had added some hallucinogenic drug to the coffee. Then, he noticed something that really bothered him; the flames in the vicar's fireplace had stopped moving. They were now quite still – as in a painting.

At this point, the vicar stood up, abandoned his pen, and, making direct eye contact with Whitt, seated himself on the edge of the table and continued his 'journal' as a direct voice communication, as if speaking to a confidant. "My parents were as attentive as their social and business demands would allow, but in truth, we had few interests in common and consequently spent little time together. So, I sought my entertainment elsewhere. But frankly, I quickly tire of the small talk found in most gatherings, unless of course, some members of that company have something more pleasurable than talk to offer." He raised his eyebrows and smiled mischievously. "A pretty woman with a well-formed figure would compensate very well." His gaze drifted upwards, and his expression changed to one of pleasurable reminiscence, accompanied by a self-satisfied smile. Whitt was feeling panicky. "That bloody coffee," he stammered.

"Frankly, I enjoy the company of the ladies most of all," confided Roddy McDowd – for Whitt no longer had any doubt that that was who he was listening to. He reached out to touch the vicar, but his hand became so frighteningly cold as it drew close to the image, that he quickly jerked it back before it could make contact, "Damn! Could it be some sort of hologram," he muttered. But a derisive laugh – seeming to emanate from somewhere inside his head – ridiculed that possibility. The vicar continued, without appearing to notice: "I particularly enjoy those ladies who have a free and uninhibited spirit. In fact, I indulge myself in such company at every opportunity. Unfortunately, that is what brought about my downfall, ruined my financial prospects, and is the reason for my present, miserable situation."

Whitt felt like a voyeur of a past life experience, but it all seemed so unbelievably real. His mind struggled to find an explanation: drugs perhaps, or hypnotism, illusion or some combination of these things. But the discomfort in his stomach, and the cackling laughter in his head, rebutted each new idea. Reverend Roddy McDowd, however, seemed completely oblivious of his distress and, as Whitt fell back into the wing chair, the vicar continued: "My father had always intended that I would inherit the family business you know, and so, once I had finished my education, he insisted that I join his company. He started me in the most junior position of course; to learn the business from the ground up, just as he had. So, I became the errand boy and general help. Most degrading!"

Visions of the streets of 18th century London passed before Whitt's eyes and he watched in shocked disbelief as the smoky image of Roddy McDowd blended with that of a young man carrying a wicker hamper. "Wine samples," said Roddy – in answer to his unspoken question – "in the hamper! Wine samples that I am to deliver to a retailer in the West End," and Whitt felt himself immersed in the new surroundings, as all traces of the vicar's kitchen disappeared.

The smells of the streets were vivid – the fresh baked bread had a tantalising aroma and the butcher's shop too had a strong, but less pleasant odour; the manner in which chickens were hung and rabbits displayed, gutted, but otherwise intact, was disgusting and unattractive. But the most pungent smell of all assailed Whitt's nostrils when they turned a corner and found themselves outside a farriery. A man in a leather apron was cradling a horse's hoof, sole uppermost, between his thighs, whilst a second man used tongs to set a hot, glowing, shoe on the animal's hoof. The resulting smoke was alarming, and the smell – like burning hair – was one that Whitt would never forget. He expected the animal to panic, and break free, but the horse, although restless, was certainly less alarmed than he, as he felt his grasp on his reality slipping away.

• • •

Boredom had set in very quickly for Roddy and he found himself taking longer and longer on his errands. He began stopping at local inns for refreshment, and, hopefully, some titillating company to relieve the monotony of his errand boy duties. Unfortunately, news of his dallying eventually reached his father who, acting on timely information, caught him in the company of a working girl in the middle of the day – and a most personal involvement. He was sent home, embarrassed and in disgrace, his income suspended, and confined to the house to contemplate the error of his sinful ways.

With no money, and his confinement, he was obliged to suffer his punishment with such good grace as he could muster. However, with a sorrowful display for her benefit, he was able to convince the young maid, to take pity on his wretched loneliness. After two weeks of self-evaluation he was allowed to resume his duties. Unfortunately, four months later, the maid's father, cap in hand, came to see his father. His unmarried daughter's shameful condition was now obvious and he made enough of the disgrace that had been brought upon his family that Roddy's father provided enough compensation to encourage a local man to marry the girl and then arranged for the newlyweds to 'have-a-place', in domestic service, with a friend of his, living some fifty miles north of London.

The gossip mill was working overtime and his father's embarrassment in the city, as also amongst his friends and neighbours, was causing him much distress. His rage was frightening and Roddy was grateful for his mother's claim that she had been on the verge of dismissing the girl herself, 'for her flagrant flirtatious attitude towards him.' It was expected that the limitation of language, plus a hard taskmaster relationship and absences from home, would teach him to be celibate, hardworking, and repent his wanton ways. So he was sent to France to be under the tutelage of one of his father's associates. However, he had a gift for speedy learning, and the willingness of some young ladies at the winery to teach him, made light of those limitations.

Unfortunately, one of those ladies was the young bride of his new employer, Monsieur Beaucaire. This man was roughly the same age as his father, yet through an arranged marriage had taken as his wife, a beautiful young lady of only eighteen years. Possibly because their ages were so similar, she confided to Roddy about her desperate unhappiness, saying that her husband treated her more like a possession than a wife. He, *of course*, had felt compelled to comfort her. He had tried to resist her affections, but the more he rejected her, the louder she would cry and eventually, for fear that her crying would alarm the servants, he gave in. Yet despite Roddy's assertions, he delighted in conveying that it had been necessary to do so more than once and the consequences of his behaviour.

"M'sieur. Beaucaire came home unexpectedly one day, and found us in bed together." He would tell his audience while fingering the thin scar that ran down his cheek. "This is a souvenir of that event. The man struck me with an ornament from the night table. Luckily I dodged most of the blow. It barely missed my eye."

Eventually he made his way back to London but his Patron's letter had preceded him and his father's moods were now fluctuating between deep depressions and towering rage. He laid into Roddy with his walking cane as soon as he saw him. Had it not been for his mother's intervention he might have killed him. His Mother managed to get him out of the house and into a friend's home. There she tended his cuts and bruises, whilst trying to find a way to keep him in the family circle. However, his Father was adamant. He was dishonoured, disavowed and disinherited. His father's attempt to allow the scandal at home to fade into distant memory had only been worsened and his father was now concerned that his relationship with Beaucaire, a cornerstone of his business, might be destroyed. His mother tried desperately to pacify her husband but he flew into a rage every time Roddy's name was mentioned.

Eventually he grew tired of coming home to a crying wife, and promised to try to find a way to remedy the situation, provided it did not add to the embarrassment that the gossip mongers were causing in the city. His first thought was to send his son to the colonies with a small allowance, on the strict condition that he never return to England. However, this distressed his wife so much that he had to give up the idea. His parents were loyal and devoted supporters of the Church and the Bishop, a personal friend and lodge brother of Mr. McDowd Sr. So, in desperation, he sought the advice of this good friend.

"Your Grace, that boy is not like normal men. Certainly not like you or me." But that was the moment that inspiration came to him. "Tell me, Your Grace, do you believe that one's character is mainly due to breeding, or training?" A scheme was forming in his mind that might well solve his problems at home, and eliminate any future responsibilities from his problem son.

His wife was shocked, when he returned home, by his change of heart. He told her: "I have been talking with our friend Bishop Mason, and we have come to the conclusion that our son should have another chance. As you know, the Bishop is a man of considerable wisdom and insight and together we have devised a plan to help save our son's soul. No man likes to abandon his own son my dear, but you must admit that the provocation has been extreme. I could not possibly survive another episode such as the last two and certainly my business could not. However, I would like to provide an opportunity for our son to redeem himself. If I could be sure that Rodney had managed to curb his appetites, and was prepared to knuckle down to a hardworking, moral, lifestyle, I might restore his allowance, and possibly reinstate him in my will, but only if his behaviour merited such action."

She had hurried to her husband's side to kiss him and tears of joy filled her eyes, as she gave thanks to the Good Lord for enlightening her husband and prompting him to welcome the return of their prodigal son. "Indeed; all thanks to our Good Lord my dear," he replied, "for it is He who will save our son. As to the return of the prodigal, that can await the proving of his repentance."

"I do not understand husband. What do you have in mind?"

"Our son, my dear, will enter the priesthood. That is if he ever wants to be a part of this family again, together with such privilege as goes with that membership. I have already made the arrangements with the Bishop. If Rodney agrees – and you can ask him tomorrow – then he will report to our church for an interview with the Bishop next Monday morning, at eight o'clock sharp. If the Bishop approves of his attitude, then Rodney will report immediately to Theological College – another favour – to begin his training. We are fortunate indeed to have a man such as the Bishop to call our friend." Roddy's mother was stunned. Her mind had gone blank. Even such a staunch defender of her son as she, had trouble believing he could modify his appetites to that extent. However, his father made it clear that this was the only solution that he would allow and she knew him well enough, to know that he'd not change his mind.

Roddy's only recourse now was to apply himself hard enough to show his penitence and so earn reinstatement in his father's will. Eventually, he believed he would control his own fortune, provided that he play his cards right in the short term, and he reasoned that once his father passed on, he could leave the church and go his own way again.

• • •

At eight a.m. sharp the following Monday morning, Roddy reported to the Bishop's office. He had always known how to impress people and so proceeded with his pious and penitent attitude to make that reverend gentlemen begin to wonder if his father was overstating his delinquent ways. Following his plan, he then studied hard, passed his examinations with flying colours, and was assigned to a small parish north of London, as an assistant to the ageing vicar. Unfortunately Father Dexter, upon catching him engaged in some lighthearted conversation with one of the young ladies of the choir – who did seem rather well disposed towards him – and, having been advised of his fondness for the fair sex, complained to the Bishop. It was decided that, given the fragile state of his morals, London was too dangerous an environment and the Bishop used his influence to transfer Roddy to a diocese in Cornwall where a vacancy had occurred through the sudden death of a vicar in a small village. So, he was 'promoted' – to his own parish – Ryeport! It was not a good beginning; neither his father nor Bishop Mason wanted him and he was soon to learn, his new Bishop, and parish, didn't want him either.

A hackney carriage took Roddy from his parent's house to the Coaching Inn and from there he began his four-day journey to Nextwest, in Cornwall, where he would report to his new master, Bishop West. It was not a good meeting. His reputation had preceded him, and Bishop West made it clear that he was there under protest. His first mistake, or indiscretion, would be his last. He was then handed off to an assistant, the 'chubby' Reverend Tubbs, who had been 'filling-in' at Ryeport since the demise of Roddy's predecessor. Tubbs arranged that they would dine together at the Nextwest manse where he would spend that night in the guest room. Dinner was pleasant and the manse was comfortable enough. Reverend Tubbs proved to be an easy going fellow who was plump, a little boring, and obviously lacking in self-confidence.

He introduced himself as: "Reverend Percival Archibald Tubbs: Tubbs by name, and 'tubby' by nature." He blushed at his feeble joke. "In informal situations I'm known as Tubby. Please feel free to use that nickname. Percival is rather much, wouldn't you agree? I'm afraid you will find your accommodation in Ryeport rather Spartan, Rodney. The village is very poor and the people are on the rough side. Not my cup of tea I'm afraid. Yours neither I suspect. However, one must make the best of things, don't you agree? I will help if I can. Beware of the Bishop however. He is not a forgiving man and very critical. I get the impression that he is not well disposed towards you. Although, I must confess, I don't know why." Tubby's expression seemed to be an invitation to enlighten him which Roddy didn't accept.

The following morning Tubby drove them to The Harbour Light Inn in Ryeport and introduced Roddy to the owner, Ernie Chandler. 'Ernie' was a large, powerfully built man, with a barrel chest and arms and legs like young trees and he seemed annoyed by their arrival. Tubby treated Roddy to lunch at the inn whilst they waited there for his housekeeper, Bessie Drew. Eventually, a robust, ruddy complexioned woman, who appeared to be in her mid-forties, arrived. She wore a patched apron, over clothing that had obviously seen better days, and her attitude was one of bored resigna-tion, leaving Roddy with the impression that she would rather be anywhere else than there. She and the innkeeper had a quiet conversation, giving occasional, disapproving, glances in their direction, without acknowledging them in any way. Eventually, the innkeeper brought her to their table, and introduced her. Mrs. Drew then took them on a hurried tour of the very basic church and Roddy's even more primitive cottage. It was a grudging, cheerless, reception and Tubby was obviously relieved to say goodbye.

"Oh, by the way," he said in parting. "You do have a pony and wagon you know. It's just like this one, and stabled at the inn, in exchange for its occasional use by the innkeeper. Actually, the pony spends most of its life grazing behind the stable. His name is 'Slondosh'. I can't imagine where that name came from – most unusual. Bye now. Come and see us if you need anything."

He smiled, waved a quick farewell, and was soon out of sight on the twisting, tree-lined road back to civilisation. Roddy watched him disappear, feeling that he'd been abandoned in hostile territory, at the mercy of his enemies. That night he ate at the inn, but was offered nothing in terms of companionship or conversation. There were no introductions. Later, his housekeeper sat across from him with a mug of ale and questioned him about his family and previous experience. Apart from that, he was ignored. Once the meal was over they walked back along the broad harbour front to the cheerless three roomed cottage. The only comforts appeared to be a dying fire and a well-worn wing chair, set on a scrap of threadbare carpet. There were few furnishings, and minimal comforts. Mrs. Drew informed him that she would come by every morning, top up the water butt, and prepare his breakfast. Lunch and supper too if he wanted, but she thought he might want to vary that by eating at the inn.

"Of course, you will also have to prepare Sunday's sermon, Father. But I imagine you already have something in mind. You must have prepared some before now." Her offhand remark and tone of voice seemed to imply that she doubted if he could write his name, let alone a sermon. His new home consisted of a bedroom, living room, and scullery. As far as provisions were concerned, there was the butt of water in the scullery and a small cupboard, which she had stocked with some bread and cheese, butter, milk and half a dozen eggs. Outside there was a woodshed and a few paces away, an outdoor privy.

Mrs. Drew put more logs on the fire, bade him goodnight, and left him alone to contemplate his good fortune and enjoy the comforts of his new home. Once she left, Roddy did find one saving grace; a small cupboard that held a few bottles of wine left by his predecessor and he resolved to taste that as soon as possible. "Just to make sure it hasn't spoiled of course," Roddy said smiling rather wearily, and raising his eyebrows. He felt abandoned, friendless, and very sorry for himself."

• • •

The Cornish coast is notorious for unpredictable, violent, storms and squalls. These conditions, coupled with the rocky coastline, and submerged rocks, make the area a particularly hazardous one in which to earn a living from the sea. During Roddy's first evening in Ryeport, there occurred just such a storm.

Ryeport's small fishing fleet – an assortment of boats ranging from twenty to thirty feet in length – had been fishing all day with poor results. 'The Lucky Lady', a thirty-foot boat, had ventured two miles farther out to sea than her closest rival, 'Sunset' – owned and manned by the Carter family. During the late afternoon The Lucky Lady had found a good-sized school of herring. The skipper, Timothy Ozmund, and his mates, Will Tarret, and Mrs. Drew's fourteen-year-old son, Mick, were so busy with their nets that they failed to notice the steadily darkening sky and sporadic gusts of wind. When these warning signs finally registered with Tim, he straightened up and looked west. Dark, ominous looking clouds were being driven towards them by a freshening wind, slowly blotting out the descending sun. The wind gusts grew stronger and the rolling swell began to develop a heavier pitch. The danger signs were now very clear. "Cast the rest loose lads; we're running for home; looks like rough weather's comin' in." The Skipper's crew mates responded quickly to the urgency in his voice, as they too cast anxious looks at the gathering clouds.

Tim looked towards the shore and saw that the other boats were already running for home. Less occupied by smaller catches, they had become aware of the signs before Tim and were already making good speed towards the harbour. Carter's 'Sunset' was still farther west than they, but closer inshore. By the time Lucky Lady's gear was stowed, and she was heading for the harbour, the sky was heavily overcast and white crests were being whipped onto increasingly high waves, and salt spray was stinging their faces. The 'Lucky Lady' was heavy with her good haul, and consequently unable to make her best speed. Tim was proud of the fact that his was the most successful boat operating out of Ryeport. Some said he was just lucky but others would admit that he was a smarter and more daring skipper than most. He would venture farther, work longer and use his seamanship and experience to improve his crew's earnings.

A flash of lightning off to the west was quickly followed by a crash of thunder. Tim tightened his grip on the tiller as his crew trimmed the boat, in an effort to squeeze every last ounce of speed from her. The weather and visibility was worsening rapidly and Tim realised that he would need the guidance of the beacon fires on either side of the harbour entrance, to guide him into the harbour's safe channel. It was during a previous storm, nearly two years ago, that one of those beacons had been doused by heavy rains, and Tim had been obliged to guess which of the two fires was lit. If it was the eastern beacon – the one on his right of the harbour entrance that was alight – he would have to steer left of it to find calm water. However, if the western beacon was the lighted one, steering left of that would commit him to disaster in the rocky bay known as Sorry Cove. On that first occasion he had reasoned that the lighted beacon would be the more easily serviced eastern one, on the right of the harbour entrance and had steered to the left of it. Unfortunately, he'd guessed wrong, and committed his boat and crew to Sorry Cove. A lightning flash had revealed his mistake, but too late for him to make a course correction. Faced with almost certain destruction on the rocks of Sorry Cove, Tim had gambled on steering his boat through the narrow gap in the western cliff that divided Sorry Cove from the safe entrance. That gap is known locally as 'The Chute'.

Tim had gambled and won. Luck had been with him that stormy evening. Despite the poor visibility, he had timed his critical right-handed turn perfectly, and his boat had ridden an incoming wave that carried it safely over the hazardous rocks just below the surface and through The Chute into safe water. Several of the local fishermen had navigated The Chute successfully in empty boats, when the tide was favourable. But Tim Ozmund is the only man that brought a loaded boat through The Chute during a storm and lived to tell the tale. In fact, his boat had been lifted so high on that incoming wave, that the top of her mast had speared the footboards of the bridge over The Chute.

The men at the inn had ridiculed Tim's story of their journey through The Chute at first but had had to 'eat crow' when the beacon master, Archer, brought Tim's masthead pennant to the inn, and told the story of how he'd found it jammed in the footboards of his bridge over The Chute. That was something that even Tim had been unaware of until then. That same pennant was flying now at the masthead of Tim's new boat, 'Lucky Lady.' Much patched and repaired, that banner was priceless to this superstitious fisherman. But Tim's first boat, 'Lucky Lass' had been smaller, and their catch had been lighter when he guided her through The Chute that stormy night. He knew better than any other skipper, the dangers of entering Sorry Cove with a heavy boat. The Chute would be a dangerous option tonight.

"Keep a sharp eye out for the beacons lads," Tim yelled. "We should see them soon." With more than a mile to go the full fury of the storm was now upon them. The sky was very dark, and the heavy driving rain stinging their faces was rendering visibility very difficult. Each man muttered a quiet prayer and Mick and Will Tarret touched the crucifix fastened to the mast as they secured their safety lines.

Joshua Cobbe's boat was the first to enter the harbour entrance. It eased into the calmer water behind the western cliff as the beacon above them blazed its brightest. Minutes later Archer's straining eyes made out the boats of Tyler, Andrews and O'Sullivan, rounding the cliff into the quieter water. Seven boats still remained outside the harbour, and still there was no light from the eastern beacon. Visibility was less than a hundred yards, in a driving rainstorm. That reduced visibility would make it impossible to correct an errant course from close inshore. Then lightning revealed the distinctive rig of Morris's ketch as it rounded the cliff into the protected water, and thunder shook the ominously dark sky. That boat was followed by one other that he could not identify, and again he looked anxiously towards the east. "Where is that eastern light? Why hasn't Rooken lit his beacon?" During another flash of lightning, and an almost simultaneous crash of thunder, Archer glimpsed shadows rounding the western cliff but he could not recognise the boats. The waves were ten feet high now and growing higher every minute. "Those boys followed each other in," he muttered. "Pity those poor buggers that were further out, especially with no second beacon to guide them. Someone from the inn should be checking on Rooken by now. I wonder what the problem is."

On that eastern cliff-top, Jamie Rooken was lying face down beside the unlit beacon. He had been sleeping beside his fireplace when that first crash of thunder had startled him from the comfort of his dreams. Jamie had lost no time in cramming his portly form into oilskins, and rushing out of his cottage and up the rough steps to his beacon. He had just reached the beacon when a sudden crushing pain in his chest robbed his lungs of air and his legs of their strength and he fell face first, onto the unlit brazier. He laid there unconscious, blood welling from a gash that ran across his cheek from chin to ear. Jamie's wife, Emily, knew nothing of her husband's problem, and he would often spend a couple of hours at his beacon, so she was not alarmed. But as she passed the seaward window, the usual reas-suring glow from his beacon wasn't there, only darkness and a feeling of dread, based on a lifetime of hard experience, gripped her. She hurried up the cliff steps, to the brazier, to find her unconscious husband, soaking wet and barely breathing. The brazier was still unlit, and Jamie's smashed oil lamp lay beside him on the ground. She could see Archer's beacon blazing brightly across the channel, and prayed that someone would come by to see why Jamie's was still unlit. Despite her husband's plight, she would have to light the brazier first – so many lives could depend on it. Frantically, she threw the wet kindling out of the brazier and replaced it with fresh dry kindling from the shelter. Then she used her lantern to light two pitch torches which she stuffed under the kindling, almost choking in panic as the driving wind and rain tried to defeat her attempts to start the fire. Archer, at the western beacon, heaved a sigh of relief as he saw the beginnings of a flame across the harbour entrance. Emily's fire was building nicely, and she was trying to help her stricken husband, when three men from the village arrived on the scene. One remained to tend the light, whilst the other two struggled down the steps, with the unconscious Jamie. Emily, meantime, was hurrying her weary legs into as fast a pace as she could manage, stumbling and falling over the rough ground to Doctor Hudson's cottage, fearing that he would be too late to save her husband.

"One beacon again," said Tim, bitterly, as he struggled to control his heavily laden boat. He shielded his eyes against the stinging rain as he stared into the darkness, searching for a clue as to which beacon was lit. "I'm getting too close to change course. Which side should I choose this time? Some lightning would help right now," he said. "If I could get a glimpse of Archer's bridge I would know which beacon is lit. I'll go left. The western beacon is always the most likely to fail, because of its exposure." He eased the tiller to starboard, bringing the boat left of the lighted beacon, as the shadowy bulk of the cliff loomed larger. "Committed now," he muttered grimly.

The hoped-for lightning flash came seconds too late. "My God; it's the West beacon. We're going into Sorry Cove again." The muscles in Tim's stomach tightened, as that brief illumination confirmed his worst fears. "Lighten the boat lads," he screamed. "Lighten ship! Lighten ship!" But his crew could not hear him for the wind and rain. They too had seen the bridge over The Chute during that flash of lightning. They 'crossed' themselves, as they looked back at their skipper. Then, as if to confirm their fears, they saw a small glow from the eastern beacon. They groaned, checked their safety lines, and tightened their hold on the rigging.

Once again, The Chute would be their only chance. They would be going in fast and the timing of their angled entry would have to be perfect. Tim would have to swing the boat almost broadside to the following waves just before The Chute. "Too late to reduce sail," he muttered as he aimed the boat a little further left, trying to compensate for the waves pushing them to the right. Timing would be critical. If he turned the boat too soon the waves would roll the broad-sided boat over, and into a trough. He could use some lightning right now but the storm didn't oblige. For a few seconds the boat would ride high on a wave and the beacon would appear at almost eye level. Then they would drop back into the trough and the beacon would seem to climb high above them on their way down. This was making the boat very hard to control. "Maybe we'll get lucky again and just break our mast on Archer's bridge," Tim muttered hopefully. Then a flash of lightning revealed that he was too far left and too close in for a hard corrective course. He tried to carefully ease the boat into the correct alignment without having the following waves roll them broadside. His first alignment had been good but he had over compensated for the drift. As the boat descended into a trough, he fought to hold his target line for that critical turn into The Chute, with only memory and the glow of the beacon to guide him. "We're going to make it!" He yelled, forcing as much conviction into his words as he could muster. "We're going to make it!"

The next wave rushed The Lucky Lady, slightly broadside, into The Chute and she was lifted high as she entered the portal, until her mast speared the footboards of Archer's bridge. A flash of lightning burnt the image of his boat, dangling by its mast from Archer's bridge and bracketed on either side by the cliffs, into Tim's memory. There was complete darkness, as the mast snapped and the boat fell. Then a following wave hammered the partly broadsided boat into the landward side of the narrow Chute, smashing in the port side before spewing the wreckage from the boat and the bridge, into the calmer water of the harbour entrance. Tim Ozmund and Will Tarret were cast free of that wreckage and were struggling in the water, but Mick Drew had been thrown head first into the cliff and then trapped underwater in a tangle of ropes and fishing nets, until another wave drove the shattered remnants of the boat into the harbour channel.

Archer, in the beacon hut above, heard the noise of the wreck and, hanging onto his safety line, he struggled to the bridge to see what had happened. He would have stepped onto the space vacated by the destroyed bridge had an opportune lightning flash not revealed the damage. Only a few footboards remained and they were dangling from the safety net on the eastern side. That lightning flash also revealed a masthead pennant, that Archer knew only too well, jammed in the remains of those dangling footboards.

His heart ached for the three popular men that manned 'The Lucky Lady'. He began yelling their names at the top of his lungs, hoping to hear an answering voice from the rocks below, but none came and it was too dark to see anything. Any would-be rescuers would have to work virtually blind in the turbulent, rock-strewn, waters around The Chute. But that would only happen if they knew a boat had been wrecked there, which of course, they didn't. And it was no longer possible for him to cross the gap and tell the villagers about the wreck. He would have to wait for a rescue party himself. Until then, he would be tending the beacon, safe and dry in the hut. He later confessed that he felt guilty just for thinking that.

A role call at the inn revealed that two boats were still missing: Tim Ozmunds's Lucky Lady, and the Carter's Sunset. Despite the best efforts of the fishermen, it was impossible to search beyond the harbour. The weather precluded the use of sail and their lanterns were all but useless in these conditions and so the boats were forced to return to the landing to await calmer weather. However, Joshua Cobbe, his brother Ben's, and O'Sullivan's boats were away at the first hint of daylight and others were close behind. Ernie stood at an attic window of his inn, his telescope focused on the remains of Archer's bridge and the hut. Smoke was still coming from the chimney but there was no sign of Archer. He wondered what had destroyed the bridge and if his friend might be lying dead or injured on the rocks below.

Now, thinking ahead, Ernie hurried to Archer's stable and harnessed the horse to the flatbed wagon, in case injured men might need to be carried to their cottages. The light and the weather were improving steadily by the time Cobbe's boat arrived at the harbourside entrance to The Chute. It was there that they found the shattered remains of The Lucky Lady. Mick Drew's broken body was visible just below the surface, held there by snagged nets and rigging. "My God; they came through The Chute again," said Cobbe, looking up at the demolished bridge. They cut Mick free and gently brought him aboard, he had been dead for hours and was freezing cold. Joshua Cobbe was choked with emotion. "Poor Bessie," he said, "First her husband and now her only son."

Then they heard a shout from O'Sullivan's boat. They had spotted two men on some rocks on the other side of the channel, further east. Will Tarret had managed to snag his safety line to a spur of rock and was lying there, on his back, with his legs under Tim's arms, and his feet hooked across his body. That desperate hold was the only thing preventing the unconscious skipper from slipping back into the water. Will was drifting in and out of consciousness himself, but resisted the rescuers effort to disengage his legs from around Tim. "It's alright Will. We've got Tim, you can let go now. Let us get you boys home." Dave O'Sullivan (Sully) was moved to tears by the injured man's refusal to let go of his friend. Eventually they managed to get Tim into Sully's boat and Morris took Will aboard his. As they turned towards the jetty Joshua Cobbe called to them: "We've got young Mick, lads. The poor lad's beyond our help." Sully called back: "Tim and Will are in a bad way. We'll get them to Doc. Hudson as fast as we can." Cobbe called to the other boats that were arriving: "Tim's boat got smashed up coming through The Chute. Young Mick is dead and Tim and Will are in bad shape, we'll get them back to Doc Hudson. See if you can find Carter and his boys."

Back at the landing Ernie had arrived with the cart and makeshift stretcher. "Where's the vicar?" he asked looking around the assembled villagers. Having been without a vicar for several weeks, no one had thought to call and advise their new vicar of the situation and he was asleep in the fireside chair in the cottage, completely unaware of the villager's latest tragedy. Then Ernie saw Jane Cobbe, Benjamin's young daughter. "Quickly Jane, run and fetch the new vicar," he called. "Hurry, there's a good girl!"

• • •

Roddy, who was totally unaware of the storm, having drunk almost two bottles of his predecessor's wine in an effort to relieve the misery of his new surroundings, was rudely awakened by someone pounding on his door, and shouting: "Vicar! Vicar!" He had a pounding headache, a miserable pain in his stomach, and a disgusting, gummy, film coating his teeth. "Just a minute," he yelled, but that shout caused a pain to run from his right shoulder, up his neck and stab his brain. He realised he was about to pay the price for overindulgence in the wine, and groaned as he struggled out of the chair where he had spent the whole night. Unfortunately, on his first step in an effort to retain his balance, he knocked a glass of wine off the table, splashing the contents over his breeches and stockings. Cursing, wet, and uncomfortable, he stumbled to the door. A flushed and anxious young girl stood outside. "Come, Vicar. Come right now," she yelled. "You're needed at the landing." She reached through the opening, grabbed his wrist, and tried to drag him through the door into the drizzling rain. Only his other hand's firm grip on the door jamb prevented that from happening.

"What's the matter? Who are you?" he asked. She ignored his question. "The jetty, come to the jetty. My daddy and the other men are looking for the missing fishermen. They need you now. Hurry! Right now, hurry!" Her voice was impatient, and she gave him another violent tug on his arm. "Let me get my coat," he said. "What fishermen?" Once he had his coat, she would brook no more delay, but got behind him and pushed him into the street. Moments later they were running through the rain together with every step he took sending a searing pain through his head to add to his misery. He had hated this place from the first moments he had set eyes on it but it seemed that every fresh minute here would build on that misery. He began to wonder if reinstatement in his father's 'will' could ever compensate for all his discomfort.

A crowd was gathered at the jetty, waiting for two boats soon to come alongside. A woman – whom he later discovered to be Archer's wife, Kathleen – was the first to recognise the limp figure in the bottom of Cobbe's boat and her hand swiftly flew to her mouth. Mick Drew's awkward posture, together with the downcast expressions on the faces of the boat's crew, confirmed her worst fears. Kathleen put an arm around Bessie Drew's shoulder just as she too, recognised the oilskin clad figure of her son, and began to weep. Gentle hands lifted the young lad onto the jetty and Bessie Drew dropped to her knees beside her son and looked up anxiously at Joshua. The big fisherman responded with a slight shake of his head and some of the women began to weep, whilst others turned away shaking their heads, as though refusing to accept this tragedy. Bessie Drew cradled her son's head in her lap as she gave a quick, despairing glance into Kathleen's sad face. Not a word was spoken; Kathleen just gave her friend a gentle squeeze, as they both knelt beside the dead boy and Mrs. Drew's tears fell uncontrollably, as she tried to clean and dry her son's face.

The other injured fishermen were now being lifted onto the jetty and one very pregnant and almost hysterical, young lady tried to get to her knees to help her man. Fortunately, there were plenty of caring neighbours to support her. Then Jane's insistent young voice demanded their attention: "I've brought the vicar!" she shouted, causing some of the crowd to turn their attention to Roddy. Then one of the men shouted angrily: "The bastard's drunk; just look at him: wine-soaked clothing and obviously the worse for drink and looking like he's spent the night boozing in a gutter. While our men were dying in the storm he sat comfortably in his cottage, getting drunk. I'll kill the bastard!" He broke from the crowd and quickly clamped his hands around Roddy's throat. Fortunately, the innkeeper was close by and pulled him off, but he was badly shaken.

"Enough of that Bannerman," said the innkeeper. "Have some thought for Bessie. She's the one having the toughest time here today." Several other men looked threatening and anxious to take over where Bannerman had left off. Mrs. Drew lifted her tear stained face to Roddy. "Why? Why did God take my son, Father? He took my husband only two years ago. Mick was all I had left; why did he have to take him too?" Then her manner abruptly changed to anger: "With all the evil people in this world, why did God have to take my son? Mick was a good boy; so tell me: why did God have to take my son?"

Roddy was totally shaken. He had anticipated meeting his parishioners after Sunday's service, in a calm and civilised introduction, but was confronted by them as an angry, grieving mob, who blamed him for their tragedy and were anxious to punish him for that in a most violent and extreme way. It was true that he had been oblivious of the storm and the disaster but he was hardly responsible for it. He dropped on his knees beside his distraught housekeeper. "I'm so terribly sorry, Mrs. Drew," he said. "I honestly knew nothing of this tragedy until moments ago. What can I do to help?" He was well aware of his shameful appearance; it was unforgiveable, especially for a man of his calling, and he felt totally wretched. But his discomfort earned him no sympathy from this devastated gathering. "I'll tell you what happened," screamed his antagonist, Bannerman – but the innkeeper, Ernie, quickly clamped a big hand over the man's mouth. "Give Bessie some peace Jack," Roddy heard him hiss into the man's ear. "We can deal with him later. Right now we can help Bessie most by helping him. She has to be our first concern today."

Bannerman, angrily tore himself free of the big man's grasp, and walked away. "I'm going home," he said, almost choking on his words. Some of the crowd patted him on the shoulder, but he shrugged them off and carried on walking. Roddy was living in a nightmare, dragged from a drunken sleep, and rushed into a situation where people were injured and dying and he was being held responsible for that. "I'm so sorry, Mrs. Drew," he repeated, and gently rested a hand on her shoulder. "I knew nothing of this tragedy. Honestly. I'm so terribly sorry. If there is anything I can possibly do to help – anything at all, please tell me."

"Tell your God to give my son's life back," she shouted angrily in his face. "That's what you can do. That's all I want from you. Tell Him I want my son back. Can you do that? We've always done right by the church and your religion and this is the response we get. I'm going home," she sobbed. "I'm taking my son home." She rose to one knee, turned her back on him, and tried to lift her son off the ground, but Ernie quickly restrained the grieving woman. "Bessie, let me carry Mick home. We'll leave the wagon for the other men to take Will and Tim home. I can carry Mick. Better this way." Bessie nodded tearfully, and the big man picked up the lad as though he were a baby. Bessie stood beside him, holding one of her son's cold hands. Ernie looked over his shoulder at Roddy. "You'd better come too vicar. I can't vouch for your safety back here." Kathleen Archer took Bessie's free hand and they walked together along the harbour front. He stumbled along behind them like a stray dog hoping for the comfort of a kind word. Ernie's daughter, Meg, was weeping at the edge of the crowd, and he called to her: "Meg. Please go to the Rooken's lass and tell Doc Hudson about the injured. You could stay there and help Mrs. Rooken for a while. Tell the doctor that Will and Tim are in a bad way."

"Alright, Dad," sobbed Meg, and hurried away.

Gentle hands lifted the injured men onto the wagon and the pregnant lady, obviously the wife of one of those men, was holding her man's hand as she stood beside the wagon. Just as they were leaving, there was a shout from beyond the jetty. Everyone turned to see a boat, with a broken mast and jury-rigged sail approaching, followed by other search boats. All three men in the damaged boat were safe and waving. "The Carters are all alright," yelled a man from one of the search boats. Ernie heaved a sigh of relief. "Well, that, at least, is good news. But what the hell am I going to do with this useless fool of a preacher."

• • •

"Whoa, Meg, hold up, girl!" Doc Hudson raised a hand to stay the teary-eyed Meg. She was half running, head down, and showing no intention of stopping as she tackled the uphill slope to Rooken's cottage. "What news, young Meg? Who are those tears for? Tell me what's going on Meg; there's a good girl."

"Oh, Doctor." Meg burst into a fresh fit of sobbing, almost choking on her words: "Mick Drew is dead and Tim Ozmund and Will Tarret are being taken to their cottages on Mr. Archer's wagon. They are hurt real bad. Dad said I should see if you could be spared from Mr. Rooken's bedside to see to the injured. I'm to stay with the Rooken's in case I can help, or run errands." The old doctor's shoulders slumped. "So I can do nothing for young Mick," he said, shaking his head, "Poor Bessie! Who is worst off Meg, Tim or Will? Did your dad say?"

"I believe it's Tim Ozmund, Doctor. No one said who was hurt most, they both looked really bad but I think Mr. Ozmund is the worst off." Doc Hudson patted the girl's copper coloured hair. "Thank you Meg. I shall go to Tim first then. I'm so sorry about young Mick lass. He was a good lad. We'll all miss him. How is his mother?"

"She was terribly upset doctor – really broken up. My dad was carrying Mick to their cottage; Mrs. Archer was with them. Oh, the new vicar too. There was not time to talk. The villagers were mad at the vicar though. They said he was drunk."

"Really! Well, thank you Meg. Please tell Mrs. Rooken I'll be back later; after I've done what I can for the other men. You're a good girl Meg. We're lucky to have you." He turned and walked towards the jetty. It seemed to Meg that he was trying to hurry, but was too tired. Then he turned and called back to her. "Any news of the Carters, Meg?"

"They're safe doctor," she replied. Doc Hudson acknowledged with a wave of his hand, and they continued on their separate ways. Emily Rooken was waiting at the door when Meg arrived and she had to retell her news. Emily sat at the table and began to cry. "It's our fault," she said. "I should've checked on Jamie earlier. They could have all been safe if I'd lit the beacon sooner." Meg put her arm around the distraught woman. "Oh, Mrs. Rooken, it's nobody's fault. No one expected your husband to collapse like that. He's always been strong. No one would have guessed he would fall ill so suddenly. You've got enough troubles of your own, don't borrow more." Emily gave a weary sigh before looking up at Meg. "You're right lass. What's done is done. I've got to look after my own troubles now." She wiped her eyes, put on a resolute expression, straightened her shoulders and walked into the bedroom to be with her husband.

About half an hour later she called excitedly: "Meg! Meg! He's stirring. Come see, lass." Meg hurried to the door. Sure enough, Jamie Rooken was moving his head and looking as though he was rousing from a deep sleep.

"Meg, Doc Hudson left some herbs and things in a bag on the dresser. He said to boil them in a cup of water and let Jamie sip it, when he comes around. Will you do that dear, please – boil the herbs that is – in a cupful of water?' Meg hurried to make the herbal tea. Meantime, Emily continued moistening Jamie's lips with a cloth soaked in brandy, giving a little squeeze every so often –  especially when she saw signs of life from her stricken husband. "Not exactly doctor's orders," she muttered. "But it's got Jamie licking 'is lips. What works can't be bad, can it? Signs of life at least."

# CHAPTER 5

## *A cold welcome*

Tom, the innkeeper's son, was waiting at the door of Mrs. Drew's cottage. "Have you got any tea made son?" His father asked. "No Sir, but the kettle is just off the boil." His words were said in a flat bewildered tone whilst staring at the limp figure in his father's arms. His shoulders slumped and in a trembling voice he asked: "Dad, Mick. Is he..?" His father nodded sadly. "It's a tragic day for us all, son." Ernie said softly. Then as Tom's jaw clenched and his eyes moistened, he quickly added: "Tom, I'm really going to need your help today. It's up to us now, to help those who are hurting too much to think for themselves. Pour some tea Tom, there's a good lad and put a good shot of brandy in each cup. There's a bottle in my coat pocket. Tom kept his face averted as he swung the kettle over the glowing embers in the fireplace. Bessie stood, silent and despondent, beside Ernie, still holding her son's hand. The innkeeper gave her a sympathetic smile and said: "Why don't I get Mick into some dry clothes Bessie? Perhaps you and Kathleen can help Tom find the makings for the tea. Me an' the vicar will look after Mick."

Bessie made no reply, but slumped into a chair, folded her arms on the table, rested her head on them and quietly wept. Ernie led Roddy into the lad's small bedroom. "I didn't want Bessie here when we cleaned Mick up," he explained. "We don't know what injuries might lay under his clothes that might add to her misery. Look through those drawers," he nodded towards a small chest of drawers. "Find some of Mick's good clothes. Let's get him looking his best before his mother sees him again." Ernie had laid the boy on the floor beside the bed, and was removing his oilskin and wet clothes.

"Find a towel and flannel vicar. Don't ask Bessie though. See if Tom knows where things are." Obediently Roddy left the room and soon returned with a bowl of water, flannel and a towel, then watched like a mindless dummy, as Ernie cleaned Mick up, placed him on his bed, dressed him, and brushed his hair. "What do you think?" Ernie asked. "We don't want Bessie any more upset than she already is."

"He looks good, clean, dry and comfortable. I don't think you could do any-more," said the vicar. He was feeling absolutely useless, unable to contribute, and with no idea of what to do or say. The innkeeper stared at him for a few seconds before saying: "Very well vicar. Roll up his wet things in the oilskin, and sneak them out to Tom. Ask him to take them back to the inn when he goes. Meg can wash them and bring them back later. Now mister preacher, you'd better think of some words of comfort for Bessie, and a prayer to say over this young man. It's time to start earning your keep! Mick was a fine young man and well-loved hereabouts. He was a fun loving, teasing young chap, full of life and good-natured mischief. Special, you might say. And – if you value your sorry arse – you'd better treat him that way." Ernie's expression was grim and, despite the softly whispered words, the underlying threat was hard to miss. "Into the kitchen now, let's get a cup of hot tea down Bessie – us too, before we tackle the rest of our problem."

Tom had poured the tea, and Roddy could smell the brandy before the cup was halfway to his mouth. Bessie didn't want any but Kathleen eventually coaxed her into taking a few sips of the heavily laced brew. Then Bessie stood, and they all followed her into her son's bedroom. Her tear stained face was devoid of all expression now. She looked vacant, as though her own life had drained away with the passing of her son – looking like a mere shell of her former self. "He looks peaceful," she said, in a listless voice. "Thank you, Ernie."

Kathleen and Tom were staring at Roddy, and Ernie gave him a stern look. So, with an empty, sickness in his stomach he broke into the silence. "Let us pray," he said and they all bowed their heads whilst he 'ad-libbed' his way through his first family bereavement. "Dear Lord. We ask for your help and guidance in this time of grief and tragic loss. It is beyond our under-standing why this much-loved son has been taken from us so early in his promising life. Our faith leads us to believe that you have a greater purpose in mind for him now and we will take such comfort from that as our limited understanding will allow. Please bring your comfort to Mick's beloved mother, as also his many friends and neighbours in our humble village. We are devastated by Mick's passing and he will be desperately missed. We accept that you have taken him to be with you, in heaven and ask that you grant us the ability to find comfort in the sure and certain knowledge, that we shall all be reunited in your own good time. We ask this in the name of Our Saviour, Jesus Christ, who taught us to pray saying: Our Father....."

As The Lord's Prayer was ending Roddy stole a quick look at Ernie, through lowered lids, and was alarmed to see the big man draw a finger across this throat. Then he gave a discreet nod towards the door and, Roddy realised his signal meant that it was their time with young Mick that was ending – not his life.

Ernie gave Bessie a gentle hug and explained that they were needed at the homes of the injured men – especially since they did not know how badly hurt they were. Bessie nodded her understanding. "Thanks for everything Ernie," she said. "You too, Father," and she sat on her son's bed. Kathleen, standing by her side, looked at the innkeeper. "I'll stay with Bessie, Ernie. Please let me know how Archer is and send someone here if he needs me." Ernie nodded. "Thanks Kathleen, I'll do that." He sent Tom to relieve his sister Meg, at Rooken's cottage, with instructions for her to return to the inn and get soup and bread ready to feed the rescue parties and families of the injured. Then he led the vicar outside saying: "It's Tim's cottage first. I'm sure he was the worst off."

When Roddy said goodbye, he made the mistake of shortening Kathleen's name to Kate – possibly because the only other Kathleen he knew preferred to be called Kate. However, Kathleen corrected him – and in a very officious manner. "Vicar, my name is Kathleen. Not Kate or Kathy. Everyone in the village calls me Kathleen and now I'll not answer to anything else. I will make an exception for you though. You can call me Mrs. Archer." He felt chastised and hastened to apologise but, whilst he struggled to explain himself, she closed the door in his face.

The grim-faced innkeeper strode off, into the drizzling rain, in the direction of the jetty. He was soon way ahead of Roddy, never looking back, and leaving him farther behind with every step. In his thin soled, silver buckled town shoes, Roddy was struggling to maintain his balance on the slippery, pebble strewn road, mainly because of the innkeeper's fast pace. He was breathing heavily, his feet were sore, and, despite the chilling rain, he was sweating profusely. Ernie turned left, into an alleyway between the rows of cottages, where Roddy was relieved to find him waiting for him. Although desperately weary, he did manage a half smile as he drew level with him. It was the first time they had been alone together all morning.

But when he turned to confront him, the anger on his face was alarming and Roddy was to be the sole recipient of his anger. "You religious bastards make me sick!" He almost spat the words at him as he thrust his face close to the alarmed vicar's. "What idiot sent a fop like you to our village, especially after our last experience? Do you realise how hard it's going to be, for me to save your sorry arse from the villagers? Where do you get the gall to lie around in your cottage, getting drunk, whilst our men are fighting for their very lives in a storm? Have you no concern for your fellow man? No compassion? Just look at you. Crumpled clothing, wine-soaked stockings, unshaven, and obviously the worse for drink. How much respect does that show for our dead and injured? What sort of leeches do they breed in those seminaries anyway? Do they teach you...teach you..." His anger was choking off his words. "Do they teach you to get drunk and ignore the problems of the people you're supposed to be helping? Or is that something you managed to learn all on your own? His rage was fearful – boiling over. Roddy felt certain that he was about to lose control, and beat him to death. He struggled for words or means to defend himself, but in the face of this powerful man's raging hostility, inspiration failed him. "For God's sake man, be reasonable," he said. But Ernie did not appear to hear him and he was in fear for his life.

"Tell me something," he raged. "What good has your bloody religion ever done for our village?" He grabbed the front of Roddy's coat in his left hand, twisted it, and with an upward, thrusting motion, slammed his back against the rock wall, pinning him there with a powerful forearm, braced across his chest. His unpleasant breath was spraying his angry words into Roddy's face as he struggled to break free. There were pains in his back from being slammed into the protruding stones in the wall but that became insignificant as he realised that his feet no longer had firm contact with the ground. Roddy began shouting back at him.

"Listen you big oaf! Listen! Don't ask questions if you've got no intention of listening to my answers! I didn't choose to come here. I wasn't even consulted, just dumped here, like an unwanted package. I'm a newly ordained priest. This is my first parish and when I arrived you treated me like a leper!

No greetings. No introduction. No words of welcome. I knew nothing of your life here. Nothing! And you did nothing to enlighten me. Beyond a grunt or two, you paid me no attention whatsoever. I was abandoned in this God-forsaken hole, where you ignored me, and made me feel like a liability. You're the head of this village but you did nothing to acquaint me with it, or anyone in it." Although Ernie was taken aback by the aggressive response, that only gained Roddy a few moments reprise.

"God-forsaken you say. Well that sums up our feelings too – though why God would forsake good people like these, I'll never know. But you're his go-between, so it's up to you to find out. And if you hope to survive around here let alone be our vicar, you'd better learn what we're about and bloody fast. The last useless fool that had your job was a drunk too. He was drunk when he fell off the dockyard wall and broke his neck one stormy night. We didn't tell the Bishop that he was drunk though because we didn't want to embarrass his daughter and family. They don't live in our village so our villagers agreed to keep his disgrace a secret.

Jack Bannerman knows about that night better than most. Jack's the man that was so interested in your neck a short while back. It was Jack who risked life and limb, during a storm, to climb down those slippery rocks to see if he could help the useless bastard. It's a slippery climb on a good day. In a storm it was asking for trouble. It's a wonder he wasn't injured himself. Jack thinks all you church people are useless drunks and leeches. And he's not alone in that." The pressure of his forearm on Roddy's chest was increasing with every word.

"If you want to know why you got a poor reception here, it's largely because of your predecessor and his preaching. The villagers got nothing useful from him. They gave money from their meagre earnings, and prayed constantly. But your God didn't listen. Maybe, He just doesn't care. Most of our fishermen fasten a crucifix to their boat's masts. They touch it and say a prayer, every time they leave harbour. But still they keep dying at sea, or on the rocks in the harbour, like poor Mick and his father and the crew of The Lucky Lady. Your religion did nothing for any of them. It demands obedience and sacrifice but gives nothing in return. Nothing!"

His white knuckled, right fist had been rising in step with his angry words and was now hovering above his shoulder. Roddy screwed up his face, anticipating those big white knuckles smashing into it and raised his left arm to protect himself. "Go ahead then. Hit me if that will make you feel better but don't blame me for the storm. I can't create a storm. I'm not from God, just one of his servants, and I'm new at the job. I'm not responsible for the mistakes of your last vicar either. He was! And I refuse to accept responsibility for his mistakes. I make enough of my own. Nor did I choose this job. If I had a choice, I wouldn't stay in this God-forsaken hole another minute!"

This highly charged atmosphere was dramatically broken by a deep, gravelly, voice. "Well, well! Spoken like a true man of the cloth. Ernie, don't scare our new vicar so. Remember poor Bessie; she has to do his laundry!" Roddy felt the pressure of the innkeeper's forearm ease as they both looked towards the owner of the voice. "Come now Ernie, let the vicar have his coat back. He looks bad enough without you screwing it up like that." The innkeeper's face broke into a grin, and he released his grip. Roddy was relieved to feel his feet in solid contact with the ground again. He looked at the tall stranger that had just saved him from what might have been a life-threatening beating and tried to restore some dignity to his dishevelled appearance. Ernie left him, striding to meet the newcomer with his hand outstretched, and a big smile on his face. "Archer, you cantankerous old bastard! I'm so glad you're safe. Have you seen Kathleen? What happened last night to wreck your bridge? How did you get back?"

"Whoa, Ernie, whoa! One thing at a time, please." Archer held up a shattered mast tip, with a torn pennant still attached. "That's what happened to the bridge. Tim's mast head came right up through it. He might have made it through The Chute again, if the bridge hadn't snagged his mast." Ernie's mouth dropped open as he touched the pennant. He was speechless. Archer continued: "Sailmaker told me that young Mick is dead and that the other two lads are in bad shape. Is that true?"

"Afraid so, Archer. We thought we might be adding you to the list of injured too. How did you get back?"

"Well, the safety netting, on the west side of the bridge, was still in pretty fair shape. What was left of the bridge was dangling from that. Tim's pennant was jammed between a couple of footboards. Sailmaker got a line across to me and I secured that to the beacon hut and used it as a safety line as I climbed across the safety net on the side of the bridge. I gathered up Tim's pennant on the way."

"Good grief man! Who would have thought Tim would go through The Chute a second time."

"I'm sure it wouldn't have been his choice Ernie. But he damn near made it." Archer looked glum as he fondled the tattered bunting. "That's the second time I've taken this pennant from that bridge, he said, despondently. Ernie took the beacon minder's elbow. "We're off to see Tim now. Why don't you come with us?"

"Sure. We can talk on the way. Then I must head up to see Jamie. Any idea how he's making out? Sailmaker said it was something wrong with his heart. Didn't look good, he said."

"That's all we know Archer. We've been at Bessie's place since the boats brought the lads back. Archer turned to Roddy. "Come vicar, you'd better join us. From what I hear, Ernie an' me must be your two best friends in this village." Roddy despondently tailed along behind the two men. There was no introduction. They arrived at Tim's cottage just as Doc Hudson was leaving. Doc clapped a hand on Archer's shoulder. "Glad you're safe Archer. You had us worried. Have you seen Kathleen?"

"Not yet Doc, but Sailmaker has gone to let her know I'm alright. I'll see her before I head up to Jamie's. How is he Doc?"

"It doesn't look good, my friend. Nothing more I can do for him until he regains consciousness – precious little even then. He's in God's hands now my friend." Archer shook his head. "What about Tim then?"

The old doctor looked downcast. "The vicar here might do more good than I, in pulling him through this. He has several broken ribs, both legs are broken and all sorts of cuts and bruises. He took a pounding on those rocks, all night long while soaked through. His legs were in that cold water all that time. The exposure would have killed most men. If he survives tonight, he'll have a long road back to health. He's not conscious yet – may never be again." Doc Hudson turned to Roddy. "See what you can do for him Father. He's a religious man. You may be able to help him. But be careful, he's a canny lad. He'll know whether you're a true man of God or just a pretender, even if he doesn't appear to be conscious."

For the first time since he had been forced into this new calling, Roddy came face-to-face with the responsibilities of the undertaking. This life wasn't his choice, merely a means to an end – a last opportunity to recover his inheritance and lost privileges. The fact that the doctor, or anyone else for that matter, might believe that a man's faith might be the deciding factor in his life or death, had never occurred to him. The fact that he might need to be the instrument of that faith – especially since he was just a pretender – was a sobering thought.

They were ushered into Tim's cottage by a neighbour but Ernie paused at the door to watch his old friend, Doc Hudson trudge wearily off to his next patient. His slumped shoulders and hanging head betrayed the man's exhaustion. It was obviously an effort for him to force his tired legs, through the drizzling rain to Will's cottage. "Every picture tells a story!" Ernie muttered as he followed the doctor's progress. "He'll be our next problem. What'll we do Archer, when poor old Doc can't handle this job anymore? What'll we do if he falls ill? Who will be able to help him? This is a hard living for a doctor; we'll never find another like him. Dedicated to the people of this village, yet content to be paid with the three F's, as he calls it: fish, firewood and favours. Poor old Doc; he badly needs to rest." Ernie closed the door, assuming that he'd been sharing his thoughts with Archer and gave Roddy a disapproving look when he realised that it was he who had overheard his words. Archer was being welcomed by the people in Tim's bedroom and hadn't heard one word of Ernie's concerns. When Archer held up the pennant there were gasps of amazement from every-body present. "He nearly made it a second time." Archer said, and had to repeat the story of how Tim's mast had wrecked the bridge. "Here, Rachel," he said, giving the pennant to Tim's pregnant wife. "This was always Tim's good luck piece. Have one of the men put it on the wall where he can see it. If he knows that it survived it may help in his recovery too."

Ernie pulled the brandy bottle from his pocket and arranged for one of the women to make some of the fortified tea that had proved so acceptable at Bessie's place. After the tea and the exchange of news, Ernie 'cued' the vicar again. A bitter resentment was growing within Roddy for this brute that had bullied him so recently. He had believed him to be his protector, when he'd saved him from Bannerman but as soon as they were alone, he too had turned on him. However, he had to concede that his cues were valuable in this unfamiliar situation and was truly grateful that Archer had come along when he did, otherwise Ernie, his first protector, might have killed him. He vowed to free himself of the control the big man had so easily gained over him, but now was not the time or place. For now, he must focus on the job at hand.

"Let us pray for God's help to heal Tim's broken body," he said. "Please kneel around Tim's bed, and join hands, so that we link Tim with all of us, in a circle. Rachel, you take one of Tim's hands in yours, and mine in your other." He nodded to Archer. "On the other side of the bed, Archer, please take Tim's other hand and join with the person on your left. We need to join us all, Tim included, in an unbroken circle." The men looked openly hostile but Ernie's warning stare scanned each face, and they kept their silence. The women, however, seemed to derive some comfort from this structured prayer arrangement and he could see they were anxious to believe in God's benevolence. Even he began to think that he might have created a healing environment. "Now, let us pray."

"Dear Lord; please hear our prayers for your faithful servant Tim Ozmund, who lies badly injured and in desperate need of your help here today. Lord, we ask that you allow Tim to draw whatever strengths he may need for his recovery, from those of us in this circle, and so speed his healing. And please, Lord, allow Tim to share his pain and suffering amongst us also, so that we may ease his burden. We ask this in the name of Our Saviour, Jesus Christ, who taught us to pray saying: Our Father..."

Roddy took a quick look at Ernie across the bed and thought he saw a look of surprised approval on the man's face. "Better than I could have hoped," he thought. "But for Tim's sake I hope it works. I'm sincere in that at least." He rose from his knees and everyone followed suit. Ernie reminded them that he was providing free soup and bread at the inn and would arrange for some to be brought to those who would be staying to care for Tim and Rachel. Then he excused them both, explaining that they still had to attend at Will's bedside, and then Jamie Rooken's. Archer joined them and they headed for Will Tarret's cottage.

Will had suffered from exposure almost as badly as Tim. But as far as broken bones were concerned he was considerably better off. He had briefly regained consciousness whilst the doctor was splinting his broken arm but quickly drifted off into a desperately needed sleep. Doc Hudson made for the door. "I have to go and see how Jamie is getting on, he sighed wearily. By God; how I hate that bloody slope up to his cottage. My legs are aching something fierce."

Roddy was puzzled. "Ernie. Does the doctor have a buggy?"

"No, can't afford it."

"Then why, in God's name, doesn't he use my wagon?"

Ernie looked crestfallen, "Because, in all the confusion, I never thought of it, I'm 'shamed to say." He called to the doctor. "Doc, the vicar has offered his pony and wagon to you. Stop at the inn and tell Tom to harness the horse up. Get something to eat and drink while he's doing that. We'll be along shortly."

The doctor turned to the vicar. "Well thank you, Father. That's most kind. I appreciate it."

"You're more than welcome Doctor. Please use it for as long, and whenever, you need it. No need to ask. If it's there, use it. I'll let Ernie know if I ever need it."

"Thank you again. Tell me, Father, how did you fare with poor Tim?" Ernie interceded. "He did very well. This is not an easy situation for a newcomer to be dropped into. But if Tim was even slightly aware, I think he would have been encouraged and grateful." Doc raised his eyebrows. "Well done, Father. That gives us an extra measure of hope. My thanks to you too, Ernie; some of your hot soup will be most welcome." He turned and left.

Roddy was getting used to his role in these situations now, and didn't need Ernie's cue at Will's cottage. They all knelt around Will's bed and basically followed the routine that they had used at Tim's. The second brandy bottle gave-up-the-ghost before they left Will's place. The fishermen making the rounds of the injured, that morning, were wearing oilskins, and reasonably dry because of it. Ernie and he had grabbed the first coats that came to hand and those coats were now heavy with absorbed water. They were a chilled and bedraggled pair as they headed for the inn. "Vicar, you look like hell." Ernie commented gruffly. "You're no oil painting yourself," he replied, and was startled by the innkeeper's short explosive laugh.

"Maybe you'll do after all," the big man said. "Why don't you go home, clean yourself up, put on some dry clothes and come back to the inn." He paused in midstride, then turned to face him. "No, on second thoughts, I'll come home with you, and wait while you clean up. We'll go back to the inn together. You might run into someone who doesn't like you, and, if you're alone..." He pulled a wry face. So they both entered the cheerless cottage. The fire had apparently been dead for hours, and the place smelled damp and unpleasantly musty. "Apart from the bloody drizzling rain," Roddy said, "I'd sooner be outside. What was it that Bannerman said: Whilst I sit in the comfort of my cottage?" Ernie's explosive laugh startled him yet again. They were both soaked through; and water was dripping off their coats, onto the stone floor of the cottage. This had been the most miserable day of his life, but he began to feel he was being extended a little forgiveness.

They entered the inn by the kitchen door. "Better that you don't go into the bar yet, vicar. No sense in tempting trouble if it can be avoided," said Ernie. He took off his sodden greatcoat, and draped it over a chair-back by the fire, then, he did the same with Roddy's. Water drained off the coat, leaving drip lines on the stone floor. As they sat with their soup, fresh bread and cheese, steam was rising from the wet garments. "Not enough time to dry them, but they may be a bit lighter when we put them on again," said Ernie. "Steamy warm too! We should have worn oilskins. How about a drink? A hair of the dog that bit you, we say. You sure look as though you could use one. Some wine perhaps."

"No thanks. I couldn't face wine right now. Perhaps a shot of that medicinal brandy if you have any left," he replied, as he downed his last piece of cheese. Ernie rose from the table and brought a fresh bottle from a cupboard. "Good stuff this," he said, pouring three fingers into two wide brimmed glasses. "I was saving it for a special occasion. But I don't think it gets more special than today, does it now? Happier maybe, but not more special." He raised his glass, and Roddy followed suit. "To those in peril on the sea," said the innkeeper, as they clinked glasses. "To those in peril on the sea," Roddy responded.

. . .

As Ernie and Roddy were savouring their brandies they could hear Joe Carter in the bar, telling the story of their adventure to those villagers that had accepted Ernie's invitation for free soup.

Joe and his two boys had made the same error as Tim, guessing that the lighted beacon was the eastern one. But, since they were farther west when the storm broke and close inshore, the wind drove them ashore long before Sorry Cove.

"It was during a lightning flash, that one o' me boys recognised a massive rock on a short piece of rock-strewn beach before a cliff. You all know the place. No safe landing there," he was saying. "An' we were too close inshore to do anything about it. I tell you lads, we thought we were done for. But talk about luck, a bloody great wave carried us up the beach, just missin' that big rock, and then just as we were about to smash into the cliff the water rushed us back to the sea. It carried our boat bouncin' an' skiddin' back down the beach, and jammed us in behind that great rock. We was wedged there. But that rock protected us from almost certain death. That bit of good luck saved our lives, so it did. All night long the waves crashed over that rock, and fell on us. We were soaked afresh by each new wave, but the rock saved us from the poundin'. Once we realised our good luck we 'uddled up together, an' used part of the fallen sail to cover us, an' waited out the storm. Early the next mornin' the storm died down and we were able to assess the damage. Our boat was wedged on some smaller rocks, a bit like a seesaw. So we weighted the stern, so's she would tip easy – then we 'ad to dump our catch, before we could drag 'er down to shallow water. We found some timber on the beach, and levered 'er around. Then we dragged 'er through the shallows 'til she floated. It cost us a good catch but that's a small price to pay for savin' our lives, and our boat. A big piece of our mast had broken off and some boards 'ad been sprung, but that was the worst of it. A jury-rigged sail, and some 'ard bailin', brought us 'ome."

That day, the villagers in Ernie's bar had christened that landmark rock: 'Carter's Rock.' Every time a fresh face appeared, the Carters were obliged to retell the story. Then the newcomer usually bought the Carter's a drink. Of course, the story was embellished with each refilling of their jugs. Ernie had a big grin on his face as he sipped his brandy. "What's so amusing?" asked Roddy. Ernie's smile grew even broader. "The Carters are a good family, fine people, but you can always count on Joe to add some colour to a story. And with each retelling it'll get bigger and more adventurous. A couple of months from now you won't recognise that story, especially, if it's a stranger that's buying Joe a pint. Anyway, those boys'll be in no fit shape to repair their boat today, possibly not tomorrow either. But they'll blame their ordeal for their terrible headaches. It couldn't possibly be the result of too much ale. Good people though very entertaining too." He laughed that same short, explosive laugh that appeared to be part of his character.

Meg was serving hot soup and biscuits to all the villagers at the inn. The food was free but not the ale. Roddy considered Ernie's generosity even more remarkable when he later discovered that he wasn't much better off than the rest of the villagers.

It was obvious that the villagers had very little money to spare, and equally obvious that Ernie would never get rich through their patronage. Roddy was soon to learn, however, that there was nobody in the village that wouldn't rush to help Ernie and what little spare cash they had was usually spent at his inn.

Ernie had drained the last of his brandy and was anxious to be on the move again. "Come on then. No time to lie about; we've got to get back to visiting the sick." He shrugged his body back into his wet greatcoat and preceded Roddy through the kitchen door. Seconds later he back-tracked, to retrieve the brandy bottle he'd left on the table, then they both trudged off to Jamie Rooken's cottage, up the long slow hill that Doc Hudson found so trying. When they arrived at Jamie's cottage, Roddy paused for a quick look at his pony and wagon. "Hello Slondosh!" he said rubbing the pony's wet head. "I bet you'd rather be in the stable nice and dry, than out in this miserable rain."

"Who introduced you two?" asked Ernie.

"Oh, Reverend Tubbs mentioned the pony and wagon as he was leaving. He didn't know where his name came from though."

"Neither do I. Stupid name if you ask me." Ernie knocked on Rooken's door and they were soon greeted by Emily. "Oh Ernie' it's good to see you. How do you do Father? Thank you both for coming," she said, but she avoided eye contact with the vicar. He realised that the story of his arrival at the jetty that morning had been spread and been discussed by the whole village. "Good news," Emily said. "Jamie is conscious and has taken a little soup. Let me take your wet coats." Doc Hudson and Archer were sitting by Jamie's bed. His complexion was ashen, but at least he was conscious. Ernie strode to the sick man's bedside. "How are you, Jamie?" Good to see you're still with us. You had us worried for a while but you're obviously on the mend now. Jamie: this is our new vicar Reverend Rodney McDowd. He's been visiting the sick and injured with me today. Not an easy first day in his new job I might add." He turned to Roddy: "Say hello to Jamie Rooken, Father. Emily, is Kathleen Archer's sister. The village has cause to be grateful to both these ladies today; we owe them a big vote of thanks.

Roddy shook hands with the Rooken's, who were stiffly polite in their responses to him. Doc Hudson, despite the blazing fire in the next room, was shivering when he looked up at the innkeeper and said, "Ernie, do you happen to have any more of that medicinal liquid that made the tea at my patient's cottages so interesting earlier." He shot an arch look at Emily. Ernie tried to look disappointed. "Well as it happens, I do have a bottle in my pocket. But I was saving it, so I was, for a special occasion."

"Well if you're looking for a special occasion Ernie: this is it, my friend. Believe me, this is it." The doctor held his arms wide and smiled his weary smile. Ernie passed the bottle to Emily, who gathered four assorted glasses and poured a generous measure into each.

"Only four glasses! Aren't you having any Emily?" murmured the ashen-faced husband. Doc Hudson laughed. "Nice try Jamie. I found Emily's brandy-soaked handkerchief before she could wash it. I think you've had enough already. That wasn't exactly doctor's orders, but it's hard to argue with success, so we'll drink to your health Jamie and then leave you in peace so you can get some good, restorative sleep." He raised his glass to Jamie and they all followed suit. "Good health Jamie Rooken and a speedy recovery!' They downed their brandies at their own pace, whilst Jamie moaned and groaned about people who came into his house just to torment a sick man.

Doc Hudson turned to Ernie again and said, "By the way Ernie. I checked on Tim again, since I had the wagon. No more medicinal tea for Rachel please. Too much medicine can be just as bad as none at all. She was feeling rather peculiar when they put her to bed. She may pay for that tonight. Not good with a baby on the way – especially with all the worry about Tim."

"Sorry, Doc. I didn't serve it, just provided the brandy. Is she going to be alright?"

"Oh I think so. I'll pay them another visit after I drop you off at Bessie's. Thank you again for the use of the wagon Father. It's a great relief for my weary legs."

"Don't mention it, Doctor." Roddy looked at Ernie and discretely put his hands together as he raised his eyebrows a little. Not discretely enough apparently. Jamie caught the signal. "We don't need no prayer makin' 'ere preacher! 'specially when I'm denied a drink in me own 'ouse and addin' insult to injury 'ave to watch you lot guzzle brandy. Me in me sick bed and all!" Jamie's voice was weak but the words were spoken with conviction.

Emily thanked Ernie and Doc Hudson gave Ernie and Roddy a ride back to Bessie's place. The doctor stopped off too. He checked her pulse and asked if she'd eaten anything. "No Doctor, couldn't face it."

"You must try Bessie. You have to keep your strength up. I don't need another patient right now." He gave her a hug. "I'll see you tomorrow my dear." Archer had arrived shortly before them, and was getting a hostile reception from his wife, Kathleen. "Thanks for sending someone else to let me know you were alright Archer," she said, "but you shouldn't flatter yourself that I was worried about you."

"Sorry Kathleen," replied her weary looking husband, "But once you knew I was safe, I felt I should see if I could do anything for them that was injured. Come on girl; you knew I was alright and you were busy too." He put his arm around his wife's shoulders and gave her a gentle squeeze. But Kathleen was intent on remaining aloof. "Is that what passes for affectionate concern where you come from?" she asked. Archer just smiled and going to Bessie's side, laid a hand on her shoulder. "I'm so sorry for your loss Bessie. We all loved young Mick. God rest his soul. If you ever need anything, you know we'll do our best to help." Bessie looked up into her friend's concerned face and put her hand on his. "I know that Archer. And I am always grateful for friends like you."

Kathleen turned to Ernie and motioned to the scullery. "I'd like a word with you three," she whispered. Once in the scullery she said: "I'll be staying here tonight. Bessie won't leave Mick's side. Not even to go to bed. When I told her I would stay tonight, she said it wasn't necessary. She said they'll be apart for a long time and she'll stay with him as long as she can. She's being strong but she's broken up inside. When Sailmaker came by to tell us Archer was safe, Bessie asked him to make Mick's coffin. Said she would like him to be buried Sunday, next to his father. Deep enough to leave room for her she said. She wants them all to be together eventually." The men all looked grim faced. Doc Hudson said: "She's strong willed alright Kathleen, but she must keep her strength up. Try and get some food down her, even if it's only soup."

"I'll do that doctor. Vicar," she said, turning to Roddy. "Bessie said that for the funeral service in the church, she'd like The Third Psalm and for the hymn: "For those in peril on the sea." She wants you to keep it short at the grave side. Jack Bannerman and Will Baker have offered to dig the grave tomorrow. They're both friends of the family. Bannerman has promised me he'll behave himself – for Bessie's sake." She raised her eyebrows a little and lowered her head as she looked at Roddy. He ignored the reference to Bannerman. "Very well, I'll see to that Mrs. Archer." Kathleen touched Ernie's arm. "Bessie wanted you and Archer and the Cobbe Brothers, to be pall bearers, Ernie. Is that alright?"

"Certainly, are the others agreed?"

"Yes."

"It's settled then. What time?"

"Right after the eleven o'clock service." Ernie looked at the vicar. "We'll talk about this later Father, to arrange the details." Roddy nodded his agreement. Doc took Kathleen's arm. "Are you alright Kathleen? You've done a great job, but it must have been a strain."

"I'm fine, Doctor. I'm the least of your worries."

"Glad to hear it girl. Then I'll say goodbye to you all and go and see how Tim and Rachel are getting along." Ernie stopped him at the door. "Bring the wagon back to the inn when you've finished Doc. You can stay at the inn for as long as you need. Tom will look after the pony and put the wagon away. Come in for something to eat when you've finished your rounds. The inn will be warmer than your empty cottage. I'll get Meg to put the warming pan in a bed for you and we'll get the wagon ready whenever you need it."

"Thanks, Ernie. Much appreciated," said the weary doctor. Darkness was falling as he left for the skipper's cottage. Archer and Kathleen remained at Bessie's after Ernie and Roddy said goodbye. "See you tomorrow Father," said Ernie. "Come to the inn for breakfast. We'll feed you there until Bessie is able to pick up her life again." Then the innkeeper headed for the inn and he carried on to his cottage. At least he'd been 'promoted' from 'the vicar' to 'Father'. He was exhausted and shivering. His clothes were soaked, and his feet were squelching water in his lightweight shoes.

• • •

As he stepped through the door, something rushed between his legs, causing him to stumble into the room, where he trod on something soft that let out a terrifying squeal. Startled, he lifted that foot and losing his balance in the process, fell to the floor, striking his face on the corner of the table on the way down. Bewildered and disoriented, he struggled to regain his feet as his eyes tried to adjust to the dark interior. A small, red glow identified the dying remains of the fire and finding the poker he stirred the smouldering embers into a small flurry of sparks and flame. Obviously, he had trodden on a cat. But as far as he knew, he had no cat. He eventually made out a pair of yellow eyes watching him warily from a dark corner beside the fireplace. His left hand was carefully examining his sore eye, but his right still clutched the poker as he advanced on the cat, who made a rush for the partially open door. He dropped the poker and caught the animal. What a fitting conclusion to the worst day of his life. "You little bastard you nearly killed me," he screamed and threw the cat into the street and slammed the door closed behind it. With the aid of the dying flames from the fire, he managed to light some candles. His heart was pounding so hard he thought it would burst through his chest. He felt absolutely wretched. Just as he collapsed into the old wing chair, the last flicker of flame, in the fire, 'popped' and died.  Finding no kindling in the log box, he was obliged to carry a candle lantern, through the rain, to the woodshed for a few sticks to restart the fire. "This night is proving a fitting ending to my first day in hell," he muttered as he revived the fire. Minutes later with the fire burning nicely; he hung his coat on a chair-back to dry in front of the fire. He was about to settle into the chair again when he realised he was hungry. The pantry brought a pleasant surprise. A note, trapped in the door read: "I made up the fire for you. I hope it lasts. There is some cold meat in the covered dish, some pickles, fresh bread and milk. You might want to heat the milk in the small saucepan, perhaps add some of my Dad's rum for good measure – it's in the cup. Goodnight. Meg Chandler."

"Well, what a pleasant surprise. And the girl can read and write too. It's a shame that the fire gave out though." He was more grateful for the goodwill than the very welcome food. But he quickly put those thoughts aside and had just comfortably seated himself by the fire with a plate of crusty bread, cold meat, and 'medicinal milk' when he heard scratching at the scullery door. "That bloody cat. Of all the nerve! Well, it can stay out there." He ate half of his meal before the scratching got the better of him. When he opened the door, the wet and bedraggled cat was sitting in the drizzling rain with one paw raised. "Meow," it said. "You look like hell!" he responded. "Alright then, come on in," he said, and stood aside for the cat to pass by him on its way to the fireplace. Once there, it sat dripping water onto the floor as it tried to lick itself dry. Roddy closed the door and picked up the towel.

"I guess I have more in common with you than most of the villagers," he said, as he began drying the cat. Then he gave him a piece of the cold meat, which he devoured ravenously. Sitting in the wing chair, he put his feet up on the stool to finish his meal and fortified milk. "Thanks Meg!" he said raising his glass. "You're a good girl for sure."

"Well, cat; what's your name I wonder? You seem better disposed towards me than anyone I've met for a few weeks now. In a way we are quite alike I suppose: unpopular, tired and hungry for affection. We could be friends.

But a friend should have a name. Until I decide what that should be, I shall call you Moggy." The cat was looking up at him. "Meow." So he gave him another piece of meat. The fire was dying again so he had to disturb the cat whilst he made the fire up one last time, before going to bed. The cat seemed to resent the disturbance and jumped into his chair to watch him work.

Putting Moggy back on his lap he watched the fire grow as he reviewed the happenings of the day looking for a way to restore his independence. He decided to talk it over with his newfound friend. "Moggy, unless I'm prepared to take charge of my life pretty soon, I may find myself dancing to other people's tunes for the rest of my life. I'm sure I could have been the late vicar of Ryeport had it not been for Ernie, and yet I might have been the late, or at least badly battered vicar, had it not been for Archer. But I believe it will be prudent to give my pride a back seat for a while. Nod your head if you agree Moggy." He gently held the cat's head and nodded it for him. "Besides, Ernie could be either a valuable friend or a bad enemy. He has too much control here to alienate him. The only way I can overcome his control over me is to gain his respect. It will take a better understanding of the village than I have now for me to do that. So, I shall take his direction and cues until I get to know my way around and gain some acceptance in the village. Obviously his needs and those of the village are closely entwined. As are mine unfortunately. But I could do worse. Bannerman would love to help me do a lot worse. I'm sure." The fire was well established now and stoked for the night, so he headed off for bed, placing Moggy in his warm seat. But just before dozing off, he felt a little pressure behind his bent knees. The cat had joined him on the bed. "Goodnight Moggy," he murmured.

• • •

Roddy awoke from a fitful sleep and a confused dream, in which something was chewing his ear. He lashed out to fend off the attacker and sent the cat flying across the room. It took a couple of minutes for his pulse to return to normal.  He would learn, however, that licking his ear with a tongue like a farrier's rasp was his idea of showing affection. But now the cat was pawing at the door. Roddy cracked it open a little and the cat rushed out. It was sunrise. Although he had promised himself that he would be up with the rest of the villagers, there was already lots of activity along the harbour front and sails were already headed for the harbour exit.

His morning ablutions were rather primitive. He poured a jug of cold water into the bowl on the washstand and splashed some onto his face. "My mother would have called that 'A cat's lick and a promise.' Well, I've certainly had the cat's lick. One ear at least should be scrupulously clean," he mused. Minutes later he tossed the water into the back yard, and lifted his coat from the chair-back, in front of the fire. It was dry, but stiff as a board and to add to his misery, there was a large scorch mark on the part closest to the fire. "Damn! It is impossible for me to get any sort of a break in this place! Well, I don't have another coat, so I'll have to make the best of it." He massaged the arms and the front of the coat trying to soften it, but no matter what he tried, it looked a mess. "It might look better if someone ironed it for me," he thought. "Meantime I'm going to look like the village rag-bag."

He reloaded the log box and stoked the fire. "So this is how poor people live!" he muttered. "Welcome to hell, Roddy." Dejected, he sat in the wing chair for a few minutes, feeling very sorry for himself. His life had been growing increasingly miserable ever since he entered the seminary but this had to be the lowest point of all. Eventually, his need for food outweighed his self-pity and he headed for the inn. Before leaving the safety of the cottage he took a cautious look around, just in case any ill-wishers might be waiting for him. All seemed clear, so he stepped out, in his uncomfortably stiff coat and shoes. Meg, who was at the kitchen window of the inn, saw him coming and waved him to the back door. "Here we go again," he thought, "Even his daughter is giving me orders now." But he couldn't feel any bitterness towards Meg after her thoughtfulness of last night.

She laughed a high, lilting, laugh that seemed to make the world a happier place, as soon as she saw his clothes. "My goodness Father, whatever have you done to your clothes – and your eye?" Her concern for his eye was so genuine, that he told her the story of last night's adventures with the cat. She couldn't stop laughing. It was so infectious he found himself laughing too. He even modelled and paraded his rag-bag outfit for her amusement. Their laughter brought Ernie into the kitchen. "What's going on here?" he said gruffly. But when he saw the state of Roddy's clothing, he too had to smile. "Well Father, you certainly don't look very smart in that coat, so I can understand why you tried to burn it. Your shoes too have seen better days. What are we to do with you? You seem to be in trouble in all areas of your life." Meg chimed in. "Oh, Dad! I can use a damp cloth and a smoothing iron on his coat. It won't take but a few minutes. I won't be able to get out all the scorch marks though. His shoes need some work too, but I fear they will fall apart if they're brushed too hard." Ernie looked thoughtful. "Well Father. It seems my daughter is prepared to help you with your coat but what will you do about your shoes? Do you have another pair?"

"I'm afraid not. I'll just have to make do with these." Ernie turned to his daughter. "Meg, I believe we have some shoes that Tom grew out of? Or have we given them away? Might we have a pair to fit the vicar?"

"I'll look, Dad," she said, and hurried away. "Your daughter is a fine young lady Ernie. You must be proud of her!"

"She'll do Father. And she's spoken for. She will likely marry Sailmaker before the year is out. Maybe you'll get the job. If you're still around that is.'

"Well, I hope to be and I would be happy to perform the ceremony of course."

"Well, we'll see."

Meg arrived with two pair of heavy shoes. They needed some work but looked very sound. "Try these on Father," she said, handing him the shoes. "We gave the best pair to Mick," she said with downcast eyes. "These were Tom's, from when he was smaller. Haven't found anyone they'd fit yet." The second pair proved a reasonable fit. "They'll clean up Father. Use some dubbin, to keep the water out and they should last you quite a while," said Ernie. "I imagine your growing years are done. As far as shoe size is concerned anyway. This matter stays between us girl," he said to his daughter. "Sure, Dad, I know that."

"Well thank you both. I'm most grateful," said Roddy.

"Meg, see what you can do for the vicar's coat. Then you'll have to be about your chores."

"Yes, Dad. Shall I put a scorch mark on the other side, just to make it look like a new style?" She laughed and her father smiled and said: "Father, we've got a busy day today. Sailmaker is making Mick's coffin. We have to make sure that the grave is dug and deep enough for Bessie's wishes. Then we have to do the rounds of the sick and injured again. At least the weather is better than yesterday. Maybe you won't have to stiffen your coat up again. If you do you'll have to learn to fix it yourself. Meg's going to be busy picking up the slack for the wives of the injured for a while."

"I understand Ernie. And I do appreciate your help." Ernie gave him a stern look. "One more thing Father; Bessie told Kathleen that after the funeral, she'd like to visit her sister in Nextwest for a couple of days. I think it would be best if you could drive her there in your wagon. It'll give you a chance to spend some time with your mates at the Church there. You might even get some help with your laundry and other needs. It will also get you out of the village while some hot-heads here cool off." Roddy didn't like the idea of having his life arranged for him but Ernie's suggestion made sense. And a few days in Nextwest might give him a chance to wind down and do a little 'personal planning'. "What about Doc Hudson?" he asked. "He needs the wagon."

"I'll arrange for Archer's cart to fill in for that job while you're away. It's not as convenient as your wagon, but we'll manage." Roddy was nodding his acceptance as Doc Hudson entered the kitchen. He looked every bit as tired as he had last night. "Good morning all. How are you, Father? Got yourself dried out yet?" He paused, looking a little embarrassed. "Your clothes I mean...Sorry. I know that you have no help, since Bessie is not available at this time."

"Oh, I'm fine Doctor. Meg has been very kind and offered her help with my more immediate needs. How are you?"

"Past my best I'm afraid. The years are taking their toll you know. Don't bounce back like I used to, I'm sorry to say. But I'll manage. I'll manage." They all sat down to breakfast together. Ernie's arthritic wife put in a rare appearance and cooked bacon and eggs and fried bread. It was tasty but very greasy. "This is the sort of breakfast we could have used yesterday," said the doctor. "Sticks to your ribs and keeps the cold out." Meg was working steadily on Roddy's coat in a corner of the kitchen. Eventually she came over and offered it for him to try on. It was not as stiff or wrinkled as it had been, and the scorch mark, was less obvious, but still there for an observant eye. "Thank you, Meg, that's wonderful. Many thanks indeed. I feel a lot more comfortable now." Doc Hudson smiled. "This village is lucky to have the Chandler family, Father. They're dedicated to our little community. They help to make the village more like one huge family really. We're grateful to have Ernie to organise us." Ernie looked a bit embarrassed. "Ready everyone? First call Doctor? You name it. The vicar and I will come with you. I'll get the wagon ready while you're getting your bag of tricks, Doc. We'll walk after the first call so you can have uninterrupted time with your patient."

"Very well," the doctor responded. "First call is Jamie. Hopefully that won't take too long, then we're off to Tim's. From there on, you may be walking gentlemen."

Jamie was much the same as he had been the previous night. Tim though had regained consciousness long enough to take a few spoonfuls of soup and for Rachel to show him the pennant that Archer had retrieved from the bridge. He had managed a weak smile at that, but drifted back to sleep almost immediately. Rachel and the Doc were both encouraged. At Rachel's request they had a small prayer then Ernie and Roddy headed off for Will Tarret's cottage.

Will was taking a little nourishment too and seemed somewhat better. He managed to shake Roddy's hand and introduce himself. Obviously no one had told him about the vicar's shortcomings of the day before. Again they said a little prayer and left to the Sailmaker's hut. The coffin was ready. Sailmaker was fitting the last of the rope handles on the sides of the box when they arrived, and a handcart was waiting to carry the coffin to Bessie's cottage. Ernie told Sailmaker: "It won't be as upsetting for Bessie if Mick is in the coffin before she wakes. If she can get a few hours sleep this morning, that'll be a good time to get everything set up. The funeral is tomorrow and we need to get this over with as quickly as possible. By the way, how is Bannerman holding up?"

"Well he still carries some bad feelings for the vicar here," replied the young man. "But he will always try to find someone to blame when things go bad. We have to remember how close he was to Mick. He tried very hard to fill in for Mick's dad when he died. Mick's death was a bigger blow to Bannerman than anyone else, except for Bessie of course. He'll cool off. But it's best to give him a wide berth and time to calm down; he's always been a hothead." Sailmaker gave Roddy a warning look and raised his eyebrows. "Jack's not the most reasonable man hereabouts. Don't listen too well, 'specially to apologies."

"The vicar's going to take Bessie to her sisters for a couple of days right after the funeral," said Ernie. "But keep that to yourself. Bannerman doesn't need to know that." Sailmaker nodded. "That's a good arrangement given the circumstances."

Bessie awoke later that afternoon to find that Sailmaker and Archer had quietly set up the coffin in her living room and Mick was settled in it.

Although Bessie was startled when she first saw the coffin she quickly recovered. "Sailmaker's done a nice job," she said. "You've all been very good to me. We should close the coffin now. I want to remember Mick from happier times."

# CHAPTER 6

## *Mick's funeral*

It was Sunday, time for his first service in his new parish of Ryeport. The villagers filled the church but they made it very obvious that this was purely out of respect for Bessie Drew and the burial of her young son. With few exceptions, the villagers avoided all eye contact with their new vicar and certainly made no attempt to speak with him. That, coupled with the innkeeper's information regarding their dissatisfaction for the church, made him anxious to comply with Mrs. Drew's request for a short funeral service. In fact, he blended his drastically short Sunday service with young Mick's funeral service. Shortening his hastily planned sermon, he commended the villagers for their compassion and mutual support in these tragic times and stressing the value of family and friends in times of such loss, proceeded to the funeral service. Meg had helped him set up the church earlier, placing the hymn books in the pews and explaining that she set numbered markers in the appropriate pages of the hymn books. "Most of the villagers can't read, but they don't want that to be obvious, so I mark the pages for them. They feel better if they can be seen to open the books and find the page. They know the hymns by heart anyway."

Mick's simple funeral went smoothly and the grief of the congregation was heartfelt and sincere. Bannerman had wanted to give the eulogy but couldn't trust himself not to break down, so Ernie eulogised the young man at length, emphasising his popularity and fun loving nature. The attentive participation of the congregation, together with their lusty singing, underscored the affection of the villagers for Bessie Drew and her lost son. Roddy wondered if he would ever be able to attract congregations like that sometime in the future – without such a tragedy of course. That could go a long way towards regaining his father's approval.

Mick's coffin had been placed on trestles in the nave, and the ladies had added wild flowers and other decorative touches to the church. It was simple, but tasteful. The pall bearers carried Mick's coffin outside and set it on two boards laid across the grave. Roddy was standing on a mound of earth at the head of the grave, bible in hand, waiting quietly for the congregation to assemble, when a blow in the back of his knees made his legs collapse and as he fell he almost slid under the coffin into the grave. He heard Ernie yell: "Bannerman," and a strong hand suddenly grabbed the back of his coat, and heaved him to his feet. "Sorry about that Vicar," said Bannerman. "I didn't notice you standing there. My spade seems to have a mind of its own this morning." Then turning his head so that his face could not be seen by the congregation, he added, in a menacing tone: "I'd much rather have dug this grave for you than young Mick. But I suppose I'd best be watchin' m'self today, for Bessie's sake." He held Roddy's arm in a bruising grip and casting his spade aside he used that free hand to roughly dust the dirt from the vicar's coat. Roddy knew he would discover fresh bruises when he undressed for bed that night.

"Well! What's this big scorch mark on your coat then, Vicar?" Bannerman whispered. "Could it be that you really are the 'Vicar from hell?'" Roddy was badly shaken and didn't know what to expect from this man after the service but tried to make it appear that he accepted the event as an accident and thanked him for his assistance. He was relieved, however, when the grim-faced innkeeper moved closer and inserted himself between he and Bannerman. Again, the service was very brief, and the coffin was gently lowered as Bessie Drew threw some flowers and a handful of earth after it. She was better composed than most of the ladies – and a few of the men – and he was impressed to see her square her shoulders and lift her head high, before giving Kathleen Archer a discreet smile and taking her arm to lead the mourners from the graveside. Bannerman and Baker remained, to close Mick's grave. The mourners followed Bessie back to the inn where refreshments had been arranged. As he joined the crowd Ernie took Roddy aside and whispered: "Father, when you've eaten, I think you should go home, freshen up and pack a bag. I'll have Tom pick up Bessie in the wagon and bring her to your cottage. That way you'll be away before anyone misses you. We'll look after your cottage." When he opened his mouth to speak Ernie held up his hand. "Yes, I know about the bloody cat. We'll look after him too."

He was being given his marching orders again, but after the latest incident with Bannerman, was pleased to accept them. At the inn, Sailmaker and Meg came over to him. "That was a good service Father," said Meg. "Yes. Well done," added Sailmaker. No one else even looked in his direction.

Less than an hour after the funeral, Bessie Drew and Roddy were on the Coach Road to Nextwest. It seemed the villagers hadn't even noticed their departure.

An hour and a half and many of Mrs. Drew's stories later, they finally spotted the small scattering of cottages that marked the approach to Nextwest and beyond them, the church steeple. "Look, Father, there's the church now," said Mrs. Drew. "My sister lives just a few streets from there. We'll soon be drinking a nice cuppa' tea and enjoying a piece of 'er apple pie. You'll soon forget this rough ride once you sample 'er pie I'll wager."

Roddy's particular appetite would not be satisfied by apple pie and tea and the company he had in mind would certainly not be appropriate for someone dressed as a clergyman but with very little money and only three days before he had to be back in Ryeport, his prospects for entertaining female company were bleak. He was beginning to believe that Ernie's suggestion, to seek the hospitality of his 'mates at the Nextwest church,' would be his only option.

Mrs. Drew began tugging at his coat sleeve. "Father, look we've been spotted by Reverend Tubbs!" Sure enough, the rotund Reverend Tubbs was hurrying down the path from the church, waving his arms frantically as he tried to attract their attention. He reined Slondosh to a stop. "Whoa boy! Whoa!"

"Ah! Reverend McDowd. I honestly thought you meant to pass us by!" The words came in breathless gasps from the flustered young clergyman as he clung to the wagon for support. "So pleased to see you again, especially when I so badly need a favour. My guardian angel must be watching over me." Roddy smiled. "I did not mean to pass you by, dear Sir but I am on my way to deliver Mrs. Drew to her sister's house, just two or three streets away. Then I intended to return and seek the pleasure of that hospitality that you offered at our last meeting. Mrs. Drew, I believe you already know Reverend Tubbs. Tubby, you will recall that this good lady looks after our church and my cottage. Myself too of course."

"Oh yes, Bessie and I are already acquainted; pleased to see you again Ma'am." Tubby extended his hand to Mrs. Drew. She smiled, shook his hand and responded: "Likewise I'm sure." Tubby turned back to Roddy. "As you know Reverend, I filled in on occasion at Ryeport after Reverend Cole's unfortunate demise, so Bessie and I are old friends. So glad to hear you planned to visit us Reverend. Very glad indeed." Tubby's smile was so genuine that Roddy felt a sense of ease and relaxation that he'd not known since he saw him last. Perhaps being away from the threats and pressures of Ryeport, he might be able to recover his wits and formulate a way to re-gain control over his life.

Tubby's voice was less breathless now. "We've a sad situation here I'm sorry to say. One of the pillars of our congregation, Mr. Whatson, passed away two days ago. He is resting in the parlour of his home only two streets away. Friends and relatives have gathered there for a last farewell. I had promised to attend to offer a few words of comfort and consolation you understand. But my horse chose this very day to throw a shoe. Now I'm embarrassingly late, I wonder if you would be so kind as to give me a lift. You appear to be going in the correct direction, and it would only be a little out of your way."

Roddy gave Mrs. Drew a questioning look, and she nodded approval. "Tubby," he said. "I regret that we also have tragic news. Mrs. Drew lost her son a couple of days ago. He was drowned when their boat was wrecked in a storm. The whole village is mourning the loss of this young man and we have just come from his funeral service. I'm taking Mrs. Drew to her sister's house for a few days of support and companionship. Tubby, this is an especially tragic loss; Mrs. Drew's husband, the young man's father, was lost in a similar accident only two years ago." Tubby turned his shocked expression to Mrs. Drew. "Oh, dear lady, I am so sorry. I had no way of knowing of course, but my problem of a lame horse should not delay your visit to your sister. Please accept my condolences for your tragic loss." Turning back to Roddy, he said: "Please carry on, Reverend. I can walk to the Whatson's. They will understand I'm sure." Mrs. Drew interjected: "Nonsense Father. A few minutes delay is no problem. Life goes on and we all have to help each other in difficult times. It'll be no trouble to give you a ride to this widda's house."

"Are you quite sure Mrs. Drew?" Tubby looked very concerned. "Of course," she responded as she extended her hand. "Up you get."

"Thank you Mrs. Drew; you are very kind, very kind indeed."

Mrs. Drew smiled and moved over to make room for the grateful Reverend Tubbs. He tipped his hat in thanks, as he settled on the bench seat. "The second street on your right please, Reverend," said Tubby. Roddy slapped the reins on Slondosh's back and they moved off. Tubby leaned forward, turned to him and said: "Reverend, seeing as you planned on visiting us, I wonder if you might consider – other plans permitting of course – to join me at the Whatson's house, on your way back here? Later we could have supper together and relax around a toasty fire with a glass of wine. How's that for a suggestion?"

"That sounds very attractive Tubby. Not that your bribe was necessary, but I will accept it gratefully nonetheless. Your accommodations here in Nextwest are certainly luxurious compared to mine." A few minutes later they had delivered a grateful, but still flustered Reverend Tubbs, to a rather grand house on Pleasant Road. It had been but a short drive from the church, which in turn, proved to be an equal distance from the house of Bessie's sister. However, the difference in affluence of the two neighbour-hoods was very marked indeed. Bessie's sister, Marie, lived in a terraced house in a working-class area close to the market place of Nextwest. The accommodations here were better than those in Ryeport though they were still a far cry from the luxury of Pleasant Road.

Roddy helped Mrs. Drew from the cart, and then hung the pony's nosebag on his head. Mrs. Drew pointed out the weighted iron ring in the back of the wagon. In the absence of a hitching rail, it was used to tether the pony. When they knocked on Marie's door she smiled and hustled them indoors, offering tea and something to eat. Roddy tried to excuse himself, offering to give the ladies privacy but they rejected his attempts to leave. Mrs. Drew quietly hugged her sister as she whispered her sad news. Marie's expression changed to shocked disbelief and horror and then she clapped both hands over her face, and burst into an uncontrollable fit of crying. It seemed an age before Mrs. Drew managed to compose her but eventually, wiping her tear stained face with her apron, Marie insisted that he stay for the inevitable 'cuppa' and a piece of pie. Mrs. Drew was right about the pie. It was excellent, and he was easily persuaded to have a second helping. The tea too was very welcome and he soon found himself relaxing in the comfort of an armchair by the fireplace and wishing that he did not have to leave to join Tubby. However, the two ladies were soon involved in details of their personal affairs, and he took that opportunity to excuse himself, promising to return before noon on Tuesday, the day after tomorrow. Minutes later he was headed for Pleasant Road and Mr. Whatson's wake.

The butler answered the door. He was an intimidating man; over six feet tall, heavily built and looked very muscular. He greeted him with that air of superior formality that so many butlers assume. "Bloody snob," Roddy thought. "Butlers are bigger snobs than their employers. They think they're smarter than their employers." He couldn't resist a smile though, because the sad truth was, they often were.

Tubby was quickly at his side, and began introducing him to the mourners; although 'mourners' hardly seemed an appropriate appellation for this crowd. Revellers might be more appropriate. A maid was providing fresh glasses of wine, or liqueur as required and she was kept very busy indeed. Mrs. Whatson proved to be a handsome, but rather hard-faced woman of around forty years. Roddy's quick look in the casket revealed that her husband was a trifle older; a trifling thirty, or possibly forty, years older. "Perhaps that is why she looks more relieved than bereaved," he thought. "Life might indeed begin at forty. Or even well before forty, if I read this lady correctly."

As Tubby droned on, and on, extolling the virtues of this generous benefactor of the church, he found his attention wandering from the countenance of the deceased and focussing instead on the quality of the clothing due to be interred on his cold body the following day. When he realised that this man was of similar height and build as himself, his interest deepened, and his imagination took over. "Tubby: do you think the widow might possibly extend her husband's charity, beyond his sad demise, to benefit others less fortunate than themselves?" Tubby appeared shocked. He lowered his head – Roddy assumed to avoid anyone reading his lips – and quietly said: "Well, I don't know old chap. She is not as charitable as he was and this hardly seems the time to broach the matter – widows grief and so on. What did you have in mind?"

"Tubby there are a lot of people in Ryeport that could really use decent clothes in which to attend church. I've heard some of them say that they feel ashamed to attend the Lords House in the same clothes they wear to take fish from the sea and God knows they're too poor to buy any. To some people, that may seem a poor reason not to attend church, but it's very real to them. I wondered if Mrs. Whatson might be prepared to give some of her husband's clothes to these needy folk. Mr. Whatson certainly has no further need for them and, judging by appearances, I doubt that she would need the sale price of secondhand clothes to sustain her." Tubby was appalled, almost panicky, as he responded. "Well, really old chap. I wouldn't have the nerve. If she were offended it could cost us dearly at the church. As I said she is not as charitable as he was. And I'm not too sure that she is at all well disposed towards me."

"Then let me ask you this Tubby. Do you know if they were close in real life? Anyone can see they were not close in age. That could mean not close physically, if you follow my meaning. Perhaps this was a political or business marriage. Do they have children that might want his clothes?"

"No, there are no children of this marriage. He has a son and a daughter from a previous marriage but they are well off and quite independent." Tubby's face was growing redder as his embarrassment grew. "Really, old chap. Should you be talking like this and at such a time?" Tubby was shuffling his feet, keeping his head down and mumbling, in his efforts to avoid attention. "Tubby," said Roddy, "his clothes obviously wouldn't fit the butler; he is twice the size of his master. If you can think of no one else, I shall ask...In the name of the poor and needy!"

"Roddy, no, I forbid it. You...."

They suddenly became aware that Mrs. Whatson's attention had been drawn to their obviously intense discussion and Tubby looked as if he wanted the earth to open up and swallow him. His panic and anxiety were almost palpable. But Roddy understood; he knew Tubby would be severely chastised by the Bishop if this influential lady was angered, even though he was not the instigator of the trouble.

"Reverend Tubbs, you seem unnaturally distressed. Can I help in any way?" Mrs. Whatson had joined them, her voice little more than a whisper but her manner was suspicious. Her pale blue eyes were probing and intense, as she scanned their faces, as if seeking to bare their innermost thoughts. Tubby coloured even more profusely as he stammered. "I, I, er I ..."

Roddy quickly interceded. "Dear Lady, I regret that my friend is embarrassed because of me. He is deeply concerned over your grief, and so sensible of the wealth of charity and goodwill that you and your dear husband have brought to his congregation, that the thought of adding one more morsel to your pain is more than he could bear. Had you seen how distressed he was, at the thought of failing you by arriving late today, I know you would understand how grieved he is over your loss."

Mrs. Whatson focused her incisive stare on Reverend Tubbs. Roddy also turned to him and said: "My friend, I should have known better than to burden you with my problems, particularly at a time of such distress. Please forgive me." Tubby gave a fleeting smile, and a quick nod, before lowering his head again. Roddy saw that they had begun to attract the attention of some of the closer mourners and realised that the involvement of a larger group might prove beneficial to a plan that was forming in his mind, so he allowed his voice to rise a little. "Please, Reverend, forget that I ever mentioned the subject."

"Just what is he supposed to forgive?" Mrs. Whatson's suspicions were aroused, and her manner insistent. It appeared that she did not appreciate being the subject of a discussion without approving the content. Pleasant platitudes aside, Tubby's embarrassment appeared to indicate that their conversation had some personal content that she was intent on understanding.

Roddy responded: "Mrs. Whatson, Revered Tubbs was telling me what a great supporter of the church and the less fortunate members of his community, your dear husband was. How he could always be counted on to support both the church and the disadvantaged. You must be very proud of him." Some of the guests – curiosity aroused – joined their group and one of them, a rather portly, and heavily whiskered gentleman, raised his glass towards the coffin and loudly cried: "Hear, hear. Let us toast the memory of our most generous friend, Obidiah Whatson: champion of our Church and the needy." It was a ragged response, but focused the attention of the whole room on 'Whiskers' and the group were now staring at him, obviously awaiting further comment. He was suddenly aware that he had, unwittingly, claimed centre stage whilst totally unprepared for it, and was embarrassed. He lowered his befuddled head, and struggled to form a fitting follow up.

Anxious not to lose the floor himself Roddy quickly sprang to his rescue. "Thank you for your words of appreciation kind Sir. Dear Lady, prompted by the sentiments of goodwill that fill this room so abundantly today, I asked Reverend Tubbs if he thought you might have the fortitude to look beyond your deep personal grief and pain, to extend your husband's generosity one last time on behalf of the needy. Reverend Tubbs – quite correctly – chastised me for my grievously poor manners and sense of timing. Please forgive me, Mrs. Whatson."

"Forgive what? You talk in riddles Sir. If I am to forgive something, surely I should be entitled to know what I am forgiving. Just what did you intend to ask me for?" The earlier impatience in her voice had hardened to steely intolerance.

He responded slowly, in a quieter voice, forcing the mourners to close in, in order to hear. "Dear Lady, I am a recently ordained vicar, and only this morning I performed my first funeral service in my new parish, the fishing village of Ryeport. The very day that I arrived in Ryeport, one of her young men died when his fishing boat was wrecked in a storm. The deceased was a much-loved young lad of only fourteen years. Today I brought his grieving mother here, to Nextwest, to visit with her sister for a day or two of companionship. Obviously these were unexpected happenings.

Ryeport buried that widow's teenaged son today. But it was only two years ago that they buried her husband. Both died in seafaring accidents whilst earning their modest living by bringing food to our tables. This was a well-loved, respected, and God-fearing family and yet they've been doubly stricken by tragedy of the most painful kind." The room had become very quiet and his quick glance revealed that he had his audience's complete attention. "My friends, our villagers lead a very hard life and are well aware that great hardship will certainly follow if they suffer the loss of a loved one – especially when that loved one is the only breadwinner. Such is the case of this poor mother today, as indeed it has been for other villagers who lost their men to the sea. Now, later in the same day, God showed me a similar tragic situation. The pain, grief, and sense of loss are so similar, and tragic, but in this case, those near and dear to the deceased are spared the added burden of poverty. I give thanks to God for that." Roddy briefly put his hands together and raised his closed eyes to the ceiling. "Amen!" responded the mourners; some struggling to put their hands together, whilst still holding on to their drinks. Roddy suddenly realised that he was preaching. "However," he continued, "once the desperation of poverty is removed, the suffering becomes more bearable. In the case of the poor, however, the grief can endure for a lifetime because their poverty becomes a daily reminder of their loss. Thank our Lord for the benefit of financial well-being that occurs in a house blessed by a charitable master."

Tubby's expression of rapt attention was fixed on him, and the room remained silent; he had their undivided attention. Even Mrs. Whatson's stern expression had relaxed, so he continued: "My friends, it is often said that charity begets good fortune, but I have never seen that more clearly evidenced than here, today.

My friend, Reverend Tubbs, would certainly have been here long before I arrived in Nextwest, had his horse not thrown a shoe. He was not expecting me. Neither of us anticipated my being here today, nor could we have predicted that I would become part of this sadly bereaved group. So, I ask you my friends: Is my being here today really a coincidence? Or do you think I was meant to be given a lesson? And, if so, was it intended that I share that lesson with you? I do know that, for me, the example of this good man, Obidiah Whatson, was an experience that I will carry with me forever. I don't believe that my being here today was pure coincidence. I'm sure that I was meant to learn from Obidiah's example, as I hope we all have and I pray that we all go from here today resolved to help our less fortunate brothers and sisters, as Obidiah did. If we do, I'm sure that we all and all we meet, will benefit from that, both in this life and the next."

All eyes in the room were on Mrs. Whatson and Roddy. His improvised little speech may have been a bit much but it had gained the full attention of the somewhat inebriated mourners. However, it was obvious that they still expected a confrontation. The party atmosphere had evaporated. Drinks had been hastily set aside and people were looking very sombre indeed – even the bleary-eyed ones and Mrs. Whatson's expression, was still taut and suspicious.

"Are you going to use this sad event to ask us for money?" It was impossible to miss the anger in her voice. Tubby took a startled step backwards and his alarm would have been plain for all to see had he not had the foresight to turn his head and feign a cough. The atmosphere was very tense. Roddy answered in a most apologetic and hurt voice. "Oh no, dear lady. I would not be so crass as to raise such an issue at a time like this. I had merely wondered if your husband – had it occurred to him – might have donated some of his clothes, for the benefit of those that have only their working clothes. Some of my villagers confess that they are ashamed to enter a house of God, wearing the same clothes that they wear when taking fish from the sea. I intended to take my friend's counsel in this matter and not mention it. But, unfortunately for me, you came to Reverend Tubb's aid as soon as you saw his anxiety. Reverend Tubbs was indeed correct, when he praised you for your charity and compassion earlier today."

There were quiet murmurs of approval: "Well done," and "God Bless you Mrs. Whatson," accompanied by some eye dabbing by the ladies and choked expressions of comfort from 'Whiskers'. However, Roddy did catch a glimpse of Goodman, the butler, standing 'offstage', just beyond the open door. He was rolling his eyes to the heavens, and looking absolutely disgusted. "Oh well, you can't win them all," he thought as he continued. "I am so sorry to have caused you such distress dear lady. Please forgive me. If you will excuse me, I shall wait for Reverend Tubbs in my wagon." Turning to Tubby, he said: "Please, take your time Reverend. And, Mrs. Whatson please be assured that I had no intention of being thoughtless or disrespectful here today. I was just overcome by these tragic events. As I said earlier, I am newly ordained, and lack my friend's experience and ability to handle such grief." There was a murmur of sympathy from the guests, followed by discreet hand clapping. 'Whiskers' laid a comforting hand on the widow's shoulder. "Do not distress yourself, Mrs. Whatson. I will be happy to provide Reverend McDowd with some clothes for his people. I am certain that many amongst us have clothing to spare, especially when we know they will provide hard working souls with the courage to communicate with their Maker. He turned to Roddy. Father, you can count on me to solicit our friends on behalf of your village. And God Bless you for opening our eyes to this opportunity to be of service."

"Hear, hear!" And more quiet hand clapping was the response from the guests. Roddy thanked 'Whiskers' for his generosity, hung his head, and made for the door. Mrs. Whatson caught up with him just as Goodman, the butler, attended. "Reverend McDowd" she murmured. "I hope that if I ever need a champion to speak for me, that I might find someone as moving as you to espouse my cause." Her whispered comment displayed some respect but her searching scrutiny left him in no doubt that she was still suspicious. Her voice grew louder – and even broke – more than once in fact. "You shall have my husband's clothes for your needy, this very day. I know Obidiah would have approved had he recognised the need. Goodman has some items already packed in a trunk; he will put them in your wagon right away. Return the trunk next week and we shall have more for you, from Obidiah's friends and mine. My husband will have no more need of them – another timely catch in her voice – and I am sure he would have approved of them going to such a worthy cause."

"Well done!" Roddy thought. He had suspected that Mrs. Whatson was an opportunist, and she had indeed seized this opportunity to draw attention to her charity in front of her friends.

"Thank you Mrs. Whatson," he said and gently took her hand and raised it to his lips. "And God Bless you. You rose through adversity and grief, to aid others less fortunate than yourself." His sidelong glance at Tubby caught him wiping his eye. It had gone better than he could have expected. Mrs. Whatson dabbed a 'kerchief' to her eye too as she took a furtive glance at her attentive guests – hoping for further appreciation of her charity perhaps? Her reward was fresh, quiet hand clapping and a comforting arm from one of the ladies. He was sure she understood that there would be ongoing recognition from her peer group, because of the unintentionally public nature of her gift. She seemed well satisfied.

Roddy bade the mourners a quick farewell and left the room. Tubby hastily followed, his cheeks still glowing, and seeming very anxious to be gone. Goodman was waiting at the front door, looking very grim. "Would you be kind enough to give me a hand with the trunk, Reverend?" Goodman's hostility towards him seemed obvious though puzzling at that time, but Roddy learned later that he had already arranged a buyer for the carefully selected clothing in the trunk. Roddy's scheming had stolen the profit of his careful planning. "Thank you, my good man," he said, as they loaded the trunk onto the wagon.

Mrs. Whatson and 'Whiskers' were watching them load the trunk. "Mr. Westerhof," she said do you think you might be able to add some of your donations to ours before next weekend. Not everyone in the village will be the same size as my husband and I, and we should try to share the benefit as evenly as possible." Tubby was looking very relieved as they drove away, but, although he did his best to appear humble and pious, Roddy felt like the cat that had swallowed the canary. His guile had provided him an escape from the prison imposed by his clerical clothing and meagre income. It was difficult to prevent a smile from spreading across his face but he had to. At least until he could get rid of Tubby. His mind was already working on that.

Tubby, on the other hand, was shaking his head in disbelief. "I can't believe how well you handled that situation. You were unbelievable. The people of your village are fortunate indeed to have such a champion. I shall be sure that the Bishop hears of this. Westerhof already has commitments from several of the guests. He plans to deliver some clothing to the Whatson's house tomorrow. You will likely go back to Ryeport with more stock than many of the shops in Nextwest. It's unbelievable and you even won over Mrs. Whatson. Isn't she a handsome woman though?" He blushed and added: "In a very Christian way, of course."

• • •

Marie had added the extra comfort of brandy to their first cup of tea and when that was finished they forgot the tea and stayed with the brandy. As they relaxed their conversation turned to the struggles of widows trying to survive in those tough times, and Bessie would learn something new about her sister. Marie, naturally concerned over Bessie's loss of income, asked: " 'ow will you manage for money now, Bessie? Bein' 'ousekeeper for a vicar in a small village can't pay very much."

"No. That won't keep body and soul together, that's for sure. I'll still clean an' dry some fish when needed, and some picklin', of course. But I've always done that, an' we still struggled, even with Mick's share from the fishin'; an' Tim's was the best earning boat in the village. I don't really know how I'll manage now. But 'ow do you manage Marie? You've 'ad no one to bring money in since your Fred died. Did 'e leave you well provided for?"

Marie laughed. "Fred couldn't provide for 'imself let alone a family. Any money 'e got was spent in the Coach 'n' 'orses. Liquid refreshment was always more important to 'im than feedin' us, or payin' the rent. If I 'adn't done some house cleanin' for well-off folks, and sold a few pies and pre-serves, we would've starved. Oh, Fred wasn't a bad man but very weak when it came to choosin' between drink and 'is responsibilities. When 'e died I was actually better off than when 'e was alive, 'cos I didn't 'ave to support 'im anymore. It was 'is drinkin' an' gamblin', that kept us strug-glin'. I even 'ad to cough-up some of me cleanin' money to pay his gamblin' debts at times. It was either that, or 'e would 'ave' ad the daylights beat out of 'im. It's true!" said Marie, in response to Bessie's shocked expression. "If I 'adn't done that 'e would 'ave 'ad more good 'idin's than a fish 'as scales. But, I don't do cleanin' no more Bessie. I bake a few pies, make some jams and pickles, an' sell 'em to local shops. Don't make much money mind, 'cos the shops want their profit too. I was 'avin' it pretty tough. 'Til someone showed me 'ow to make a little extra on the side." She tried to appear casual and read Bessie's expression before breaking eye contact.

"Marie! You don't mean..."

Marie laughed, "Oh, Bessie, of course not. Look at me. If I wanted to earn money that way, I wouldn't get many takers, would I? Let's face it, girl, men want young things for that and then they prefer 'em good-lookin', an' big busted. No Bess, I just act as an agent for people who sell stuff. You know that spare room I've got, in the back? Well, I rent it out – as a store-room – and I also hold some stock for them. Customers give this bloke orders for goods, and then the customer brings me a numbered chit, an' I give 'em the goods that match the chit from me back room. At the end of the week – provided that I've done some business of course, I get extra money with the weekly rent in exchange for the chits." Bessie looked horrified. "That doesn't sound honest, Marie. What are you doin'? If it was 'onest, they would sell the goods an' take the money themselves. They wouldn't need you, and this numbered chit business. It looks like you will take the blame for them if things go wrong."

"Well, Bess. Who's to say what's 'onest and what's not. Do you think rich people get that way by being 'onest? Maybe 'onest people stay poor while the dis'onest rich get richer. Lots of people 'ereabouts don't see no 'arm in makin' a few extra bob on the side. Providin' you're not 'urtin' anybody that is. 'specially if it's the only way to stay out of the poor'ouse; where's the 'arm in that?"

Bessie was very worried. "Marie, I think you must be mixed up with thieves. You could end up getting yourself killed girl. They'd 'ave no problem shuttin' you up, if they thought that you might let on what you were doin'. What kind of goods are you talking about?"

"'ere: come and see," said Marie. She led her sister to a back room cluttered with old furniture and boxes. "This is junk," said Bessie, "no one would pay good money for this." "No, not this," said Marie. She lit a lamp and gave it to Bessie whilst she moved an old Welsh dresser away from a wall. She pulled at a black post which, at first glance, seemed to be a load bearing support for a ceiling beam but which proved to be the edge of a door disguised as a section of the beam and plaster wall. The 'wall' swung open, revealing a deep cupboard. Marie took the lamp from Bessie and, grabbed her sister's wrist, and pulled her into the deep cupboard after her. Marie then passed the lamp along shelves stacked with fancy glassware, French lace, bolts of silk and – even more enlightening – earthenware jugs and glass bottles bearing fancy labels. There were even three small kegs.

Bessie's mouth was hanging open. "Smugglers," she gasped.

Marie stared at Bessie, startled by the panic she could hear in her voice. "I know it's not strictly legal," she said. "But if the only way I can survive is by depriving the King of a little tax money, I have to do it. What good would it possibly do 'im if I starve to death? 'e won't get any richer by me dyin', will 'e?"

Bessie said: "But if you're caught, Marie, they'll 'ang you."

"If I die from starvation, I'll be just as dead," responded Marie.

"Oh, Marie! I'm scared. I've already lost me 'usband and me son. I don't want to lose you too."

"Well, neither your 'usband, nor Mick were smugglin', but they died anyway. None of us know when our number's gonna come up, girl. Besides, this is well organised. I'll be alright. Give it some thought Bessie. I might be able to get them to find a little job for you, if you want." Bessie shuddered. "Let's get out of here Marie. Before someone comes."

Marie managed a grim little smile. "It's safe Bessie. Don't worry." They closed the hinged section of the wall, replaced the Welsh dresser, and returned to the comfort of the living room.

"That junk, as you call it, is part of that bloke's cover story," said Marie. "Every so often he brings repaired or broken furniture here for storage. But sometimes an old cupboard or chest of drawers will 'ave somethin' special inside – she gave Bessie a broad wink as she touched a finger to the side of her nose – that stuff goes in me secret cupboard. Then 'e takes some of 'is other old furniture away, to repair it. And sometimes someone will bring me a chit for that bit of furniture. They look it over, take it away and I get paid again. Honest money those times. And, quite often, when people pick up stuff, they'll buy a pie or two. After all, I'm just a poor widda' woman with a spare room, tryin' to make ends meet. Oh, don't worry so Bessie; I've never seen you look so miserable. I wish I'd never told you now. I didn't mean to worry you; just thought that it might be a way for you to earn a little money." The ladies took comfort in another glass of brandy.

Bessie held up her glass. "Is this...?"

Marie just smiled and nodded. "Couldn't afford it otherwise."

• • •

Roddy guided Slondosh into the stable yard behind the manse and the groom met them as they alighted from the wagon. He patted Slondosh affectionately and took him out of the shafts, talking softly to him all the while, then led him to the stable. He seemed to have a particular affection for the pony and, apart from a touch of his cap, paid them no attention.

"Fletcher loves animals," explained Tubby, "Slondosh in particular. The Church actually bought the horse from him. His father used to make and repair furniture you see, and Slondosh used to pull his wagon. It seems they were a good team, and the animal was well loved. When he died, Fletcher's father left his business to him, but the son was not the fine craftsman his father was, and ended up having to sell the shop, tools, horse and cart too and came to work for the church. He'd always hoped that he could keep Slondosh here, but the Bishop wouldn't hear of it. Pity really. Look at them, you'd swear the horse understood every word he says, wouldn't you?"

Tubby followed the groom, calling: "Fletcher, Reverend McDowd will be staying with us for a couple of days. I know that you'll look after Slondosh very well but would you also have the trunk taken to the guest room when you've finished with the pony?"

"Aye, Zur." Fletcher touched his cap, and carried on talking to the pony.

"Come, Roddy, let's get a glass of wine and a snack." Tubby led the way into the comfortable living room of the manse. "Why did you want the trunk taken to your room Roddy; wouldn't it be better left on the wagon to await your return to Ryeport?"

"Well, I would like to see what's in it Tubby and I don't know how well the clothes will fare if left outside in the trunk overnight. They might get wet if the trunk isn't watertight."

The wine and the supper were excellent but after a couple of glasses, Roddy excused himself, claiming fatigue from the trials of the past week. That gave him some time alone, behind closed doors, to try his new wardrobe. His casual assessment of Mr. Whatson's size and build proved quite accurate. They were indeed, very similar in height and build. The shoes and the other clothing fitted so well that no one would suspect they were not made for him. One coat in particular, although quite conservative, was particularly flattering. It was dark grey, with trimmed edges on the pockets and lapels. A pair of light grey breeches and stockings and black shoes with silver buckles complimented it very well. He began to feel more like his, pre-seminary self. The clothes were more conservative than his own taste, but certainly classy and more flattering than his clerical garb. Then he found the piece that he really liked. It was a hunter green velvet waistcoat with a modest gold trim at the pockets. "Classy," he muttered as he posed before the mirror. "You look nothing like a cleric now Roddy. More like a successful businessman."

He carefully folded this set of clothes, and set them in his own case, so that they would not form part of the donation – just in case the Bishop wanted to see them. He was ready for his first 'social outing' since entering the seminary – provided he could excuse himself from the manse for an overnight stay, without rousing suspicion. The Bishop must never learn of the lifestyle he was planning outside his clerical duties. He had to be very discreet and Tubby could easily give away his secret, without knowing he had one. Fortunately, he hadn't seen the clothes, so it was unlikely he would ever recognise them. If Westerhof and his friends could come up with enough clothing of other sizes, this whole chestfull could possibly be his. But that really was dreaming. The donation had been so public, that he doubted he could keep it all for himself. All he needed now was a reason to leave the manse – on his own of course – so that his drought of titillating company could end. He would need to find suitable lodging, preferably in another small town, to avoid being recognised by locals.

He awoke the following morning, Monday, to a bright clear sky. His mood too was sunny and lighthearted as he went down to breakfast, certain that he had the beginnings of a good 'escape plan' and confidant that he could solve any problems that might arise. Tubby was already seated at the breakfast table, but looking very glum. "Cheer-up Tubby, it's a fine-looking day. Why the sad face?" Tubby looked at him and shook his head, dismally. "I fear that you will not like my news, Roddy. I hardly know how to begin."

"Begin at the beginning, my friend. Surely things can't be that bad."

"Very well; the Bishop noticed your wagon in the yard when he came in last night. He wanted to know where you were and what you were doing here. I told him that you had gone to bed, about the tragedy in Ryeport and also about our visit to the Whatson's. I thought that he would be pleased with your initiatives but the further I got into the story the more angry he became. He said you had no right soliciting handouts – especially in our parish – and particularly from people like the Whatsons. He said you were an embarrassment to the church in general, and to him in particular. Roddy, he was furious. He wants all of the clothes that are donated brought here, for sale locally. The proceeds are to go into the church funds, for distribution to the needy of Nextwest, as he sees fit. He also wants to see you as soon as you've had breakfast. He is eating in his rooms. I'm so sorry, Roddy. Nothing I said would calm him down. I fear that I may have made too much of your success with the people at Whatson's wake. He intends to go to the funeral today and said he will straighten things out with Mrs.

Whatson. Reverend Watkins, the senior vicar here will conduct the service. I am to attend, but you are not to be there. I'm so sorry. I didn't know what to say or do. It seemed that everything I said just made things worse, so I just shut up and nodded my head. He really doesn't like you at all, Roddy. Be careful when you see him. I fear you are on thin ice, though I can't imagine why."

Roddy listened to this with a growing sense of loss. All of his hopes and plans had been destroyed out of hand. He really wished that Tubby had said nothing about the events at the Whatson's. Although he knew his intentions were good and that the Bishop would have undoubtedly learned about the situation when he attended the funeral anyway. His breakfast was relegated to a quick and miserable affair and he asked the housekeeper to let him know when the Bishop had finished his breakfast. He then waited outside his office like an errant schoolboy awaiting punishment, for almost an hour. When he finally called him in, his expression left him in no doubt that he was in for trouble. "What's all this I hear about you begging from the widow of one of our most influential church members? Where did you get the temerity to just come into this parish and accost my people? Is there no end to your arrogance McDowd?"

"Your Grace: I had no intention of embarrassing you, or in any way offending members of your congregation. I believe that Reverend Tubbs has told you of the tragedy in Ryeport and how difficult it is to get these people into church because of their loss of faith. I was merely trying to find ways of rebuilding their confidence, hoping to create opportunities to help them regain their lost faith."

"Nonsense; this was grandstanding, pure and simple and I will not tolerate it. You had no business in Nextwest anyway. Your place is in Ryeport, especially now, in view of their problems there. This was a heaven-sent opportunity for you to be of service but you ran away. You can pack your things, pick up Mrs. Drew and return to Ryeport immediately. And make sure that you leave the clothing that was donated. It will be sold here, for the benefit of the poor of this parish, where the donations originated."

"Very well Your Grace. I shall be ready within half an hour but Mrs. Drew will not be ready until late afternoon. She is visiting relatives here to acquaint them of her loss. I apologise most sincerely for any perceived harm that I may have caused. I can assure you that I was acting in what I thought were the best interests of my congregation."

"Don't think, you aren't suitably equipped for it. Just do as you are told." But he paused, looking thoughtful for a few seconds. "Come to think of it; it might be better if you apologised to Mrs. Whatson and her friends personally. I don't see why I should spare you that embarrassment by allowing you to run away again. Report to Reverend Tubbs. Tell him that you are to pick up Mrs. Drew immediately after the funeral, then return to Ryeport."

"Yes Your Grace; as you wish," and he left the room.

At the funeral Mrs. Whatson looked respectfully elegant. Tubby's eyes followed her every move. His admiration for the lady was so obvious that people were looking from one to the other, wondering if they were missing something. The Bishop was first in line to offer his condolences and also his help in any business matters if she so wished. The rest of them followed him in paying their respects. Reverend Watkins performed a very practised and efficient service, after which the mourners made their way to their carriages, preparing to return to the Whatson's house for refreshments. "Oh! Reverend McDowd!" Roddy saw the Bishop flush with anger as Mrs. Whatson called to him and he quickly joined him as he went to her. "Yes, Ma'am," said Roddy.

"Reverend, please see Goodman when we get back to the house. He has some boxes for you to take back to Ryeport. I believe Mister Westerhof also has some for you."

The Bishop preempted his reply. "Mrs. Whatson, I only heard of Reverend McDowd's inappropriate solicitations for clothing donations, late last night. I apologise most humbly for any embarrassment or hurt that he caused you by this thoughtless behaviour. I have also instructed him to offer his personal apology in this matter. I hope that you will not consider this incident typical of our concern and affection for yourself, and your friends." Mrs. Whatson's face was partially masked by a fine black veil, but even so it was obvious that she was taken by surprise.

Roddy stepped forward and made a small courtly bow. "Mrs. Whatson, I do apologise, most humbly indeed, for my actions of yesterday. I ask that you consider my inexperience in these matters and would be sincerely grateful if you would accept my apology." Then turning towards the Bishop, he said: "Your Grace: I also thank you for your correction in this matter and for giving me the opportunity to apologise to this good lady." Then he promptly stepped back. They had not noticed Westerhof join their group but he now moved to Mrs. Whatson's side. "I certainly don't believe any apology is called for," he said. What do you say, Mrs. Whatson?"

"No, I certainly don't believe any apology is necessary either, Your Grace. In our eyes, Reverend McDowd was an excellent representative of your church, and we intended to commend you for raising such a compassionate man to your staff. He moved all of us who were present and we all felt closer to our church and our faith because of him. No apology required. Indeed, a 'thank you' from us would seem more appropriate." She smiled rather weakly, and raised the back of her hand to her forehead. Westerhof quickly took her arm. "Come my dear, let us get you to your carriage. Reverend McDowd, I'll see you at the house."

"I'm sorry Sir, but I have to leave immediately, for Ryeport."

Westerhof paused. "Then what will become of the clothing that we have gathered?"

"His Grace has asked that it be delivered to your church here."

"Oh, I see. Then he will deliver it to Ryeport for you?"

"I can't presume to answer for His Grace, Sir."

Westerhof turned to the Bishop: "Well, Your Grace, perhaps you will be kind enough to let me know what is to become of the clothing?" Westerhof made firm eye contact with the Bishop.

"Certainly, Mister Westerhof: it seemed more appropriate to me that your gifts should benefit the poor of our congregation. I intended to sell them for the benefit of our congregation's needy people."

"Oh!" Mrs. Whatson and Westerhof halted in their slow promenade towards the carriages. "Well, that is not why we donated the clothing. Was it dear lady?" Westerhof was looking intently at Mrs. Whatson, who seemed to have made a remarkable recovery. "No. It most certainly was not," she replied. "We were actually looking forward to attending Ryeport's church one Sunday in the hope of seeing for ourselves how our less fortunate brothers and sisters had benefited from our help." The Bishop was caught off-guard. "Well, I'm sure you will understand that the villagers are not really suited to the quality of clothing that you good people have made available. The items are not likely to fit either."

Westerhof had no wine befuddling his brain right now. "Well, I'm afraid that does not suit, Your Grace. Our donors all had visions of these good people – who risk their lives daily to provide food for our tables – setting up a sewing circle, and altering the clothing to fit the church going villagers. The clothes will surely help them feel more respectful, and at ease, in the house of God." Another small group of donors had caught up with their assembly, and were adding: "Hear, hear!" Mrs. Whatson sounded annoyed. "Surely, Your Grace, you would have no objection to the clothes going to the people for whose benefit they were donated?"

"Certainly not, dear lady; if that is your wish, then so be it." The Bishop looked flustered.

"It's settled then. Reverend McDowd. Please attend the house with your wagon. Goodman will help load the clothing for you. And, sometime in the next few weeks, I would appreciate a progress report on the alterations etcetera. Then, other commitments permitting, we would appreciate an invitation to attend a service in Ryeport, to see the good people in their 'Sunday best' as my friend so eloquently put it." Mrs. Whatson turned to Westerhof. "Come, Sir, we have guests to attend to. Good day to you gentlemen." The Bishop glared at Roddy. "Do you see the embarrassment and trouble that you have caused me now? I'll not forget this."

"I'm so sorry, Your Grace. I only apologised – as you instructed."

# CHAPTER 7

## *Miss Prudence unmasks the vicar*

Pleading urgent duties, Bishop West excused himself from the gathering at the Whatson's house and returned to the manse in his carriage, taking Reverend Watkins with him and leaving Tubby and Roddy to finalise arrangements with the Whatson's regarding the donated clothing. They would then have to walk back to the manse for the wagon. Westerhof clapped a heavy hand on Roddy's shoulder, smiled, and said: "It seemed to me old chap that the Bishop was trying to steal the fruits of your idea."

"Oh, I think not, Sir. I fear that my lack of worldly wisdom led me where wiser minds would not go. The Bishop is far more experienced than I. I'm sure that he could provide many examples that would prove that actions, such as mine, were detrimental to the greater good of the congregation."

"Diplomatic to the last, eh? Well, let me tell you ,young man, your compassion for your villagers has made an impression here. We would welcome your invitation for some of us to attend one of your services, once your people feel more comfortable in their new clothing that is. Sunday best and all that."

"Thank you, Sir. I'm sure the villagers would welcome the opportunity to meet you. How do we thank the various donors for the clothing? Could you provide us with a list, so we could write and express our appreciation?"

"Not necessary old chap. By all means, send a line or two to Mrs. Whatson. She can read your letter to our friends at her next gathering. If we can find more clothing, or indeed any other items that may be of use, we'll let you know and you can arrange collection."

"Well; thank you again, Sir. God Bless you for your charity and compassion. If you would excuse me now, Sir, Reverend Tubbs and I have to leave now and walk to the manse to collect my wagon. I had arranged a few errands when I thought that I was not coming back here. Would it be convenient if I picked up the clothing about four o'clock? That is about the time that I was to pick up Mrs. Drew – the lady who lost her son last week."

"That will be fine. Most of these people will be here for an hour or so. Some are staying for supper – myself included."

"I'll wish you a good afternoon then Sir. Thank you again. I hope to see you later." Tubby and Roddy left, intending to go back to the church for his wagon, but, after a few paces, Tubby stopped and, looking thoughtful, said: "I think it might be wise Roddy, if you let me get the wagon. I could meet you at Mrs. Drew's sisters. Then you could drop me back at the church on the way to your other errands. Let's allow the Bishop some time to cool off, before your next meeting. I'm afraid you've upstaged him – in a venue of his own choosing too." Tubby couldn't restrain a smile. "He's not a very forgiving man. I hope that doesn't sound uncharitable. His Grace has a quick mind. He could have instructed Fletcher to bring your wagon to the Whatson's. I'm sure he would have thought of it. Better you avoid him for a while. I'll have Fletcher put the trunk of clothing and your bag, in the wagon."

"Here we go again," thought Roddy. "Everyone wants to get rid of me. No matter where I go, they just harness up the rig and send me away." But he had to admit that Tubby's suggestion was a good one. An hour later he dropped Tubby back at the manse, and headed out to the West End of town to explore the opportunities for future social adventures. First though, he needed somewhere private to change into his new clothes. He pulled the wagon into a lonely copse and quickly changed, then, feeling less conspicuous, continued west along the Coach Road, eventually arriving at a small inn on the western outskirts of Nextwest. 'The White Hart' was not nearly as busy as 'the Coach and Horses' but did appear well maintained. It was early afternoon, however, so it would be difficult to assess what the evening clientele might be. He sat with a pot of ale, enjoying his new civilian identity but decided that this was dangerously close to Nextwest and he might easily be recognised here. He had just dismissed any idea of seeking female company here, when a very attractive and well-dressed young lady approached the table. She stood, looking at him curiously for a few seconds, before saying: "Excuse me Sir. Would you mind if I joined you for a few moments?" Roddy rose from his seat feeling elated by this chance encounter. "It would be my pleasure, Ma'am. My name is Rodney Jacob; is there some way I could be of service?"

"Really! At first I thought I was looking at a younger version of my Grandfather: Obidiah Whatson. But, perhaps that is because you're wearing his clothes." She fixed eye contact and awaited his reaction. His stomach churned, as he felt the blood rush to his face. He was lost for a response – so she continued: "When I saw you earlier today from my carriage window, at Grandfather's funeral, you were dressed as a cleric and in the company of Bishop West. I could have sworn they called you Reverend McDowd. You appear to be flying false colours, Sir!" His heart was pounding. Less than half an hour since his change of clothes, and his deception was already unmasked. "You must be mistaken dear lady. There has to be more than one set of clothes like this."

"Possibly, but only one waistcoat like that, where my own stitching replaced the top button. It doesn't quite match you see. The replacement is slightly larger than the others and, unlike the rest, has a small design on it. Closest match I could find in my button box at the time. Grandfather often met me here for lunch. I must confess that when you first walked in, I nearly fainted. I thought Grandfather had been reincarnated; in a younger frame of course; and yet it was only a few hours ago that I saw him buried."

He hung his head, unable to believe the coincidence that had trapped him. "Alright, Miss. You have found me out; I confess my duplicity. I am actually here hoping to locate a long lost relative. Not a very nice man, I might add. His name is Albert Carson. He is aware that I am a vicar in this area, and would avoid me if he could. He owes my father a considerable sum of money and fled London to avoid repayment. I was in the area for your Grandfather's funeral, and thought I would borrow some of your Grandfather's clothes – which his wife donated for our villagers use – to make some enquiries and see if I might find him. Incidentally I don't remember seeing you at the funeral."

"I stayed in my carriage," she replied. "Mrs. Whatson, doesn't like me. You may have noticed that she is somewhat younger than my Grandfather. Some people – those with nasty, suspicious, minds – say she only married Grandfather for his money. I happen to be a founding member of that club. In fact, she and I have had several discussions concerning their relationship, and as a result, she assured me that she would arrange for

Grandfather to disown and disinherit me because I was far too outspoken on the matter. That would be the second time I'd been cut off from family fortune. On the first occasion, it was my parents that disowned me, because they didn't approve of the man I wanted to marry. They said he was a waster and a philanderer. Time served to prove them right. Unfortunately, I was young and naive at the time and thought I knew better. Once my money was gone, he left me – exactly as my parents said he would. We never married of course. He always had a reason to wait. Obviously, he was more worldly wise than I. As a consequence, my parents considered me a fallen woman – a disgrace to the family name. Only Grandfather looked beyond my youthful mistake, and took the trouble to make sure I was safe. He ensured that I had a respectable place to stay and a modest income. Actually, he pays for my rooms here. So, as you might expect, Grandfather and I were very close. Now that he's gone of course, I'm not sure of my future. I'm sure that Helena, the good Mrs. Whatson, will do her best to make sure I don't have one.

It was shortly after Grandfather set me up here that he met Helena. She objected to sharing him or his money. However, Grandfather continued to pay for my room and board, and used to meet me here quite regularly. As I said: the rest of the family had disowned me. I am an embarrassment." She paused, thoughtfully, possibly anticipating a response. But Roddy was too shaken to comment. Again she continued: "If you're wondering why I, a complete stranger, would feel free to share all this personal information, it's because you too are obviously an embarrassment. A cleric in disguise, not well thought of by his Bishop and who, I now discover, is using an assumed name and wearing my deceased Grandfather's clothes. So, answer me and please be honest this time. Why are you dressed in my dead Grandfather's clothes?"

He tried to cover his shock at her direct and blunt attack by feigning a laugh. "You are the most direct person I have ever met."

"I've been told that before. Please answer the question."

Despite the fact that she had uncovered his disguise, and embarrassed him, there was an air about this young lady that he found attractive and exciting. True; she was aggressive, and confrontational, but she was also courageous, honest, and straightforward. Under these circumstances, he would have expected any woman to send for the constable before confronting him. Somehow he believed that he could trust her. In truth, he had no other option. So, omitting most of his individual history, he gave a brief overview of how he had been forced into the clerical life and was now striving to regain his inheritance, whilst covertly seeking the company of people who were less stuffy and more sociable than his present vocation approved.

"Now that's a more plausible story," she said. "But I don't believe a word of it. Once you're caught out in a lie, everything else you say has to be suspect. But you are quite good at making up stories and in a very spontaneous manner too – quite entertaining really."

He smiled. "May I buy you a drink? Or would you be so gracious as to join me for a meal? What I've just told you is actually true. And you are now one of two people, outside of many a day's journey, privy to that truth. Somehow I find that strangely liberating, although I would prefer that you not share that information with anyone else. Too much exposure of that truth would not be good for my wellbeing. I must confess though, that it's a weight off my mind to be able to converse freely with someone without further pretence. Thank you for that at least. Of course you have completely destroyed my hopes of a relaxing afternoon. And I was really looking forward to enjoying this free time, without the limitations of my religious apparel. But I suppose that loss is no less than I deserve for wearing your Grandfather's clothes. As to my future in the church – which is absolutely essential if I am to retain that faint hope of regaining my inheritance – my subterfuge has placed me entirely in your hands." He spread his hands wide in a gesture of submission. "Bishop West would welcome a reason to remove me from his staff. And yes, he is the second person, locally, who knows my history."

She looked at him in silence for a while, as if trying to gauge his sincerity. "Tell me, just how did you come by my Grandfather's clothes?"

She smiled as he described his theatrics at the Whatson's. "My name is Prudence," she said "Prudence Mercer. Which of your aliases should I call you by?"

"Your choice," he responded. "My full name is Rodney Jacob McDowd. I answer to Roddy amongst my friends and acquaintances."

"This place is too public, Roddy," she said. "Join me in my rooms upstairs and we can have a glass of sherry whilst you fill in the gaps in your story."

"Might that not compromise your reputation?" he asked.

"Not if no one knows about it. There is a second staircase, outside, at the rear of the building. I'll use the indoor one. You can leave by the front door and use the outside staircase. Suite 3. Don't knock. That would advertise the fact that I'm having company. Just walk in. I am expecting you after all."

He walked around the back of The White Hart and found the outdoor staircase and suddenly remembered Slondosh. He had stayed longer than he first intended and not put the feedbag on him. So retracing his steps he hung the nosebag on his faithful steed, and then returned to the rear staircase and climbed to the next floor. The door to suite 3 was unlocked and, as instructed, he stepped in. But, then, he heard a man's voice from the next room. The voice sounded familiar, but he could not place it immediately.

"So we've brought the run forward by two days. Your consignment will be waiting at the usual spot for pickup. The box marked with a fleur-de-lis in the corner is to be delivered immediately to Mister Lawson. He wants it for a special dinner later in the week. Don't wait for payment; I'll take care of that."

"Smuggler talk," he thought, recognising the term 'the run'. He must be in the wrong room. He turned to tiptoe out and had almost made it, when a sudden draught slammed the door shut. That noise brought Mrs. Whatson's butler, Goodman, in from the other room. He stopped dead in his tracks as soon as he saw Roddy. Then, in an ominous voice, he said: "Nice waistcoat, Reverend. Since you enjoy my late employer's clothes so much, perhaps you should also share his present accommodations. I'd be pleased to arrange that." He stepped between Roddy and the door blocking any chance to escape, before continuing. "I was on my way out of town when I spotted your wagon in the yard. That wasn't very smart of you really, if you were trying to be inconspicuous, I mean. That style of wagon is well known in these parts as the choice of the clergy. I thought I should warn my friend, Miss Prudence, about you, and stopped by." He leaned against the door. "Of course, I had no way of knowing that you were about to enter her rooms, and would overhear our conversation. I realise now that she was trying to stop my speaking when she raised a finger to her lips. I thought she merely wanted me to be quieter. You really should learn to knock, Reverend. It's only good manners after all. Good manners that could have saved your life."

"Sorry for that," Roddy said. "But Miss Prudence told me not to knock. Didn't want her nosy neighbours to know she had company. What remarks are you talking about? Were you making uncomplimentary remarks about me?"

"Nice try. But I can't afford to take the chance that you may not have heard."

Prudence stepped between them. "No need to worry about the vicar John. I have enough information on him to be sure he'll keep his mouth shut. Don't I, Roddy?"

"Yes, you do. But, kindly tell me what you're talking about? If you two are 'keeping company', as the saying goes, who cares?"

"Well, something like that," she said, "but not that. You certainly have an uncanny knack of being in the wrong place at the wrong time, Roddy." Goodman looked very threatening.

"Well Prudence, it appears that you set me up for this one," replied the vicar.

She went to the sideboard and poured three sherries. "Let's all sit down and have a little chat," she said, handing glasses to Goodman and Roddy. "Roddy, you told me it was liberating not to have to bother with pretence any longer. I would suggest that this is a good time for you to exercise that freedom. John here has a short fuse and a reputation for hard, and nasty, decisions. First, tell us what you heard. Then tell us how you feel about what you heard. Above all else – be believable."

Roddy sat waiting for some divine inspiration but knew it wouldn't come. He wasn't a member of the right team. Hell, he wasn't a member of any team. "Alright, I heard John here talking about moving 'the run' forward by two days and you having to deliver a box marked with a fleur-de-lis as soon as you could. That's it. I believe that is smuggler talk so I have to assume that you two must be involved in smuggling. That answers the first question. As to how I feel about that: I don't give a damn. It's none of my business. I'd like to believe that people don't get killed or hurt as a result of you people making illegal money. That would be my only concern. As I told you, Prudence, the church was not my career choice. However, I have to stay with it until I can earn my way back in my Father's good books and regain my lost inheritance. Along the way, because I realise that regaining my Father's goodwill will take a long time, I would like to enjoy some of the more pleasant things in life. Things denied me by present vocation and previously enjoyed; some pleasant female company for instance, and a life that offers decent food and comfortable accommodations. Perhaps even a friend or two that I could truly relax with, instead of always having to play the righteous, servile, ninny. That's it! Believe me or not; that's the truth."

There was a prolonged silence. Prudence and Goodman exchanged glances a couple of times but nothing was said for a few minutes. Eventually, Prudence broke the silence. "I believe him. He won't go squealing to the Revenuers."

"I'm not so sure," Goodman was giving him a fixed, unpleasant stare. "Why on earth should we take the chance? If you're wrong, it will mean both our necks."

"Then let's bring him aboard. Make him part of the crew. Then he'd have to keep his mouth shut."

"I don't think he'd be of any use to us. Why take a chance for no good reason?"

"Because I don't think we should attract attention to this area right now. We don't need King's men investigating the death of a priest. It could make life very difficult."

Roddy interrupted. "Thank you both for taking such an active interest in my life. Do you think I might be consulted though, instead of having you two talk over my head all the time?"

"Nothing that you could say would be relevant here," Goodman said in a dismissive manner.

"Well, relevant or not. I don't want to be part of your bloody smuggling ring. If news of that ever got out, my inheritance would be gone for good. I have just one thin chance of recovering that and I'm going to need all the luck I can get, just to keep that chance alive."

"You're going to need more than luck just to keep yourself alive," Goodman responded. It seemed he had already made his mind up as far as Roddy's future was concerned.

Prudence spoke up. "Well, either he lives or I'm out. I don't want any involvement in violence. And none of us need the added risk of an investigation just now. That would be bad for all concerned. We could all end up in the hands of the King's men."

"Are you serious?" Goodman demanded, looking at her as though she'd lost her mind.

"Yes! And that's my last word on it. Find a means to keep him under watchful eyes if you want. He won't know who your watchers are. If he should make a suspicious move, you could arrange one of your fatal accidents then. Until then, leave well enough alone. In the meantime, we have some leverage that might prove useful."

Goodman was silent for a while. Then he stood up, put his empty glass on the sideboard and turned back to Roddy. "You've got away with it this time preacher. But don't you ever give me the slightest reason to think I've made a mistake. There will be no discussion next time, just a quick solution. As far as an investigation is concerned, there won't be one. They'll never find your body. By the sound of things you have a reputation for being unreliable. I doubt anyone would bother to look for you for very long." He turned his attention to Prudence. "Bye, Pru; remember what I told you. I'll arrange for watchers to keep an eye on this preacher. I believe we've just made a big mistake." Goodman pointed a threatening finger at him. "That won't happen twice!" He left without another word. Prudence and Roddy were silent for a while. He sat there holding his empty glass, with his elbows on his knees. "I'm not sure if I trust Goodman to merely have me watched. It sounds to me as though he'd rather have me killed," he said.

"Well, he does have a reputation for acting first, and – sometimes – asking questions afterward in matters like this. But I'm pretty sure you're safe for now. I'm sorry about his unexpected visit. I did try to stop him talking, and get to the door before you showed up but he held my arm and just kept talking. I'll admit I was a bit annoyed when I first saw you wearing Grandfather's clothes but not mad enough to want you killed for it." She smiled and he believed her.

"It wasn't your fault Prudence. As you said, I do have an unhappy knack for being in the wrong place at the wrong time. Where do we go from here?"

"Well, why don't we get back to our original intention of having you fill in the blanks in your story? The better I know you the better chance I have of keeping Goodman under control." She poured another sherry and they sat and talked for another hour or so whilst Roddy elaborated on his sorry tale. By wearing 'Grandfather's clothes' he had given Prudence unusual leverage but it was actually a relief to finally have a confidant and he felt comfortable sharing with her. Or was it because of the sherry? Finally he excused himself, explaining that he had to pick up Mrs. Drew, and the clothing, at the Whatson's. He also needed to change back into clerical garb. But he wasn't looking forward to seeing Goodman again at Whatson's house and said so.

"No need to worry about that. He was on his way out of town, remember. He won't be back at the Whatson's until late tonight. Just be sure that you don't mention anything about what you've heard here. Not to anybody. You will never know who may be listening, or who his watchers may be."

• • •

Mrs. Drew's face was a little flushed when Roddy collected her from Marie's, and when he commented on her high colour, she bristled up and said: "That sounds to me like the pot's calling the kettle black." Until then he hadn't noticed the smell of brandy on her breath but, obviously, she had sensed that he'd had a drink or two. He thought it safer to ignore her comment and change the topic. Despite their poor beginnings he was developing a strong regard for this stoic lady and hoped that they might become friends. "Mrs. Drew, are you good with needle and thread?" She gave him a searching look and replied: "Why'd you ask?"

"Well, I wondered if you might be willing to exercise such talent for a good cause. Help with some alterations, resize some clothing to fit, and things like that."

"I've always given help in a good cause. Not likely to stop now. What's it all about? That scorched coat of yours?"

"Actually no, I have no replacement for that."

"Yes, you do. Reverend Cole's coat is still in the closet at your cottage. I'd have to cut it down to fit you, but I can manage that."

"Well thank you, Mrs. Drew. I would certainly appreciate that. I've been the target of a few disparaging remarks lately. The Bishop said I looked like a burnt offering."

Mrs. Drew laughed. "I can see why. You certainly aren't as well turned out as the preachers I'm used to."

"Well thank you for those comforting words Mrs. Drew, but actually I was thinking that we could use the talents of a good seamstress to benefit the people of the village."

"How so?"

"Better I show you rather than try to explain," Roddy said.

On arrival at the Whatsons, they were greeted by Westerhof. There were several bundles of clothing lining one wall. He was shocked by the amount, and Westerhof revelled in his astonishment. "Can you handle this little lot Father?" he asked.

"Not I," he replied. "But I'm hoping Mrs. Drew can," and quickly introduced his bemused housekeeper. Westerhof's smile faded, when he learned that Mrs. Drew was the lady who had so recently lost her son. "Please accept my sincere condolences, Mrs. Drew. Reverend McDowd has informed us of the tragedy in Ryeport. We are all so very sorry for your loss. I shall pray for our Good Lord to help and comfort you in this sad time. How are you managing?"

Mrs. Drew was shocked by the sincerity and warmth, of her reception. Roddy allowed Westerhof to explain the bundles of clothing, and how they were a gift to the villagers. She turned to him in concern. "I may be good with needle and thread Father, but I'm no magician. I'd need a lot of help with this lot."

"How about a sewing circle?" he suggested. "Surely other ladies in the village would help? There must be others that can sew?"

"Now that's a good idea," she said. "We can chat around someone's kitchen table instead of at the well." She smiled at Westerhof. "Thank you so much, Sir," she said. "This really will be a great gift to the villagers." He beamed. "It's our pleasure, Ma'am. It truly is a great pleasure. We shall stay in touch." So they loaded the wagon and took their leave. They were about a mile out of town when Mrs. Drew broke the silence with a sudden laugh. "Any good with a needle and thread," she said, and punched the vicar on the shoulder. "Ouch."

Once in Ryeport they carried the bundles into the church. Roddy was explaining to Mrs. Drew some of the events that led up to the donations of clothing – leaving out his personal motivation of course. "This could be a real help to the villagers," she said. "But there might be a problem with their pride. They're very independent you know. They won't like the idea of charity. Takin' other people's cast offs as it were. That could ruin the whole idea."

"Then why don't we let them buy the clothes?" he said. Mrs. Drew laughed. "What with, shirt buttons?"

"Suppose we say you negotiated a great deal on their behalf, provided you took the whole consignment. We could say that they were intended to be sold for the benefit of the poor in Nextwest, but, if you agreed to take the whole lot, the cost would be...er...let me see...contributions to the poor box at Nextwest Church. All donations should be modest and anonymous and for the benefit of the poor in Nextwest."

"Well now, that might work! Now the villagers are the ones who are being charitable rather than the other way around. I like that. That might work, but why me? You're the one that arranged all this."

"Mrs. Drew. You know that I am held in very low regard in the village and I understand why. It could sour the whole deal if the villagers thought that I had a hand in it. Let's proceed as I said. You take credit for the idea, because that's the best way to benefit the village. I'll have to earn their respect some other way and that will take time."

"Very well then Father. But the first item for alteration is Reverend Cole's coat."

They unloaded the clothing and made their way back to the inn. Mrs. Drew was certain that was what Ernie would have wanted so, of course, that was the way it had to be. Ernie joined them for supper in the kitchen. He listened to Mrs. Drew's recounting of the events of the past days and she swore him to secrecy concerning Roddy's part in the clothing donations. "That can't hurt," thought Roddy. "I'm not blowing-my-own-horn, and, although he's sworn to secrecy, he is still in a position to influence people's behaviour towards me."

"Well done Father, Ernie said as he patted him on the shoulder. We'll keep your secret."

"How are the injured and the sick faring? Roddy asked. "I was chastised by the Bishop for leaving the village when I might have been of service here." Ernie responded with a derisive grunt. "What does he know about what's best for this village? We've not seen him here for almost ten years. Most of the villagers wouldn't know him if he did show his face. That assistant of his, the little fat one, is the only one we've seen from Nextwest. And he doesn't stay a minute longer than he has to. Anyway, regarding the sick and injured, there has been improvement all around. Except for Doc Hudson, that is. I'm afraid this affair has really taken a toll on him. Tim is sitting up and taking nourishment now and so is Jamie. Not that they look that good mind you. But at least there is some improvement. Rachel said, that when Tim first saw his pennant pinned to the wall, he smiled and said: 'Lucky lady's still with us – in spirit anyway!' Then he went back to sleep. When he woke up again he seemed much better. Archer must understand that man really well. Will is doing best of all three. He actually gets up for a little while each day. Sits by the fire and eats his meals. These boys are tough Father. Believe me they're tough. The exposure alone would have killed most men. Even Doc Hudson shakes his head in disbelief. He gives you some credit for their recovery. Only the women buy into that though. You've still got a long way to go with the men."

"I'm well aware of that. It looks as though I will have to bear the blame for all the wrongs of the past as well as my own. So be it. Tomorrow, I'll see if I can get Sailmaker to show me something of the harbour. Time I got to know what this place is all about." Ernie raised his eyebrows. "That could be a good start. First thing first though. You and I will go on our rounds of the sick in a few minutes. Then we'll have a chat about the harbour. By the way Father, that blasted cat of yours won't leave the woodshed. He hisses at anyone who tries to move him. Meg's the only one who can get close. She gave him some scraps from the kitchen, but cats never go hungry around here. There's always fish."

The sick rounds confirmed Ernie's report of improvement, and all were amenable to a short prayer of thanks, except Jamie Rooken of course. Emily on the other hand followed them outside, and asked if they could have a short prayer on their own. "And could we all join hands like you did for the other boys?" she said. "I know that Jamie won't be part of the circle but it's better that than nothing." Of course, they agreed and she seemed more content when they left. On the next morning, Mrs. Drew came by to make breakfast and take care of the other chores in the cottage. "I'll be talking to the women at the well later," she said. "Then we'll see who will come and help with the clothing. First we should see who can get into the clothes without alterations. Then we'll see how we can best fit the others. Better to let the people choose and alter their own clothes where possible. I'll help those that can't help themselves." Roddy nodded his head, glad to be free of the business, then excused himself and left for Sailmaker's hut. He hid the clothes that Prudence had seen him wear at The White Hart.

Sailmaker was busy caulking the seams of a small boat, but greeted him affably. "How are you Father? Did you enjoy your visit to Nextwest? Bessie says you made a good impression there."

"I wouldn't go that far Stephen. But some goodwill might come of it. Mrs. Drew needed the break and I'm sure the visit did her good. Stephen, I believe that I should get to know more about the village and the hazards our men face, both at sea and in getting back into the harbour. I was hoping you might be able to help me with that, since you seem to be the only one who will give me the time of day around here."

"Oh, I'm sure that's not true Father. The time-of-day thing I mean. Anyway, I'd be pleased to show you around. Give me a few minutes to finish this seam and, if you wish, we can take my dinghy for a trip around the harbour right away."

"That would be most appreciated, Stephen. Thank you."

"By the way, Father," he said, smiling, "No one calls me Stephen since my mother died, I'm known as 'Sailmaker'. That's a nickname I got when I was just a kid, when Dad helped me make new sails for my first boat."

"Very well then. Sailmaker it is." They shook hands on it.

They spent the next three hours pulling Sailmaker's dinghy around the harbour. They even went through 'The Chute', into Sorry Cove. The weather was calm and they came back into the harbour the same way. Sailmaker explained in detail, how Lucky Lady had come through The Chute, pointing overhead to where the boat had jammed her mast into Archer's bridge. Then he showed Roddy where some wreckage of The Lucky Lady had been found, with Mick still trapped in it. They then went across the channel to the place where Will had kept Tim from slipping into the water and after that, went back out to sea through the 'dogleg'; the same entrance that the fishing boats used. Sailmaker pointed out another danger; a rocky spine that extended from the eastern cliff, into the sea. "We call that ridge 'The Dragon's Tail'. You can see why. It looks as though a dragon buried its head and shoulders in the cliff, leaving just its back half and spiky tail trailing into the sea. That's the hazard where Bannerman wrecked his boat a couple of years ago. It's beyond repair. Now he works as crew on the Sullivan's boat. That's a hard knock for someone as independent as he is and he's been harder to get along with ever since. We should arrange for you to go out with one of the fishing boats, Father. You could see the whole business of leaving harbour, fishing, and getting back in. It's a lot tougher than other harbours along this coast. But it is also miles closer to some of the better fishing. So you have to take the good with the bad. I'm sure one of the Cobbe brothers would take you along. They're good people. Not as quick to judge, as some folk around here."

"That would be most appreciated," said Roddy. "When do you think that could happen?"

"I'll have a chat with them when they get in tonight, and let you know."

The vicar thanked Sailmaker and returned to his cottage. It was time to work on Sunday's sermon. The fresh air and unaccustomed exercise had taken its toll however and he awoke with his head on the table and a crick in his neck. The paper was still blank but he gave up and went to bed.

The following morning he was startled from a deep sleep by a hammering on his door, and a booming voice yelling: "Wakey, wakey, rise and shine! The sun is up, the morning's fine!" This was repeated several times before he managed to get to the door. "What's all the noise for? What is the trouble?" He dreaded the answer, because the last time he had been awakened by an outsider it had been the morning of the disaster and his first encounter with Bannerman. He was confronted with a burly fellow, with a big smile on his ruddy face, who filled the doorway. "Name's Benjamin Cobbe. Sailmaker says you wanted to experience a day's fishing, and the return to the harbour. Well, I'm your man."

Roddy rubbed his eyes. "Good to meet you Benjamin, but why all this racket? Are you always this noisy? I thought the cottage was coming down around my ears."

The big man grew larger. "Well, my little girl, Jane, says you're hard to wake." She's the youngster that brought you down to the landing if you remember."

"How could I forget? But Sailmaker said he would let me know when he could arrange the trip."

"Well, it's arranged. No time like the present. Nice day too, by the looks of things. It may not be as nice on an arranged day. Get yourself into something warm. I've got oilskins for you in case of need. Got food on board too, arranged extra just for you. Step lively now, Father; I'd like to get out there before the fish get too smart. They travel in schools you know."

"But..."

"No buts Father; it's got to be today. Eat in the boat, on the way out." He stepped through the door, and propelled him towards the bedroom. "Hurry now. I hate being the last boat out! Warm clothes now." So began Roddy's first trip outside the harbour. There was a small swell running but otherwise the weather was quite pleasant. Benjamin introduced him to his two sons, John and Sam, as they boarded his boat. They were soon in the dogleg channel leading to the sea. "What's with all this: Wakey, wakey business?" asked Roddy. "You said the sun was up. It certainly wasn't up when you were trying to break my door down earlier."

Benjamin just laughed. "The sun's always up somewhere Father. You just weren't in a position to see it." He grinned as he raised his eyebrows. "And, if I'd wanted to break your door down, it would be very draughty in your place right now. Look yonder, Father. That's where we found Tim and Will. I believe Sailmaker already showed you that. When we round this dogleg you will see The Dragon's Tail. You know, Sailmaker had to work fast to repair Archer's bridge. He managed that whilst you were in Nextwest. Depending on the catch, we might be coming back late tonight. If so, you should get a fair idea of how the beacons look from seaward."

His sons broke-out breakfast from a hamper, and they ate that on the way to the fishing grounds. Benjamin Cobbe kept up a running commentary on local landmarks, including the full story of Carter's Rock. "That was quite a stroke of luck," he said. "Wouldn't want to try that a second time." It was a bright day, and very pleasant out there but he was soon chilled. He didn't have the warm clothing that the Cobbe's had. And certainly wasn't as hardened or as strong as they were. Benjamin had him put on the oilskin coat to keep the wind off. Hauling in the wet nets proved to be heavier work than he had expected. His stomach, back, and thigh muscles started complaining very early on, and his hands soon became raw from the chafing ropes. Salt water and rough ropes were punishing his soft flesh and he caught a few knowing looks passing between the family when they saw him pause to inspect his hands. He was determined not to complain, and tried to find ways to reduce chafing the broken blisters where possible.

Eventually Benjamin was satisfied with the days haul, and began looking eastward for his landmarks. The nets were stowed and the boat turned for shore just as the light began to fade. They were still a few miles from the harbour when darkness reduced the landmarks to a series of blurred shadows. Benjamin gave the vicar a nudge with his elbow. "Look yonder Father! There goes the first beacon now. It will build to a considerable light shortly." Then he saw a flicker of flame from another of the taller shadows. That too quickly grew to a bright beacon. "That's Archer's beacon," said Benjamin. "Can you imagine trying to find the harbour entrance, rather than Sorry Cove, if you had only one beacon to guide you? Especially in heavy seas and with a strong wind pushing you, whipping spindrift in your face? I tell you Father: Tim did a great job, even with a bad guess, the night we lost young Mick. He almost made it through The Chute even so. If his mast hadn't speared Archer's bridge, he might have made it through."

They saw the faint stern lights of a couple of other boats pass between the beacons ahead of them. Soon they were part of a straggling line of boats following each other into the safe channel. Benjamin pointed out the similarities between the east and west cliff structures. "Not much to choose between 'em is there? And this is a clear night."

"Look left now Father," he said, after they had been in the narrow channel for a short while. Another beacon had come into view, in the harbour itself. "That's The Harbour Light," Benjamin said. "We steer towards it as soon as we see it. There are submerged rocks on our starboard side. Steering to that light keeps us in the deepest part of the channel all the way into the harbour. That's how the inn got its name of course." There were helpers waiting for them at the landing and the boat was unloaded fairly quickly. "Took longer than that to get the damned fish aboard, didn't it Father?" Benjamin was smiling as he patted him on the back. "Thank you for your help today. Bessie will have supper ready for you I expect. Why don't you hustle away, and get to it."

"Thank you Benjamin, and you too, John and Sam, for your help and hospitality today. That was a most enlightening experience." He took off the oilskin coat, folded it, and dropped it in the stern seats. He was dead beat, cold, and sorer than he had ever been in his whole life. Even so, he was grateful for the goodwill that he'd experienced that day. Even more grateful that he'd survived the day, and that the experience was over. He was dragging his weary body along the jetty, almost asleep on his feet, when Benjamin's booming voice rang out: "I'll pick you up same time tomorrow Father." Roddy stopped dead in his tracks, lost for words, and turned his frozen body towards the boat. Ben was standing there, straight faced, hands on his hips, watching him, as he struggled to find an excuse that wouldn't embarrass him too much. Suddenly, he and his boys exploded with laughter. "I'm only joking Father. I just wanted to see your reaction. You did well today."

Roddy managed a weak smile as he raised a weary hand in a feeble wave. "Thanks, Benjamin. You had me worried there for a while."

Supper was ready when he got to the cottage. But first, Mrs. Drew bathed his hands in warm water. Then she bound them with strips of clean cloth before she sat him by the fire with a large bowl of steaming hot stew. "Those hands were never meant for such rough work Father. You were only supposed to go along for the ride you know." She poured him a large glass of wine, and sat across from him, on the other side of the fireplace, as she watched him eat. "This is a marvellous stew, Mrs. Drew. The wine too, it's really luxurious. You're spoiling me."

She started to tell him about the arrangements she had made for the sewing circle but Roddy nodded off and she had to dive to catch the bowl as it slid from his lap. Roddy slept for almost an hour before she roused him and suggested that he'd be more comfortable in bed. Just before dozing off he felt a slight pressure behind his knees; Moggy was re-establishing his spot on the bed.

• • •

Apart from his fishing trip, the two weeks following his return to Ryeport were quite uneventful. Mrs. Drew organised her sewing group and the ladies chose clothes, made their alterations, and chatted an awful lot. Those that couldn't sew very well ended up making tea and snacks for the rest. It proved to be good therapy for Mrs. Drew, who was kept very busy. A lot of the clothes were far too dressy for the villagers, and the women removed lots of lace and ornamentation. In the waste-not-want-not economy of the village, this was set aside for other projects.

Roddy spent more time in the harbour with Sailmaker, and also on the cliff-top overlooking the harbour entrance. An idea was taking shape in his mind but he was unsure of how to turn the idea into a practical plan. The church attendance had improved a little and, on the following Sunday, they had more than thirty people in the congregation. It was mostly women and children, but he was especially grateful for the support of a few men; namely Ernie, Sailmaker, Benjamin Cobbe and his brother Joshua, who attended with their families. Doc Hudson and Archer were there too. Maybe he was making a little progress after all. No one had threatened his life for more than two weeks.

Some of the congregation were looking smarter too. Burly Benjamin Cobbe was wearing a coat that he was sure he had seen on Westerhof. Mrs. Drew told him that his sons were also waiting for some alterations to be completed. It was the women though that stood out the most. And they were certainly less selfconscious in their new clothes than the men. But even Ernie was wearing a fancy shirt, smart new breeches and stockings. Mrs. Drew was all smiles, and waved to him as she entered the church, gesturing towards the congregation. Obviously she was pleased with the efforts of her sewing circle. The service went well. Hymns had been chosen by Mrs.

Drew, and Doc Hudson read the lesson. Roddy made a point of keeping his participation short and focused on matters the community could identify with. He praised all of the villagers for their commitment to each other and community projects and made sure to give full credit for the impressive recovery of their sick and injured, to God's compassion and Doc Hudson's skill and dedication. The congregation may be growing, but there was a long way to go before it would impress his father.

The service was well under way when the door of the church opened and Emily Rooken half dragged an embarrassed looking Jamie through the door. Everybody turned to face the late arrivals and everyone stood in stunned silence for a few moments. Roddy expected to see Jamie bolt out through the doorway at any moment. Then he noticed that he too was wearing a smart jacket, vest, new breeches and stockings. Mrs. Drew began a quiet clapping and that was quickly taken up by the rest of the congregation. Jamie, looking very sheepish, and Emily, both nodded in recognition, before moving to a pew. Of course Roddy made a point of welcoming them and was about to continue with the service when Emily stood, and asked if she might make a request. "Could we have a special prayer for those still recovering from their illness and injuries?" She asked. "And, could we all join hands during that prayer, same as the folks did around the sick beds, after the storm?"

"That's a wonderful suggestion, Emily," replied Roddy. "Why don't we do that now?" He went down to the floor and stood between the front pews and held out both hands. Ernie's daughter, Meg, took one and Mrs. Drew the other. Soon the connections were made through all the pews with Emily moving into the aisle to complete the circle at the far end of their small group. "Let us bow our heads and pray," he said and followed the same routine that he had used around the sick beds of the injured, again ending with The Lord's Prayer.

After the service concluded, the congregation did not hasten from the church as with previous services, but remained, talking in small groups. One such group had gathered around Jamie Rooken, clapping him on the shoulder, congratulating him on his recovery and his smart appearance, as they shook his hand. Roddy found himself studying this congregation with an interest he'd never experienced before. How well paired Emily and Jamie Rooken appeared to be! Both were short, stocky, and rather plump. Emily was about five feet two, and Jamie roughly two inches taller. Both had ruddy complexions, and cheerful faces. They gave one the impression of a matched set. Certainly, family likeness would never come to mind when comparing Emily and her sister. Kathleen was taller, about five feet six inches, with a lean build and a rather pale complexion. Her husband, Archer, looked about five feet ten and, but for his arthritis, which caused him to stoop, might have been six feet tall. Kathleen was certainly more aloof, than her rosy-cheeked, outgoing sister. Her husband too, had a somewhat distant and critical manner. Another matched set, but quite a contrast from the Rookens.

Emily detached herself from that group to come and speak with him. "I wanted to thank you, Father. Jamie is so much better. I think the prayers did a lot for 'is recovery. I told 'im 'ow we'd formed a circle outside the cottage that day, after 'is attack. I told 'im that, even though 'e wasn't part of it, the prayer circle 'elped 'im. 'e was annoyed at first. Said we was makin' 'im a laughin' stock. But 'e calmed down when 'e saw 'ow mad I was. You'd be dead but for me Jamie Rooken, I said. So don't you give me no lip. Then I got Meg to sit with 'im while I went to Bessie's sewing circle. I found some clothes that would fit 'im – with a little adjustment of course. Jamie didn't want any part of it. Charity, 'e called it." Emily's face took on an impatient, slightly angry, expression. "Charity, my arse, I said! Oops!" She clapped a hand over her mouth. "Sorry, Father. I paid for those clothes with my savin's' I said. Every last penny went in the Nextwest's poor box. Just so you could look respectable in church and able to give thanks for still bein' alive.

'I ain't goin' to no church,' 'e says. 'Oh yes you are I says or you can start looking after yourself from 'ere on. I'll move out!" She shrugged and made an apologetic gesture. 'e knows I wouldn't, o' course. But 'e needed some-thin' – some excuse – to justify a change of 'eart ye see. Anyway, 'ere 'e is. First time in church for many a year – 'cept for weddin's and funerals o' course. Poor old Archer, nearly 'ad a fit. Said 'e would 'ave bet money that Jamie would never go to church for a regular service. Thank you, Father. You bein' 'ere 'as 'elped turn 'im around. 'e won't admit it mind. But it's true." She smiled as she reached out and gave his arm a gentle squeeze and promptly left to rejoin her friends.

Bessie Drew informed Roddy later that, at the wish of the sewing circle, she had put a box in the church entrance marked: 'Donations to Nextwest's Poor Fund.' People could donate as much as they pleased, and anonymously. Obviously the villager's pride was protected, now that they were paying for clothes, as evidenced by Emily's remarks. Roddy's conscience prodded him to contribute too, and rather generously.

He looked around this small congregation and wondered who amongst them might be smugglers and who might be John Goodman's 'watcher'. The Whatson's butler was never far from his mind. But then, neither was Prudence. His mind's eye would often picture her willowy figure and pretty face when he ought to have been concentrating on his clerical duties. And the memory of her assertive, teasing, manner always put a smile on his face. She was never far from his mind.

# CHAPTER 8

## *Bridget – a woman scorned*

Despite the fact that this had been his best day ever in Ryeport, sleep came slowly to Roddy that night. He could not find the peace of mind that would allow him to rest. No matter how he tried to dismiss them from his mind, a jumble of thoughts concerning the boats' re-entry into the harbour persisted. He was sure there had to be a better way to identify the safe entrance than to have two vulnerable beacons. After all, both of the latest tragedies had come about because one of the two beacons had failed. "Reduce the dependence from two to one, and you should halve the risk," he reasoned. "Isn't that right Moggy?" But he got no help from the cat. He was already in 'the-land-of-nod'.

He was up early the following morning and had gathered sketching materials in a bag before Mrs. Drew arrived to make breakfast. She found him sitting on the floor, sliding back and forth on an old scrap of carpet, whilst staring up at a box that he had placed on the tabletop. On the side of the box facing him, he had drawn a large crucifix and set the salt and pepper pots in front of the box, one on the left side of the crucifix, and the other on the right. He was determined to explore the persistent thoughts that had ruined the last night's sleep, at a practical level. For that, he would first need to discuss his thoughts with Sailmaker. After that he would pay a visit to the eastern cliff-top, where it overlooked the Dragons Tail.

"My, my, we are up early today. Is there a problem with the bed Father? Did the cat wet it or something?" Mrs. Drew asked the questions with raised eyebrows. Her surprise at seeing him up and about so early was understandable but she still thought to modify the common sarcastic remark of a wet bed, in case it might offend him. "No. Mrs. Drew. I wouldn't expect such bad conduct from Moggy. He's far too refined a creature for that. I just wanted to get an early start on a project that I need Sailmaker's help with. Good morning, by the way."

"Good morning to you, Sir." She gave a mock curtsey before adding. "By the way: Is there a charge for using the chairs now? Or are you just scratching an itch? Oops! Sorry, I didn't mean to be rude." Roddy laughed. It was a relief to have someone feel comfortable enough with him to share a joke. The formal, arm's length, relationship accorded most clergy plus the ill will that still distanced him from most of the villagers, had denied him the pleasures of friendly banter. He really missed that. "No problem Mrs. Drew. I am pleased that you share your good humour with me. As to my sitting on the floor, I was just trying to test an idea I had about the beacons. But I will need Sailmaker's help, so I must get to him before he gets too busy."

Half an hour later he was trotting off to Sailmaker's hut. "Good morning Sailmaker! Tell me: why not one beacon rather than two? If there was only one there would not be the confusion of whether to go right or left, would there? Surely the last two accidents would have been avoided, wouldn't they?" Sailmaker was a little taken aback by his unexpected arrival and the flurry of questions, and took a few moments to respond. "No Father. You can't say they would have been avoided. If Jamie had been the one beacon master, there wouldn't have been any light at all would there? Also, steering midway between two lights is easier than trying to judge how far left or right you might be from a single light and, even more important, it lets you know the direction you are approaching the light from."

"Well, you could always use two men for the one beacon. It wouldn't cost any more than it does now, and, if one fell sick, the second could take over."

"There's still the problem of avoiding The Dragon's Tail, and judging where the deeper water is! If you centre the boat between the lights you can be sure of sufficient draft. Be a lot easier if it weren't for the jagged rocks that line the edge of the deep water."

"Oh. I missed that. Of course. Sorry."

"That's alright Father. These ideas have all been kicked around before, and will be again I'm sure."

"Suppose the light were, indoors, bright enough, and positioned so that you set your bearings directly on one light?"

"Like one of the new lighthouses that people are talking about?"

"Yes, something like that."

"We could never raise the money to build such a light. And it would still be a single light. You need two points of reference for reliable guidance and lighthouses only warn you of a hazard really. You don't use them to guide you into a narrow harbour entrance. And, once again, a single light would appear the same from any point within a large radius. You wouldn't know if you were too close to shore, whether you were east or west of it."

"Suppose you could take a true bearing from a single light?"

"Good trick Father. How do you propose to do that?"

"I'm not sure yet."

Sailmaker raised his hands in despair. "Father, I'm sorry. I have to finish repairing the nets. When you've worked out your idea – let me know. Right now I have to get back to work." His manner was impatient.

"Sailmaker, I need your help. Could you spare me some time on the eastern cliff-top in the near future?"

"To do what, Father? This problem has been gone over many times by better seamen than you or me, believe me. The two beacons is the best idea so far, despite the two failures!"

"I've got an idea for a single light to guide the boats in. But I need to test it. I want to make a large crucifix, wrap it in oily rags, position it on the cliff-top, and set light to it. I need to be at sea when the cross is lit and a seaman to steer a boat by it. Just to see what the possibilities are."

"Leave it alone Father. The two beacons are good. The villagers are working on a backup system to check that they are always lit. They'll come up with something soon, believe me."

Roddy was deflated. His best hope for some cooperation, wasn't even giving him a reasonable hearing. "It's not just the beacons, Sailmaker. I'm trying to marry two benefits into this idea. Look." He pulled his sketch from the bag.

"See here. I want to build a church on the cliff-top with a big window in the seaward wall, shaped like a crucifix. Behind the window would be a lot of oil lamps that would show a bright light out to sea in all weathers. There would be no problems with wet wood or having to struggle across Archer's bridge or up Rooken's slippery steps in bad weather. We could even arrange a window facing the inn, so that people would always know when the light was lit."

Sailmaker shrugged, and gave a despairing smile. "Nice dream vicar. Where would the money come from? I've already told you that we could never build a lighthouse. What you're suggesting could cost far more. Apart from that, we're still stuck with the single light. And, of course, there's no way the Bishop would consider a new church for our little village. Especially with the attendance we get."

"Look Sailmaker; as far as the single light is concerned, the lighted cross would only appear complete if you stayed in the safe channel. Veer left or right and a corresponding arm of the cross would appear shortened. See these two blocks I've drawn either side of the crucifix? As the boat moves out of proper alignment to the cross, the blocks would obscure part of the cross."

Sailmaker studied the drawing. It did seem that he was getting interested. Then, suddenly, he straightened up. "Nice dreaming Father. It might work. Be tricky to get it right. Then there's The Dragon's Tail to contend with. And, the biggest obstacle of all – no one would pay for it. The Bishop certainly wouldn't approve it, and the village doesn't have such money. You could buy the whole village for less than it would cost to build that church. Then there's the ongoing cost of oil for the lamps. That would be expensive." Roddy felt his shoulders slump.

Sailmaker stood up, stretched, and patted his shoulder. "Nice try though, Father. It seems that you really do have the village at heart. By the way, Benjamin said you did a good job on the fishing trip, for a land lubber that is." He smiled, "Benjamin said you didn't complain once while you were out and he knew you were hurting. He was impressed. Well done!"

"Well thank you for arranging that trip Sailmaker. But, let's get back to the light. Leave the money side of things to me. Maybe I can, maybe I can't, arrange the money. We'll never know if we don't try. In the meantime though, let's get back to my earlier question. Can you spare me a little time for my test? Please." Sailmaker looked down at his shoes for a few seconds. "Well, you are really persistent, aren't you? I'll most likely be laughed at for days, when the village finds out what you're up to. But, alright, I'll give you a hand this time. I'm sure we can have Meg light the cross for us."

It was Roddy's turn to smile. "Thanks, Sailmaker. Nothing ventured, nothing gained. I appreciate your help and support, believe me."

Sailmaker gave him a big grin. "You're a much different man than Reverend Cole, that's for sure. Different too from what we first thought of you that morning of the rescue. You really are trying to help the village, even if your ideas are a bit crazy. But I can't help you today. I've promised these nets for tomorrow, and there's lots of work left to do. I'll have to set something up with Meg too. What size does this cross have to be?"

"Maybe fifteen feet tall. Might need to get even taller. Depends on how it looks from outside the harbour."

Sailmaker smiled, and shook his head. "Alright, I'll see what I can round up in the way of lumber. I'll see you in a couple of days vicar. Not before. I'm just too busy."

"Thanks, Sailmaker. I'm going to the cliff-top now, to see if I can get a start on positioning the cross. Bye!" Sailmaker was chuckling, and shaking his head as he returned to working on the nets. He thought the vicar was crazy but at least he was going to help. He was right about the money of course. Roddy doubted that Bishop West would support minor repairs in the present church, let alone build a new one. So how could he arrange the money? First he would wait to see if his idea showed any merit, then he'd worry about the money. One problem at a time was quite sufficient.

. . .

Two days had passed since Sailmaker had agreed to help with the 'fiery cross' idea and Roddy was growing impatient. However, during that time, a problem had surfaced that threatened all his efforts at reinstatement in his father's will. He badly needed his housekeeper's insights, but didn't know how to approach her on what was a most embarrassing subject. Mrs. Drew had seated herself at the kitchen table and was finishing the alterations to a black coat that had once belonged to his predecessor. She had always intended his 'new' coat to be her first job in the sewing circle, and was always apologising for the delay. The excitement caused by the donated clothes, and the demand for her help had swept aside all her good intentions. He assured her that there was no problem.

Mrs. Drew was working quietly as he gazed out the window, trying to summon the courage to present his new problem without embarrassing himself, or her. Beyond the window, drizzling rain was forming tiny puddles all over the gravel pathway. From time to time, a little puddle would overflow and migrate to another one, causing that to do the same. Of course, the deepest puddle had formed in the depression in front of his doorstep and it was too large for him to jump over it. "Of course," he grumbled, "just one more comfort to my new home." Roddy shook his head, and mentally chastised himself for allowing such a small distraction to take his mind off his bigger, more urgent, problem.

He desperately needed Mrs. Drew to respect his confidence regarding this new problem, and was unsure how much he would be able to rely on that. He took a seat opposite his industrious housekeeper, and, resting his arms on the table, leaned towards her, quietly clearing his throat to attract her attention. He was so nervous he feared she would hear his stomach churning. She looked up and gave him a brief smile. So, he began: "Mrs. Drew, I would appreciate your advice on a very delicate matter. But, before I say anything, Mrs. Drew, I must know that I can count on your absolute, and confidential, silence concerning this very, very, delicate matter." There was a prolonged silence. Mrs. Drew's expression was very solemn and she paused in her stitching and looked at him attentively. His discomfort caused him to lower his voice again. "I need your assurance that you will mention nothing, or even hint of this, to anyone." Another silence. "Mrs. Drew?"

"Oh! Sorry, Father." She had been studying his face so intently that she now wore a frown of her own, almost as though his anxiety was contagious. "I thought you were going to tell me about the problem Father. Yes, of course, you can rely on me. I've been serving the Church for many years now, and 'ad to keep many a secret." The atmosphere was as sombre as the grave.

He gave a small sigh of relief. "Thank you, Mrs. Drew. Mrs. Drew, I've had a very disturbing visit from a young woman named Bridget."

Mrs. Drew's solemn expression lingered for maybe two or three seconds longer before she exploded with laughter, completely shattering the solemn atmosphere. He sat upright, startled, and offended, by her unexpected outburst. His shock and displeasure must have been very evident, because she did try to compose herself, but, even so, little grins and snorts of suppressed laughter, threatened to spark a fresh outburst of hilarity. Her struggles were so amusing they became contagious and despite his annoyance, he could not suppress a smile of his own. He had never seen anyone laugh so uncontrollably.

"Ahh-ooh! I'm so sorry Father. I'm not laughing at you. 'onest!" Then she was off again, having to wipe tears from her eyes. His impatience began to reassert itself. "Really, Mrs. Drew, I would expect better from you. This is a very serious matter. It seems that I have made a grave mistake in seeking your advice on this subject. If I am really such a huge joke I would certainly appreciate your sharing it with me. God knows, I've had little enough merriment in recent months and certainly nothing to match the scale of your amusement."

Mrs. Drew heaved another big sigh and took a deep breath. "Oooh! I'm so sorry, Father. I will explain later, but please, do go on. Believe me; I will be able to help ye better once I know more about Bridget's visit. And please, be patient. I know ye will understand once I'm able to explain. You see I'm already keeping a secret that involves Bridget." She dabbed at her eyes once more, as a tentative smile, suddenly broadened, and her eyes sparkled.

"Mrs. Drew, this woman is not normal." Now that remark itself was not funny. So it must have been his bewildered expression, or possibly her secret knowledge, but his housekeeper's smile blossomed again. However, it gradually wilted under his impatient stare. "Please, Mrs. Drew, do not make fun of those less fortunate than we. Remember: There but for the grace of God…"

"Oh, I think not Father. Not in this case," she said, and exploded into another fit of laughter, and had to wipe her eyes again. Gradually, her laughter subsided into a series of smiles and chuckles. "I'm not making fun of 'er Father. 'onest I'm not. I'm really sorry that I've got the giggles. I promise you'll understand, but I must know what 'appened, during 'er visit' before I can break a confidence I'm already keepin.'"

Roddy considered her amused expression for several seconds before proceeding. Certainly, her expression was serious and attentive. "Very well then! Mrs. Drew, this lady came here after supper last evening, seeking my advice and help. She said that Reverend Cole used to help her and…" He stood up feeling embarrassed and humiliated.

"Oh no! No, please, do sit down Father. Believe me. I know better than you 'ow serious and important the matter is. And I promise you, I'll not mention one word of what you tell me to another soul. I promise. I promise." She crossed her heart before dabbing at her eyes with a scrap of waste material from the altered coat. He sat down again, but studied Mrs. Drew's face for a long time before continuing, wondering if his youth was an impediment to his housekeeper being able to take him seriously. "Very well then. As I said before: Bridget claimed that the last vicar helped her on a regular basis and she wanted me to be the provider of that help now that he was gone. I told her that I would certainly do my best to satisfy her needs and that seemed to please her... Mrs. Drew, please wipe that smile from your face. You really are trying my patience. I fear I shall have to seek my solutions with a more sober confidant. Something I am most reluctant to try." Mrs. Drew dried her eyes with a handkerchief, then wadded it and placed it in the palm of the hand that covered her mouth – trying to make the action seem casual and relaxed. So he continued:

"Bridget retrieved a book concealed behind the bookshelf and drew the curtains. I was at a loss to understand what was going on. She handed the book to me. Inside was a tape measure. I asked her what these things were for, and she said that Reverend Cole used it to record her progress. But she couldn't read. I would have to read the book to understand.

When I opened the book, I found a series of dates in the left margin, with groups of numbers alongside them in columns. The columns were headed with initials. The entries made no sense to me and, I must confess, I struggled for several minutes in an effort to understand the purpose of the record. When I looked up from the book this lady was standing before me, stark naked. To say that I was shaken is the understatement of the century."

Roddy rose from his chair, raising his eyes and hands to the ceiling. "Mrs. Drew. What in heaven's name is wrong with this woman?" Mrs. Drew's eyes were watering as she struggled to keep her composure. He was certain that his expression was not one of amusement. However, having gone this far he was determined to finish. "I turned my back on Bridget and told her to put her clothes back on. She started to cry. 'But you said you would help me,' she cried. 'I need to be forgiven, and blessed.'

"Her words made no sense to me, and I was terrified that someone would come to the door. Eventually though, she put her clothes back on, crying all the while. I opened the curtains again and sat down, trying to gather my senses, and make some sense of the situation. Mrs. Drew, the sweat was running down my back like a small river. And it was cold in here. It's always cold in here! I told her that I would have to study Reverend Cole's book before I could consider the matter any further. I had to push her out into the street, and even then she made me promise to discuss the matter with her again, after service on Sunday. However, Mrs. Drew, it seems to me that you know a great deal about this Bridget woman and I insist you enlighten me. I could get no sense from her and was obliged to send her on her way crying. God knows what people in the street must have thought." His housekeeper dried her eyes once more, but seemed under control at last.

"Very well, Father…The fact that Reverend Cole was givin' special 'elp to Bridget was supposed to be a secret just between those two. But it's a secret that the 'ole village was keepin', just to save embarrassing the vicar's daughter and 'er family. Now that Bridget's involved you, I feel free to tell you what used to 'appen in this cottage. But you must also keep this between us. She raised her eyebrows and looked at him in a questioning manner. He nodded. "Certainly, Mrs. Drew; you have my word on it."

His housekeeper was better composed now, and began to explain. "Like I said, what used to transpire in 'ere was intended to be a secret between Reverend Cole and Bridget. That shows you just 'ow little that poor man knew about Bridget and 'is 'flock'– as 'e liked to call 'is congregation. The whole village knew about poor 'simple' Bridget and the vicar because she would tell all us women at the well about 'ow 'e 'elped and 'blessed' 'er. Reverend Cole's wife was dead three years before Bridget sought 'is 'elp. And poor, simple, Bridget will never get to be any man's wife. Certainly lots of men wanted 'er, but no man wanted 'er, as a wife. That was why she sought the vicar's 'elp in the first place.' And who could find fault? 'e was a widowa' an' she was a spinster. Live and let live, where there's no 'arm done, we say."

The smile reappeared. " 'e gave more 'elp than she could've 'oped for!" Mrs. Drew had to stifle another short explosive laugh before she could continue. He didn't need any pictures drawn to understand his housekeeper now and he was sure she read that very clearly in his face. Now, it was he having difficulty maintaining a serious expression.

Mrs. Drew continued: "You see, it all began when Bridget confessed all of the wickedly intimate events of 'er life, to Reverend Cole. 'ow some of the men talked about 'er to their friends and 'ow, as the word got around, more men came around. She would cry to the vicar and ask for forgiveness, for not being strong enough to resist them. She said 'e used to scold, and then console 'er. Then they would pray together for 'er greater moral strength and 'e would tell 'er that: provided she did 'er best to improve, and was truly repentant, she would be forgiven. Father Cole told 'er that 'er problems were not really 'er fault. She was being tested, 'e said. Provided she tried 'er best each day, she would gradually improve, and the mistakes she made along the way would be forgiven, but she 'ad to be truly repentant, an' try to improve."

Mrs. Drew continued: "Well, once Reverend Cole told Bridget that she wasn't responsible, she kep' on doin' it with whoever came around. We all figured she liked bein' tested. And, whenever she felt 'guilty', she would trot back to the vicar and tell 'im 'ow she'd 'stumbled'. 'er descriptions of what the men did with 'er certainly disturbed a lot of the women. You know, I really don't think 'disturb' is a strong enough word. Some of the women were openly envious. Bridget really liked that. Father Cole's wife had been dead for three years and we would often see 'im studyin' some of the young'ns in ways that seemed a bit unseemly – for a man of the cloth anyway. Eventually the vicar decided that prayers and kind words weren't working for Bridget. 'e would have to punish her to get the message across." Mrs Drew's smile grew even bigger. "It started with 'im spankin' 'er but Bridget wondered 'ow she would satisfy 'er wicked need and resist the men once she was away from 'im. You can almost guess the rest. 'e said it wouldn't be right for 'er to go back to being 'used' that way, by those lecherous men. That made a sinner of 'er, and adulterers of some of them. So, provided that she promised that it remained their secret, 'e would sacrifice 'imself. In the interests of 'is flock. 'e would satisfy 'er wicked need 'imself. Just to remove the temptation from her and the other sinners. She should consider this 'is special, personal, 'blessing'.

But he stressed the villagers must never learn of 'is sacrifice on their behalf, for that would endanger everyone involved. But, at the well, she would go into great detail every time she 'ad a blessing'. And she swore everyone there to the same secrecy that she'd agreed to with Reverend Cole.

You can see how often he 'blessed' her from the dates in the book. Although they all laughed when she told 'er stories, I can tell you there were a few red and thoughtful faces around that well." Mrs. Drew and Roddy both lapsed into fits of laughter.

After much dabbing of her eyes, Mrs. Drew continued. "The guilt and the worry of being found out must've eaten away at 'im though. Eventually, 'e must 'ave realised the whole village knew. 'e began drinking too much, got slack about preparin' new sermons, an' started repeating old ones. It got worse as time went on. Sometimes 'e would be drunk when 'e was givin' 'is sermons and would talk gibberish. Once, 'e even fell out of the pulpit. Fortunately there was only one young couple left in the church at the time: Meg an' Sailmaker. The rest of the congregation 'ad already left when 'e dozed off during a hymn a few minutes before.

The giggling and the snippy remarks must've made it obvious to 'im, that 'e was found out. The sniggering from the others must 'ave confirmed that 'is 'secret' was out. The poor man never mentioned anything to me though. It was a shame really. Doc 'udson believes it was Bridget's need to tell the women about all their 'carryin' on that was responsible for 'is death. Reverend Cole did ask to be transferred, but the Bishop refused. 'is life must've become unbearable, although no one ever 'eard him complain. Then, one stormy night, 'e walked off the end of the dock wall. Doc 'udson recorded it as an accident. 'e made no mention of 'is drinkin' in 'is report to the Bishop. 'e wanted to spare the vicar's daughter any embarrassment.

"Poor Bridget; she was raised to be a 'good girl'. But nature gave 'er a weak mind and the lustful needs of a 'bad girl'. An attentive young 'usband would've likely solved 'er problem. But she realised it was unlikely she'd ever be someone's wife. She wasn't as smart or capable as the other women. That's why she settled for whatever she could get that first time, in Archer's stable. She used to 'elp Archer feed the 'orse and 'is chickens you see. 'e used to pay 'er with eggs and firewood. Nothing else; I'm certain of that. Archer's a strict and 'onest man. Most women would 'ave avoided the stable after that first time, when one of Archer's callers 'ad found 'er there alone, but she didn't. In fact she found excuses to go there. Said she liked the smell of the 'ay." Mrs. Drew's giggles came back again. "I've been in Archer's stable, you can't smell the 'ay for 'orse shit! Oops!' She clapped a hand over her mouth. "Sorry, Father! Forgot meself for a moment. Bridget told us about that first time, and many other times, many, many times over, but she never named any of the men. We all 'ad our suspicions o' course and some asked 'er to name the men. But she never would.

"And, although she tried to appear secretive, it was only for Reverend Cole's benefit.  In 'er own mind, she felt that what she was doing was alright, provided that she said she was sorry, and 'e forgave her." Mrs. Drew's contagious smile broadened. "And she always 'as 'er sore arse as a reminder that she'd done 'er penance."

Mrs. Drew was quite proud of the fact that she'd confined herself to nothing but a big grin over this last remark. But when she saw Roddy stifling his own laughter, she pointed at him and collapsed onto the kitchen table, close to hysterics. He gave up trying to control his own amusement. His mind was flooded with mental images of these two people playing their little games, in this very room. Gradually their laughter subsided, and Mrs. Drew heaved a couple of long deep sighs before continuing. "Like I said, she never did name any of the men. And it was obvious that there's been quite a few. Some of the womenfolk were mad about that, but others seemed relieved. None of them knew for sure whose men were involved. Some, of course, 'ad reason to suspect their own men but they kept quiet.

"In the beginnin', I'm sure that Father Cole must've convinced 'imself that 'e could provide a more kindly and understandin' solution to 'er needs. It didn't 'urt 'is needs either." Her grin grew bigger than ever. "I can imagine 'im sayin' that. More understandin' I mean. 'e really was a kind man but very lonely after 'is wife died. 'is only daughter 'ad married and moved away. 'e never did 'ave much in common with the people around 'ere. Certainly 'e was kind to Bridget, in private anyway. In public 'e gave 'er no more than a passing glance durin' their affair. For 'er that relationship was the most important thing in 'er life. She didn't go back to Archer's stable anymore. And that made the women of the village 'appier. She seemed to be out-of-the-market to all except Father Cole and that made the women feel less threatened. And they still 'ad Bridget's stories, to entertain 'em, at the well.

"The 'ole village got used to her sayin': 'I'm just a poor, simple minded, girl and God knows I can't 'elp the mistakes I make.' You'll likely 'ear 'er say that yourself one day. Maybe more than you want to."

Her smile quickly faded when she saw by his expression that he didn't consider that allusion as funny as her others. "Yes, very simple is poor Bridget, but sly as a fox. You mark my words, Father. Spiteful too, if she thinks you're makin' fun of 'er. She was always mean, if she thought you meant to do 'er wrong, or ridicule 'er. I remember Violet tellin' a joke at the well one day, and everyone laughin' except Bridget. She 'adn't understood the joke. Everyone else looked at 'er – wondering when she would get it – but she thought they'd all been laughin' at 'er an' blamed the woman who told the joke. You could see it in 'er face, plain as day before she stormed off. When Violet took 'er buckets of water home from the well the next day, she used 'er usual short cut: some stone steps between the cottages just a few paces from the well. She stepped on some small round pebbles on the top step, and 'er feet flew out from under 'er. She fell, real awkward down several steps before she stopped. 'er 'ead was badly cut and she 'ad some broken ribs and terrible bruises. It was weeks before she was able to carry water from the well again. We all took turns in getting 'er daily water, all except Bridget that is. The only place to get those round pebbles is from the riverbed at the other end of the village near Archer's stable. When we asked Bridget if she knew 'ow the pebbles got there, she said: 'No....But God pays debts without money. Don't 'e?' We're all sure Bridget was responsible. You'll need to watch that one Father. You mark my words." Mrs. Drew finished sewing the last button on the altered coat, bit through the thread, and pushed the needle into a spool of thread before dropping it into her needlework basket. Then she stood, and folded the coat over her arm.

"It's not nice to be ignored y' know, much better to be popular. But, this is your problem now Father, that's for sure. You're younger an' much more attractive than Father Cole and a bachelor too. In Bridget's mind you'd be Reverend Cole's natural replacement. I would bet that she spends a lot of time thinking about the pleasures of that new relationship. This cottage is a lot more comfortable than Archer's stable and a lot less stinky. She won't be in any 'urry to go back to that even if she does like the smell of 'ay." This time her smile was fleeting, almost apologetic.

Her mind had obviously progressed beyond the humour caused by his remarks whilst innocent of Bridget's special relationship with Reverend Cole. Mrs. Drew's expression was now very sober indeed and left him in no doubt that he had a major problem. Her words had worsened his growing sense of danger. He respected Mrs. Drew's judgement in matters relating to the people of the village. Of course, she was not aware, of the special reasons that made it imperative that he stay clear of any scandal. Her concern was only for his situation with the church and the village. They were developing a good friendship, however, and he sensed that her regard for him went beyond that of housekeeper and employer. Perhaps she needed a replacement 'someone' to care about, someone to substitute for her son.

He moved from the table to the fireplace, and slumped into the battered old wing chair, to stare into the slumbering fire. However, he found no comfort, or inspiration there. Irritably, he reached out with the toe of his once elegant, but now battered shoe, and jarred the dying logs into a small flurry of sparks and flames. A solution to the Bridget problem would be hard to find.

• • •

At the first hint of daylight, he sprang from his bed, grateful for the opportunity to occupy his mind with thoughts other than those that had ruined his nights rest. He rejuvenated the dying fire, put the kettle on, and was enjoying his first cup of tea when Mrs. Drew made her appearance.

"Well, good morning Father. You're up and about early this mornin'. Is everythin' alright?"

"Yes, Mrs. Drew. Just couldn't help thinking about the Bridget problem. I didn't get much sleep actually. Good morning to you too, by the way."

"Did you come up with any ideas then?"

"I'm afraid not. Your colourful description of that young woman's vindictive personality really got me worried though. I know that Bishop West would welcome any excuse to sack me. He's made it perfectly clear that I am on thin ice with him – especially since the donated clothing incident."

"Well then, we will have to put our minds to it. We'll find a way, don't you worry. Maybe Ernie 'n' Doc 'udson should have a word with the Bishop before any trouble starts."

"Oh no, Mrs. Drew. Let's keep the Bishop out of this, Ernie and Doc too. This must stay strictly between us."

"Alright, Father; if you say so."

• • •

Roddy had just finished breakfast when Sailmaker knocked on his door. "Good mornin', Father. We're ready to help build your fiery cross," he said. Archer's cart, loaded with two long, slender trees that trailed off the back of the cart by about ten feet was outside the cottage and Meg was sitting on the bench seat, with a big smile on her pretty face. "I've got extra spurs and ropes, some old sailcloth and a tub of oily waste," said Sailmaker, as he turned his head to smile at Meg. The bright morning sun was reflecting highlights off the girl's shiny, copper coloured hair and he doubted that any artist could do justice to the picture she presented. Her teasing smile might indicate that she shared Sailmaker's opinion – that the vicar's idea was crazy – but even so, there was no implied criticism in her happy personality.

"Good morning Meg," he said. "Thank you for helping with this little test of mine. Although, I can see from your expression, that you think me as stupid as your beau does."

"Hey! I didn't say you were stupid Father," protested Sailmaker. "Crazy maybe, but not stupid." He was in a very happy frame of mind, as he always was whenever Meg was around. "There's a very fine line between stupid and crazy," Roddy replied. Meg couldn't suppress a chuckle, and Sailmaker was obviously very pleased to have her company for their little experiment on the cliff-top.

"My Dad's going to come to see how we're managing later on," said Meg. "I had to tell him what we're doing, just to get out of some of my chores." Roddy groaned. "Oh no! I suppose the whole village knows what the stupid vicar is up to then?"

"Not the whole village," chuckled Sailmaker. "Some of them are away fishing. But they will know soon enough when we light the cross. Or did you think that no one would notice a fifteen-foot tall cross, burning brightly, on the cliff-top, on a dark night, Father?"

"Oh, let's get on with it," said Roddy as he climbed onto the cart. Of course, curtains were pulled aside as they travelled through the village. Villagers that they passed pointed and giggled as the trio made their way to the cliff-top. "Well, maybe the congregation will be larger on Sunday. There must be plenty of people who would welcome the opportunity to poke fun at the idiot with the crazy ideas, whilst he spouts off in the pulpit," he said.

"Wouldn't be surprised Father. Wouldn't be surprised at all," said Sailmaker as he gave his giggling girlfriend a big smile. "Us two have had a few laughs in church before now, at Father Cole's expense mostly. This is a new experience though – a new play and a new cast." He laughed again and then patted Roddy on the shoulder "Don't worry Father. You're gaining support in the village. There are more people giving you credit, for trying to help, than those that are against you. Meg's Dad, for one, is supporting you lately. That's quite a change of heart considering how you two got along when you first met. Then there's Bessie; she's a staunch champion of yours, and people around here respect her opinion, and Ernie's. Mind you, I like your crazy ideas myself. It's good to have something different to look forward to. It breaks the monotony around here. And we might even get a few laughs."

At the cliff-top Sailmaker checked Roddy's siting of the cross and moved the base some twenty feet to the west. Then they began gathering stones to make a rock crib to support the base of the cross. Sailmaker wired the horizontal member to the upright tree and attached some ropes, with which to pull the cross up into place. "We will have to anchor these ropes as guy lines, to steady the cross Father. I've tried to keep the flames away from the ropes by using wire for the first few feet closest to the cross but it will eventually collapse. We'll be lucky if we get half an hour before the whole thing falls apart."

The cross was wrapped in sailcloth and soaked with tar oil when Ernie and Archer arrived. Ernie was bright and cheerful and obviously in good humour. "Good morning, Father, Sailmaker. Are you about ready for the fiery cross yet?" Archer surveyed the scene with his usual critical expression. "Waste of time and effort, is this. It won't last but a few minutes once it's lit and it'll be useless for guiding the boats home."

"This isn't meant to guide the boats home, Archer," said Roddy. "This is just to help me gauge if this size of cross might be suitable for some plans I have. If it shows promise, we'll try and build something permanent. Something that's protected from the elements."

"Humpf!" was his only response. Ernie smiled. Although he seemed equally doubtful about the project, he was unwilling to criticise. "Are you ready to hoist the cross then Sailmaker?" he asked.

"Just about. I need to set up some anchor points for the guy lines, is all." Half an hour later the cross was erected and secured. A small crowd of villagers had gathered in the area, and they were pointing and chuckling at the cross, and making jokes. The vicar's expression was not a happy one. Ernie smilingly clapped a huge hand on his shoulder, and turned him away from the amused villagers. "Come now Father, there's not much entertainment to be had in this little village of ours. This is a more fascinating event than the arrival of the stagecoach and that's the highlight of the week as a rule. Let them have their fun. Join in. They'll think more of you for that, than if you walk around with a sour face."

So, taking the advice Roddy turned to face the small crowd, holding the lapels of his coat, and, adopting the mannerisms and the voice of a fairground barker, cried out: "Ladies and Gentlemen! I give you our latest Ryeport spectacle: 'The fiery cross!' " He used both hands to indicate the oil-soaked structure. "This was conceived purely for your amusement, by the crazy vicar of Ryeport. Our spectacular opening – and closing – performance will be after sundown tonight. In the meantime I take great pleasure in introducing our fine cast of players, and ask them to take a bow. Please hold your applause until the introductions are completed. I give you: The Ryeport Players."

And so the crew of helpers were introduced as though they were a cast of players. Ernie and Sailmaker joined in the spirit of the act and gave exaggerated bows to their audience. Meg too, with the forefinger of her right hand held coyly under her chin, curtsied deeply – held a fold in her dress with her left – before exploding with laughter. Archer was the only spoiler to the act and he stomped off muttering about the foolishness of some people who had nothing better to do with their time. So, Roddy introduced him whilst he was stalking off, as though he was the villain of the piece, following him offstage as he twirled an imaginary moustache and 'humphing' and muttering. The crowd laughed, and broke into applause. Then he asked the cast to come forward for a second round of applause. "Ladies and Gentlemen, I give you The Ryeport Players!" Ernie laughed, and added: "The players are to be my guests at the inn. The rest of you can buy your own ale. This is more fun than a lot of the stagecoach stories and the day's not over yet."

About half an hour before sunset, Roddy helped Sailmaker row his small boat out of the harbour. The sea was calm, with only a sliver of crescent moon to lighten the night when Sailmaker and Roddy took up position about a quarter of a mile out from the harbour entrance. They signalled Ernie and Meg when they were just off The Dragon's Tail. Ernie lit the cross and it was soon blazing fiercely. The beacons were already lit.

Sailmaker first directed the boat straight at the cross, then moved right and left to observe how well the blinds would mask parts of the cross. Roddy signalled the cliff-top, and the blinds were moved closer together. But they were not tall enough to be effective at obscuring the horizontal arm of the cross until they were too close inshore. Even so, there was reason for hope. The cross was certainly a distinctive and spectacular sight. Obviously it would need a lot more work, but the potential was there. Roddy was kept busy making notes about the positioning of the blinds and the cross itself.

Some incoming fishing boats hailed them as they drew close, wanting to know what was going on and some of the men crossed themselves at the sight of the blazing crucifix, obviously disturbed by the unexpected spectacle. Sailmaker promised to tell them the whole story at the inn. He knew that would please Ernie. The fiery cross was quite striking while it lasted, but, as Sailmaker had predicted, it lasted less than half an hour, collapsing in a shower of sparks and small flames as the junction of the cross burnt through. However, most of the village had turned out to watch and they cheered and applauded The Ryeport Players, both on the cliff-top and at the jetty, when Sailmaker brought his boat alongside.

Later, at the inn, the vicar was obliged to explain their actions, and give a small demonstration of what he thought might be possible as far as a church/lighthouse was concerned. Although there was some interest at first it quickly waned when Archer pointed out that no one would pay to build a new church in Ryeport, let alone such a distinctive one. The idea was quickly relegated to the category of crazy dreaming. Ernie was smiling though and he did his best to keep the topic alive. Finally, Roddy went home to modify his sketches. Moggy sat on the table watching him draw and occasionally swatting at his pencil. At least he was company, of a sort. And, he never criticised.

# CHAPTER 9

## *The coachman's tale*

The villagers had lost interest in the 'fiery cross', quickly accepting Archer's comments regarding both the effectiveness and the financial prospects of ever completing such a project. Nevertheless, Roddy busied himself with diagrams and sketches, trying to make the most of the sparse information gleaned from their short-lived experiment. His knowledge of geometry and navigation was very thin, but he was convinced that his idea had merit. However, having trouble developing a convincing presentation, he worked late into the night, finally going to bed with little to show for all the efforts of the 'Ryeport Players'. The following morning, he was awakened by the appetising smell of bacon frying. Moggy had already abandoned the bed in the hope of tasty scraps from the kitchen. His own taste buds were excited too, and Mrs. Drew's hearty breakfast of fried bread, eggs and bacon, soon got his morning off to a good start.

Since their trip to Nextwest, he had suggested that Mrs. Drew join him for breakfast. He suspected that without someone else to cook for, she would most likely miss or skimp on meals. She had been pleased to agree, mainly, he suspected, for the relief it gave her meagre income, but he hoped that she also enjoyed having some company. He was also able to learn more about the village during their meals together. Their conversations were usually enlightening, and this day was no exception. Before she left Mrs. Drew was explaining that some of the fishing boats would periodically sell smoked and pickled fish in the small villages along the coast, usually east of Ryeport. Such trips lasted two to three days and once their stock was sold, the boats would return home, fishing on the way. It was a way to earn a little extra money to help them through lean periods, and today was the start of such an event.

Mrs. Drew had now left and he was left alone, labouring over his next sermon when he heard the sound of a post horn announcing the arrival of the stagecoach. He was tempted to abandon the sermon and hurry to the inn for news of the outside world, and perhaps an entertaining tale from the coachmen. His days had become a monotonous routine and any diversion was most welcome. Ernie, always eager for the opportunity to sell extra ale and food, had encouraged the stagecoach drivers to detour to Ryeport whenever they could find an opportunity to do so. As an incentive, he would provide the coachmen with free food and ale, in exchange for news and stories and they took advantage of his offer at every opportunity.

The post horn was a sure summons for those out of sight of the inn. Ernie had made it clear to the coachmen that their 'celebrity' status at the inn, together with the benefits that went with it, were dependant on the money spent by locals that wanted to hear their news or stories. Roddy rose from his seat and struggled with his yearning for a change of pace before reluctantly returning to his task. "I can't believe how desperate I've become for fresh news or company since I've been here," he moaned. "However, I must get this sermon finished. And I still have to solve the Bridget problem."

At the inn Meg had cut fresh bread and cheese, cold meats, and prepared a dish of pickles, whilst her father ushered the coachmen to a table where they could be clearly seen by all. The driver took a leather mail pouch from his companion and handed it to Ernie. "For Cap'n Hawksworth, Ernie. This is gettin' t' be pretty reg'lar. Are you expectin' 'im t'day?"

Ernie shook his head as he took the pouch. "No, but he might be expecting this. I'll see he gets it. Here, have a drink to wet your whistle." He placed tankards in front of the two men. "What news from the outside world lads, anything interesting?" The driver took a long pull at the ale and wiped his mouth on the grimy cuff of his sleeve. "Aye, there's some worrisome goin' on 'ereabouts, that's for sure." He looked around, checking to ensure that his audience was paying attention, before taking another long drink from the tankard. Ernie was getting impatient. "Well, out with it man" But the driver wasn't to be hurried, and drained the last of his ale in a very deliberate manner, before returning the tankard to the table as he maintained eye contact with Ernie. "Aye, there's somethin' worrisome afoot right enough."

Ernie's lips tightened a little as, taking the hint, he refilled the jug and topped up the relief driver's too, just in time to stop him following his partner's lead. Meg put food in front of the driver and his mate, and Ernie waved an arm in his daughter's direction as she returned to the bar. "There's good tasty food at the bar for you people who'd like a bite. Meg'll take your orders and put it on your tab! Let's give these fellows a chance to eat before they give us their news." Then, rolling his eyes to the ceiling in mock despair, he said: "Because, I know they're too well-mannered to talk with their mouths full." He had created a quiet period for the villagers to fill whilst they waited for the drivers to finish eating. Hopefully that would tempt the locals to eat too. A sudden flurry of activity at the bar seemed to relax the innkeeper however, and he gave the driver a nod.

The driver pointed to his well-filled cheeks, and held that finger in the air. Everyone seemed to be hanging on his every move, and he obviously enjoyed the attention. One more swig at the tankard and he began. "Smugglers!" he said, and followed that with a long pause. "Well, what about 'em." Ernie had been satisfied with the activity at the bar, and was now as anxious as his clients for the story.

"There's a bloke come down from London," said the driver. "Corby, 'is name is. I dropped 'im at the Coach an' 'orses yesterday. Didn't know ooh or what 'e was then, o' course. Found that out later." He took another pull at the jug, to keep his audience waiting a while longer, obviously, intent on 'dragging out' his story. "Well, we pulls into the yard, and the passengers gets out an' drifts into the inn to put the feeding on. Good grub too, old man Shields keeps a good 'ouse 'e does."

"Get on with it man." Ernie was tiring of the driver 'milking' the situation.

"Alright, Ernie, keep your shirt on. Just makin' a comment, that's all. Anyway, after I'd 'ad somethin' to eat, and a couple o' pints, I went back to the coach, like I always does. Once the 'orses are put away y'see, the coach is nice 'n' quiet – private like. So I usually get inside, an' get me 'ead down for a while, just to let the meal go down." He looked at his companion, who nodded his confirmation. "Anyway, I'd only been there a few minutes when I 'ears footsteps. So I lift up a bit to look out the wind'a – real careful like – to see who it is. It's a young city gent. Carried 'imself like an officer, 'e did." The coachman squared his shoulders and tipped his nose in the air, in imitation. "'e looks all around the yard and then starts walkin' towards the coach. I quickly lays down and makes out I'm asleep. But before 'e gets to the coach, I 'ear more footsteps, and a voice I recognise as one o' me passengers.' 'Manning?' Me passenger calls out. 'Aye Sir,' says the posh gent. 'Mr. Corby, I presume?'

'Correct.' I 'ear Corby come closer to the coach, an' stop, just a couple o' steps from where I was layin.

'It's a pleasure to meet you, Sir,' this bloke Manning says. 'Your reputation in the service precedes you.' 'e says, real posh, like. 'Congratulations on your recent success on the east coast.'

Corby, soundin' a bit annoyed, sez: 'Quiet man, someone might be listenin."

'Oh, we are quite alone, Sir! The stablemen have put the horses away and are eating their lunch. There's no one else due in the yard.'

'What about the coachmen? Will they be coming out?'

'I looked into the bar a few minutes ago Sir. They were still eating. They'll not be out again until the stablemen put up the fresh team.' Manning sez. 'When the coach is ready, they'll let the driver know. But that won't be for an hour or so, Sir. The coach isn't due out 'til two o'clock.'

'Very well then, tell me about the informer,' sez Corby.

'I don't know much about him, Sir. Captain Whitestone is keeping his identity secret. It seems that the informer is still working with the smugglers and the captain doesn't want to risk him being discovered. 'e sez, 'e could be the source of valuable information in the future.'

'I see. But you are certain of the time and the place of the next run?"'

Ernie smiled, as he watched the driver 'play' the parts of the two men, squaring his shoulders and tipping his nose in the air, when he spoke Manning's words, and lowering his head and pulling a grim face when he played Corby. He'd obviously practised this performance and, when he remembered, he took pains to pronounce his aitches – actually over emphasising them – when speaking as Manning. "'Oh yes, Sir,' sez this bloke, Manning. 'Our scouts found kindling and pitch torches for lighting warning fires Sir – all hidden under hedges at the site. Pathways up the cliff have been cleared of loose stones, and squared off to provide better footing. There are also some heavy ringbolts anchored to the cliff at strategic places. It looks as though they've been put there to secure lifting tackle. It would be too difficult to carry contraband up that steep cliff, the captain says. So, it appears they plan to hoist the goods up the cliff to a waiting shore party on the cliff-top. It would have to be a valuable cargo to go to this much trouble, Sir.'

'Will we be able to snare them all do you think? Could they 'ave seen your men checking the site?' sez Corby.

'Yes, Sir. To your first question that is,' sez Manning. 'We're certain that we can get them all. None of our people have been near the place since we confirmed it as their intended landing site. But we do have the area under constant watch from the woods on the north side of the road. We have two men, in deep cover, with spyglasses. The smugglers should have no suspicion they've been betrayed.'

'What about our men? Do we have enough?' Corby said.

'Yes Sir,' sez Manning. 'and more men are arriving discretely, every day, from three counties. They're drifting into local villages, in ones and twos to avoid suspicion. We also have men watching suspects all day, every day. That has been going on for nearly a week now. There is also a force of fifty militiamen on the pretence of being on exercise, camped within an hour's march. A fast cutter has also been dispatched to a concealed location just west of the landing beach. She will close the exit from the bay on our signal. Revenue cutters from the two closest divisions will be hidden close by too. We'll have them surrounded Sir. The cutters will prevent the smugglers from putting back to sea and the militia will seal off any escape by land. These smugglers will rue the day they chose to deprive the King of his lawful dues, that's for sure.'

'Well done!' sez Corby. 'Now, I understand that you have horses available, so that I can soon meet Captain Whitestone.'

'Yes, Sir. They're in the stable. Thursday night we'll teach these rogues a lesson that will reverberate throughout the country. We think we have the Spotsman under surveillance too, Sir. Our informer tells us that he never gets involved with the actual run ashore, but he doesn't know if the Spotsman is actually the head man in the ring. He gave us three names, one of them being his contact. All three are being watched around the clock. If the Spotsman isn't their top man, we have ways to persuade the other prisoners to identify him.'

'Good! I'd like to inspect the arrangements for myself of course, but discretely. We don't want anyone, other than yourself and Whitestone, to know that I'm here. That alone might warn them off.'" The coach driver had been lowering his head and speaking in hoarse, confidential tones in an effort to add more drama to his story and his audience was intent on his every word, being very quiet and attentive. Now he raised his head and looked from his empty pot then to Ernie, then back again to his pot. Ernie, dutifully, refilled it. The driver's mate looked crestfallen. "I don't know what you've done to deserve a fresh pint," the innkeeper said to the mate and indicated the driver. "He did all the talking – and took all the risks." But he topped up the man's pot anyway.

"Aye," said the driver. "an' I might not be 'ere today if that officer 'ad taken another step towards the coach, 'e'd 'ave looked right down on me, so 'e would. Most likely, 'e'd 'ave arrested me, as a smuggler's spy. Thursday's gonna be a bad day for the 'trade' 'ereabouts, you mark my words. Some local necks will be stretchin' some of the King's rope I'm thinkin'."

He swallowed the rest of his ale, followed that with a piece of cheese, a pickle and a loud belch. "Beggin' yer pardon m'dear," he said to Mrs. Drew. "Be kind enough to blame Ernie's gassy ale for me bad manners." He stood up and swatted his mate with his hat. "Come on then, you layabout. We're runnin' be'ind our time now. We've got to make that up. You check the luggage. I'll check the 'arness, an' we'll be on our way. Thank you innkeeper, for your kind 'ospitality I'm sure." Then, surveying the unusually quiet group, he said: "Now, I'm trustin' you lot to keep our little bit o' news secret. My life's in your 'ands, so it is. That's 'ow much I trust ye. At least, I 'ope I can trust ye." He fingered his neck thoughtfully. "This may not be the prettiest neck 'ereabouts, but I don't think it would look any better for being a couple of inches longer."

When the coachmen left the bar the patrons remained unusually quiet. Nobody spoke until jingling harness and the clatter of hooves announced the departure of the coach. That seemed to give the coachman's audience leave to scurry away and carry the news to the rest of the village. Their sombre attitude, however, was in stark contrast to the noisy banter and laughter that usually resulted from the coachmen's visits.

Alone in the bar now, Ernie and Bessie Drew were looking at each other in stunned silence, obviously concerned. "This is bad news Bessie," Ernie was shaking his head as he spoke. "Hawksworth was talking about this man Corby the other night. Right here in the bar. Didn't mention him by name, mind you, but it's obvious it's the same man the coachman was talking about. Hawksworth says he's ruthless in dealing with smugglers. Lots of 'traders' back east have been hung because of him. Doesn't matter he says, if you were in on the run – delivering, or just buying, he'll hunt you down. Hawksworth said this bloke's determined to make everyone too scared to even think about being involved with the trade. He's made a real name for himself back east, he said. And I'm not too sure about Hawksworth either; he was trying to get me talking about local smugglers. He didn't ask any direct questions mind you. You might think he was just making idle conversation but I'm pretty sure he's a revenuer. People need to watch what they say around him. He seems friendly enough. Buys drink for lads in the bar and all but I think he's just trying to get them talking about the trade. I've heard him make some stupid statements about smuggling in these parts. But I think he does that deliberately, hoping to be corrected. That way, he might get an idea about who is 'in-the-know'. People need to watch him, Bessie. We might lose some of our own villagers in this net. The Custom people would likely have spies posted, watching for clues and having an informer gives them a big advantage. If the smugglers ever find out who the informer is," he drew a finger across his throat, "he won't last long." Bessie was nervously twisting her apron with one hand as she placed her unfinished ale on the bar with the other. "It looks bad Ernie; we should try and get the word out. Do you know any villagers who might be involved in the trade? It seems there's no time to warn those already at sea."

Ernie gave her a wry smile. "I've got my suspicions Bessie, but that's all. The word will be out already. You saw the people scuttle out of here as soon as the coach left. It might be that this was just a story by the coachmen. They could even be spies too. Maybe Hawksworth and his friends are hiding outside, watching to see who runs where. Now there's a thought!" Ernie went to the door and looked around. "No one in sight," he called to Bessie. "Cripes! Now I've got the jitters."

"I've got to go, Ernie," Bessie said, and squeezed past him in the doorway. "The vicar will be wondering where I am."

"Bessie, you've not finished your ale." But Bessie appeared not to hear; she was almost running as she headed for Roddy's cottage. Her haste was nervous and indecisive and on reaching the cottage she paused, looking towards the harbour, as if unsure of what to do. Finally, she muttered. "Give 'im a chance girl, can't see it making things any worse," and she rapped, on the door and walked in. Ernie had been watching her erratic progress and looked very puzzled. As she walked into the cottage he shrugged and said: "Oh well, shouldn't waste good ale", and finished Bessie's ale with one long swallow.

Roddy was sitting with his quill pen poised in his right hand, still working at his sermon, when Mrs. Drew entered the cottage. "Hello, Mrs. Drew. Were the coachmen entertaining today? I didn't hear any laughter. Good Lord woman, are you alright? You look as though you've had the fright of your life."

Bessie sat at the table facing him and looking very grim. She nodded. "I'm alright Father." She looked down at her clasped hands for a few seconds, uncomfortably aware of his focused attention.

"Mrs. Drew?"

"Father, a little while ago you asked if you could trust me to keep a secret. At this very table. Remember?"

"Yes, of course, I remember Mrs. Drew. Has something happened with Bridget?"

"No Father." She held her hand up to silence him. "Please. Can I ask you for some advice now and ask you to keep secret the things that I will tell you?"

"Of course," he nodded to emphasise his agreement. There were a few moments of awkward silence before she said, "I don't know where to begin."

"Try the beginning."

"No, I'll start with the coachman's story," she said, and recounted the events at the inn, including Ernie's comments. Roddy listened intently, watching his housekeeper's agitation grow with every fresh disclosure. "So you see, Father, if any of the village lads are involved its most likely those already at sea. They could be picking up trade goods on their way 'ome after selling their smoked fish and the like. I hadn't thought of it before, but it's a good opportunity to meet suppliers at sea and bring in trade goods while lookin' like they're returnin' from 'onest business. But this time, they can't be warned off because the Revenuers know the time, and the landin' beach. The smugglers will land the goods, and the revenue cutters will close the bay be'ind 'em. And the Customs men will be 'idden on the cliff in front of 'em, just waitin' for 'em to come ashore. They won't stand a chance. This is all because of the informer. What can we do? What can anyone do?" Suddenly her expression changed and she looked very scared. "Oh Father,

I shouldn't 'ave told you. You're a man of the church. You must believe the Customs men are in the right." She clapped both hands to her face looking at him anxiously.

Roddy got up walked around the table, and put an arm around her shoulders. "Relax Mrs. Drew; I'm on your side. If our villagers are involved, and you don't know for sure that they are, we have to find a way to warn them. As for believing the Revenuers are in the right, well, I've seen how difficult it is to support a family here by hard work alone. If smuggling's the only way to keep your family fed and clothed, and provided there's no violence, smuggling seems to me to be a lesser evil than having good men hung for merely depriving the King of a little tax money Now, those opinions of mine are another secret between us. Agreed?" Bessie nodded. The relief on her face was plain to see but she pulled at the collar of her dress, as though it were too tight around her neck. "There's more, Father."

He had been about to return to his seat but turned to face her again. His housekeeper's voice was hushed. "I'm involved too. Well, my sister actually and I only found out when you took me to Nextwest. She's not involved in the run of course. Marie just receives and delivers some goods for a little extra money. She needs it, to make ends meet. Times are 'ard for 'er, Father. There's been no man in 'er life for seven years now. She took on this little bit of 'trade' business to 'elp pay the rent. She wanted me to get involved too, for the same reason. The villagers have been good to me, Ernie in particular but there's only so much they can do, an' I don't want to be a burden. The church pays me a little, of course, but a body couldn't live on it. I get a little money for cleanin' fish too. But that's only when they need extra 'elp."

"Bessie – may I call you Bessie?"

"Of course."

"Bessie, we'll work something out. Who could I talk to in the village that might be able to get a boat out to meet our fishermen, and warn them?"

"No one, Father; all the workin' boats are at sea. There's Sailmaker's small dinghy, of course. But that's no good for heavy seas. It's only suitable for around the 'arbour really."

"Is he likely to be sympathetic to the Crown or the villagers Bessie?"

"I can't say for sure Father. But he's a good friend; I think he'd put the village first."

"Then he'll be my first choice, Bessie. I like him too. He's been helping me understand the village and its problems. I'll go down to his shop and see if I can get some advice. I'll be careful with my questions though because I don't know for sure how people will respond in matters like this."

Roddy's mind was in turmoil. It was essential for him to stay out of trouble and now it seemed that some of his congregation, including his newly won friend, Bessie, were at risk in this Customs ambush. He hurried to the east side of the harbour where Sailmaker's rigging shop was located. Three villagers were talking with him, but, as soon as it became obvious that Roddy was headed there, the group broke up, leaving Sailmaker to face him alone. He was sitting on a keg splicing an eye into a ropes-end and looked up as he drew close.

"Good day to you Father. To what do I owe the pleasure of this visit, another crazy idea perhaps?"

"Hello, Sailmaker. Sorry if I drove your friends away. I seem to have that effect on lots of people hereabouts. It's as though I had the plague or something equally distasteful."

"Oh, they were just passing the time of day, Father. Just about ran out of things to say when you showed up. Something I can help you with?" He set the splice aside and rose up, stretching to ease his stiff muscles.

Roddy removed his hat and sat on the keg that he'd just vacated. He was wearing Tom's old hand-me-down shoes, which he hadn't yet broken in, and his feet were sore. "I hope you don't mind me stealing your seat Sailmaker but my legs and feet ache so. I imagine that you've heard the news brought by the coachmen. Were you at the inn by any chance?"

"No Father. They've started to repeat some of their old stories now. I do get tired of hearing them re-hash the same old stuff. The coachmen haven't had too much news lately. But they don't miss an opportunity to squeeze free food and ale from Ernie – often using stale stories to do that. Anyway, I thought I'd give it a miss today. But the chaps that just left were telling me I missed a real piece of news this time."

Roddy stood up, thoughtfully weighing his words carefully before speaking. The villagers were showing some improvement in their attitude towards him; with Sailmaker, Ernie and Bessie Drew being the ones he felt most comfortable with. But he still didn't know them very well, and was unsure if he should confide in Sailmaker.

*From the author's sketchbook*

"I felt the same way about the coachmen's stories Sailmaker. But Mrs. Drew just gave me their news, and I'm very concerned. It seems that some of our villagers might be in danger. Is that possible?"

"Oh Father, I don't think you should worry about that. I'm sure that everything will be alright." Sailmaker's manner was dismissive, and reminded him of when he first asked for his help with the fiery cross. He began to feel angry; the heat rose in his face and he felt his muscles tense. "Now see here Sailmaker, I realise I'm still an outsider in this village, and regarded as a useless, preaching, sponger, satisfied with the easy life of a do-nothing vicar, but I am genuinely concerned for the people of this village. So please, don't you treat me like a fool. If Mrs. Drew is concerned, then we should all be concerned. She knows the people here better than most – or wouldn't you agree?" His anger obviously surprised Sailmaker. He was used to him meekly accepting the off-handed treatment that most villagers doled out to him. Still bristling, Roddy continued: "I've been told that some of our men, already at sea, might be involved. Also, that Revenuers are watching the landing site and that will prevent the warning-off fire from being lit. That's true isn't it?"

"Well, I don't think you should assume that any of our villagers are involved." Sailmaker was waffling and Roddy got the feeling that he was unsure of how much he could confide in him. "I don't just assume," he replied. "I'm bloody sure, some are! There wouldn't be so much concern amongst the villagers otherwise. I'd bet that was exactly what you and your friends were talking about when I turned up."

"Well, we were talking about the coachman's story."

"Of course you were. I imagine that's just about all anybody is talking about today. Now look, it doesn't bother me if some of our people make some extra money by smuggling. Provided no violence is involved, that is. I couldn't condone that. I certainly don't consider that depriving the King of a little tax money is as great a sin as breaking a man's neck at the end of a rope, especially if that was the only way to feed his family. I'm not blind. I can see how hard it is for our villagers to eke out a living here and I certainly wouldn't inform on them to some Revenue officer. Our people need their families to eat reasonably well, and stay warm and healthy. If that deprives the King of a few guineas, I really don't care." He realised that his manner was intense and that Sailmaker hadn't seen this side of him before and was looking at him as though he was a complete stranger.

"Look, Father, no disrespect, but what do you think you could do on the villagers behalf? You could even get arrested yourself. Especially if a revenuer heard what you just said."

"I realise that. I also know that I'm putting myself in your hands by saying these things. I have to trust you because some people, who matter to me, are in danger, and you happen to be one of the few people around here that will give me the time of day."

"What do you suggest then Father?"

"I don't know yet. I'm new at this. Tell me what you know about the warning-off signal."

"Well, I don't know first-hand you understand," he said cautiously, "but I'm told that the smugglers place men to watch for any Customs or militia men in the area where the goods are to be run ashore. If they see anything suspicious, they're supposed to light a bonfire on the cliff above the landing site, and then, run for cover. Because there's always a chance the weather could wet their kindling, they sometimes prepare pitch torches and protect some dry kindling near the place where the fire would have to be lit. Obviously they don't build the fire before they have to. That would really tip their hand. In fact, if you're caught preparing such a fire, that alone would convict you. From the coachman's story, it seems that the Revenuers have discovered the hidden makings of the fire for this run. I'd expect them to leave everything undisturbed, and remain hidden until after the shore party had given the all-clear signal to the smuggler's boats – generally they'd use a shuttered lantern. The Revenue men would only reveal themselves to prevent the smugglers from lighting the signal fire. Once the boats hit the beach, the Revenuers would arrest the shore party, and the smugglers would walk in to the trap, thinkin' all was safe. Revenue cutters would then come in behind their boats, preventing them from putting back to sea. It would be a very successful ambush."

Roddy was puzzled. "Why can't we take a boat out to warn them instead of lighting a fire?"

"Because we don't know where they are. They aren't in the habit of telling people what they're about, let alone give details of when and where. Chances are we'd miss 'em if we went looking. There's a lot of water out there to hide in and we'd likely get arrested ourselves. There are also the cutters to worry about. They're a lot faster than any fishing boat and well-armed. You can bet they're hiding in some cove or inlet already and our boats could never outrun them."

"Does the fire have to be in the same vicinity as the landing spot?"

"Well somewhere reasonably close, otherwise the smugglers might think a barn or haystack was on fire."

Roddy sat holding his head in his hands. "Sailmaker, we have to do something." He stood up and began pacing. "They will be landing in the dark right?"

"Well that's what smugglers usually do," said Sailmaker, sarcastically, "but, according to people that claim they can read the signs, there'll likely be a little moonlight, and clear skies." Roddy stopped pacing and turned to Sailmaker. "What about a fire at sea? Surely the boats wouldn't come ashore if there was a fire out there, somewhere off the landing beach. Even if it was a genuine, accidental fire on board a boat for instance, the smugglers would have to give up the idea of running ashore because the fire would attract too much attention. The Revenuers wouldn't be able to put out a fire out at sea and if the cutters tried to do it, they would give themselves away."

"How do you suggest we start a fire at sea?"

"An old boat maybe, loaded with dry wood and tar. Or a raft perhaps."

"And how would we get away from the burning boat without a Revenue cutter seizing us? Always supposing we could find an old boat that someone is willing to give us?"

"Oh I don't know," Roddy snapped angrily. "I'm new at this." His frustration was showing. "Couldn't a raft be towed into position, with the fire set to burn under cover for a while – long enough for someone to get away?"

"Possibly, but remember the Revenue cutters. They'll be watching the shoreline and any harbour the smugglers might make a run for. And we don't have a boat to burn, or time to build a raft. The run is tomorrow night, remember."

"Tomorrow night, I thought it was tonight?"

"No, it's tomorrow."

"But Mrs. Drew thought it was tonight. Isn't that what the coachman said?"

"Well it's not tonight, it's tomorrow for sure."

"How do you know that?"

"Father, I just know that. And I can't tell you how I know." Sailmaker drew a finger across his throat.

"My God; you're involved too!"

"No, not really, but I do have more reliable information." Then he hung his head as he said: "I did sell some lifting tackle and I had to go to a cliff-top, above the landing beach, and install it. I suppose that means I am a little involved. Not in the run itself, mind you. I want no part of any smuggling and you are now the only person in the village who knows about my rigging the tackle, except for one other person that is. Now I'm in your hands." Sailmaker looked up, and from his expression, Roddy could see he already regretted telling him so much. He was dumbstruck. "For God's sake man, stop telling me what we can't do, and tell me what we can do. Your life is on the line here, as much as any of the smugglers." Sailmaker looked at him despairingly for a few moments before saying: "Well, there is Bannerman's old boat. It has a broken keel, and a couple of holes in it, and no rudder. It'll never sail again – although Bannerman would never admit that. He's determined he'll fix it up someday. He doesn't like working someone else's boat. He's not that impressed with you either, Father. If he knew you wanted to burn his boat, he'd likely make sure you were in it when that happened." He looked at Roddy with an expression of genuine concern but Roddy ignored Sailmaker's warning. "Will Bannerman's boat float?"

"Not without some repairs. And even then, not for long. If the weather gets up, it wouldn't last more than a few minutes."

"Can we fix it up so it would last long enough for a bonfire aboard? Something like a Viking funeral?" Sailmaker gave him a grim smile. "Another crazy idea Father? It might last long enough for our funeral. But how do we get it out of the harbour without the Revenue cutter spotting us? They will be looking for sails remember, they show up in the moonlight and there will be lookouts everywhere. We'd be spotted for sure. And any boat will get boarded tomorrow night."

"Where should the signal fire be lit? What area?"

"About three miles west of Sorry Cove."

"Aha! Sorry, Cove. You believe the Revenue cutters would be watching the harbours – but would they be watching Sorry Cove? Would they notice a boat, without sails? Couldn't your dinghy be rowed through The Chute, and tow the fireboat into position? Someone could anchor it, light it up, and then row back home the same way. Surely the Revenuers will not be watching Sorry Cove. And there would be no sail to reflect the moonlight." Sailmaker remained silent. "Well?" Roddy's impatience was getting the better of him. Sailmaker raised a silencing hand. "Be quiet man; I'm thinking." Roddy complied, realising that he'd proposed a possible but difficult solution. It seemed like an eternity before Sailmaker looked up again. "I think we may be able to do it."

"Great," said Roddy. "Let's get to it." Sailmaker's hand was raised again. "Be quiet for a minute!" Now it was his turn to be impatient. "Listen to how we might do it, and what's involved. First: I think I can put a couple of patches on Bannerman's old boat. It won't be pretty, but we're going to burn it anyway. I'll have to seal any open seams too. Maybe punch in some oakum, or patch the damaged parts with oilskin, or copper tingles. She's been dry for months and, even without the holes, she'd leak like a sieve." Sailmaker was thinking aloud, and appeared oblivious of him now. He was visualising whether a botched repair might keep the boat afloat long enough for their purposes. "The broken keel won't matter much for this trip," he said, "provided I can make it watertight. We could fill the boat with kindling and scrap pieces of sail, soaked with tar and oil. The toughest part of the job will be lighting it up and getting away without being spotted. Maybe I could set a little gunpowder amongst some kindling. Fasten one end of a fuse into the powder and leave the other end hanging over her stern. Then we could anchor the boat in position, light the fuse and row like hell for The Chute. The fuse will ignite the powder and cause a small explosion that should scatter flaming pieces through the rest of the oil-soaked sail and wood. By then we should be out of sight, unless the cutter spots us. I feel pretty sure Hawksworth is a revenuer too. The mail pouch delivered today was most likely instructions for him to pay close attention to the village, so we don't want him seeing what we're up to. Or see us coming or going." Sailmaker's mind then seemed to return to his present surroundings.

"My little dinghy will have a job pulling Bannerman's old broken boat, and it will yaw and drag real bad. It's a much heavier boat than mine. It'll be heavy going even with both of us on the oars. Also it will take some time to get the boat ready, but the tide will be on the ebb and it'll be dark when we have to leave. That'll help. There's another problem though. Not all of the fishing boats will be away overnight. Some are still fishing locally. If any boats come in early, we wouldn't want them to see us towing Bannerman's boat. They'd talk about it at the inn. Hawksworth will remember that when our warning fire is lit. That alone could get us hung." He'd been excited by Sailmaker's idea but now caught his concern. "Hawksworth; I'd forgotten about him. He's expected at The Harbour Light to pick up his mail bag. If you're right about him, and I think you could be, then he'll be watching the shore and harbour. He may even have some hidden help. This may not be such a good idea. You could be arrested and likely hang alongside the smugglers."

"Not just me Father. I can't manage this alone. Your neck would stretch as well as mine if we're caught. Or do you want to back out now?"

The vicar hesitated, this attempt to warn the smugglers had suddenly taken a dangerous turn for him personally. He managed a grim little smile. "No, Sailmaker. I won't back out. But we must arrange for someone to keep Hawksworth's nose away from the harbour or we could well play into their hands. Can you think of a way of doing that?"

"Not right now but we'll have to come up with something."

"Do you think Ernie might help us? Or would he side with the Revenuers?" Sailmaker laughed. "Ernie wants no part of any smuggling. A friend of his, another innkeeper, east of here, was hung a couple of years ago. That left his family absolutely destitute. Ernie's first concern is always his family. If he knew I was involved with smuggling, I'm sure my hope of marrying Meg would be gone. But, if he thought Customs men, or anyone else for that matter would harm the village, he'd fight them all single handed!"

"I see. Then where do we start? And when?"

"First, Father, you must go back to Bessie. Tell her that we have a way to warn off the boats but we need her to keep Hawksworth away from the harbour this evening. Get Ernie involved if she has to, but only if she has to. I don't think it will be a problem. Hawksworth rarely comes down here anyway." He held a forefinger over his lips. "But don't tell Bessie what we are going to do. The less she knows the smaller the chance she might let something slip accidentally. Then, get back here as fast as you can. I'm going to see just how much work I have to do on Bannerman's boat. He won't be pleased, he always intended to repair it. We'll be killing a dream of his with this Viking funeral of yours. Everyone else knows it will never be fit for fishing again but he'd never agree. I'll put a couple of quick patches on the hull, then we'll tow it into The Chute tonight and beach it in Sorry Cove. I'll finish the repairs there tomorrow. You have a talk with Bessie now, while I check out the boat. Hurry now, get Bessie working, then get back here as fast as you can. Once the boat is patched, I'll go for supper at the inn. You should make an appearance about that time too. We must keep our usual routines as far as possible; Hawksworth may be watching. Then tomorrow night, you get back here about nine o'clock, and we'll arrange this 'Viking Funeral' of yours."

"Good man," Roddy said and clapped him on the shoulder before hurrying back to Bessie. Sailmaker was shaking his head when he left, saying. "Now who would have believed that?"

 Bessie was pacing nervously when Roddy entered the cottage. She turned to face him. "Well, Father?" She asked, anxiously.

"It's alright Mrs. Drew – Bessie. We have a way to warn off the boats. But we need someone to make sure Hawksworth doesn't wander down to the harbour area until after dark. Do you think you could keep him occupied at the inn, if he looks like he's going to do that?"

"Why?"

"Well, we think he may be a Revenue spy. What we're doing will take some preparation and, if he sees, or gets wind of it, he'll become suspicious. If he should even remember what he saw here – even after the run – it'll be enough to get us arrested."

"What are you going to do?"

"I promised I wouldn't tell you. Sailmaker thinks that if this thing goes badly you'd be better off not knowing anything. And I think that's wise too."

"Sounds like you don't trust me to keep my mouth shut."

"Not true Bessie. I'd trust you more than anyone."

"Well Father, warning off the men at sea is good but what about the shore parties, and distributors. How do we warn them?"

He threw his hands in the air. "Well, you certainly come up with some tricky questions Bessie. Please, try to remember, I'm a vicar, not a smuggler. What am I supposed to know about smuggling?"

"Sorry, Father. I don't have anyone else to turn to. And I'm really worried about my sister. And time is short. I've got to warn her tonight somehow."

"Not tonight Bessie. The run is tomorrow."

"No, it's tonight vicar. The coachman said so."

"No Bessie it's tomorrow. There is a more reliable source than the coachman."

"Oh no!" Bessie clapped a hand over her mouth. "Not Sailmaker. He's not in on it too?"

"No Bessie. But he does have more reliable information. That's all! Now, you go and keep an eye on Hawksworth for us. He could be a problem. Leave the rest to us Bessie and don't tell anyone about this. The run is tomorrow night, not tonight. But don't tell that to anyone else either. Not even Ernie. Let them believe you think it's tonight too.' She looked downcast. "Bessie, it is safer if people believe it is tonight. If anyone should question you, you must have the same information as everyone else, alright? You should not know anything more than what you heard from the coachman. The only information anyone should have is from his tale."

"Alright! I'll stay with the coachman's story about the run."

"That's right. Don't let on that you know – or even suspect – anything different. Tomorrow we'll go to Nextwest and warn the smugglers there. Don't say anything to Ernie about this unless you absolutely have to. Sailmaker says Ernie is dead set against smuggling. If Hawksworth is content to drink and chat with the villagers, you won't need to do anything. We just don't need him getting nosy around the harbour tonight. If he looks like he's going for a walk around the village, see if you can get Ernie talking to him. Try and keep him at the inn. Now Bessie, I've got to go and help Sailmaker. We'll come up with something for the shore parties. We'll talk about that later tonight; I promise." Bessie hesitated for a few moments, then with a last anxious look at him she left the cottage and headed for the inn. He hurried back to Sailmaker's hut. Sailmaker was cutting up an old oilskin coat. "I thought you'd be repairing Bannerman's boat," he grumbled.

"This is part of it, Father. I'm making some gaskets and patches to cover the holes. I'll put some tingles, over or under these where I need to. It'll be a real botched up job. Good thing we're going to burn it. I wouldn't want anyone thinking this a true sample of my work."

"What can I do?" Sailmaker ignored the question and asked: "What did Bessie say?"

"Oh yes. She's at the inn now. If she needs to, she will talk to Ernie, and try to warn us if things aren't safe. Hawksworth doesn't usually come down here anyway but I suppose his mail could be giving him different orders."

"Very well Father, you can chop some dry kindling from that scrap pile over there. Cut up the pieces of scrap sail by the door too, and put everything into those wicker baskets, and we'll take them down to my boat."

Roddy started his chores straight away. "When will you actually start repairing the boat?" he asked.

Sailmaker responded testily: "When I'm ready Father. I have to prepare the materials for the bloody job first." His impatient manner betrayed the strain he was feeling. Then, in a softer tone: "Sorry Father. This is going to be a real scramble and I'm not sure it will work. In a few minutes we'll go down to the The Landing. Fortunately Bannerman pulled his old boat way up the beach and turned it upside down over some beams. It's out of sight of the inn and harbour front. You'll have to help me right the boat once I have these outside patches on. Bannerman covered his boat with an old sail and it looks a bit like a tent right now. So I'll also have to make some sort of frame and cover it with that same old sail from Bannerman's boat, just as a disguise. Hopefully, no one will give it a second look. We'll also have to take some rollers, so we can roll her over the beach into the water. She's high and dry right now, so she'll take on water for sure. We'll have to see how much. This may not work you know. I've no idea how much work it might take just to keep the water out. One more thing; take this adze with you when we go. You can chop the name off the bow and stern, just in case the Revenuers try to read it before the boat burns completely."

By the time Sailmaker finished his patching job daylight was fading fast but a crude frame, covered with an old sail was now sitting where Bannerman's old boat had been and the patched and tarry vessel was sitting on rollers awaiting its trip to the water. "We have to get the boat into The Chute as soon as it's dark enough that people on the harbour front won't see us, and before any boats return," said Sailmaker. "We can't afford for anyone to see us dragging it around, especially Bannerman! If we are seen, it'll ruin everything. If the Revenuers don't get us – Bannerman will. I think we'd fare better at the hands of the King's men. Certainly, you would!" Sailmaker climbed partway up the cliff behind his hut, where he had a view of the dogleg channel that led to the sea. "No sails in the channel," he called quietly.

Visibility was now at a level where they could no longer make out any detail along the harbour front. "Let's go Father," said Sailmaker. "Put your back into it. We have to hurry; a boat could be turning into the channel at any time." They grunted and heaved Bannerman's heavy boat, gradually moving it over the rollers towards the water and stopping periodically to take rollers from behind the boat and place them under the front. He was not in as good physical condition as Sailmaker, and certainly not as capable of avoiding the tarred patches. "Father – you look like hell!" Sailmaker was smiling as he made the remark, and Roddy realised that he and Ernie had been talking. "You're no oil painting yourself," he answered. They both laughed and suddenly, the bow floated. One last push and she was free of the rollers and fully afloat. A quick inspection revealed some leaks, but nothing that should prevent them from getting the boat into Sorry Cove. Sailmaker splashed through the water to his dinghy and dragged her, stern first, to the bow of Bannerman's boat. "Quick as you can, Father. Dump the rollers into my dinghy and the kindling and other junk into the fire boat." Sailmaker secured the bow line from Bannerman's boat to the stern of his dinghy. "Hurry Father – into my boat – smartly now."

Roddy splashed through the water and plunged into an unexpected deep hole. When he resurfaced Sailmaker grabbed the back of his coat and dragged him aboard the dinghy. He was grinning broadly as he said: "By the way Father, there's a deep hole just there." Roddy was not amused and only just managed to grab his hat as it floated by. "Have you rowed before, Father?"

"A little."

"Good, take the bow position and try and stay in time with me. This is a very dangerous time, we couldn't come up with a believable story if anyone should challenge us now so put your back into it. We don't know when somebody might show up." The area around Sailmaker's hut was rarely busy and with the boats all being at sea there was little likelihood of anyone coming to this area. But people did sometimes appear, unannounced, just to chat, as they had that very morning. So they sweated and heaved, towing that lumbering, heavy boat, across the harbour, through The Chute and into Sorry Cove. There, it would be out of sight from any casual observer and no one had reason to enter The Chute itself.

Sailmaker was securing the fireboat's bow line to a spur of rock as he said: "Quietly now Father; Archer will already be in his hut above us. Any noise might make him look over the side of his bridge. Then he might spot the boat. He wouldn't have reason to look down here as a rule and it'll be too dark for him to see the boat when he leaves tonight. If he decides to take fresh wood to the hut in the morning though, we could have a problem. If he does see it, he's sure to get someone from the inn to check it out. It could even be Bannerman!"

It wasn't hard for Roddy to be quiet; he barely had enough breath to speak. But he did manage to whisper: "By the way Sailmaker, Bessie and I will be going to Nextwest tomorrow. We have to warn the smugglers there or all our efforts may go for naught. And if the Customs men catch any that know of your involvement...." He spread his arms despairingly. Sailmaker lowered his head, when he raised it again there was a grim, mirthless, smile on his face. "They sent three men to help me set up the tackle. Then I had to show them how to take it apart, and set it up again. Obviously they will know me." He gave a weary despondent sigh, before saying: "Back to my dock now Father, fast as we can. Keep a sharp eye out for other boats before we leave The Chute. If anyone sees us once we're clear of The Chute, we'll say that I've been showing you around the harbour again, because you want to review a few things for your new church, alright?"

"Alright." They were tying up at Sailmaker's when moonlight showed them a sail in the dogleg channel. Sailmaker pointed and said: "See how the moonlight shows up the sails, Father. Luck was with us tonight." Roddy could hear the relief in his voice. Now, let's get back to the hut and see if we can clean some of that tar off you. You should have worn some old clothes. You're a real candidate for Bessie's sewing circle that's for sure. People will wonder what sort of a vicar the Bishop has sent them." But with the aid of some lamp oil they cleaned most of the tar off his skin and clothes.

They arranged to meet back at Sailmaker's hut at nine o'clock the following night. Sailmaker gave him some old clothes to wear for their fireboat adventure the following evening. In the morning he would re-examine his repairs, prepare more materials, and load up the fire boat with flammables. He planned to set the fuse before they towed it out of the Cove, so that they'd be all set to drag Bannerman's old wreck to the spot where they would anchor and burn it. Hopefully, they wouldn't be stopped by the Revenue cutter, because they could never lie their way out of that situation.

"How do you intend to warn the smugglers ashore about the trap – especially since they're already being watched by the Customs men? And how would you know who to warn? Is there something you're not telling me?" asked Sailmaker.

"I'm not sure yet but I have good reason to believe that one of the people I met in Nextwest is a smuggler," he responded grimly. "Enjoy your supper at the inn Sailmaker, but keep your ears open for signs of trouble. I'll go back to my cottage and clean up. I may see you at the inn later. Depends on what Bessie discovered about Hawksworth. I'm famished, tired too. Not used to all this hard work." He didn't mention the nasty sick feeling he had in his stomach. He knew full well that that wasn't hunger. He'd experienced fear often enough recently to recognise the signs. Now that their first frantic preparations were over the dangers he'd involved himself in were registering loud and clear. He had never intended to get involved in warning the smugglers personally. Someone more capable than he was supposed to take whatever risks that might be involved. Hell – it was none of his business. He wasn't even a smuggler.

# CHAPTER 10

## *Warn the smugglers*

Bessie was pounding on his bedroom door at first light. "Breakfast is on the table," she yelled through the partially opened door. "And Tom will 'ave your wagon 'ere in a few minutes. We 'ave to get going, Father; there's no time to lie-a-bed." He quickly splashed some water on his face, and dressed in the last of his clerical garments that weren't tar stained or scorched. He needed to look somewhat presentable for a trip to Nextwest, where he might be unfortunate enough to bump into Bishop West. They were soon on their way and, of course, the first question out of Bessie's mouth was: " 'ow are we going to find a smuggler to tell about the ambush, Father?"

"Bessie, do you remember the butler at the Whatson's house?"

"No. You did mention 'im, but 'e wasn't there when we picked up the clothing, Father. I know Mr. Westerhof though. I remember 'im."

"It's the butler I'm concerned with, Bessie. He's a smuggler."

She gasped. " 'ow do you know that?"

"I overheard a conversation that I wasn't meant to. He, the butler, realised that I'd overheard, and threatened to kill me. In fact, it was only the intervention of another smuggler that saved me. The butler's name is Goodman. We have to get our information to him. I believe he's highly placed in their organisation."

"Well, I can go and see 'im as soon as we get to Nextwest. That'll solve our problem then. Should put you in 'is 'good books' too."

"Not so fast, Bessie. The informer may have named him. Goodman could quite likely be one of those being watched by the Revenue officers. If so, anyone visiting him would be under suspicion too. So that visitor would need an obviously legitimate reason to call at the house. It must appear to be a call that the Customs men wouldn't consider revealing themselves over."

"What about the clothes? I could deliver our letter of thanks and ask if they 'ad anymore clothes?"

"That's a good idea, Bessie, except that it might force the officers to reveal themselves. They wouldn't know what you were doing there until they read your letter. They might even think the letter to be a coded smuggler's communication. No! Your reason for knocking on Goodman's door has to look so routine and innocent, that they would only watch – but not challenge you. Bessie, I was wondering how many pies and preserves your sister might have available this morning. Do you have any idea?"

"I've no idea, Father. 'ungry are you? She'd 'ave a few, I would imagine. She starts bakin' early most mornin's."

"Bessie, I think you and Marie should go into business for yourselves: selling pies and preserves door to door." She looked at him as though he'd lost his mind. "Some other time, Father; let's warn the smugglers first."

"That's just what we'd be doing, Bessie." Peddling pies door to door will just be our cover, a way to disguise the real reason for your visit and make it seem innocent. If you borrow this wagon, load it with pies and preserves and then go peddling door to door, you will meet Goodman on the same terms as the rest of your customers on that street."

"Ooh! Now I get it. The pie business is just a blind."

"Yes, but for it to be believable, you would have to be patient. Start at one end of the street and work your way along. Continue on even after you have been to Goodman's house. It must look as though going to his house was just another, innocent sales call. If anyone should ask you what you're doing – most probably a Revenue officer – you could honestly say that you and Marie are widows trying to earn money by selling her pies and preserves, door to door. What do you think? Could you do it?"

"Could I do it? I think it's a great idea. Could I still give 'im the letter for Mrs. Whatson?"

"No, Bessie. Stay with the pies and preserves. If a Revenue spy sees you passing notes, they will most likely be all over the pair of you. You must be careful."

*From the author's sketchbook*

"I see. So, do we go straight to Marie's or stop at the manse first?"

"Straight to Marie's. We'll discuss the details there."

. . .

Marie gave them a welcoming smile as she ushered them into her warm kitchen, full of the tantalising smell of baked goods. Her smile quickly faded, however, when she heard their news, and she fell into the fireside chair holding her suddenly pale face in both hands. "My God, Bessie," she said in a hushed and fearful voice, "What'll I do now?"

"Well, Marie, the Father here has suggested that we go into business together. 'ow many pies and jars of preserves 'ave you got that are ready for sale?"

"What are you talking about, girl?' said the bewildered Marie. Bessie gave her sister a reassuring smile and placed a hand on her shoulder, whilst she explained their plan. "Relax, Marie; this is just a way to warn the smugglers in Nextwest, without raisin' suspicion. The vicar is lendin' us his wagon, so I can use the pie peddlin' to meet the smugglers without raisin' suspicion. I'll drop the vicar off at the manse, and pick 'im up again when I'm finished." Marie was looking at her sister as though she were a total stranger. Bessie gave her a gentle shake. "Come on, girl; time's a wastin'. 'ow many pies do you 'ave? I'll need boxes to put the stuff in, a plate and a knife too, so I can give tasters."

Marie rose slowly from her chair, her gaze darting fearfully, first to the vicar, and then back to her sister. They had given her no time to absorb this life-threatening news and now she was being forced to respond to it without having time to weigh the possibly deadly consequences. She had every right to be scared. Then, in a flat, confused tone, she said: "I've got about a dozen pies. I baked last night for delivery to the shops this mornin'. There are more in the oven now. There's a few jam tarts and lots of preserves. Boxes are in the back. This means I'll have to bake some more for the shop on the corner." A frown creased her brow and in a more assertive tone she said: "I can't' let them down. They're my steady customers."

Within half an hour the wagon was loaded, and they were headed for the manse. Bessie's smile looked a little forced as she handed Roddy the box of money that had resulted from the clothing donations to their village. He was concerned and feeling very guilty about the risk his scheme would place on Bessie. However, it would have been suspicious for a vicar to be peddling door to door. If Bessie was nervous about the dangers of her upcoming subterfuge, his stoic housekeeper didn't say. She just picked up the reins, gave a little wave, and headed for Pleasant Avenue. He was sending this good-hearted woman into a dangerous situation where he would be in no position to help or coach her whilst he relaxed in the comfort of the manse. However, he was more nervous than words could describe, so 'relaxed' was hardly a true description of his condition. He felt nauseous and his stomach was in turmoil as he wondered how Mrs. Drew might handle a possible confrontation with a Revenue officer. She was a self-assured and determined woman but this was asking a lot of her. Nevertheless, he would have to hide his anxiety from Tubby, and wait for his co-conspirator's return.

"What a wonderful surprise!" His greeting left him in no doubt that Reverend Tubbs was genuinely pleased to see him. "Come in, come in. Have you eaten? It is so early; you must have been on the road at first light." The stableman, Fletcher, stood in the driveway, obviously disappointed, as he watched Bessie drive off with Slondosh. Then he returned to the stables without giving them a second glance. Tubby followed Roddy's gaze as he watched Fletcher walk away. "He can be a surly fellow, Roddy. I think that was part of his problem when he tried to take over his father's business."

Over a glass of wine, Roddy explained the business of the donations to Tubby and gave him the proceeds, together with Bessie's letter to Mrs. Whatson. "I thought you might be kind enough to deliver that for us, Tubby. You could then fill in any detail that Mrs. Drew might have left out of her letter." He described the gradual return to the church of many of the congregation, with particular stress on the Jamie Rooken incident. Tubby was most impressed. "I shall be most pleased to convey these good tidings to Mrs. Whatson. The fruits of her generosity are most gratifying. Most gratifying, indeed! I think I will ask her to give this news to the Bishop though. He would find it more acceptable coming from her, you understand?" He gave Roddy a knowing wink.

He was too nervous to enjoy the wine, or Tubby's company. What if Goodman wasn't available? He might already be engaged elsewhere, marshalling his shore parties and so on. If that were the case, he would have to try to contact Prudence. But he was reluctant to expose her to any danger. Concern for others was a new and unpleasant experience for him, so he hastily ascribed that to his personal needs.

• • •

Having spent a disturbing night worrying about Archer spotting Bannerman's old boat in Sorry Cove, Sailmaker hurried to the inn at first light. He hoped that Ernie might know how Archer planned to spend this day. However, guile was never Sailmaker's strong point, and his inquiries were clumsy enough to rouse the canny innkeeper's natural curiosity. "What's your problem, Sailmaker? Why are you so concerned about Archer?" Ernie tried to appear casual and unconcerned as he asked the question avoiding direct eye contact, while he continued cleaning the bar and putting jugs away.

"Oh, I'm not really concerned, Ernie. I just wondered if he might be going to the beacon hut today. I thought you might know if he planned to restock his firewood or something." Ernie stopped working and gave Sailmaker a stern look. "How the hell can I help you, Sailmaker, when I don't know what you're up to? Archer will be up and about already. Ask him yourself. Stop beating about the bush. I can hold my tongue if that's what's worrying you." Ernie's short fuse had started to glow, and bit-by-bit, he wheedled the story of the 'fireboat' from his prospective son-in-law. Sailmaker began well enough, telling Ernie that, because of the coachman's story the vicar was concerned that some villagers might be caught in the Customs officer's ambush. Finally, Ernie said: "Is that why Bessie kept Hawksworth chatting last evening?" Under Ernie's incisive questioning, Sailmaker eventually disclosed all their plans for Bannerman's boat and their struggles of the night before.

"You see, Ernie, we were lucky that Archer was in the hut before we towed Bannerman's boat into The Chute. Now I need to keep Archer, or anyone else for that matter, from looking down from the bridge until I'm finished repairing the boat. If one of our boats returns early and someone stares directly into The Chute, we could still have a problem." Sailmaker hung his head, already regretting that he'd involved Ernie, and wondering if this might end their rescue mission. Even more devastating to him, Ernie might forbid him to see Meg anymore. But that could be inevitable if his good relationship with his future father-in-law should collapse.

"It looks like you and the vicar are becoming quite chummy," said Ernie, studying Sailmaker as if he were a suspicious stranger. The innkeeper's expression was grim, lips pursed, one eyebrow raised, and his muscular arms folded across his chest. Under his penetrating stare, Sailmaker knew he was being re-evaluated. "Come now, Ernie. He needed some help trying to save any villagers that might be involved. It's not like we are the best of mates."

"Nothing wrong with that if you were. Seems to me the vicar is working hard for the folks hereabouts and his best efforts are outside the pulpit. Now he's putting his life at risk too. It appears he's a better man than any of us gave him credit for." Sailmaker shuffled his feet a little. "Yeah, I know. But most folks hereabouts still won't give him the time of day."

"Well, that'll change. But I'm not sure Bannerman will change fast enough to save the vicar's neck if he discovers his boat's about to go up in flames."

"Well, I put a frame under the old sail he used to cover his boat, so it looks like his boat's still there. But if Bannerman is caught by the King's cutters, his boat will be the least of his worries," responded Sailmaker. "Right now his boat is in shallow water in Sorry Cove and she's taken on more water than I'd hoped. She'll need a lot more work if we are to get her to the anchor point before she sinks. That would put paid to any chance of warning off the smugglers. I've got to work on her again today. That'll mean some noise and if Archer is in the beacon hut, he's bound to hear me." Archer chose that very moment to walk into the bar. "Did I hear my name mentioned?" His unsmiling face took on a more suspicious expression than usual, as he scanned the two men's faces.

"Eavesdroppers never hear any good about themselves, Archer. You shouldn't earwig." Ernie's quick retort was intended to buy him some time whilst he thought up a more appropriate response.

"Well, I'd like to know why you were discussing me. Or doesn't it bear repeating?"

Ernie took up the challenge. "You're a suspicious old bugger, Archer. Sailmaker was asking about you and wondering how you were handling the firewood situation, now that Jamie's too sick to work with you. How's your new mate, Higgins, working out? Does he help you cut and load as well as tend Jamie's beacon?"

Aye, that he does and we're well stocked now. I thought I might clean up the stable today, after I've tidied up the beacon hut, that is." Ernie shot a quick glance at Sailmaker. "Well, I was hoping that you might be able to cut some wood for me, Archer. I don't like my woodpile to get too low and I particularly need some short stuff, maybe a foot long, for smaller fires, you know. I like small fires for simmering stews and suchlike – any chance?"

"Well, you don't need it today, do you?" Ernie faked a glum expression. "I can manage, but I'll sure need it tomorrow. I wanted to try out the shorter logs today, to see how they work out for simmering soup and stock pots, for instance."

"I guess I could cut you some from the pile at the stable. One load do?"

"That'd be great, Archer. Won't it spoil your plans for cleaning up the beacon hut though?"

"No, that can wait for a day or so. There's plenty of wood in there; that's the main thing." Sailmaker lowered his head, to prevent Archer from seeing the relief on his face. Archer looked from Ernie to Sailmaker, then back again. "What I really called in for was to see if you had any more news on this smuggling thing." Archer continued scanning their faces as he spoke.

"No, not really. Bessie and the vicar are in Nextwest today though. Maybe they'll hear something while they're there," answered Ernie.

"Doubt it. By the sounds of things, this bloke Corby runs a tight ship. Surprised really that the coachman heard what he did. Wouldn't want to be in his shoes if Corby ever finds out he blabbed all that information over a couple of jugs at your inn. Maybe he's even told the tale elsewhere. Maybe even in Nextwest. Not too smart really. Well, I'll be off to cut your wood, Ernie. See you boys later." Archer waved and left.

"Ernie, that was great. Thank you." Sailmaker's gratitude was heartfelt. "Now I'd better get about my business too, and not waste any more time."

Ernie raised his hand. "Hold up a minute, young fella. I don't like the idea of you being involved with the smugglers. Does Meg know?" Sailmaker shuffled his feet, fidgeting self-consciously. "I'm not involved in the actual smuggling, Ernie. I sold 'em some tackle, but that's all. It will pay well, and I was hoping to earn some money for when Meg and me get married. When Bannerman asked me to quote for that tackle, I didn't know it was for smugglers. But once they took me to the site and showed me what they wanted to be done, it was all too obvious." He shrugged, and raised his arms in a gesture of despair. "Then, of course, it was too dangerous to back out. I knew too much."

"So why did the vicar and Bessie rush off to Nextwest so unexpectedly?"

"The vicar believes he knows someone in Nextwest who might be involved in smuggling. He wanted to warn them. He's worried that if they're caught, they might give up some of our men in exchange for an easier sentence."

"Who is involved, Sailmaker?"

"Ernie, I honestly don't know. Neither does the vicar. Mind you, I've got my suspicions. I would think Bannerman must be, because he recommended me to the smugglers for the rigging job. That means the Sullivans have to be in on it too. It's their boat after all."

Ernie pursed his lips. "When's the vicar due back?" Sailmaker shrugged. "Bessie told me they were going to Nextwest to give money, for the donated clothes, to the Nextwest Poor Box. Most likely to see Bessie's sister too."

"Will he be back in time to help you? And more to the point, do you think the vicar can handle his share of this 'fireboat' business tonight?"

"Well, Ernie, it was his idea, and so far, he's surprised us all when he starts something that we think is crazy. But if it doesn't work, we might just as well have signed a confession. We'll all be caught, for sure!"

• • •

Sailmaker rowed his skiff into The Chute. It was loaded with a tar bucket and patching materials. He was hoping to seal the boat from the inside, because he wouldn't be able to drag it to a beach and turn it over on his own. He was worried, alone, and vulnerable on this dangerous mission. On examining Bannerman's boat, he found that the area of the broken keel was the biggest reason for the extra water and an overwhelming sense of dread came over him as he re-examined the battered hull. How could he possibly fix the leaks in time for tonight's dangerous venture, especially without the vicar's help?

He looked around him, seeing Sorry Cove in a new light today. It had always been a dangerous wasteland as far as the villagers were concerned but today it had become his opportunistic hideaway. Without this dangerous, rock-strewn bay, the secrecy needed for this mission would have been impossible. Looking up at the cliff, he noticed an overhang that shielded part of the beach from Archer's bridge. "I wish I'd noticed that last night," he muttered. "We could've pulled the boat under there, and it would have been hidden from above." Lots of soaked kindling and canvas was floating in the water; he would have to bail out, and he shook his head miserably. "None of this will burn now, and even if I load fresh kindling into her, she'll be too wet to set afire by the time we get her in place. And that's provided she doesn't sink on the way." Panic was setting in and he was tempted to abandon the whole idea. If he was discovered, he would be arrested as a smuggler's accomplice, with possibly fatal consequences. After another long re-examining of the boat, he threw up his hands in an attitude of surrender. "I have to find a way to turn this bloody thing over."

"Need a hand?' The unexpected voice made him jump, and sent his heart racing as he turned to face the speaker. The innkeeper was standing under the overhang of the cliff, wearing a big smile. "You shouldn't be talking to yourself, lad," he said. "You'll only get silly answers."

"Ernie! You scared the hell out of me." Sailmaker put his hands on his knees and took a few deep breaths.

"Good. It's about time somebody did. This is a scary thing you're doing. You should have considered all the risks before letting the vicar talk you into it."

"Ernie. You know the story. What else could I do?"

"Alright then; I'll give you a hand. I told my family I was going to see Doc Hudson. Then I told Doc that I'd come to see him because I needed to disappear for a couple of hours." Ernie smiled broadly as he recalled that meeting and said: "Doc gave me a funny look, closed his eyes, and waved his fingers in front of my face, like this:" Ernie wiggled his fingers in Sailmaker's face, and said: "Alacazam, Alacazeer! Make our Ernie disappear." Then Doc opened his eyes, looked at me, all puzzled like, and said: I'll try again," and repeated his finger-wiggling bit. When I asked him what the hell he was doing, Doc opened his eyes and said: 'Ernie, I tried, but you're still here! I don't think I'm much good at making people disappear. Do you think a pointy hat might help?'" Ernie gave a little laugh. "Anyway, Doc agreed to cover for me – by disappearing too. He's gone off to read, on a secluded piece of beach that he uses when he needs some time alone, and took my bottle of rum with him. As far as anyone else is concerned, we will have been there together all day if need be. I'll slip back there when we're done here. Then Doc an' me will stagger home together, three sheets-in-the-wind." Ernie smiled. "Alright then, Sailmaker. Let's get to it. Bannerman's old boat always was a heavy, lumbering, old bitch. I figured you'd need a hand, and then I remembered this overhang and how concerned you were that no one should see you working on the boat. So here I am. What say we bale her out and drag the beast over there out of sight from The Chute and the bridge? Then we can flip her over and I'll give you a hand with the caulking."

"Bless you, Ernie. I was getting scared when I saw how much water she'd taken on. I'll bale her out, after I've tossed this kindling out. It's soaked." Half an hour later, the boat was concealed under the overhang, and turned bottom-up once more. Without the time pressure of the day before, Sailmaker did a better job of closing the wounds on the hull. He punched oakum into some of the worst seams, without bothering to make it pretty, but he had to reinforce the broken keel because that was where most of the water was getting in. When he'd finished, the area around the keel looked like a solid block of pitch with pieces of wood sticking out of it. But it would hold out the water now, provided a heavy sea didn't twist it, that was.

Ernie had brought some food with him, and they took a break before righting the boat again and coating the insides with tar before pulling the rollers under her. After testing for leaks, they filled the boat with fresh kindling and dry flotsam from the beach. "Can you manage now, Sailmaker? With the vicar's help, I mean." Ernie looked concerned as he studied the heavy boat.

"Let's give her a trial shove," Sailmaker replied. The boat was heavy but he moved it fairly easily on the rollers, then pulled it back under the overhang. "The flood tide will help," said Ernie. "You'll not have far to push her come dark. And by the time you need to get going, you'll catch the ebb tide. That'll help too. In the meantime, she's out of sight from above and the harbour."

"I was counting on the ebb tide, Ernie. Thanks, we can manage now," replied Sailmaker.

"Good. Then I'll be off to join my friend Doc Hudson for my share of that rum bottle," said the innkeeper. "Good luck tonight, Sailmaker. I'll keep an eye out for the vicar. If he doesn't show, I'll find some way to get down here."

"No, Ernie! You mustn't do that. You have a family to consider and the village needs you. Promise me you won't get involved, for Meg's sake."

"I think you should have thought of Meg before you got involved, Sailmaker. She would be upset if she knew about your part in this business."

"Sorry, Ernie, but I honestly didn't know I would be working for smugglers. It was good money and I wanted that so's Meg and me could get a better start when we got married." Ernie pulled a sad face. "You be careful too, lad; that 'good money' should've tipped you off that it wasn't an honest job. I'm off to see Doc now. If you get up to the inn before the vicar gets back, remember to ask where I am," and with that, he strode off in the direction of Doc Hudson's hideaway.

Sailmaker cautiously took his dinghy through The Chute, making sure no one saw him enter the harbour from there. Back at his rigging shop, he lighted a sample piece of fuse, making sure it was reliable. Then, struck by an afterthought, he scooped up a bucketful of stones from the ground outside and went back to the powder keg. He poured some powder and stones onto pieces of canvas. Then he gathered the edges of the canvas and tied them into bags. When he was satisfied, he took his supplies to his dinghy, protected them with another piece of old sail, and went to the inn. "Where's Ernie?" he asked. "I could do with a jug of ale and something to eat." Archer appeared at his shoulder. "I've been asking the same question," he said. "You heard him this morning: crying for more wood. Now when I bring it – as a special favour like, 'cos I'm not short of things to do – he's not here. What's more, he doesn't need any more bloody wood. He's got plenty of short bits out back. He got me goin' for no good reason, so 'e did. Then he buggers off on some pleasure jaunt."

"I guess he just forgot, Archer. It happens to all of us at times when things come up unexpected like. Can't foresee everything you know," Sailmaker gave the beacon master a friendly smile. Archer wasn't in a forgiving mood, however. "Yeah well, while I'm out there working hard for no good reason, he's off pissin'-it-up with 'is old friend, Doc Hudson. I could have used a break myself. I'd have gone with him if he'd asked me. Miserable old sod!" With that he stomped off, scowling. "Wait 'til he wants another favour!" he called over his shoulder.

• • •

On arrival at Pleasant Road, Bessie spent a little time rearranging her pies and preserves to display them more openly at the rear of the wagon. That gave her another opportunity to survey the area for possible Revenue spies. She paid special attention to one particular jar of jam that was marked with a small cross on the paper cover. The vicar had been most emphatic that that jar was for Goodman's eyes only. There must be no mistake about that. If anyone else wanted to buy it, she was to say that it was marked with a cross because there was some mould on the jam, because the wax covering hadn't made a complete seal. Bessie filled a large wicker basket that Marie had lent her, and she was ready. She had her story down pat: Two widowed sisters trying to start a new business to earn a living, and so on. This was a trial run, to see if the residents were interested enough to make it worth-while to establish a regular route. She had chosen this street for the trial because the people here were wealthy enough to buy these items, rather than have to make their own. If Goodman was not interested in talking to her, she was to say that a gentleman that wore a green velvet waistcoat, that he'd admired recently, said it was a matter of life or death that he listen to her advice about 'watchers'. She was not to identify the vicar, except as a man who wore a green waistcoat, and even then, only to Goodman. Bessie had never seen Goodman, but the vicar had given her a good description of him. He had refused to elaborate about the green velvet waistcoat but she trusted him well enough to respect his request and not question him about that. "Be sure you are talking to the right man," he'd said. Well, now she was prepared as she'd ever be, so she took a deep breath, ignored the butterflies in her stomach and took one last look around as she muttered the vicar's caution: "Don't be obvious about it, but do be very observant and do your best to appear casual."

The first house on Pleasant Road was a rather grand affair and Bessie felt her tension rising as she walked to the tradesman's entrance. Her knock was answered by a thin woman, with a miserable countenance, dressed in a plain, very formal, dark green dress with a starched white collar. "Well?"

"Good morning, Ma'am. My name's Bessie Drew. Me and my sister are offerin' fresh baked pies and preserves, carefully made, with the best ingredients, to customers in this area. I wondered, Ma'am, if I could tempt you to try one of our delicious pies today?" Bessie moved her basket forward for the woman's inspection. "Don't bother me with your peddled goods, woman. Be off with you. We have our own cook." The miserable woman closed the door in Bessie's face; her shoulders slumped and she held her head low for a few moments. "Well, that was a good start," she said, and as she trudged back to the waiting pony, she casually scanned for people who might appear to have no real business on the street. "Nothin' seems out of place 'ere," she grumbled. "Except me!" She crossed the street and repeated her approach there. This time the reception was better, but the end result was the same. "No thank you, we have our own cook."

"At least they were more polite about gettin' rid of me," she muttered. The third house was better. Not quite as grand as the first two, but the plump housekeeper was smiling when she opened the door. "Well, those pies certainly look delicious," she said. "We do have our own cook, of course, but pies and the like are not her specialty. Could I try a piece perhaps?"

"Certainly, Ma'am," replied Bessie, grateful for the friendly attitude. She cut a narrow slice, and handed it to the woman on a piece of waxed paper. "Mmm. That really is very good. I'll take this one and another apple pie, please." Bessie hurried back to the wagon for the extra pie but was embarrassed when she had no money to make change when the woman paid her. "No matter, dear," said her customer, "give me a jar of pickles instead." Will you be coming around on a regular basis?"

"Oh yes, Ma'am, provided that people want me to, of course."

"Well, I'm certainly interested. Stop by next week if you are able." Bessie put the money in her apron pocket, thanked the lady and left. Making the sale had helped validate her cover, but she was worried that Goodman might leave his house before she got there. It was still three houses away and she was working both sides of the street. That thought brought on a sense of panic. She made another sale: two pies, two jars of pickles and two jars of jam. Now she would have to move Slondosh and his feedbag along the street a little. She sold another pie, a jar of jam, and some pickled onions at the next house, had a bad reception at the next two and then she was at Goodman's – or rather the Whatson's – house. She made a big show of tidying up the goods in the wagon and reloading her basket, as she surveyed her surroundings for any 'watchers'. There was a gardener in the grounds of the house across from the Whatson's. He was working with a spade, but something didn't seem quite right with his attitude. Fighting off her fears about Goodman leaving, she decided to visit that house first, and check out the gardener, before going to Goodman's. Carrying her basket, she approached the gardener first. "Good morning, friend," she said cheerily. "You're workin' 'ard I see. Lovely garden."

The gardener seemed caught off-guard. "Mornin," he responded. He looked awkward, and unsure of himself.

Bessie noted that he'd not really dug much ground at all, merely disturbed the soil around some of the plants. "You must be a professional gardener to get results like this," she said. "Been a long time in this business, 'ave ye?"

"A few years now," he replied.

"Just weedin', are you?"

"Yes, just weeding."

"I'd love a Begonia like this one. I could never get mine to bloom," she said.

"Are they usually 'ard to grow?"

"Yeah, you've got to know what you're doing."

"Oh, well, I'd better stay with my bakin' then. I'm startin' a new business you know, tryin' to make ends meet. I'm a widda', y'see. Lost me 'usband a couple of years back. I'm selling pies and preserves. Is there a cook in the 'ouse or should I talk to the 'ousekeeper? Perhaps you would like to buy a pie to take 'ome? They're nice and fresh. Want a taste?"

"No, I've got to finish up here. The lady of the house will be after me otherwise."

"Oh, alright then," and Bessie walked up to the house. The woman who answered the door seemed nervous as Bessie went through her introduction and offered a taste. The woman declined with a wave of her hand but she did buy a jar of jam. Bessie got the impression that the woman made the purchase just to get rid of her. "I love your garden" she said. "Makes all the difference when you've got a professional gardener, don't it?"

"Thank you. He's not…well, he's not our regular gardener. I usually do the work myself."

"Well, you do a lovely job." Bessie smiled, said goodbye, and crossed the road to the Whatson's house. A young maid answered the door and Bessie's heart was in her mouth. What if Goodman wasn't in after all this effort? "Is the butler available?" she asked.

"Who shall I say is enquiring?" asked the girl, in a condescending manner. She eyed Bessie's basket rather disdainfully. "We have our own cook, you know, and he won't talk to peddlers."

"Actually, a friend of 'is told me 'e wanted to try our baked goods."

"Oh! What was the friend's name?"

"Ooh! I've forgotten 'is name. On the tip of me tongue it was, but I can't recall it now. But the butler will know 'im. He told me your butler complimented 'im on 'is green velvet waistcoat when they last met, right after the funeral for the master of your 'ouse, that was."

"I can't bother him with this," said the girl, and moved to close the door. Bessie put her basket in the opening to prevent that and, in a more assertive manner, she said: "The gentleman in the green waistcoat told me your butler would be very annoyed if I didn't show 'im my goods."

"I'm sure he'd be more impressed if you remembered his friend's name."

"Well, I'm sure 'e'll be even more impressed, and bloody annoyed too, when 'e finds out you didn't give 'im my message." Bessie's mouth was set in a grim line. Her annoyance at having this prissy little maid talking down to her had her dander up, and it was showing. "Wait here," the girl said impatiently, tipping her nose in the air. Bessie fussed with the basket of goods, which now included the jar with the cross marked on it. A few minutes passed before the door opened and Goodman's large frame filled the doorway. There was no mistaking him from the vicar's description. Bessie could see the maid hovering in the background, obviously waiting to enjoy Goodman giving this pedlar the rough edge of his tongue. "Well?" Goodman's expression left Bessie in no doubt that this could go badly. She moved to hide her face from the maid and whispered: "This is a very private matter," inclining her head towards the girl. Goodman turned to the maid. "Be about your business." The girl scowled and scurried away.

"My basket of pies and preserves is just a cover," said Bessie. "I'm here to warn you that an ambush has been set by the revenuers. The warning beacon is discovered and is being watched and so are you. You have an informer in your group who has given up the date and time of the run." Goodman eyed her suspiciously. If he was at all alarmed, he didn't show it. "What are you talking about, woman? I've got no time for silly games."

"You'll 'ave plenty of time to regret that decision while you wait for them to 'ang you. You'd best listen to me now. Otherwise me and me sister will likely 'ang right alongside you. Otherwise, I wouldn't care." Bessie had her anger under control now that all her efforts were about to be wasted. She lifted her basket, to give the impression that he was looking at her goods. "Don't raise your head," she said. "Keep looking in the basket. We're being watched. Examine the goods. Take the jar with the cross on the cover indoors. There's a message under the cover. Take it and read it. Then, from be'ind your curtains, look across the street at their gardener. Only 'e ain't no gardener. 'e doesn't know a Begonia from a Rhododendron. I just checked. The woman of the 'ouse says she does the gardenin' usually but stopped short of telling me that the fool with the spade is a revenuer. Take the jar of jam into the house, read the message under the cover in private, and then destroy it. Then come back and see me. Here, take the whole basket. It'll look better." She thrust the basket at him. Goodman stared at her for a few seconds, before taking the basket indoors. Bessie waited on the step, counting the money in her apron pocket and trying to look unconcerned, but her stomach felt as though a thousand insects were cavorting in there. She wondered if the watcher could see how scared she was. Goodman had to believe her if the shore party was to be saved. That included Marie, and now herself, if Corby's ruthless reputation was true.

Goodman ripped the waxed paper off the preserve jar. On a paper beneath it, the vicar had written: 'Because I overheard too much at The White Hart, you were having me watched. But you have been betrayed by an informer in your group. Listen to the peddler. It's a matter of life and death.' Goodman crumpled the note and stuffed it in his pocket. The preserves were still sealed under a sound layer of wax and had not soiled the paper. He went to the window and cautiously peered between the curtains at the 'gardener' across the street. He seemed to be in the same spot where he'd noticed him hours ago. It was true that the woman usually worked the garden herself. Mrs. Whatson had told him rather scornfully that the woman claimed it was her hobby. He went outside to Bessie and returned an almost empty basket. "It seems I have to listen to you," he said. "So talk."

"Then make it look as though you are going to buy something more. At least appear interested. Both our necks are at risk here. Did you see the 'gardener'"?

"Yes. He's been there for two days, and most of the time, he works that same spot now that you mention it and I've never seen him turn his back to this house." So Bessie told Goodman the coachman's story and they walked to the wagon, where he inspected her wares before walking back again with more goods. Bessie told him that arrangements had been made to warn off the boats, but that they didn't know how to warn the crews on shore. Goodman picked up a jar of preserves and waved it at her, doing his best to look like a buyer. He positioned himself between her and the 'gardener' so the man couldn't see his face. "Why would the preacher help smugglers?" he asked. "He told me that he wanted no part of the trade. So why risk his neck – and yours – for smugglers now?"

"Because some people 'e cares about are involved – my sister for one. She holds goods for one of your blokes, in 'er spare room. Mostly, the vicar wants to save 'er and any villagers that might be involved. He's got to help you in order to help them. So just consider yourself lucky." Goodman studied her face for a few seconds before replying.

"There's a carpenter's shop at the bottom of Church Street. Go there now, and talk to Godfrey – your sister knows him: a skinny fellow, with a scar over his left eye. Tell him: "The cat's amongst the ducks." You don't have to say anything more. He'll do the rest. Give him that message, and he'll take care of all the people involved on shore. Give me a taste of that pie. We have to hang this out for a few more minutes." Bessie obliged, and Goodman made an event of sampling the pie at the back of the wagon.

"Have your sister give you an old chair from her back room. Take it to Godfrey – as a cover for your real reason for going there. After you've given Godfrey the message, you go on home. Leave the chair with Godfrey. Tell the preacher I won't forget this."

"The cat's amongst the pigeons," Bessie said. "The correct sayin' is 'The cat's amongst the pigeons.'"

"If you say that, you could end up getting your throat cut, my girl." Goodman's expression was grim. "We changed the word to trip up imposters. Remember: The cat's amongst the ducks. Ducks – not pigeons. We use code phrases that could be incorporated in conversation, but alter a key word or two." Bessie swallowed hard and repeated the modified saying for Goodman's approval.

"Fine! But remember, you can only use that once. After today we'll change it and we won't be telling you about the change!" They walked back to the house, and Goodman gave her money for the goods.

"Now be off with you. There's no time to waste."

"I can't just rush off. That would be too suspicious. I have to continue on down the street 'til I've sold my goods. Otherwise, your 'gardener' friend will put two and two together and this will all go for naught."

"Alright then, go back to your cart one more time. I'll send the maid up. Give her what's left of your preserves. Keep enough goods to knock on one or two more doors, or until you're sold out, or can hide what's left. Then bugger-off to Church Street. And remember DUCKS! Not pigeons."

One more thing, and this is very important. The man that was supposed to tend the warning-off fire fell off his roof last night and broke a leg. Godfrey's runner will be warning him because he doesn't know we had to use someone else for the warning fire. Our new man didn't know where to pick up the cart though, so a young lady of the vicar's acquaintance agreed to show him, and help with the warning fire. They will take over the hay cart from the bloke with the broken leg, somewhere west of Nextwest – the lady knows where. It's essential that you stop that wagon before it turns into the field where the warning fire would be lit. There is some lifting tackle hidden under the hay on that cart. If the revenuers discover that, it will be as good as a confession. All of your efforts today will have been wasted. The site of that warning fire is on your way home, just west of Pringle's farm. You are our only chance to warn them because I left their route and timing up to them. It's essential that you get ahead of them and stop them before they turn into that field. The lady on the cart will be disguised as a farm boy."

Goodman opened his purse and they went through the pretence of calculating the price of the goods he'd purchased. He gave Bessie more than adequate coin to cover the cost. "Tell the vicar I said: 'Welcome aboard.' " He forced a quick smile, and then left her. Minutes later the prissy maid arrived, scowling, and carrying a large basket. Bessie loaded the basket so that it was off balance with most of the weight at one end. She then walked Slondosh to the next house, with a big grin on her face as looking over her shoulder she watched the girl struggle up the pathway with the basket banging against her legs. The two pies left on the cart were sold at the next house. Then Bessie made a big show of tidying up the back of the cart and turning the boxes upside down, to help watchers conclude that she'd sold out. She sat for a few moments, counting her money and trying not to look hurried. Then she slapped the reins on the pony's back and headed for her sister's place.

Marie ran from the house as Bessie brought the wagon to a stop. She looked flustered and very anxious. "Oh, Bessie; what happened? Are you alright?" Bessie smiled. "Shh! Everythin's fine, Marie. Try to remember – I was out sellin' pies an' preserves; it's not supposed to have been a matter of life and death, girl." She tipped the money from her sales onto Marie's table. "Not a bad mornin's work, Marie, considerin' it was just a few 'ouses. I think this will be worth lookin' into once we've got our bigger problem worked out." Marie looked at the money with both hands clasped over her mouth. But her mind quickly returned to their present danger. "What about the other thing?"

"Get me a broken chair from your back room, Marie. I have to take it to a carpenter at the bottom of Church Street and give him a message. I must 'urry." Marie looked startled. "That's Godfrey. That's the bloke that brought the stuff 'ere in the first place – the same bloke who rents my back room. What will 'e want with a broken chair?"

"Never mind, Marie; it's just a cover. It's to make it look like I've got a legitimate reason to go there, because 'e's most likely bein' watched too. Hurry, girl, time's precious. The boxes were quickly removed from the wagon and replaced by a broken chair." "Now, if anyone should ask why I'm taking a chair to Godfrey's, I'm just doin' you a favour, 'cos I've got the wagon today. Godfrey asked you to take it to 'is shop – remember?" Bessie's wide-eyed expression and raised eyebrows triggered a light in Marie's mind. "Oh! I get it, another cover story."

"That's right. Now I must rush off. Be back shortly." The last building at the bottom of Church Street proved to be an ill-kept workshop. A sign over the door proclaimed: 'Godfrey's Carpentry Shop'. Bessie carried the chair in but the shop was empty. She called out: " 'ello! 'ello! Anyone about? I've got an urgent job 'ere!" No answer. She felt the butterflies start to dance in her stomach again. What if this bloke Godfrey was out somewhere? She couldn't go back to Goodman. She called out again, louder this time, and started banging a chair leg on the counter. " 'ello! 'ello! Service! I need service 'ere." She heard a door creak upstairs, and a scruffy individual appeared, and lazily descended the rough staircase. "Alright! Alright! he said. "Keep your shirt on. You're makin' enough noise to wake the bloody dead."

"Oh! So that's where you came from," said Bessie. "Back from the dead! No wonder you took so long and look so bad." Godfrey rubbed his unshaven chin, and then his eyes. He appeared to have wakened from a deep sleep. "What's all the racket about? An' what are you doin' with one o' my chairs?" Bessie ignored the question. Hers was more important. "Are you Godfrey?"

"Yes. I'm Godfrey. An' what are you doin' with one of my chairs?"

"I'm here to tell you: 'The cat's amongst the ducks,' " said Bessie.

"You mean the cat's amongst the pigeons," responded Godfrey, eyeing her suspiciously.

"NO! I mean the cat's amongst the ducks. I was told I'd likely get my throat cut if I said pigeons." Godfrey stared at her silently for a few seconds. "Who are you?"

"You don't need to know that. A big man of your acquaintance said all I had to tell you was: 'The cat's amongst the ducks.' Oh, there is one more thing. I think you're bein' watched. I spotted a couple of layabouts up the street that look like they've got no business bein' there. So, be careful."

Godfrey looked stunned for a moment. "Alright! Leave the chair. "It'll be ready next week sometime. I've got an urgent appointment." With that, he disappeared through a back door. Bessie hesitated for a few moments, gathering her composure. She had no sense of having accomplished her task or that the shore party would be safe now, including her sister and herself. She thought about the two 'layabouts' up the street – seemingly with nothing better to do than waste time chatting. They were just sitting on a garden wall and looking down the street. She wondered if Godfrey would have noticed them. Back at Marie's, she quickly told her sister all that had transpired and declining a cup of tea, she drove off to the manse. She had an urgent message for the vicar concerning a 'lady-of-his-acquaintance'.

On her way back to the manse, Bessie saw Godfrey push a handcart into the front yard of the Coach and Horses and hurry inside. "Looks like 'e's doin' somethin' about them bloody ducks," she muttered. She turned into the church driveway where Fletcher attended Slondosh as soon as she arrived. He was about to take the horse out of the shafts, when Bessie stopped him. "We aren't stopping,'" she said. "No time. I have to get Reverend McDowd and hurry back to Ryeport." Minutes later she and the vicar were back on the road, leaving a perplexed looking Reverend Tubbs, and a disgruntled stableman, staring after them.

Roddy listened to Bessie's account of her morning's experiences with growing admiration. He was amazed at how well she had handled the unforeseen problems that could have prevented her from getting the message to Goodman, and then to Godfrey. The biggest surprise was that Prudence, disguised as a farm boy, was riding a hay wagon, and was to be responsible for both the warning-off fire, and the delivery of some incriminating tackle. She was driving into a trap. He had to prevent that. But where could he intercept her? He had no idea of their route or timing. It was now mid-afternoon. Their only information was that she and her driver had to collect the cart, from somewhere west of Nextwest. "Surely, Bessie," said the vicar, "we must be hours ahead of the hay cart." Bessie nodded, "I would think so, Father. Got a long wait ahead of us, I expect. They wouldn't need the warning-off fire until well after dark." Despite that sound reasoning, the vicar was nervous. He slapped the reins on Slondosh's back, and the pony picked up the pace, quickly leaving the streets of

Nextwest behind them. He couldn't afford to be late, so they planned to drive until they saw the barn on Pringle's farm. Bessie was well acquainted with that landmark. They would then pull over, and wait for the hay wagon. Bessie said that would place them at least a mile west of Pringle's barn and the warning fire and out of sight of the ambush party.

They were about five miles east of Nextwest, when they got their first glimpse of the hay wagon. It was cresting the hill about a mile ahead of them. The vicar groaned. "My God, Bessie, they're already ahead of us. I thought we would have to sit and wait for them to catch up. Didn't Goodman say they would be here sometime in the late afternoon?"

"That's what he said, Father. They must've 'ad a change of plan."

"Bessie, we've got no idea where the fire is supposed to be," said the vicar. "Just west of Pringle's farm means nothing to me. They might be there right now. We could already be too late." Then the cart disappeared over the crest of the hill. "Well, Father," responded Bessie, "I know where Pringle's farm is. We can only do our best. What will you say when we catch up to them?"

"That'll depend on whether or not they are arrested by then. Stop worrying, Father. You look guilty enough to get us both arrested." The vicar slapped the reins on Slondosh's back again. "Giddup, boy!" Slondosh was moving so quickly they were badly bounced around by the rough road. Bessie had a white-knuckle grip on the armrest, and both feet braced tightly against the dashboard. "If you wanted to look suspicious, Father, you couldn't do a much better job," she said, anxiously. "No one in their right mind would go as fast on such a bad road. Slack off a bit." The vicar slowed their pace as they crested another rise in the road and then they saw the hay wagon again. It was much closer now, maybe a quarter mile away. The vicar groaned. "Did you see that flash of red, Bessie, in the trees beyond the hay cart?"

"Yes, Father," she said, "Redcoats. In the trees. That'll be the ambush. They'll be hiding right opposite the entrance to the field. And there's Pringle's barn. Not far past the wagon. I don't think they've seen the soldiers.

The vicar slapped the reins again and poor old Slondosh broke into another trot. Over the next rise, they saw the cart was less than a hundred yards ahead. Pringle's barn was looming larger but there was no sign of the red-coats. Then they saw a rutted pathway, between the hay cart and Pringle's barn. The pathway turned right, into a scrubby field. "That must be the place, Father," said Bessie, pointing.

"Don't point now, Bessie. For God's sake, don't point!"

"Sorry."

They caught up with the cart about fifty yards short of the turn-off. The vicar was yelling: "Hello, the wagon! Hello, the wagon!" Bessie was looking at him as though he were mad. "Whoa, Slondosh! Whoa!" The driver of the wagon was a scruffy individual, about fifty years old, wearing a traditional farmer's smock and a grubby cloth hat. His companion was a slightly built youngster, dressed in much the same way, but with a larger cloth hat pulled low over his ears. Now that he had stopped them, the vicar didn't know what to say. He thought he heard movement behind the hedge on his left and that meant the Customs men were only feet away. "What's all the bloody noise about then?" said the driver, apparently annoyed by their interruption. The vicar called loudly: "This hay has to go to Archer's stable. Not the inn, as previously arranged."

"What are you talking about?" said the driver. "I don't know nothing about no bloody stable."

"Of course you don't. That's why we're here to correct you."

"Correct me? Correct me? Now you see 'ere..." The driver was rising from the seat, and looking hostile. "Preacher or not, you're not goin' to correct me, or tell me what to do." There was more rustling from behind the hedge. Then Bessie piped up. "If you don't deliver this hay to the proper place, you'll really put the cat amongst the ducks."

"You mean pigeons, Missus. The sayin' is: 'Put the cat amongst the pigeons.' And you can mind your own business too." It appeared the driver relished confrontation. The young lad gave the vicar a brief nod, tugged at the driver's sleeve and whispered in his ear. "Well, no one told me about no bloody stable," said the driver. "I was told it was to go to the inn! I'm sick of bein' the last one told, so I am. I do all the bloody work and I'm the last to 'ear about any changes. It's always the bloody same. Treat me like bloody dirt, so they do. Well, I've 'ad enough of it."

"Well, you had the original instruction correct," said the vicar. "We tried to change them before you left but we didn't expect you to get such an early start. Sorry, if we offended you." The vicar touched his hat as he nodded to the young lad. He would never have recognised Prudence from the grimy face beneath the farmer's hat. Then, as he watched, she cuffed her nose on her sleeve – not very lady-like. "If you follow us into the village," continued the vicar, "we'll lead you to the right stable. The innkeeper would have been upset if you had dropped the hay in his yard, and he'd had to move it. Sorry about the confusion."

The vicar was expecting the redcoats to challenge them at any moment and his stomach was in turmoil. They were close enough to have heard every word and he wondered if they were 'buying' his little act. Their best hope now was that the soldiers were anxious not to reveal themselves to the wrong party. So they moved on, at the more leisurely pace of the hay wagon, holding their breaths and dreading the sound of horses, or running soldiers behind them. But all was quiet. They realised, however, that when no one else showed up to 'tend the warning fire', the soldiers would be suspicious of them. But that would buy them some time to concoct a reasonable story. "We'll arrive in Ryeport sometime after four o'clock," said the vicar to Bessie. We'll go straight to Archer's stable. That was not a good choice. I hope he won't be there. I don't know if I could get him to side with us on this."

"He's got no regular routine," said Bessie. "If you want to avoid a confrontation, maybe we'd better go on ahead, and see if we can arrange something." And so, the vicar allowed the hay cart to draw alongside, and told the driver they were going on ahead to let the people know that delivery would arrive early. The first person they saw as they approached the Harbourfront was Archer. His expression was black as coal and he was muttering to himself as he hobbled, stiffly, in the direction of his stable. Bessie shook her head. "Somethin's upset 'im pretty bad, Father. Don't talk to 'im now. He's a strictly honest man and has no sympathy for smugglers. We shouldn't take the hay to his stable."

"The cart is only minutes behind us, Bessie," replied the vicar. "And I'd bet a Revenue spy won't be far behind that." At that moment, Sailmaker emerged from the inn, looking very cheerful. "Hello, Bessie, Father. How did things go in Nextwest?" The vicar quickly got down from the wagon and explained about the hay cart. Sailmaker's smile was quickly replaced by a very worried expression. "Archer will not be helpful," he said. "He's annoyed with Ernie about some firewood. Change the delivery back to the inn. Ernie's not here right now, but he would back us up. Archer is a lost cause today. I don't know how Ernie will ever calm him down. Archer's a good man, but holds a grudge forever if he thinks he's been slighted." Then they saw the hay cart approaching. Even at its slow pace, it was less than five minutes away and now there was a rider following it. The vicar groaned. Bessie said: "Sailmaker, why don't you stop the cart? Say you want to check the 'ay and make sure it's the right batch for Archer's stable. He's fussy about 'is 'ay. Then say it's not good enough for Archer's horse and it must be the stuff that Ernie ordered for 'is animals beddin'. Then 'ave it delivered to Ernie's stable."

"Who will pay for it?" Sailmaker was looking anxiously from Bessie to the vicar; the hay wagon was almost there. "I'll pay for it," said the vicar. "Get Meg to pay the driver and I'll pay her back as soon as he leaves."

"But, Father…" Sailmaker was worried about the money causing a confrontation. The vicar raised his hand. "Sailmaker, there's no more time. Please – do as Bessie suggested. Bessie, please go to the inn and get Meg on side with this. No time for any more changes. We can't argue this in front of a Revenue officer." "Alright," she said, but as Sailmaker turned towards the hay cart, she grabbed his sleeve and said: "There's some tackle under the hay. The revenuer mustn't see that come off the cart." Sailmaker clapped a hand to his forehead and groaned. Less than a minute later, the hay cart came to a stop, behind the vicar's wagon, and the horseman following rode up alongside. "Good day to you all," he said, with a smile. "Fine weather we're having, wouldn't you agree?"

# CHAPTER 11

## *The fireboat*

Doc Hudson's secret hideaway was a natural cavity in the seaward side of the cliff, where time and weather had sculpted and smoothed a well-proportioned seat with one wide armrest. "Nature made this just for me," Doc had said to Ernie when he had first shown his friend his secret hideaway. Now, when he returned from helping Sailmaker, Ernie arrived to find his friend sleeping there. Doc's head was slumped onto his right shoulder, and he was snoring quietly. His left hand still retained a light grip on the neck of the rum bottle resting in his lap and his book lay open on the wide armrest, where a gentle breeze was idly flipping its pages back and forth, as though searching for a particular passage. Ernie feigned a cough, and the doctor's heavy eyelids opened slowly. He grunted as he struggled to rouse himself, and sit up straight. "Ah! Ernie, my non-vap'ros frien'. Tell me again, jush why did you want to di...disappear." Doc lifted the badly depleted rum bottle and stared at it in disbelief for a few seconds, before laying it back in his lap.

"Oh, Doc, it's a long story and not very interesting. You look as though you need a good sleep, old friend. Maybe I should get you home." The doctor ignored his offer. "Not intreshtin', you shay. Lots of unit'...reshtin' things happening here'bouts shince the coachman told hi...hish...shtory." Doc was not prepared to be put off, despite the effects of the rum. "Well, if you must know, Doc, Sailmaker needed a hand with a heavy job. One that he doesn't want talked about."

"Like pasching up Bannerman's old boat, you mean?"

Ernie couldn't conceal his surprise, and joined his friend on his rocky seat. "Now how in heaven's name would you know about that?"

"Well, when you lef' me, you headed for Sh...Sh..Shorry Cove. I was a bit sc...scared tha..that my shpell might work... but after a delay." He smiled... a silly little smile. "Shumtimes happens, you know. I...I dinn't wan' you to di...dishappear in Shorry Cove. I might not never find you again... to bring you back, y'shee. So I followed you. A...at a dishcreet dishtance, of course. But you dinn't dishappear. So that was alright!" He raised his arms wearily and gave a little smile. "But I couldn' hear what you two were shaying, and got bored. I decided that my borrel" – he waved the half empty bottle at Ernie – "and a good book would be more int'reshing'. Sho, here I am. In the cum...comfort of my shecluded hideaway – a rock – a bloody big rock." He frowned, and smiled at the same time, as though unsure which was appropriate.

"You old sneak, you!" Ernie was amused by his friend's drunken humour, but although he felt guilty for having inadvertently exposed Sailmaker's secret, he knew the doctor would never reveal what he'd seen. "Oh, Ernie," Doc said. "No one knows you were there but m..me. I akshooly kep' wasch for you for a while. But that got bor...borin' too You know that ol' boat of Bannerman's will never be any good. It wasn't a good boat, even 'fore it got blown onto Drag'n's Tail. I cahn...cahn she why you're wastin' your time on it."

"Doc, I would be happier, and I think it would be a lot safer for all concerned, if you forgot you ever saw Bannerman's old boat in Sorry Cove. Or Sailmaker and me, come to that."

"My lips are sh..shealed," said the drunken doctor and dramatically pinched them together with his thumb and forefinger, leaving his pinky raised elegantly to the sky. "Have a drink, ol' frien'," he said, and passed the bottle to the innkeeper.

Ernie held the bottle at arm's length, pulling a face as he noted just how much the doctor had already drunk, before he took a swig himself. "We'll need to be seen together, Doc. By the villagers, I mean. And remember, we've been together all day."

"Of coursh we have. Couldn' get thish drunk in lesh time than that!" responded the doctor, argumentatively. "But you've got some ca...catch... catchin' up t'do, young man. I'm at leasht half a borrel ahead of you. Not that I'm braggin' of course." He belched loudly. "S...Scuuuse me!" Ernie took another swig from the bottle, before saying: "Doc, I'm sorry, but I really must get back to the inn. I've been away much longer than I intended. Do you think we could get to the road so we could be seen going to your cottage? I need people to see us together."

"Ernie – p..pee..people might talk, you know," but I'd crawl over a stony beach to oblige you, ol' fr'en'. An' it sheems thash jus' wha' I'll have to do, 'cooos I shore as hell cahn walk." The innkeeper helped his friend to his feet, and Doc draped one arm across Ernie's shoulders, and together they tackled the stony incline up to the doctor's cottage. They were almost there when Ernie's son, Tom, came running to meet them. "Dad, we've got a problem. Oh, sorry, Doctor. Good afternoon, Sir." Tom knuckled his forehead in salute.

"Goo' afternoon to you too...young Tom. At leash..I think it'll be a berrer afternoon than it will be a tomorrow morning.'" The doctor wearily closed his eyes as his legs sagged a little. Ernie strengthened his hold around the doctor's waist. "Just a minute, Tom," he said. Let's get the doctor indoors. Then we can talk."

"Easy for you to shay," said the doctor, with his eyes still closed.

Ernie held the doctor up, and Tom stepped past him to the open door. Minutes later the doctor was lying on his bed, snoring peacefully. Ernie removed his spectacles and shoes, and covered him with a blanket.

"Now, Tom: What's up?"

"The vicar's back, Dad. Bessie Drew too. A cart load of hay followed them in, and a horseman too. The horseman is a well-dressed gent, and acting – sort of nosy. They're outside the inn right now. Sailmaker is saying the hay ain't good enough for Archer but it'll do for bedding for our animals and wants it unloaded into our barn. We didn't know what to do, Dad. Mrs. Drew is askin' Meg to pay for the hay. She says – on the quiet like – the vicar will give you back the money tomorrow. Seems he doesn't want the stranger to think you don't know about it."

Ernie's expression was grim. "So, Bessie is in on this business too, is she? "Yes, Sir. The carter is Jed Pringle. He says he was supposed to deliver it to Archer's stable and he's real miserable. Says he's fed up with people changing their minds. The stranger's watching every move they make, Dad, like he's lookin' to find something. He's walkin' his horse all around the cart and looking at the hay as though he's never seen any before."

"No arguments, Tom. Tell Meg to pay for the hay. If Bessie wants us to pay for the hay, then that's what we'll do. You go ahead of me, lad. If anyone asks – yes, I did order some bedding hay. I guess it was from Pringle. Just say I forgot to tell you about it. Say I was thinking of sharing it with Archer. Ask Bessie from whom I ordered it but keep that quiet too, Tom. I don't want anyone thinking I didn't know about it! Alright, son?"

Tom looked puzzled. "Alright, Dad. What's this all about then?"

"I really don't know myself, Tom. When I find out, I'll let you know. Off you go. Hurry now. I'll follow you after I've checked on the doctor one more time." Doc Hudson was sleeping comfortably when a very weary Ernie finally left for the inn. He was tired and certainly not drunk, but he did manage to give that appearance, every so often, faking a stumble to create the impression that he was a little 'under the weather'.

Back at the inn, Tom was whispering to Meg. "It's alright, Meg. Dad says to pay for the hay. He just forgot to tell us about it." So they both went outside, to pay the carter. The stranger watched them carefully. Tom announced to the group: "Dad forgot to tell us about the hay. He expected to be here when it arrived. He's been with Doc Hudson, but Doc's not too well and Dad had to put him to bed before he could leave. Back the cart up to the stable please, Mr. Pringle." Tom was taking charge now.

"Not before I get my money," said the carter.

"Here's your money. Make sure you count it, you miserable old man," said Meg, dumping a handful of coins into Pringle's hand. He counted the coins, grunted, and then took the horse's bridle, but had to wait for the vicar to move his wagon out of the way before backing up the hay cart. "I'll help you unload," said Sailmaker, and moved to the rear of the cart. The stranger immediately moved his horse to a position where he could watch the unloading. Ernie, seeming a little unsteady on his feet, appeared just in time to see Bessie Drew and the vicar exchange anxious glances. "Hey, what's with all these people then? What's going on?" Ernie yelled. "If I knew I was providing entertainment, I'd have charged admission. You been paid yet?" he called to Pringle.

"Yeah, finally! Gettin' paid 'round 'ere is like pullin' teeth."

"Then get to the unloadin," said Ernie. "We're not going to do your job for you."

"You're bloody drunk," said the carter, and moved to confront the innkeeper.

"Not so drunk I couldn't sort you out," responded the innkeeper. The carter gave Ernie a provocative shove, so Ernie responded with a shove of his own. Their heads knocked together and the carter held Ernie close whilst they wrestled a little. Eventually, they broke free and Ernie shoved Pringle to arms' length and punched him. The carter though managed to 'ride' the blow, and responded with a light punch of his own. The unloading was forgotten, and the crowd, including the horseman, turned to watch the fun. Everyone's attention was suddenly concentrated on the two antagonists. Sailmaker grabbed the vicar's sleeve. "Quickly now, but don't make a noise or let him see. While everyone's watching the fight, help me lift the spars out without letting them scrape. For God's sake; don't let them scrape! Sorry, Father – but, please – don't let them scrape or we'll be done like dinner."

Ernie and the carter were wrestling each other, yelling insults, throwing the occasional punch, and getting farther away from the hay cart with each step. The excited crowd followed them waiting anxiously for the first telling blow to be struck. Under cover of this distraction, Sailmaker and the vicar quietly drew a shallow wooden box, full of pulley blocks, out from under the hay, and laid it against the inside wall of the barn, close by the stable doors. All attention was still focused on the shoving match but since no heavy blows had yet been struck, interest was waning. The two antagonists still looked very menacing, but tired. Bessie gave the vicar a 'hurry-up' signal before stumbling and falling against the stranger's horse. The horse shied, causing the horseman to focus his attention on her and his mount. That allowed the vicar and Sailmaker to carry two long poles into the stable whilst the horseman calmed his horse. Ernie and Pringle's shoving match had now degraded into a war of words, punctuated by an occasional shove, and the crowd's original excitement was fading to boredom. Inside the stable, Sailmaker threw some sacks over the ropes and tackle. "That's where Ernie always keeps his tackle", he said with a wink. "Let's watch the fight." Then, he and the vicar, both a little breathless, leaned on the rear of the cart, trying to appear as though they'd never moved since the confrontation began.

Having assured himself that Mrs. Drew was alright and since the fight was over, the horseman reined his horse around and returned his interest to the hay cart. Sailmaker began unloading the hay. A couple of villagers joined in and they began dumping the loose hay in a vacant stall. There were just two or three inches of hay left on the floor of the cart when Sailmaker called: "That'll do, lads."

"What about the rest of it then?" asked the vicar. "Just watch," whispered Sailmaker. It hadn't been a big load, so the chore had been quickly completed. Pringle was climbing back on the cart's bench seat, and Ernie was almost at the inn when Sailmaker yelled: "We're all done here, Mr. Pringle! Off you go."

"Hold!" called the horseman, as he dismounted and walked to the back of the cart. Using his sword, he pushed the loose hay aside, shifting it all, before re-sheathing the weapon. Then he bent and looked under the cart.

"Wotcher lookin' for mate, Christmas?" Pringle yelled derisively. His guarded glances during the shoving match had confirmed that the lifting tackle had been safely taken off, and Prudence had also given him the 'all-clear' signal. "You can 'ave that last bit of 'ay, if you want, Mister," said Pringle. "No charge. Feed it to your nag. 'e looks as though 'e could use a good feed." Then he gave a loud laugh and shouted over his shoulder: "You can tell that overgrown tub-o-lard that if 'e's prepared to stay sober for a while, I'll come back and sort 'im out, proper like. 'e got lucky today. Me muvver taught me to never 'urt wimmin or drunks."

"Good job Ernie didn't hear that," said Sailmaker as he and the vicar merged with the crowd making their way into the inn. Sailmaker gave the vicar a wink, and then addressed the horseman as they stood at the bar. "What was all that business with the last bit of hay, Sir?" he asked. "Oh, I thought I saw a rat. Can't stand rats – killed a few in my time," replied the horseman as he tapped the hilt of his sword. As he took his ale from Meg, he said: "That was a lot of fuss over a small amount of poor-quality hay, wouldn't you say? It looked to me that it was only fit for burning."

"That wasn't about the 'ay," interrupted Bessie. "More a matter of 'ow you talk to people. More fights over that than anything else 'round 'ere." The stranger turned to face her. "I hope you are quite recovered from your fall, Ma'am. I was worried that my horse might shy and hurt you. You are Mrs. Drew, I believe?"

"Oh, I'm fine, thank you, Sir. I just stubbed me toe an' tripped. Sorry if I startled your 'orse or caused you any concern. And yes, I'm Mrs. Drew. And who might you be?"

"My name is Whitestone, Ma'am. Julian Whitestone, at your service." He touched his hat, smiled, and gave a small bow.

"Oh! And what brings you to Ryeport, Mister Whitestone?"

"Just passing by really. Saw the inn's sign on the Coach Road, and fancied some refreshment. You get around quite a bit yourself, Mrs. Drew. I'm sure I saw you in Nextwest this morning. Selling pies, I believe?"

"That's right, Sir." Bessie's face lit up in a big smile and she appeared genuinely pleased to have been recognised. "Me an' me sister are thinkin' of doin' that on a regular basis. She's been sellin' pies to local shops for a couple of years now, but we got the idea that we might make more money by sellin' direct, door to door. We're both widda's, y'see, and 'ave to find a way to earn a better livin'." She hesitated for a few seconds, looking puzzled. "I don't remember seein' you in Nextwest though."

"I was indoors, visiting a friend in Pleasant Road, and saw you through the window. Nice neighbourhood, Pleasant Road."

"Oh yes, very nice. And what do you do for a livin'? If you don't mind me askin'."

"I'm a writer. I'm very interested in people and places. I like to watch how people interact. The people here are very colourful and aggressive. Take this incident today, for example. Two grown men coming to blows over a little hay."

"If you think that was aggressive, you've led a sheltered life," responded Bessie, with a shrug.

"I'm sorry, Mrs. Drew," said Whitestone, raising his eyebrows in surprise; "I meant no offence." He swallowed the last of his ale, saluted Bessie by touching his riding crop to his hat, then turned and left the inn. The patrons of the bar watched his departure most intently. "Gone but not forgotten," muttered Bessie. "If 'e's a writer, then I'm the queen of Sheba. Wonder which 'ouse 'e was watchin' me from? Most likely the one with the gard'ner. 'ow would 'e know me name though? I don't recall tellin' that woman me name." Meanwhile, Ernie and the vicar were conversing in quiet but intent whispers at the far end of the bar. "What the hell is going on here today?" Ernie was saying. "This smells like smugglers' business. And that horseman? I'd bet good money he was a Customs officer. And how did I get saddled with buying a load of poor-quality hay that I don't want?"

The vicar looked downcast. "Sorry, Ernie. It seems that the coachman was right about an ambush being set for the smugglers. We went to Nextwest to get the word out about the ambush. That old hay was intended to be left in the field in case it was needed for the warning-off fire. That field was on the Coach Road, not far from Pringle's farm. Bessie and I were worried in case some of our villagers might be involved with the smuggling, and, as you know, the Customs men intended to thoroughly question anyone that might have a connection to the smugglers. We had to stop the cart from driving into that field or the soldiers waiting in the bushes on the north side of the road would have arrested them. We caught a glimpse of uniforms as we crested a hill whilst we were trying to catch up with the cart. We had to stop the cart going into that field without making it look suspicious and that was right under the soldier's noses. I didn't have time to come up with a better story. I didn't mean to involve you, Ernie, honestly. We intended to take the hay to Archer's barn but we saw him as we entered the village, and his expression was as black as thunder. But thanks to you, it all worked out. That fight was unexpected and a very fortunate distraction. It saved the day for us – and the smugglers." Some locals began to make their way towards the furtive looking pair, hoping to 'get in' on what appeared 'inside' information. Ernie quickly cut off the conversation and took the vicar by the elbow and steered him outside. "You and I have to have a serious talk, vicar. In private! I didn't realise you were involved with the smugglers. This business could be very dangerous to people I care about."

"I'm not involved, Ernie, only trying to save some villagers who might be."

"Well, you'd better rethink tonight's adventure with Sailmaker," said the innkeeper. "This visit today, from a bloke that looks, and acts, like a Revenue man, has raised the danger level." The vicar looked shocked. "Oh, yes, I know about the Viking funeral," said Ernie. "If I hadn't known, we'd never have pulled off this little bit of play acting today. Jed Pringle and me go back a long way. He gave me a wink with his first shove, and said: 'I need a distraction, Ernie, well away from the hay cart. Let's fake a fight.' So I followed his lead, and we drew the horseman's attention away from the hay cart without me even knowing what the hell that was all about. But the look on Sailmaker's face told me there was something on that cart that he didn't want the horseman to see." The two men stood outside the inn, watching the horseman mount his horse, and follow the hay cart. "Looks like he wants a chat with Pringle," said the vicar.

"Oh, he'll get no more than a grunt or two from Jed," said Ernie, giving his usual short explosive laugh. "Jed's a bit rough around the edges, but a good sort at heart. He's always said: 'The less you say, the less you'll have to apologise for.' That horseman won't get much from him."

The village was strangely quiet after the hay cart incident. Not that it was ever a particularly noisy place but a guarded sense of unease had replaced the villagers' usual relaxed attitudes and banter. They all realised that something significant had happened there today but most had no idea just what that might be, and the few that did were keeping their mouths shut. Ernie was grim faced as he walked behind the bar to tap a fresh keg of ale. He was concerned that this new, troublesome state of affairs might endanger his friends and family. Those thoughts were soon driven from his mind, however, when Archer appeared. Ernie groaned as the beacon minder bellied-up to the bar because Sailmaker had already warned him of Archer's displeasure concerning the rush order of unnecessary firewood. The innkeeper poured a jug of ale and set it on the bar before his scowling friend.

"I don't remember ordering ale," Archer said, setting his lips in a grim line. But Ernie had had enough aggravation today and his temper was seeking some release and he said angrily: "Before you start, Archer, let's get one thing straight. You've got your troubles and I've got mine. Sometimes I have to attend to mine without asking your permission. That doesn't mean we can't be good friends. Good friends understand that there are times when a body has to attend to business without consulting them. I always figured you were such a friend. Was I wrong?" Archer drew back, obviously taken aback by Ernie's preemptive attack. "I don't know what you're talking about."

"Yes, you do. You're upset because I wasn't here when you brought the wood. Then you were upset because I didn't invite you to join Doc and me for a drink. Doc just happened to be feeling low and needed some quiet time, and someone to listen whilst he 'dumped-his-bucket.' God knows he had good cause. It wasn't a party. Next time we'll be pleased to have you come along. If there'd been time to ask you, you could have come this time! Alright?"

"Please your bloody self. I was just going to ask what all the commotion was about over a load of hay. I didn't order any hay."

"Did you get any hay?"

"No."

"Then drink your bloody ale and forget about the hay. The ale's on me. Then give me some quiet time, friend. I've got a bad headache."

"Well, friend, when your headache's gone, perhaps you could tell me more about the hay. Meantime, I can pay for my own bloody ale." Archer slapped the coins down on the counter and took his ale and offended ego to a vacant table in a far corner of the bar. Sailmaker came in, making a beeline for Ernie but did a quick about-turn when he saw the anger on the innkeeper's face. But Ernie was not letting him escape that easily. "Sailmaker! Have you eaten?" Sailmaker turned to face the innkeeper. "No, Sir. Not yet."

"Get around to the kitchen then. Meg has a meal ready for you." In the kitchen, Sailmaker found Bessie Drew and the vicar seated at the table, with Meg already serving them. Sailmaker slumped onto the bench opposite the vicar. "Boy, what a day," he said.

"Yeah! What a day!" echoed Bessie and the vicar, in almost perfect unison.

"I've had one hell of a day," said Sailmaker.

"I'll bet your day was not as bad as ours," said Bessie in an argumentative tone.

Ernie came in from the bar, just in time to hear this last piece of the conversation. "Oh, you poor, hard-done-by, sorry looking bunch. Anyone would think you were the only ones that'd had a bad day." All four sulked into silence until startled by Meg's unexpected peal of laughter. "Oh, you poor dears. Cheer up for heaven's sake! There's another day tomorrow. Maybe it'll be better, or maybe it'll be so bad, it'll make today seem good." She placed a steaming bowl of stew in front of the new arrivals and set a plate of freshly baked bread in the centre of the table as she said: "You don't look so hard done by to me."

Sailmaker dipped a crust of bread into his stew as he said: "The day's not over yet." Ernie, obviously not amused by his daughter's comments and amusement, gave her a warning glare. Then he turned his grim expression to the vicar. "We need to have a talk, Father. In the short time you have been here, our little village has been turned upside down." The vicar responded wearily: "Why don't we all meet at my cottage after we've eaten? We can talk there without fear of interruption." And so it was that half an hour later, the same foursome was seated around the vicar's table as Bessie poured them some wine. "This is almost the last of Reverend Cole's stock," she said in a concerned voice.

"That's the least of our worries," responded Ernie curtly, as he assumed the role of chairman. "It's time for us all to lay our cards on the table. No holding back. It seems that some of us, through no fault of our own, are in danger and this all seemed to start with the coachman's story. I for one want to know what this danger is and who is involved. A lot of innocent people could be hurt if we aren't very careful so let's have it. You start, Father. You seem to be at the centre of all this." He folded his arms and leaned back in his chair, glaring at the vicar.

And so, the vicar told the little group of his efforts to warn the smugglers because of Bessie's concern over the coachman's story. Then, of course, Ernie wanted to know how it was the vicar knew whom to contact, in order to warn the smugglers. So the vicar touched on the story of Mister Whatson's funeral; Sailmaker's eyes widened at that. He was the only member of the group unaware of the vicar's involvement in that piece of business. The vicar did not disclose his ulterior motives, of course, or his personal attraction to Mr. Whatson's clothes. But he did confess that, because of the unpleasant events of recent days, he had been desperate for some time alone and had gone to The White Hart, for a meal. While there he had been unfortunate enough to overhear a man discussing a smuggling run and had been dis-covered. He explained that the smuggler had threatened his life and how he had been saved by the intervention of a second smuggler, who insisted that there be no violence, for fear of attracting the attention of the authorities. He made no reference to Prudence, nor did he identify Goodman in any way. He told them that the smuggler had warned him that he would be watched and if they even suspected him of disclosing anything that he'd overheard, he would pay with his life. Because of that incident, he knew where to find one of those smugglers and that he was the man that he and Bessie intended to warn. It had never been his intention to protect the people who had threat-ened his life, only any villagers that might be involved.

Bessie was next. She confessed that since the coachman's story, she had been worried about her sister because of her small part in handling smuggled goods. A risk that Marie had accepted only because of a desperate need to improve her meagre income. Bessie also said that she too was considering similar involvement because she too badly needed more money. She went on to describe how she had undertaken the door to door peddler's role in order to warn the smugglers – right under the noses of the watching Revenue officers. Her eyes took on a very visible shine, and her cheeks were flushed with excitement as she described the day's events, in a very animated manner. It was obvious to them all that, despite her earlier complaints of a hard day, she had enjoyed that excitement. The group looked at 'their' Bessie as though she were a stranger. They had never seen her in this light before. Her colour deepened even more when she realised how intent they were on her guilty little story. So, in a more hushed, but defiant, tone, she confessed that the danger, and her spontaneous improvisations, had thrilled her. "It made me feel more alive somehow. Selling the pies and preserves was fun too. But the risk taking invigorated me. It was more exciting than the peddlin.'"

Then it was Sailmaker's turn. He explained how he had been offered the chance to make some extra money by supplying tackle. But declared that he had no idea he would be working for smugglers until he was taken to the site to quote on the job. Once he had been to the site to evaluate the task, of course, the truth was obvious. By then though, he would not have been allowed to back out. He knew too much.

Ernie confessed his suspicions that some of the villagers had been involved in smuggling and today, those suspicions had been confirmed. But he was surprised and alarmed to find that Sailmaker, the vicar and Bessie were involved too. Now, by association, he too was involved. The risk to his family was something he was anxious to avoid. He also expressed his concern over the extremely dangerous task that Sailmaker and the vicar were to undertake that night by burning Bannerman's old boat, to create a 'warning-off' fire. This was all news to Bessie, and she sat with both hands clasped over her mouth, as she learned just how her two friends proposed to warn the smugglers at sea.

"So, now we are all partners-in-crime." Ernie sipped his wine and sat back in his chair as he surveyed his accomplices. "Not what I wanted. Not what I wanted at all." He gave Sailmaker a reprimanding look. "I'd sooner see Meg married to a poor man than a rich one left dangling from a gibbet. You can't support a family very well from that lofty position."

"Well, I certainly didn't want any part of this either," said the vicar.

"Me neither," said Bessie. "But it did make a break from cleanin' and smokin' fish or cleanin' 'ouse and cooking." Again, she was surprised by the startled looks from her companions and, as her cheeks glowed a few shades redder, she added: "No offence, Father." The group was looking at her with a mixture of surprise and awe but said nothing. Bessie averted her shining eyes from her companions, and focused instead on the wine glasses. "Time for a refill," she said, and topped them up.

"Who do you suspect, Ernie? In the village, I mean." Sailmaker was looking anxious. "It would only take one slip of the tongue to hang us all possibly."

"Well, Bannerman seems to be the most likely suspect. He's single, has always been a risk taker, and he needs money for a new boat, especially after tonight. I've noticed too that when the boats leave for an overnight stay – selling their smoked fish and such – the Sullivans' boat was always the last one back. They claim they always go on a binge and drink away some of the proceeds of their sales. But Bannerman and the Sullivans have never been big drinkers. And I've noticed that since the Sullivans took Bannerman on as crew, they all seem better off than their catches would justify.

"As far as tonight is concerned, we really need to be sure that nobody in the village knows what you two are up to – no one at all. One careless remark could put us all away. So, I'll give you two a hand tonight. You'll need some help with that heavy old boat." Ernie was leaning on the table now, looking anxiously at Sailmaker. "No you won't, Ernie," said the vicar. "Thank you for the offer but that mustn't happen. Everything has to appear normal tonight, especially after this business with the hay cart. You need to be seen pouring beer and handing out cheese and pickles. Just like always." Sailmaker agreed.

"The vicar's right, Ernie. You must stay in plain sight tonight. You've done more than your share today. And, if anything should go wrong and we get caught, you must be as surprised as anyone else in the village. You have a family to protect. You're no smuggler. And should we get arrested, we'll never involve you. Will we, Father?" He raised his eyebrows at the vicar.

"No. We will confess that we operated on our own. By the way, should anyone want to know what this meeting was all about, let us say that it was to discuss my crazy idea for the new church that I want to see built in Ryeport. Just confine any of your answers to what you already know. If anyone wants to get specific, just leave them with the impression that we spent most of our time drinking Reverend Cole's wine." They all nodded in agreement. The group finished their drinks, and quietly dispersed. Sailmaker and the vicar arranged to meet after dark in Sorry Cove. Sailmaker would take his dinghy through The Chute, and the vicar was to arrive there by the same route that Ernie and Doc had used earlier. But first, Ernie and the vicar would visit the doctor, right after the meeting. After that, they would go their separate ways. After leaving the doctor, Ernie would take a bottle of rum to Archer's beacon hut and do his best to repair their bruised friendship. That would also enable him to keep Archer from getting inquisitive if Bannerman's old boat complained too loudly about being refloated.

Bessie would pay a social visit to Kathleen Archer. That way she could feed some misinformation to the Archers about their meeting, without leaking anything about the night's dangerous mission to this strictly honest couple. Now, since the conspirators were all aware of each other's various parts in the scheme, they would be able to avoid speculative comments they might later regret. The vicar was concerned about Doc Hudson's knowledge of Bannerman's boat in Sorry Cove. "The number of people who are aware of our involvement is growing dangerously large," he commented to Ernie. "Don't worry about Doc," said the innkeeper. "He's the best keeper of secrets I've ever known. And I know that because people, who later confided in me, have told me: the only other person that had known of their secret was Doc Hudson. But if I ever tried to get him to confirm anything, he always claimed he knew nothing about it, and Doc is my closest friend. And a great friend of the village too, I might add!" Ernie's tone was most forceful.

The doctor still appeared unwell when he opened the door to them. "My God, Ernie, I'm too old for this sort of drinking," he said. "I feel awfu'." His speech was still impaired and his balance unsteady. "I'm not feeling at all well. I must try to remember these awfu' consequences whilst I'm enjoyin' the drink. Why cahn' I do that? Shorry you have to see me like this, Father. Do you think the devil has me firmbly in his grashp?"

"Well, Doctor, if he has, I know you will soon wriggle out of it, just as we all have from time to time. You've done far too much good for the scales to remain tipped in his favour for very long." Ernie made up some vile looking concoction, from raw eggs, tomatoes, pepper and whatever else he'd been able to find in the doctor's pantry. It looked revolting. Ernie insisted that this would make the doctor better. From Doc's expression, it seemed he doubted that but he swallowed the concoction anyway. "Godda do what Doctor Ernie shez," he said and then promptly stumbled to the back door and threw up. They cleaned him up and saw him safely to bed. Before he left Doc's cottage, the vicar changed into the work clothes that Sailmaker had lent him, depositing his clerical clothing between a wardrobe and the wall in the doctor's bedroom. The doctor seemed too ill to notice.

Ernie shook the vicar's hand as he directed him to the stony path that would lead him to Sorry Cove and the dangerous mission that he and Sailmaker were about to undertake. "Good luck, Father. Be very careful. I've got the feeling that a lot of people will be grateful for your actions tonight." The vicar felt his stomach sour as Ernie's comments underscored the immediacy of the dangerous task he and Sailmaker were about to under-take. "Thanks, Ernie. We'll be alright." Sailmaker was securing the bowline from Bannerman's boat to a cleat on the transom of his dinghy when the vicar arrived. "Glad you could make it, Father. I was starting to feel lonely."

"You've accomplished a lot today, Sailmaker. Ernie told me about the troubles you've had. Is there anything left for me to do?"

"No, Father, all is ready."

"Good. Then I'll be off home."

Sailmaker laughed quietly. "Fat chance, Father. You're stuck with your share of tonight's little adventure." The vicar smiled. "One more thing, Sailmaker, from hereon we do not use each other's names. No names at all. In case we are overheard."

"Good idea. We might as well push off now. Quiet as you can from here on. I heard Ernie calling Archer just before you got here. I'm sure he'll keep him occupied but we'd better not make any unnecessary noise. Help me push her into deeper water so she floats easy. Then we'll tow her out. She's holding the water out pretty good considering the state she was in. Everything seems to be in our favour tonight. The boat's holding up, we have an ebb tide and just enough moonlight."

Slowly, they towed Bannerman's old boat out of Sorry Cove, then along the rocky coastline, heading west towards the anchor point that Sailmaker had chosen for the warning-off fire. Every so often they would pause, and listen for suspicious noises. So far, all was quiet. Lady Luck was with them. Sailmaker spotted a white sail reflecting the moonlight, and they hid in the shadow of a cliff until it passed out of sight behind the cliff of Archer's beacon. "See how the sail shows up in the moonlight?" said Sailmaker. "The watchmen on the Revenue boats would have no trouble spotting that. Some of the smugglers back east are using dark sails now. I'm told that the Dutch smugglers started that trick. Are you warm enough?"

"Yes, thanks to the clothes you lent me. I changed at Doc's place. The night is reasonably warm. I'm just too scared to enjoy it. Do you think anyone might hear our oars? It seems to me they are making too much splashing noise."

"No, they're not too bad. Unless there's a cutter tucked away in the shoreline somewhere, we should be safe enough. What little noise we make will be lost in the background of small noises. We have plenty of time, so we'll go slower from here on. Keep a sharp eye out along the coastline, just in case. Once we get closer, we'll hide in the shadow of the cliff until we're ready to anchor the boat, and light her up." A few minutes later, Sailmaker pointed out the landing beach for the smuggling run. "We'll wait in the shadows here. We're about an hour early. Would you like some cheese and pickles?"

"You've got an awfully big appetite for pickles, Sailmaker. I've never known anyone as keen on pickles as you."

"You just broke your own rule. No names, remember?"

"Sorry! And yes, please, I'd love some cheese and pickles."

"I brought some rum too, to warm us up." They sat quietly, enjoying the comfort of their simple snack, whilst listening alertly for noises from the cliff above them. "This is a difficult beach for a smuggling run," said Sailmaker, in a hushed voice. "The Revenuers would never have expected anyone to try and run goods ashore here. That's the reason the smugglers chose it, of course. They squared off some natural steps in the rocks, making it possible to climb safely to the top of the cliff, but it's still not easy enough for carrying goods up. It's far too dangerous. So they came up with the idea of lifting the goods from the beach to the cliff-top using tackle but they needed someone to organise a portable system. One they could take apart and hide once they'd finished that night's work. That's when Bannerman asked me if I'd like to make some money. He didn't mention that it was smugglers' business though or I would never have agreed. Ernie is dead set against smugglers. I was amazed that he helped me with the boat and even more amazed that I'm still allowed to see Meg. Maybe that's because he would have to explain to her why he forbade it." Sailmaker raised one hand as he cocked his head on one side, listening. "Those Revenue officers must be suspicious by now. The warning-off party should have made an appearance long ago. There are no houses hereabouts. Pringle's farm is the closest place. It was Jed Pringle who was driving the hay wagon today but I've no idea who the young lad was. Can you hear anything, Father?"

"Only the breeze, and water lapping around the rocks."

"Look! Out there, off to the west." Sailmaker pointed. "Sails; most likely a Revenue cutter; see the long bowsprit? She's rounding the headland. She'll hide there, I imagine. They know the smugglers will be coming from the east. She'll wait for a signal from the Revenuers ashore, I bet. Let's get the fireboat in place. Quietly now! Dip your oars carefully." Slowly, they moved out from the safety of the cliff's shadow into an area faintly lit by a thin sliver of moon, all the while expecting a challenge from the cliff above, but none came. The attention of the soldiers ashore must have been focused on the road, anticipating the arrival of the warning – of crew and the smuggler's dispersal team.

About half a mile offshore, Sailmaker gently lowered two makeshift anchors from Bannerman's boat – just ropes secured to flat slabs of rock – one at the stern and the other from the bow. "I want to keep the bow facing towards the shore," he said. "I'll be lighting the fuse at the stern and I don't want the soldiers to see anything suspicious until we're well away from here." He lifted an upturned box in the centre of Bannerman's boat, revealing a tray of gunpowder surrounded by slivers of wood and scraps of oiled canvas. He splashed more lamp oil on the driftwood and spars that he'd piled around a short, improvised 'mast' that had created a large conical, well-ventilated woodpile. Sailmaker pushed one end of a long length of fuse deep into the gunpowder. The trailing end had already been fastened around the inside of the gunwale, leaving the free end dangling about two inches over the stern of the condemned boat. They were all set. The two men kept a wary eye towards the shore. Then Sailmaker looked to the vicar. "All set?" The vicar nodded and passed their shuttered lantern to Sailmaker who used that to carefully ignite the fuse.

"Let's go, quietly now," said Sailmaker and they pulled carefully, but strongly, back to the shadow of the cliff. From there they would hug the coastline all the way back to the safety of Sorry Cove. A slight breeze sprang up, rippling the water. "We'll wait a while, to be sure the boat lights up," whispered Sailmaker. They sat in the shadows for a couple of minutes but there was no sign of a flame from the fireboat. "How long will it take?" queried the vicar.

"It should have lit by now," responded Sailmaker anxiously. They waited, breathless, for a couple more minutes but there was still no sign of a light from the fireboat. "That has to light up soon. The smugglers should be in position to see it shortly. We won't see them for a while because we're close inshore, and Archer's cliff is blocking our view to the east." The next five minutes seemed like an eternity, but there was still no sign of a flame from the fireboat. "Could that fuse have gone out?" The vicar's voice was hushed and worried.

"No reason for that. It was good dry fuse; I tried it. If it doesn't light soon, it will be too late. If it doesn't burn, the smugglers will be caught and the boat will be discovered and identified too. Then they'll be looking for the owner. Then we'll be 'gonners,' for sure."

"We'll have to go back," said the vicar, in a despairing voice.

"We'll be in full view of the militia on the cliff-top if the boat lights up while we're out there." There was a trace of panic in Sailmaker's voice. All his careful preparations had gone for naught. "We've no choice," responded the vicar. "Perhaps I could swim out there and relight it."

"Are you crazy?" was Sailmaker's hushed reply. "The soldiers will line up on the cliff-top and use you for target practice. Besides, you'd have nothing to light it with. You can't swim and keep the lantern dry." The despair in his voice was frightening. They had to relight the boat – but how? "Without the fuse, it will be a suicide mission," said Sailmaker. "Let's row back out there," replied the vicar. "Find out what's happened. We must relight it somehow; otherwise, they'll trace the boat back to the village." Sailmaker's response was shaky. "If we have to light it up directly, we'll be caught for sure because the fire will light us up too. I timed that length of fuse to give us time to pull the dinghy out of the circle of firelight."

"We have to get back out there and check it out," the vicar said. "I'm a strong swimmer. You must leave me behind to light up the boat, then pull the dinghy back to the shadow of the cliff as quickly as you can. After I've lit the boat, I'll swim underwater for a while, come up for air, then go under again. If the soldiers start down the cliff, you must leave me. Just get back to the inn. You need to be seen there tonight. I'll follow you as soon as I can. A swimmer will be a lot harder to spot than the dinghy. Almost impossible, I'd say. I'll wait 'til you get into the cliff's shadow before I light it up."

"That's a long swim, in cold water. What will you do if you reach the shore and I'm gone? There's no continuous beach back to Sorry Cove. You'd have to climb the cliff, and the soldiers would be waiting, for sure." Sailmaker was shaking his head.

"I'll head back to Doc Hudson's somehow. That's where my cleric's clothes are. I think Doc would back me up if I say I've been there all night. If Hawksworth is around, maybe someone could drop a hint that I was worried about Doc. Come on, let's go. The longer we wait the more danger-ous it will be."

They pulled out from the cliff's shadow once more, feeling far more vulnerable this time. Their heads jerked nervously around, to face any new sound. "Quiet," hissed Sailmaker, as caution suffered in their anxiety for haste, and the oars splashed more noisily than they had on the first trip. On arriving at the fireboat, they discovered that the fuse had burnt all along the gunwale but the end that Sailmaker had plugged into the gunpowder had been dragged out by a length of timber that had fallen from the conical pile around the mast. That end of the fuse was now lying beside the timber, in the water. Sailmaker groaned. "Only a wet piece of fuse left. What rotten luck. We're done for." The vicar was peeling off his clothes. "No, we're not. Hang the lantern on the stern of Bannerman's boat. Then you hurry for the cliff, just as I said."

"But, Father..."

"No more 'buts', my friend. There's no time left. Just do it. If I'm spotted, you must run for home. Don't wait for me or we could both get caught." Sailmaker hesitated. "Go, man! Go!" The vicar demanded impatiently. "Before I freeze to death. I can't light the boat up until you are back in the shadows. So hurry." Sailmaker reluctantly pulled away, leaving a quiet: "Good luck," floating on the chilly air.

The vicar waited until the paler shape of the dinghy blended with the shadow of the cliff, then lifted the lantern over the stern and opened the shutter. Then he fed a scrap of oiled canvas to the flame. His teeth were chattering and that part of his body that was exposed to the breeze was desperately cold. It was little warmer in the water but at least he was spared the chilling breeze. It seemed like an eternity before the canvas lit, and a wave of despair began to sweep over him. Then suddenly, there was a quiet 'whoosh', and the canvas burst into flame.

Startled, he dropped the flaming canvas, and there was a second 'whoosh', as more scraps of canvas caught. He tossed a flaming scrap into the centre of the boat, aiming at the small box of gunpowder that Sailmaker had intended to scatter flaming kindling all over the boat but he missed. Then there was a shout from the cliff-top. He could do no more. He was out of time. He slipped under the water and began swimming eastward, parallel to the shore and away from the boat. He didn't want to resurface until he was out of the immediate circle of light created by the fire. Nor did he want to surface in the line of sight of soldiers looking at the fire. It was time now to save himself. He came up for air just in time to hear the gunpowder box explode. A few pieces of flaming kindling flew over his head. "Well, at least the fire is lit," he thought, as the centre of the boat erupted in flames. He dove again, this time heading more towards the shore. When he resurfaced, he looked back at the fireboat, which was now burning fiercely. On the cliff-top, soldiers were silhouetted against the sky and some were scrambling down the cliff, stripping off clothing as they went. But they were almost a quarter of a mile away. He dove again, but when he resurfaced this time, he found himself within the expanding circle of firelight. He had misjudged his bearings, and was farther west than he'd intended, and closer to the soldiers on the beach. There was a sudden shout and some of them were pointing. He took a fresh bearing, and dove under once more. When he came up for air, he was farther east, but closer to the beach and there were fresh shouts from the soldiers. The sound of a musket shot was quickly followed by others. He had been spotted, and balls began splashing into the water only feet away. He went under again, this time heading directly east. He felt sick. How could he possibly escape now?

*Story continues in*

BOOK TWO

# THE CURSE OF THE SEAHORSE

# ABOUT THE AUTHOR

Les was born in London, England in 1930. He, and his wife Joyce, immigrated to Ontario, Canada in 1965 where they raised their family in the scenic Hockley Valley.

Les was always a gifted storyteller who entertained family and friends regularly with his embellished versions of classic fairy tales and a host of made up words that he used to make every day conversation more colourful.

His first novel became a labour of love during his retirement years and was nearing completion when he suffered a serious stroke which robbed him of his wonderful communication skills. Happily with the help of his family, the original version, *The Fo'c's'le Door*, was published in 2013 and he was able to hold a copy in his hands prior to his death in 2016.

It is a long and captivating mystery involving adventures in smuggling, murder and the supernatural and met with great reviews from those who read it.

*The Ryeport Redemption* is a republication by his family of the original novel, with the help of a new publisher, in order to give this wonderful adventure the recognition it deserves. It is an opportunity for them to complete this part of his legacy and share their Dad's imagination and storytelling skills with the world in honour of his memory.

lescribb.com
https://www.facebook.com/AuthorLesCribb/

With every donation, a voice will be given to
the creativity that lies within the hearts of
our children living with diverse challenges.

By making this difference, children that may
not have been given the opportunity to have their
Heart Heard will have the freedom to create
beautiful works of art and musical creations.

*Donate by visiting*

**HeartstobeHeard.com**

We thank you.